Dear Reader,

I've lost track of how many of you have written to me over the years asking for a trilogy. I had to wait until the right story came along, but I am delighted to tell you that it finally did and you are holding it in your hands. *Eclipse Bay* is the first book in a three-book series that tells the stories of the Hartes and the Madisons of Eclipse Bay, Oregon. Like the two that follow, it is filled with romance and family relationships. I had a tremendous amount of fun writing the books. I hope you will enjoy reading them.

This is the perfect opportunity to take a moment to thank each and every one of you—longtime fans and new readers alike—for the support and enthusiasm you have given to my novels. I have often felt that, if we met in person, we would find it easy to be friends. I suspect that we have a lot in common when it comes to our world views, our belief in the value of family and the power of love. That's a great basis for a lasting relationship, don't you think?

Here's to our future together!

Sincerely,

Jayne Ann Krentz

Turn the page for reviews of Jayne Ann Krentz's previous novels . . .

ECLIPSE BAY

Jayne Ann Krentz

JOVE BOOKS, NEW YORK

THE BERKLEY PUBLISHING GROUP
Published by the Penguin Group
Penguin Group (USA) Inc.
375 Hudson Street, New York, New York 10014, USA
Penguin Group (Canada), 90 Eglinton Avenue East, Suite 700, Toronto, Ontario M4P 2Y3, Canada
(a division of Pearson Penguin Canada Inc.)
Penguin Books Ltd., 80 Strand, London WC2R 0RL, England
Penguin Group Ireland, 25 St. Stephen's Green, Dublin 2, Ireland (a division of Penguin Books Ltd.)
Penguin Group (Australia), 250 Camberwell Road, Camberwell, Victoria 3124, Australia
(a division of Pearson Australia Group Pty. Ltd.)
Penguin Books India Pvt. Ltd., 11 Community Centre, Panchsheel Park, New Delhi—110 017, India
Penguin Group (NZ), 67 Apollo Drive, Rosedale, North Shore 0632, New Zealand
(a division of Pearson New Zealand Ltd.)
Penguin Books (South Africa) (Pty.) Ltd., 24 Sturdee Avenue, Rosebank, Johannesburg 2196, South Africa

Penguin Books Ltd., Registered Offices: 80 Strand, London WC2R 0RL, England

ECLIPSE BAY

A Jove Book / published by arrangement with the author

PRINTING HISTORY
Jove mass-market edition / June 2000
Special $4.99 edition / January 2008

ISBN: 978-0-515-14416-1

JOVE®
Jove Books are published by The Berkley Publishing Group,
a division of Penguin Group (USA) Inc.,
375 Hudson Street, New York, New York 10014.
JOVE is a registered trademark of Penguin Group (USA) Inc.
The "J" design is a trademark belonging to Penguin Group (USA) Inc.

PRINTED IN THE UNITED STATES OF AMERICA

10 9 8 7 6 5 4 3 2 1

Dedication

For Supreme Webscholar Cissy and the wonderful gang at *www.jayneannkrentz.com*

You all said you wanted a series . . .

prologue

Eclipse Bay, Oregon
Midnight, eight years earlier . . .

"It's going to be a long walk home."

The voice was low and rough around the edges, unmistakably masculine. The kind of voice that sent little shivers down a woman's spine. It came out of the bottomless shadows near the base of Eclipse Arch, the stone monolith that dominated this secluded stretch of rocky beach.

Hannah Harte jerked her gaze away from the sight of Perry Decatur's disappearing taillights and spun around. Her pulse, already beating briskly as a result of the unpleasant tussle in the front seat, shifted into high gear.

Maybe getting out of the car had not been one of her brighter ideas. This stretch of Bayview Drive was a very lonely place at this hour of the night. Nice going, Hannah, she thought. The old frying-pan-into-the-fire trick. And you're supposed to be so sensible and cautious. The one who never takes chances. The one who never gets into trouble.

"Who's there?" She edged back a step and prepared to run.

The man on the beach sauntered casually out of the dense darkness of the arched rock and stepped into the cold light of the late-summer moon. He was less than twenty feet away.

"You're a Harte," he said. Cold, ironic amusement filtered through the words. "Don't you recongnize a no-good, low-down, untrustworthy Madison on sight?"

She took in the stark profile, the glint of silver light on midnight-dark hair, and the air of arrogant, prowling grace. She didn't need the additional clues of a leather jacket, a black crew-neck T-shirt, and jeans.

Rafe Madison. Her generation's most notorious member of the disreputable, thoroughly scandalous Madison clan. For three generations, ever since the legendary street fight between Mitchell Madison and Sullivan Harte in front of Fulton's Supermarket, the Hartes had dutifully warned their offspring not to get involved with the wild, unruly Madisons.

Rafe had apparently made it a point to live up to his family's scandalous heritage. The product of an affair between his sculptor father and a model, Rafe had been orphaned along with his brother at the tender age of nine. Both boys had been raised by their disreputable grandfather, Mitchell, who was, according to Hannah's mother, in no way qualified to be a father.

Rafe had blossomed into the quintessential bad boy, but he had somehow managed, by the skin of his teeth, to stay out of jail. As far as most people in Eclipse Bay were concerned, it was only a matter of time before he wound up behind bars.

He was twenty-four, four years older than herself, Hannah thought. It was common knowledge that his grandfather was furious with him because he had dropped out of college in the middle of his sophomore year. Rafe had done a short stint in the military, and from all accounts, he had managed to prove all the recruitment posters wrong and emerge with no marketable skills. Word had it that this summer Mitchell was trying to coerce him into going to work for his older brother, Gabe, who was attempting, against all odds, to revive the family business. No one expected Gabe to succeed in that endeavor.

Although she and her family spent every summer and many weekends and vacations here in Eclipse Bay, Hannah had had no direct contact with Rafe while she was growing up. The four years' difference in their ages had, until tonight, served to keep their orbits safely separated, even in this small seaside community where both families had deep roots. Four years was a chasm when one was a kid.

But tonight was her twentieth birthday. In the fall she would start her junior year of college in Portland. For some reason the four years between herself and Rafe Madison no longer seemed an impenetrable barrier.

Her first reaction to the realization that he had witnessed the struggle in the front seat of Perry's car was overwhelming mortification. Hartes did not indulge in public scenes. Just her dumb luck to have a Madison hanging around when she broke that unwritten rule. Anger warred with acute embarrassment.

"Do you do this a lot?" she asked gruffly.

"Do what a lot?"

"Hide behind large rocks in order to spy on people who want to have private conversations?"

"You've got to admit that the entertainment options in this town are a little limited."

"I suppose that's especially true if you've got a severely *limited* concept of what constitutes entertainment."

Everyone knew that Rafe's motorcycle was frequently spotted in the small parking lot behind Virgil's Adult Books and Video Arcade. "What do you do when you're not being a voyeur?"

"A voyeur?" He whistled softly. "That's a fancy word for a Peeping Tom, isn't it?"

She stiffened. "Yes, it is."

"Thought so. Wasn't absolutely sure, though. I dropped out of college before we got to some of the more up-scale words."

He was mocking her. She knew it, but she was not certain how to deal with it.

"I wouldn't brag about leaving school if I were you." She clutched her purse more tightly in front of her body, as if it were a magic shield she could use to ward off any demonic vibes Rafe might be emitting. "My father says that it's too bad you blew off your future like that. He says you have potential."

Rafe's teeth flashed briefly in a sardonic grin. "Lots of people have said that over the years, starting with my first-grade teacher. But they've all concluded that I won't ever live up to whatever potential I've got."

"You're an adult now. It's your responsibility to make your life work properly. You can't blame your failure on others."

"I never do that," he assured her earnestly. "I'm proud to say that I am solely to blame for my own screwups."

She was out of her depth here. She tightened her grip on the purse and took another step back.

"You sort of implied that you and the guy who just took off came here to talk privately." His words pursued her in the darkness. "But I didn't get the feeling that the two of you were having what you'd call a meaningful conversation. Who was the jerk, anyway?"

For some oblique reason she felt compelled to defend

Perry, who, unlike Rafe Madison, would amount to something someday. Or maybe it was her own self-image she wanted to protect. She did not like to think of herself as the kind of woman who dated jerks.

Not that Perry was a jerk. He was a budding academic.

"His name is Perry Decatur," she said coolly. "He's a grad student at Chamberlain. Not that it's any of your business."

"Guess he thought the evening was going to end a little differently."

"Perry's okay. He just got a little pushy tonight, that's all."

"Pushy, huh? Is that what you call it?" Rafe gave an easy shrug. "Well, it looked like you pushed back pretty good. For a minute there, I thought you might need a little help, but then I realized that you were handling him just fine on your own."

"Perry is hardly the violent type." Outrage flared. "He's a grad student, for crying out loud. He plans to teach political science."

"Is that right? Since when is politics a science?"

She was pretty sure that was a rhetorical question. "He expects to be offered a position on the faculty at Chamberlain as soon as he gets his Ph.D."

"Well, shoot. If I'd known that, I wouldn't have worried about you even half a minute while the two of you were staging that arm-wrestling contest. I mean, a guy who's going for his Ph.D. and plans to become a hot-shot professor at Chamberlain wouldn't try to force himself on a woman. Don't know what I was thinking."

She was profoundly grateful for the simple fact that it was midnight. At least Rafe could not see the hot color she was almost sure was staining her face a vivid shade of pink. "There's no call to be sarcastic. Perry and I had a disagreement, that's all."

"So, do you date a lot of jerks?"

"Stop calling Perry a jerk."

"I was just curious. Can't blame me under the circumstances, can you?"

"Yes, I can and I do." She glared. "You're being deliberately obnoxious."

"But not quite as obnoxious as the jerk, huh? I haven't even touched you."

"Oh, shut up. I'm going home."

"I hate to mention it, but you are standing alone here on an isolated stretch of road in the middle of the night. Like I said, it's going to be a long walk back to your folks' place."

She seized the only weak point she could find in his logic. "I'm not alone."

In the pale moonlight, his smile gleamed dangerously. "We both know that as far as your family is concerned, the fact that I'm here with you makes your situation worse than being alone. I'm a Madison, remember?"

She raised her chin. "I don't give a darn about that stupid feud. Ancient history, as far as I'm concerned."

"Right. Ancient history. But you know what they say about history. Those who don't learn from it are condemned to relive it."

Startled, she stared at him. "You sound just like Aunt Isabel. She's always saying things like that."

"I know."

Hannah was floored. "You've talked to my aunt?"

"She talks to me." He raised one shoulder in another dismissive gesture. "I do some work around that big house of hers sometimes. She's a nice old lady. A little strange, but then, she is a Harte."

She wondered what her parents would say if they discovered that Aunt Isabel hired Rafe to do odd jobs around Dreamscape. "I guess that explains where you picked up the quote."

"You didn't think I'd actually read it in a book, did you?"

"Everyone knows you do most of your reading at Virgil Nash's porn shop." Lord, she sounded prissy. "I doubt that you'd find a quote like that in any of the books or magazines he stocks."

Rafe was silent for a beat, as if her comment had surprised him. But he recovered immediately. "Right. Mostly I just look at the pictures, anyhow."

"I believe it."

"I'll bet the jerk reads a lot."

Quite suddenly she'd had enough. It was time to level this playing field. Rafe Madison had four years and a lifetime of experience on her, but she was a Harte. She could hold her own against a Madison.

"If you didn't come here to play some voyeuristic games," she said coldly, "what are you doing at Eclipse Arch at this time of night?"

"Same thing you are," he said very smoothly. "My date and I had a little disagreement, and she kicked me out of her car."

Hannah was astonished. "Kaitlin Sadler threw you out of her car because you wouldn't have sex with her?"

"We didn't argue about having sex," he said with devastating honesty. "We argued about the fact that she's dating other guys."

"I see." It was no secret that Kaitlin had been seeing other men. "I hear she wants to marry someone who can take her away from Eclipse Bay."

"You heard right. Obviously I'm not in a position to do that, what with my failure to achieve my full potential and all."

"Obviously."

"Hell, I don't even have a steady job."

"I don't suppose Kaitlin would consider flipping veggie burgers at Snow's Café a position with a lot of guaranteed upward mobility," Hannah mused.

"No, she doesn't. She made that real clear."

Hannah was appalled to realize that she felt an insidious little tendril of sympathy for him. "You've got to admit that you certainly can't afford to keep her in the style to which she wants to become accustomed."

"I know. But I thought we had an understanding that while we were seeing each other, neither of us would fool around with anyone else."

"Kaitlin, I take it, didn't share that understanding?"

"Nope. She said she didn't want to be tied down to me. Made it clear that her first priority was finding a rich husband. Naturally, I was crushed to learn that I was nothing more than a plaything for her."

"Yeah. Crushed."

"Hey, Madisons have feelings too."

"Really?" she murmured. "I've never heard that."

"The family likes to keep it quiet."

"I'm not surprised. Sort of ruins the image."

"Yeah. You know, you'd be surprised how irritating it is to date a woman who is actively hunting elsewhere for a wealthy husband."

"Kaitlin's definitely active," Hannah said neutrally. "Everyone in town knows it."

Rafe smiled thinly. "As of tonight she can be active with someone else."

"I suppose she was upset when you told her you didn't want to continue in the role of, uh, plaything?"

"She was pissed as hell."

She tried to read his face in the shadows, but it was impossible to tell what he was thinking or feeling. Assuming that is, that he was thinking or feeling anything at all.

"I get the impression that you are not particularly devastated by the breakup in your relationship," she ventured cautiously.

"Sure, I'm devastated. I just told you, I'm a sensitive guy. But I'll get over it."

"What about Kaitlin?"

"Worrying about Kaitlin's feelings is not real high on my list of priorities at the moment."

Hannah gazed at him in amazement. "You mean you've actually *got* a list of priorities?"

"Okay, so it isn't a computer-generated five-year master plan like the one you've probably got tacked up on your bedroom wall. But some of us have to make it up as we go along."

She winced at the thought of the list of personal goals she had made for herself at the start of the summer. It was, indeed, hanging on the bulletin board over her dresser. It was an updated, more finely tuned version of the list she had made when she graduated from high school. Formulating objectives and then plotting a course to reach those objectives was second nature to her. Everyone in her family was trained to be organized and forward-looking. As her father, Hamilton, was fond of saying, an unplanned life was a messy life.

Madisons, on the other hand, were notorious for their propensity to be driven by quixotic obsessions, quirky desires, and the occasional wild hair. When a Madison was consumed by a passion, people said, nothing was allowed to get in the way. Rafe's casual attitude toward the breakup with Kaitlin Sadler tonight was convincing evidence that she did not rank as his passion.

"Okay, I'll bite," Hannah said, still uncertain about

whether or not Rafe was teasing her. "What's on your list of priorities?"

For a moment she thought he was not going to respond. Then he shoved his hands deeper into the pockets of his leather motorcycle jacket and turned slightly to face the bay.

"I don't think my plans would be of much interest to you," he said laconically. "It's not like I'm going to get a Ph.D. or anything."

She watched him, unwillingly fascinated now. "Tell me."

He fell silent for a moment. She had the impression that he was engaged in some kind of internal debate.

"My grandfather says that when I'm not busy screwing around I have a head for business," he said eventually. "He wants me to go to work for Gabe."

"But you don't want to do that?"

"Madison Commercial is Gabe's baby. He's in charge, and that's the way it has to be. We get along okay, but I learned a few things about myself in the army. One of them was that I'm not cut out to take orders."

"No surprise there, I guess."

Rafe took one hand out of his pocket, scooped up a small stone, and sent it skipping out across the dark water of the bay. "I want to do my own thing."

"I can understand that."

He glanced over his shoulder. "You do?"

"I don't want to work in a corporation or a bureaucracy either," she said quietly. "I'm going to open my own business as soon as I graduate."

"Got it all planned, huh?"

"Not entirely. But by the time I get out of college I should have most of the details nailed down. What about you? What's your chief objective?"

"To stay out of jail."

"That's certainly an impressive career goal. I'll bet you need to study for years and years and probably do an internship and a residency as well in order to achieve that objective."

"Everyone I know seems to think that not ending up in prison will be a major accomplishment for me." He swung back around to look at her. "What about you? What kind of business are you planning to open, Ms. Most Likely to Achieve?"

She took a few steps across the pebbly beach and sank down on a rock. "I'm not sure yet. I'm still researching possibilities. I've been talking to my dad. He says that the secret is to carve out a small niche in the service sector. One that big companies can't fill because of their size."

"Something along the lines of outcall massage, or maybe one of those private escort services?"

"Very funny."

"I've seen the ads in the Yellow Pages. You know, the ones aimed at traveling businessmen and conventioneers. *Discreet personal services offered in the privacy of your hotel room.*"

"You know, your sense of humor is as limited as your idea of an evening's entertainment."

"Well, what do you expect from a guy who doesn't have his Ph.D.?"

"Too much, obviously." She drew up her knees and wrapped her arms around them.

He moved to stand next to her rock. "Sorry. I shouldn't have teased you like that."

"Forget it."

"I'm sure you'll find your niche or whatever. Good luck."

"Thanks."

"Is marriage on your list of personal objectives?"

She glanced up at him, startled. "Well, yes, of course."

"I guess you'll probably marry someone like the jerk, right?"

She sighed. "I was never serious about Perry. He was just someone to have fun with this summer." She wrinkled her nose. "Not that he turned out to be a lot of fun tonight."

"Definitely not Mr. Right."

"No."

"Bet you've got a long list of requirements that Mr. Right will have to meet before you agree to marry him, don't you?"

The dry question made her uncomfortable. "So, I know what I want in a husband. So what? Just because you don't make long-range plans doesn't mean everyone else has to play their life by ear."

"True." Without warning, he dropped down onto the rock beside her. The movement was easy, almost catlike. "Tell me, what kind of hoops will Mr. Right have to jump through before you'll agree to marry him?"

Stung, she held up one hand and ticked off the basics. "He'll be intelligent, well educated, a graduate of a good school, and successful in his field. He'll also be loyal, honorable, decent, and trustworthy."

"No criminal record?"

"Definitely no criminal record." She held up her other hand and continued down the list. "He'll be dependable, kind, sensitive, and capable of making a commitment. Someone I can talk to. Someone who shares my interests and goals. That's very important, you know."

"Uh-huh."

"He'll also get along well with my family, love animals, and be very supportive of my career."

Rafe lounged back on his elbows. "But other than that, just an ordinary guy?"

For some inexplicable reason his mockery hurt. "You think I'm asking too much?"

He smiled faintly. "Get real. The guy you're looking for doesn't exist. Or if he does, he'll have some fatal flaw that you didn't expect."

"Is that so?" She narrowed her eyes. "How about your Ms. Right? Got any idea of what she'll be like?"

"No. Doubt if there is one. Not that it matters."

"Because you're not interested in a monogamous commitment?" she asked acidly.

"No, because the men in my family aren't much good when it comes to marriage. Figure the odds are against me getting lucky."

She could hardly argue that point. His grandfather's four spectacularly failed marriages were common knowledge. Rafe's father, Sinclair, had had two wives before he had engaged in the tumultuous affair with his model that had produced his sons. The assumption was that if he had not died in the motorcycle accident, Sinclair would have racked up a string of divorces and affairs that would have made Mitchell's record pale in comparison.

"Marriage should not be viewed as a lottery or a crapshoot," she said sternly. "It's a serious step, and it should be treated in a logical, rational manner."

"You think it's that easy?"

"I never said it's easy. I said it should be approached with intelligence and sound common sense."

"Where's the fun in that?"

She gritted her teeth. "You're teasing me again."

"Face it—we Madisons don't usually do things that involve common sense. We probably lack that gene."

"Don't give me that garbage. I'm serious about this, Rafe. I refuse to believe that you can't change what you see as your destiny."

He slanted her an appraising glance. "You really think I could be the one to break the mold?"

"If you want to break it badly enough, yes, I really think you can do it."

"Amazing. Who would have thought a Harte would be such a dreamer?"

"All right, what *are* you going to do with your life?"

"Well," he drawled, "I've noticed that the cult and guru businesses are profitable."

"Get serious. You've got your whole life ahead of you. Don't throw it away. Think about what you want. Make some concrete plans. Develop solid goals and then work toward them."

"You don't think my present career objective is a worthy goal?"

"Staying out of jail is okay as far as it goes. But it's not enough, Rafe. You know it isn't enough."

"Maybe not, but it's all I've got at the moment." He glanced at his watch. The dial glowed in the moonlight. "I think it's time that you went home."

Automatically she looked at her own watch. "Good grief, it's after one. It's going to take at least half an hour to walk home from here. I've got to get going."

He came up off the rock in a fluid movement. "I'll walk with you."

"That's not necessary."

"Yes it is. I'm a Madison and you're a Harte."

"So what?"

"So, if something were to happen to you between here and your place and your folks found out that I was the last guy to see you, I'd get the blame, for sure."

She smiled. "And maybe get tossed into jail by Chief Yates?"

"Yeah. And that would put a real crimp in the only viable career plan I've got at the moment."

The broad, semicircular sweep of the bay began in the distance behind Hannah, near the treacherous waters of Hidden Cove. It ended somewhere up ahead in the darkness, at a jutting piece of land known as Sundown Point. There were no streetlamps on the long, curving bluff road that rimmed the restless waters of Eclipse Bay. The sparse lights of the pier, the marina, and the town's tiny business district lay more than two miles to the rear, in the direction of Hidden Cove.

Up ahead, Hannah could make out only a vast pool of darkness. Sundown Point was invisible in the all-enveloping night. She knew that a handful of cottages and homes were scattered along the heavily wooded bluffs, but she saw no illuminated windows. Her family's summer place was nearly a mile from here, perched over a small, sheltered cove. Her aunt's big house, Dreamscape, was at least another half mile beyond that.

It was, indeed, going to be a long walk.

She glanced back over her shoulder. The faint glare of a well-lit parking lot could be seen on the hillside. It emanated from a clearing in the trees above the town. The parking facility belonged to the Eclipse Bay Policy Studies Institute, a recently established think tank that had been built close to Chamberlain College.

"My parents are up there at the institute tonight," she said at one point, just for something to say. "They're attending the reception for Trevor Thornley."

"The hotshot who's running for the state legislature?"

"Yes." She was surprised that he was aware of Thornley's campaign. He didn't seem like the type who paid attention to politics. But she refrained from making that observation aloud. "It looks like the event is running late. I may even get home ahead of Mom and Dad."

"Lucky for you, hmm? You won't have to go into a

lot of awkward explanations about why you came home with me instead of the jerk tonight."

She glanced at him, surprised. "I'll tell them what happened in the morning."

He slapped his forehead with the heel of his palm. "That's right, I keep forgetting. I'm with Ms. Goody Two-Shoes here. Of course you'll tell your parents that you spent the night on the beach with me."

Shock brought her to a sudden halt. "I did *not* spend the night on the beach with you, Rafe Madison. And if you dare tell your friends down at the Total Eclipse Bar and Grill that I did, I swear I will . . . I will *sue* you. Or something."

"Don't worry," he muttered. "I'm not planning to announce to the whole town that we did it under Eclipse Arch."

"You'd better not." She gripped her purse more tightly and started walking quicker. The sooner she got back to the house, the better.

Rafe fell into step beside her again. She was intensely aware of him. She had walked this road many times over the years, but never at this hour. Crime was minimal in Eclipse Bay, but not completely absent, especially during the summer when out-of-town visitors flocked to the beach. She was very glad to have company tonight. The long walk home alone would have been more than a little nerve-racking.

Half an hour later they reached the tree-lined drive that led to the Harte summer cottage. Rafe walked her to the porch steps and stopped.

"This is as far as I go," he said. "Good night, Hannah."

She went up one step and paused. It struck her that the strange interlude was over. A wistful sensation trickled through her. She stomped on it with all the ruthlessness she could muster. It was okay to have a few romantic fantasies about Rafe Madison. He was the most notorious male in town, after all—at least, the most notorious in her age group. But you couldn't get serious about a guy like this. There was no future in it.

"Thanks for seeing me home," she said.

"No problem. Not like I had anything better to do tonight." In the yellow glare of the porch light his eyes were enigmatic pools. "Good luck with that five-year plan of yours."

Impulsively she touched the sleeve of his jacket. "Think about making some plans of your own Rafe. Don't screw up your whole life."

He grinned. Without warning he leaned forward and brushed a quick, stunningly chaste kiss across her mouth. "A man's got to capitalize on his strong points, and I'm so damn good at screwing up."

The brief, casual kiss caught her off guard. Heat infused her whole body. It was followed by a tingling sensation. She covered the awkward moment by hurrying up the rest of the front steps.

At the door she paused to dig out her key. Her hand trembled slightly as she unlocked the door. When she finally got into the house, she turned to look back at Rafe. He was still standing there, watching her. She raised one hand in farewell and then quickly closed the door.

The rumble of voices awakened her the next morning. She opened her eyes and found herself gazing into a wall of fog.

Morning mist was a regular feature of summer and early fall. It would likely burn off by noon, although the cloud cover might last all day. With luck there would be enough scattered sunshine to drive the temperature into the mid-seventies in the afternoon, but that was the most that could be expected. Nobody came to Eclipse Bay to get a tan. Southern California beaches catered to those who liked to fry their bare skin in the glow of the big nuke in the sky. The wild, rugged beaches of the Oregon coast were for people who preferred to put on a windbreaker and brave the morning fog to explore tidal pools and rocky shoreline caves. They were for those who appreciated adventurous walks along high, windswept bluffs and views of seething seawater churning in stony cauldrons at the bottom of steep cliffs.

The voices downstairs grew louder. Her parents were talking to someone in the kitchen. A man. She could not make out the words, but the conversation sounded tense.

She listened for a while, curiosity growing swiftly. Who would come calling at this hour? Then she caught a name. Rafe Madison.

"Oh, damn."

She tossed aside the covers, scrambled out of bed, and hurriedly pulled on her jeans and a gray turtleneck. She stepped into a pair of loafers, ran a brush through her hair, and headed for the stairs.

She found her parents at the kitchen table with a balding, heavy-bellied man she recognized instantly.

"Chief Yates."

"'Morning, Hannah." Phil Yates nodded in his ponderous fashion. He had been the only law enforcement in town for as long as Hannah could recall, but this was the first time he had ever come to the Harte cottage.

She masked her uneasiness with a bright smile and turned to her parents for an explanation. A single glance was enough to tell her that something was terribly wrong.

Elaine Harte's attractive face was tight with anxiety. Hampton's jaw was set in a grim line. A formless dread wafted through Hannah. It was as if a ghost had brushed up against her.

"What is it?" she asked with an urgency that made her father's eyes narrow behind his glasses.

"I was just about to come upstairs and wake you, dear," Elaine said quietly. "Chief Yates has some bad news."

For one horrifying instant Hannah had a vision of Rafe lying sprawled on Bayview Drive, the victim of a hit-and-run. He'd had an even longer walk home last night than she'd had.

She went to the table and gripped the back of the empty chair. "What happened?"

"Kaitlin Sadler was found dead at Hidden Cove this morning," her father said in somber tones.

"Oh, my God." Not Rafe, then. He was safe. Hannah sank down into the chair. Then the name registered. "Kaitlin Sadler?"

"Looks like an accident," Yates said. "Apparently she fell from the path above the cliffs. But I've got to ask you a few questions."

Something in his voice got Hannah's full attention. Rafe was okay, but his girlfriend was dead. It didn't take a genius to figure out why Chief Yates had come here today. When a woman died under mysterious circumstances, the cops always came looking for the boyfriend or the husband first. Her brother had told her that.

Hamilton studied her with a troubled look. "There seems to be some confusion, Hannah. Phil says that Kaitlin was on a date with Rafe Madison last night. But Rafe told Yates that he was with you last night at about the time that Kaitlin died."

"We explained to Phil that that was not possible," Elaine said crisply. "You were with that nice young man from Chamberlain College. Perry Decatur."

Yates cleared his throat. "Well, now, I talked to Mr. Decatur. He says that's not quite true."

Hamilton flicked an irritated glance at Yates's broad,

patient face. "We also told him that even if you hadn't been with Decatur, you were highly unlikely to have been anywhere near Rafe Madison."

"I'm well aware of the fact that Hartes don't socialize with Madisons," Yates rumbled. "But young Rafe swears he was with Hannah here, and I got to check out his story."

The full implications of what he was saying finally hit Hannah. "I don't understand. You just said Kaitlin's death was an accident. Is there some question about how she died?"

"Can't rule out the possibility that she jumped." Yates wrapped one ham-size fist around a mug of coffee. "That girl always was kind of high-strung."

Elaine frowned. "She comes from an unfortunate family situation, but I never heard anyone suggest that she might be suicidal."

Yates sipped his coffee. "There's another possibility." They all looked at him expectantly.

"There may have been an argument," Yates said quietly.

"My God," Elaine whispered. "Are you saying she might have been pushed off the path?"

Hannah planted her hands on the table "Wait a second. Are you suggesting that Rafe Madison killed Kaitlin?"

"Could have been an accident," Yates said. "Like I said, maybe they got into a fight."

"But that's crazy. Why would Rafe do such a thing?"

"Word around town is that he didn't like the fact that she was seeing other men," Yates said.

"Yes, but—"

Hamilton looked at her. "Rafe is trying to use you for an alibi, honey. I don't like him dragging you into this one damn bit. But I'll deal with that later."

"Dad, listen to me—"

"Right now you just need to tell Yates where you were last night between midnight and two this morning."

Hannah braced herself for the explosion she knew would follow. "I was with Rafe Madison."

Kaitlin Sadler's death was officially ruled an accident three days later. It took a lot longer for the firestorm of gossip to fade. The news that Hannah had been with Rafe Madison the night Kaitlin died swept through the small community with the force of a tsunami. Few believed for a moment that the pair had engaged only in casual conversation.

The one person who seemed genuinely happy about the fact that Rafe and Hannah had spent two whole hours together on a moonlit beach was Hannah's great-aunt Isabel Harte.

At eighty-three, Isabel was the sole self-avowed romantic in the family. She was a retired professor of English lit who had never married. She lived alone at Dreamscape, the huge three-story mansion her father had built with the fortune he had made in fishing.

It was Isabel who had provided the seed funding for Harte-Madison, the commercial real estate development company founded by Sullivan Harte and Mitchell Madison all those years ago. The bitter feud that had destroyed the firm as well as the friendship between Sullivan and Mitchell was a source of frustration and disappointment to Isabel. She still harbored dreams of ending the rift that had shattered the partnership and ignited the hostility between the two men.

Hannah was very fond of her great-aunt. She was also well aware that her parents had been trying to get Isabel to sell Dreamscape and move into an apartment in Portland. But Isabel refused to budge.

On the fourth day of the seething rumors, Isabel sat with Elaine Harte in the Harte family kitchen.

"It's so romantic," Isabel said, blithely indifferent to Elaine's exasperated expression. "Just like Romeo and Juliet."

"That's ridiculous," Elaine gasped.

"Darn right," Hannah said from the doorway. "We all know what happened to Romeo and Juliet. A very nasty ending, if you ask me."

"This would be Romeo and Juliet with the right ending," Isabel said, unperturbed. "A happy conclusion that would end the long-standing feud between the two families."

Elaine raised her eyes to the heavens. "Sullivan and Mitchell are engaged in a feud, Isabel. The rest of us just ignore each other. Rafe Madison has no real interest in a nice girl like Hannah."

"Gee, thanks, Mom." Hannah went to the counter to pour herself a cup of coffee. "Why don't you just label me boring and be done with it?"

Elaine gave her a repressive look. "You know perfectly well what I meant."

"I sure do, Mom." Hannah made a face. "And you're absolutely right. Rafe doesn't have any interest in me. I'm not his type."

Isabel's vivid blue eyes brightened with interest. "Whatever do you mean, dear?"

Hannah smiled wryly. "Rafe thinks I'm a prim, prissy, goody-goody overachiever."

"What do you think about him?" Isabel asked quickly.

"I think he's wasting his life. Told him so, too. The only thing we had in common the other night when we ran into each other on the beach was the fact that we both had to walk home after a bad date. Trust me, seduction was the last thing on his mind."

"Unfortunately, almost no one in town believes that," Elaine said grimly. "I'm told that Kaitlin Sadler's brother believes far worse. He's convinced that Rafe really did shove Kaitlin over that cliff and later seduced you in an effort to persuade you to cover up for him."

"I know," Hannah said. "Poor Dell. He's lost his sister, and all everyone can talk about is how Rafe spent the night making wild, passionate love to me on the beach."

Isabel's eyes lit with speculative interest. "I don't suppose that he actually did—?"

"No, he did not," Hannah said brusquely. "I told you, all we did was talk."

Elaine shook her head. "I believe you, dear. And I'm relieved to know that Rafe was nowhere near Kaitlin at the time she died. I just wish that he had found someone else to give him his alibi that night. I'm afraid it's going to be a long time before people stop talking about this unfortunate affair."

"Actually it's kind of weird when you think about it," Pamela said the next day over veggie burgers and French fries at Snow's Café. "I mean, what are the odds that either you or I would ever spend a couple of hours on a beach with a guy like Rafe Madison?"

Hannah eyed her friend over the top of the bun. Pamela attended Chamberlain College. She had her sights set on a career teaching English literature to undergraduates. She already wore the uniform of the successful young academic: black tights, chunky black shoes, a long black skirt, a slouchy jacket, and glasses with thin frames. Her shoulder-length brown hair was held at her nape with a mock-tortoiseshell clip.

"I admit the odds are not high." Hannah took a mouthful of her tofu burger. "It was just one of those things. I owe it all to Perry Decatur."

Pamela made a face. "So much for your mom's opinion of Perry. She was so sure he was the nice, upwardly mobile type."

"He's definitely committed to upward mobility. Probably go far in the academic world."

"But not a nice guy, huh?"

"Smooth. Slick." Hannah thought back to the scuffle in the front seat and shuddered. "Not nice."

Pamela glanced around the crowded café. Apparently satisfied that no one could overhear, she leaned across the table and lowered her voice. "So what really did happen between you and Rafe Madison?"

"Nothing. I told you, we just talked. That's all."

Pamela's eyes clouded with disappointment. "That's all? Honest truth?"

Hannah briefly considered the insignificant good-night kiss Rafe had given her. "Pretty much."

Pamela flopped back in her chair. "Too bad."

"Think so?"

"Sure. Intelligent, educated, clearheaded women like us know better than to marry guys like Rafe Madison. But that doesn't mean it wouldn't be fun to fool around with one."

"A little hard on the reputation, especially in a town like Eclipse Bay. Trust me, I know this now. After those infamous two hours on the beach with Rafe Madison, my image as a nice girl has plummeted to somewhere in the vicinity of zero."

"The least you could have done for yourself was have a good time on the way down."

Rafe phoned the day he left town. Hannah was alone in the house at the time. When she heard his voice on the other end of the line she had a feeling he knew that her parents had driven into Eclipse Bay together.

"I owe you," he said without preamble.

"No, you do not owe me." She clutched the instrument very tightly. His voice was as sexy on the phone as it was at midnight on a shadowed beach. "I just told the truth, that's all."

"Is everything that simple for you, Miss Voted Most Likely to Succeed? Black and white? True or false?"

"In this case it is, yes."

"You don't care that everyone in town thinks I did a lot more than hold your hand that night?"

She sought refuge in irrefutable fact. "You didn't even hold my hand."

There was a short beat of silence on the other end of the line. She wondered if he was thinking about that meaningless little kiss he had given her just before he sent her into the house. It was certainly on her mind.

"Whatever," he said eventually. "But I still owe you."

"Forget it. No big deal. Besides, to be honest, I owe you."

"How's that?"

"I am no longer known around town as Miss Boring Goody Two-Shoes."

There was another beat of silence. "You're definitely not boring."

She was not sure what to say to that. She wrapped the cord around her hand and kept her mouth shut. It was an exercise in self-discipline.

"Hannah?"

"Yes?"

"I meant what I said last night. Good luck with that five-year plan of yours. I hope things work out the way you want. Hope you do okay with your own business."

He paused. "Hope you find a guy who meets all those requirements on that list, too."

He sounded sincere, she thought.

"Rafe?"

"Yeah?"

"I meant what I said to you that night, too. Get a life."

chapter 1

Portland, Oregon
The present . . .

The long, pearl-studded train of the creamy candlelight-satin wedding gown cascaded in graceful folds behind the bride as she glided to a halt in front of the altar. She smiled demurely at the groom through a gossamer cloud of veil. The organ music trailed off. A respectful hush fell. The minister cleared his throat.

"Well, that's it for me," Hannah murmured to her assistant as they retreated to the portico in front of the church. "I'm out of here. You can handle the receiving line. The limo is ready. Keep an eye on the four-year-old nephew. He'll probably make another grab for the bride's train when she walks back down the aisle. See you at the reception."

"It's so perfect." Carla Groves seized a tissue and dabbed at her eyes. She peeked back into the church. "The flowers, the candles. Everything. The bride looks as if she just stepped out of a fantasy."

"I don't know how to tell you this, Carla, but you

aren't going to last long in this business if you weep every time you send a bride up the aisle."

"But she's so beautiful. Practically glowing."

"Uh-huh." Hannah snapped the lock on her briefcase. "Looks even better this time than she did the last time. Probably because her budget was much larger. She did very well in the divorce settlement, you know. Had a great lawyer."

Carla rolled her eyes. "You're such a cynic, Hannah."

"No, I'm not. I agree with you. Jennifer Ballinger does make a lovely bride. And a very profitable one for Weddings by Harte. This is her second marriage with us, and I have every expectation that in a couple of years she'll come back to this firm for her third. Nothing like a repeat customer, I always say."

At five-thirty that evening, Hannah stepped out of the elevator into a corridor decorated in shades of tasteful beige and walked down the hall toward the door of her apartment. Her footsteps were hushed by the thick, pale carpeting, but the door of the suite next to hers opened before she reached it.

Winston rushed out to greet her with as much enthusiasm as a properly bred Schnauzer considered appropriate to exhibit upon such occasions. As always, the sight of the small, elegant, salt-and-pepper dog hurrying toward her lowered Hannah's stress level by several degrees.

She smiled as she crouched to scratch Winston behind the ears. He gave a discreetly muffled whine, quivered with pleasure, and licked her hand.

"Hello, pal. Sorry I'm late. Been a long day."

Winston looked up at her through a fringe of long, silvery lashes, understanding in his intelligent eyes.

Mrs. Blankenship struck her head around the edge of

the door. "Oh, there you are, dear. Winston was starting to get a trifle anxious. How did the wedding go?"

"Nothing out of the ordinary. The usual number of snafus at the reception. The caterer turned up with a cheese tart instead of the asparagus canapés that the bride had selected. The photographer helped himself to a couple of glasses of champagne and started to flirt with the bartender. The flower girl came very close to getting into a food fight with the four-year-old nephew."

"Just the usual, then." Mrs. Blankenship nodded wisely. She always loved to hear about the weddings. "But I'm sure you nipped all the potential disasters in the bud behind the scenes."

"That's what I get paid to do." Hannah leaned down to pat Winston, who bounced around her high heels. "I think the bride was satisfied. As far as she was concerned, everything went off as if the whole thing had been staged by a computer."

Mrs. Blankenship pursed her lips. "I don't think that's an appropriate image, dear. The thought of a computer-generated wedding is really quite dreadful. It sounds so cold. Weddings are supposed to evoke all sorts of wonderful emotions, after all."

"Trust me, Mrs. Blankenship, behind the scenes, a well-managed wedding has a lot in common with a launch of the space shuttle."

"You know, dear, I hate to mention this, but you've become increasingly cynical ever since you ended your engagement last year. It's so sad to see a young, healthy, vibrant woman like you turn jaded. Maybe you took on too much when you signed up for all those evening classes at the college."

"Mrs. Blankenship—"

"You've been working much too hard for the past year. Perhaps you need a vacation. Go someplace where you can relax and regain your interest in your business and your social life."

"I have no social life to revive, Mrs. Blankenship. And as for my career, nothing will ever make me starry-eyed about my business. The only weddings that I actually enjoy doing are those in which I know for a fact that the couple met through my sister's agency. At least I can feel reasonably confident that those marriages have a good chance of lasting."

"Yes, your sister does have a knack for matchmaking, doesn't she?" Mrs. Blankenship got a dreamy expression in her eyes. "She obviously has a wonderful sense of intuition when it comes to that sort of thing."

"I hate to disillusion you, Mrs. Blankenship, but Lillian uses a computer, not her intuition." Hannah dug her keys out of her massive shoulder bag. "Does Winston need a walk right away?"

"No, dear, we just got back from our walkies," Mrs. Blankenship said.

"Great." Hannah went to her own door and unlocked it, Winston trotting eagerly at her heels. "Thanks again, Mrs. Blankenship."

"Anytime, dear." Mrs. Blankenship paused. "You know, you really should consider taking some time off. Your busy season is finished. You could slip away for a while."

"Funny you should mention that, Mrs. Blankenship. I was just thinking the same thing."

Mrs. Blankenship beamed. "I'm so glad to hear that. You really haven't been quite the same since your engagement ended."

"Several people have mentioned that." Hannah opened her door. "One theory is that I have been possessed by an alien entity."

"I beg your pardon?"

"Never mind. Good night, Mrs. Blankenship."

"Good night, dear."

Hannah stepped into the small hallway, waited until Winston came inside, and then swiftly shut the door. She flipped on the lights.

"Give me a minute to change, Winston. Then I'll find us both something to eat."

In the bedroom she stripped off the jacket and skirt of her blue business suit, then pulled on a pair of black leggings and a cozy cowl-necked tunic and slipped into a pair of ballet-style flats. Pausing for a moment in front of the mirror, she brushed her hair behind her ears and anchored it with a narrow band.

When she was ready, she padded back down the hall into the kitchen and dug one of the expensive, specially formulated dog bones out of a box for Winston. The Schnauzer took it very politely from her fingers.

"Enjoy."

Winston needed no further urging. He set to work on the bone vigorously.

Hannah opened the refrigerator and meditated on the sparse contents for a moment. After a while she removed a hunk of sheep's-milk feta cheese and a nearly empty bottle of Chardonnay.

She arranged her small haul on a tray and carried it into the second bedroom, where she maintained a home office. Winston followed, the remains of his bone wedged firmly between his jaws. Sinking down onto the high-backed chair, Hannah propped her feet on the corner of the desk and munched a cracker with some of the cheese on it.

Winston took up his customary position on the floor beside the desk chair. Muted crunching sounds ensued.

"Brace yourself, Winston." Hannah reached for the

phone. "I'm going to check my messages. Who knows what excitement awaits us?"

The automated answering service surrendered three offerings. The first was from a florist, reporting that the orchids Hannah had ordered for the Cooke-Anderson wedding were going to cost more than expected.

"I told the client that they would be expensive."

The second message was from her brother, Nick, letting her know that he had just mailed the manuscript of the most recent addition to his successful suspense series to the editor. "I'm taking Carson to Disneyland, and then we're going on down to Phoenix to see Sullivan and Rachel. Probably be gone for most of the month. You know how to reach me if you need me."

"It's about time he married again," Hannah said to Winston. "Amelia has been gone for three years now. He and little Carson have been alone long enough."

Winston jiggled his brows.

"Yes, I know. I'm a fine one to talk."

She punched the key for the last message . . . and nearly fell off her chair when she heard Rafe Madison's unmistakable, bottom-of-the-sea voice. Her heels came down off the desk with a small thud. She sucked in a half-strangled breath and sat forward abruptly. The Chardonnay sloshed wildly in the glass. Several drops went over the rim and hit Winston between his ears.

He looked up from his bone with a puzzled expression.

"Sorry, Winston." She grabbed a napkin and blotted the wine off the top of his head. "I was a little stunned there for a second, but I don't think I'm going to faint or anything."

She tossed the napkin into the wastebasket, inhaled slowly, and took a steadying swallow of wine.

She had not heard his voice in eight years, and although this time around it was only a recording, it had the same impact on her tonight as it had the last time. Small flashes of electrical energy snapped through her nerve endings. Her stomach seemed to float in midair.

"This is Rafe Madison . . ."

The last conversation she'd had with him flitted through her mind. *Good luck with that five-year plan of yours. I hope things work out the way you want.*

She wondered if he'd ever gotten his act together.

". . . Got the message you sent through your lawyer. The answer is no. Looks like we've got a few things to talk about, and I don't plan to do it through our attorneys. See you in Eclipse Bay."

"No?" The old memories went up in smoke and the present came crashing back. She stabbed the replay key.

". . . The answer is no. . . . See you in Eclipse Bay."

She had not misunderstood. His answer to her offer was loud and clear.

"I think I've got a problem, Winston."

She dropped the bombshell on her sister the following morning.

"What do you mean, he refuses to sell?" Lillian demanded on the other end of the line. "That house belonged to *our* great-aunt, not his. He can't refuse to sell."

Hannah listened to the muffled sounds of a printer in the background. Lillian was hard at work. She ran her matchmaking firm, Private Arrangements, out of an office in a high-rise located only a few blocks away from the one in which Hannah and Winston lived.

"You were there when Isabel's will was read," Hannah reminded her wearily. "She left the house equally to Rafe and me. The lawyer says he can do whatever he wants to do with his half."

"Hmm. Maybe you didn't offer him enough money."

"The negotiations didn't even get that far. I just sent a message to him through the lawyer telling him that I would be willing to buy out his half of the house. I expected him to come back with a price."

"What on earth do you suppose he plans to do with half of Dreamscape?" Lillian mused.

"Who knows?" Hannah frowned at the array of wedding photos that decorated her office wall. "But I have plans for Dreamscape, and I'm certainly not going to let him stand in my way."

"You're going to meet with him in Eclipse Bay, aren't you?"

"Doesn't look like I've got much choice. I want Dreamscape. Somehow I've got to talk him out of his share of the place."

"We haven't heard much about Rafe in recent years. Just that he got married and divorced."

Hannah thought about her midnight conversation with Rafe. *The men in my family aren't much good when it comes to marriage. . . . Figure the odds are against me getting lucky . . .*

"Divorce is a Madison family tradition," she said quietly.

"Unfortunately, it's a very common tradition for a lot of families these days." Lillian made a *tut-tut* sound. "I don't know why so many people refuse to see the obvious. Marriage is a partnership. It should be entered into the same way one would go into any serious business arrangement. All the factors should be examined from every angle before a commitment is made."

"Lillian—"

"There's a staggering amount of scientific evidence that suggests that couples who are properly matched using modern psychological tests and personality inventories are far more likely to succeed at marriage than those who let their emotions—"

"Enough, Lillian. I've heard your professional pitch before, remember?"

"Sorry. You know me. I get a little carried away sometimes." Lillian hesitated. "About Rafe Madison—"

"What about him?"

"Think he's changed?"

"How should I know?" Hannah rose, phone in hand, and went to the window. "Wonder if he achieved his big career objective?"

"Didn't know he had one."

"Oh, he had one, all right." Hannah studied the view of the bridge-studded Willamette River. "His great ambition was to stay out of jail."

"Given the direction in which everyone seemed to think he was headed eight years ago, that would have been a major accomplishment."

"I'm sure we would have heard if he had gone to prison." Hannah tightened her grip on the phone. "That kind of news would have been hot gossip in Eclipse Bay."

"Ah, but as far as we know, he hasn't been back to Eclipse Bay very often since Kaitlin Sadler died. According to Mom and Dad, he makes a couple of short weekend visits to see his grandfather every few months and that's it. How would anyone know if he'd done time?"

"I think he was too smart to end up in prison," Hannah said.

"Smart does not always equate with common sense. We're both in the marriage business. We see smart people do dumb things every day."

"True."

Lillian paused. "You're still serious about your plans for Dreamscape?"

"Very."

"I was afraid of that. My advice is don't let Rafe know you've got your heart set on turning Dreamscape into an inn."

"Why not?"

Lillian made an exasperated sound. "Use your head. If he figures out just how badly you want the place, he'll hold out for a whopping price for his half."

"I'll be careful how much I say. I'm a Harte, remember? I can be cool."

"Do that," Lillian said dryly. "You know, something tells me that it's a good thing that Mom and Dad went on that monthlong cruise. If they knew that you were getting ready to go toe-to-toe with Rafe Madison over Dreamscape, they'd descend on Eclipse Bay like avenging angels."

"Speaking of family interference, I'm counting on you to keep quiet about my decision to go to Eclipse Bay for a while. I want some time to work things out with Rafe. That won't be possible if I'm inundated with helpful Hartes."

"I'll keep quiet," Lillian sighed. "I still can't imagine what Aunt Isabel was thinking. Ever since Rafe used you as his alibi for the night Kaitlin Sadler died, she was obsessed with the notion that the two of you were the Romeo and Juliet of the Harte-Madison feud."

"Rafe didn't *use* me as his alibi," Hannah said. "I *was* his alibi."

"There's a difference?"

"Oh, yes," Hannah said. "There's a difference."

chapter 2

The weird part was that he had never intended to come back for more than an occasional overnight stay, just the obligatory duty visits to check up on Mitchell. Now he was determined to carve out his future here in Eclipse Bay.

Go figure.

Rafe propped one sneaker-clad foot on the bottom rail of the second-story veranda that wrapped around the big house. He braced his elbows on the top rail and watched the sporty little lipstick-red Honda turn into the long drive.

He hadn't had a lot of ambitions eight years ago. He'd only known that he had to stop screwing up. Something of a challenge, given where he was coming from. He'd achieved his primary objective, he thought, as he watched the rakish red car come closer. He'd managed to stay out of jail.

He wondered if Hannah would be impressed.

The crimson vehicle came to a halt next to his silver

Porsche. An intense rush of anticipation swept through him. He watched the door on the driver's side of the Honda open.

The first thing he noticed when Hannah got out of the car was that her amber-brown hair was shorter. Eight years ago it had fallen well below her shoulders. Today it was cut in a sleek, sophisticated curve that angled along the line of her jaw.

She didn't look as if she had gained any weight in the intervening years, but there was something different about her figure. The black trousers and snug-fitting black top she wore revealed a fit, lithe body with a small waist, gently flared hips, and discreetly curved breasts. It took him a few seconds to decide that the difference was the sophisticated confidence with which she carried herself. She had seemed painfully young and naïve that night on the beach. Still a girl in some ways. She was a woman now.

She paused, holding the car door open, and leaned down slightly to speak to someone in the front seat. From his vantage point on the upper veranda he could not see who had accompanied her. Sharp disappointment gripped him. For some reason he had assumed that she would be alone. What the hell had he expected? He'd heard that her engagement had blown up a year ago, but that was no reason to think she hadn't gotten serious about someone else in the meantime.

The passenger door did not open. Instead, Hannah stepped back to allow an elegantly trimmed gray Schnauzer to bound out of the car.

Relief whipped through Rafe. Not a boyfriend, after all. Just a mutt. He could handle a dog.

Sensing Rafe's presence on the veranda, the Schnauzer came to a sudden halt and looked up at him. Rafe waited for the little beast to start yapping wildly in typical froufrou-dog style. But the Schnauzer did not bark. Instead, he gazed up at Rafe with an air of watchful stillness.

Okay, so maybe this was not a totally froufrou dog.

Hannah looked up to see what had captured her dog's attention. The light of the late-afternoon sun glinted on her stylish sunglasses.

"Hello, Rafe."

That cool reserve hadn't been in her voice eight years ago, he thought.

"Been a while," he said neutrally.

"Yes, it has," she said. "I've been wondering, did you ever get a life?"

"Depends on your definition. What about you? The five-year plan turn out the way you expected?"

"Not exactly." She moved one hand in a graceful gesture to indicate the big house. "You're going to be difficult about his, aren't you?"

"Yeah."

She nodded. "Had a feeling you would."

She went up the front steps and disappeared into the house. The Schnauzer gave Rafe one last, assessing look and followed Hannah inside.

He found her standing in the solarium, arms folded beneath her breasts. She smiled coolly, but her shoulders were angled. She was braced for battle. When Rafe walked into the glass-walled room, the Schnauzer glanced up from an exploration of a potted palm.

"Nice dog." Rafe crouched and held out his hand.

"His name is Winston," Hannah said crisply.

"Hello, Winston."

With great dignity, the Schnauzer crossed the tiled floor to where Rafe waited and sniffed politely. Apparently satisfied that the proprieties had been observed, he sat back on his haunches and looked up at Hannah.

Rafe got to his feet. "I think your dog likes me."

She did not look pleased. "Winston is always well behaved. I wouldn't read too much into it if I were you."

"Right. Maybe he's waiting until my back is turned to go for my throat. How long have you had him?"

"A couple of years."

Rafe nodded. "Outlasted your fiancé, huh? Lucky dog."

Her mouth tightened. "I'm not here to talk about Winston or my ex-fiancé."

"Whatever. Want some coffee?"

She hesitated. "All right."

"Don't fall all over yourself."

She trailed after him down the hall into the big, old-fashioned kitchen. Winston trotted briskly at her heels, pausing here and there to investigate a corner or a piece of furniture.

"How did you hear about my engagement?" Hannah asked. Irritation made the question as brittle as thin ice.

"You know how gossip travels between the Hartes and the Madisons."

"In other words, Aunt Isabel told you."

"Yeah." He set the kettle on the stove. "Sent me a note right after the breakup. She seemed delighted. Guess Mr. Right fell a little short in her view."

Hannah watched him intently. "How long have you been here at Dreamscape?"

"Got in late last night." He spooned coffee into the tall glass pot.

She glanced at the French press coffeemaker he was using. "Isabel never made her coffee in one of those. She always used a regular drip machine."

"This is mine. I brought it with me."

"I see." She eyed the gleaming stainless-steel vegetable steamer on the counter. "That's not Isabel's either."

"No."

Frowning, she walked to the pantry and opened the door. He knew what she saw inside. The supplies he had brought with him included several boxes of his favorite brand of dried pasta in a variety of shapes, a bottle of twelve-year-old balsamic vinegar, and a package of capers preserved in salt. There was also a supply of dried herbs and chiles and some French lentils.

Hannah closed the pantry door very firmly. "You've certainly made yourself right at home."

"Why not? Half this place is mine now."

"Lillian was right," she said tightly. "I can't imagine what Isabel was thinking when she made out her will."

He poured boiling water into the pot. "You know damn well what she was thinking."

"Romeo and Juliet."

He set the kettle down. "With a more upbeat ending."

"I am prepared to make you a fair-market offer for your share of Dreamscape."

"Forget it." He smiled slightly. "I'm not interested."

She met his gaze across the width of the kitchen. There was steel in her eyes. "Do you intend to make me an offer for my half?"

He lounged against the counter. "Are you open to one?"

"No. I have plans for Dreamscape."

"What a coincidence. So do I."

She gave him a speculative look. "Looks like we have a problem."

"Think so?"

"How long are you going to stay here in Eclipse Bay?"

He shrugged and turned back to finish the coffee. "As long as it takes."

"You can afford to just drop everything and move back here to Eclipse Bay for an unspecified period of time?"

"Nothing holding me in San Diego."

"That's where you've been all these years?" Her tone was one of unwilling curiosity.

Just had to ask, he thought. As if she couldn't help herself. Good sign. Maybe.

"For the most part," he said easily.

He pressed the plunger down to trap the grounds in the bottom of the pot. Then he glanced at Hannah over his shoulder. She was watching him with an enigmatic expression.

"What about you?" he prodded softly. "How long do you intend to stay here in Eclipse Bay?"

Her brows rose. "For as long as it takes."

"There are three floors. Plenty of bedrooms and baths. Take your pick."

"You're staying here?"

"Sure, why not?"

"Then I think I'll use my folks' place," she said coolly.

What had he expected? That would have been too easy, anyway. Nothing ever came easy to him. He had a talent for doing things the hard way.

"Suit yourself," he said. "But this is Eclipse Bay. You're a Harte and I'm a Madison, and by now everyone knows Isabel left Dreamscape to both of us."

"So?"

"So, people are going to talk, regardless of where you choose to sleep."

She watched him pour the coffee. When he handed her the mug, her fingers brushed against his. He savored the small thrill, wondered if she felt anything at all.

She turned away a little too quickly and paced to the far end of the counter.

"Let's go back into the solarium." He led the way out of the kitchen. "We can sit down out there."

Hannah said nothing, but she trailed after him. He watched her settle neatly onto a cushioned white wicker lounger. Winston sauntered into the sunroom, found a satisfactory place near the window, and flopped down on his belly. He rested his muzzle on his front paws and watched Rafe through feathery brows.

Hannah turned the mug between her palms. "What exactly do you plan to do with Dreamscape?"

"I'm going to open an inn and restaurant."

Her mouth fell open. She stared at him, her eyes widening in astonishment.

"You're going to do *what*?" Somewhere between a screech and a choking sound.

"You heard me," he said mildly.

"You can't be serious," she sputtered. "That's *my* plan. At least, the inn part is my plan." She hesitated, frowning. "I hadn't thought about adding a restaurant."

"You should have thought about it. The reputation of any hotel is greatly enhanced by a high-quality restaurant."

"No offense, but as I recall, your idea of a high-class establishment when you lived here was the Total Eclipse Bar and Grill. I seriously doubt that any place that uses the slogan *Where the sun don't shine* is going to show up in your better grade of guidebook."

"The Total Eclipse has its place in the grand scheme of things."

"I'll take your word for it." She eyed him. "Just what do you know about running an inn and a restaurant?"

"I worked at a five-star place down in San Diego for a while."

"Terrific." She gave him an icy look. "You've worked in a hotel, so you think you can run one?"

"I'll admit I'm stronger in the food-and-beverage area than I am on the innkeeping side."

"What did you do at this five-star place in San Diego? Wait tables?"

"Among other things," he said. "What about you? Know anything about the innkeeping business?"

"As a matter of fact, I've been taking intensive classes in hotel management for nearly a year. Ever since I got the idea of turning Dreamscape into an inn."

"Is that so? And just where did you get the brilliant notion of converting this place into a hotel?"

She hesitated. "Aunt Isabel and I started talking about it a year ago."

He whistled softly. "What an astonishing coincidence."

"Don't tell me." Hannah's jaw was very tight now. "She mentioned the idea to you at about the same time, right?"

"Right."

Hannah tapped a neatly manicured nail against the side of her glass. "Let me make something very clear. This isn't an impulse or a flash-in-the-pan idea for me. I've done a lot of thinking and planning during the past year. I've made my decision. I'm going to sell Weddings by Harte and open this inn. I'm absolutely committed to this project."

"What a coincidence," he said again.

"Let's get real here. Sooner or later we're going to have to come to some agreement about what to do with Dreamscape."

He settled deeper into his chair and looked out over the bay. "I'm in no rush."

She gave him a frozen smile. "I noticed."

chapter 3

Snow's Café had changed little in eight years. Whenever she stepped inside, Hannah always felt as if she had entered a time warp. The colorful posters on the walls were always the same—a mix of classic rock band ads and pithy sayings that reflected the conspiracy theories of the owner, Arizona Snow. The large one over the cash register summed up Arizona's worldview. The illustration showed two bug-eyed space aliens in heavy-metal attire. They were armed with futuristic weaponry. The slogan underneath read, *We're from the government and we're here to help.*

The café was the main hangout for the faculty and students of nearby Chamberlain College. The Eclipse Bay Policy Studies Institute was not far away, but the think tank staff tended to avoid Snow's. It was no secret that since the day the institute had opened its doors Arizona had viewed the facility with deep suspicion. She was convinced that whatever was going on there constituted a dangerous threat to all those who cherished a free society.

"Over here, Hannah." Pamela's face lit up in welcome. Pamela McCallister was now on the faculty of the English department at Chamberlain, and over the years her upwardly mobile path through the thorny territory of higher education had been marked by subtle but highly significant changes of fashion. She still wore a lot of black, but there was less of the romantic poetess about her now and more of the trendy professional. Her hair was much shorter, marking her shift from student to faculty status. The voluminous bag she carried was made of much more expensive material than the one she had favored eight years ago.

"Sorry I'm late." Hannah gave her a quick hug before sliding into the booth across from her. "I stopped by Dreamscape, and then I had to take my dog and my luggage to my folks' cottage."

Pamela gave her a knowing look. "You're not staying at Dreamscape?"

"Rafe got there ahead of me."

"I heard his car was seen parked in the drive all last night."

"He's definitely taken up residence." Hannah snapped the well-worn, plastic-coated menu out of the slot behind the napkin holder. "I think he's working on the premise that possession is nine-tenths of the law."

"Well, well, well." Pamela looked deeply intrigued. "This is going to be interesting."

"Think so?"

"Yes, indeed. Can't wait to see how it plays out." Pamela's eyes gleamed behind the lenses of her glasses. "And just think, the whole town will be watching."

"I'm glad everyone else finds this mess so amusing." Hannah glanced at the menu and saw that it hadn't changed in eight years, either. It still featured the same eclectic but curiously inspired assortment of vegetarian burgers, French fries, pizzas, quesadillas, and noodle dishes. "I can assure you that from where I'm sitting, there's nothing remotely entertaining about it. Rafe made it clear this afternoon that he's going to be a problem."

"He always was a problem, as I recall." Pamela propped her elbows on the yellow Formica tabletop and rested her chin on her folded hands. "So, tell me. Has he changed much?"

"No. He's driving a Porsche these days instead of a motorcycle, but as far as I can tell, he still has no visible means of support."

"Hmm."

Hannah looked up sharply from the menu. "What does 'hmm' mean?"

"There's been some talk that he might have been dabbling in a few less-than-legal activities during the past eight years."

"Great. You think I'm sharing Aunt Isabel's inheritance with a gangster?"

"No one's really sure, you understand. But you've got to admit, the Porsche is a little hard to explain."

Hannah thought about that for a few seconds. "Well, one thing's for certain. Whatever he's been up to in the past few years, he still views me as a prissy overachiever. Not exactly the basis for a lasting relationship."

"Who's talking duration?"

"I refuse to allow you to live out your prurient fantasies vicariously through me, Pam." Hannah sighed. "I guess I'll know soon enough whether or not he's changed. If he starts spending his evenings down at the Total Eclipse, I'll get a very big clue, won't I?"

"I'd say that would be a hint, yes."

"Let's change the subject." Hannah dropped the menu on the table. "Brad and the kids?"

"The kids are great." Pamela's eyes softened and lit up with enthusiasm. "I promised them you'd come to dinner soon."

"I'll be there with bells on."

"And Brad? Did he get that joint appointment at the institute yet?"

Pamela's smile faded. "We thought we were going to have some excellent news on that front to announce later this month. But now we're not so sure."

"Something go wrong?"

"You could say that. The something is named Perry Decatur. As far as we can tell, he's the one blocking the appointment. He's been jealous of Brad for years. Probably afraid that if Brad joins the staff at the institute, he'll be put in the shade."

Hannah sat back in surprise. "I didn't know Perry worked at the institute."

"I thought I told you. He left his position at Chamberlain six months ago. His title is Vice President of Finance and Administration. Brings in big donors. Everyone assumes he's got his eye on becoming director one of these days."

Hannah shook her head in wry disgust. "Perry always was a fast talker."

"Never thought you'd come back here for good." Jed Steadman sat forward in the wicker chair and clasped his hands lightly between his knees. "Figured that with the way things were between you and your grandfather, you'd want to stay clear of Eclipse Bay as much as possible."

Rafe stacked his feet on the railing, rocked back in his chair, and took a swallow of beer from the bottle he had brought from the kitchen. "One thing I've learned in the past eight years: Never say never."

"I hear you." Jed watched a seagull ride a current of air above the cliffs. "Life takes some twists and turns sometimes. I thought I'd be long gone by now myself."

"That's right. Your big plan was to get a job as a foreign correspondent with one of the big-city dailies. What happened?"

"A man has to be flexible or he'll miss out on some incredible opportunities. When Ed Bolton said he would sell the *Journal* to me a few years ago, I jumped at the chance. As editor and owner, I get to run my own show."

"A lot to be said for that."

"You got that right." Jed slanted him a sidelong glance. "Judging by the Porsche outside, you've done okay for yourself."

Rafe took another swallow of beer. "Managed to stay out of jail."

Jed gave a short bark of laughter. "Almost forgot. Not doing time behind bars was your big career objective, wasn't it?"

Rafe raised the beer bottle in a mocking salute. "And here I am today, a resounding success in my chosen field. A lesson for wayward youth across this great land."

"Exactly what *is* your chosen field?" Jed's eyes glinted with curiosity. "No offense, but I never heard that you ever actually got yourself what folks like to call a real job."

"I get by."

"I've noticed." Jed watched him intently. "There's talk going around that you maybe found some, shall we say, unconventional ways to accomplish that."

"You're starting to sound like a reporter, Jed."

Jed held up his hands, palms out. "Okay, I get the

point. No more questions in that area. Can't blame me for asking. I am in the newspaper business, after all."

They sat in companionable silence for a few minutes.

"Heard you and Connie split up a couple of years ago," Rafe said eventually. "Sorry."

"It was a mistake." Jed glanced down at his clasped hands and then looked up. "She went back to Seattle. Couldn't take small-town life. She's remarried."

Rafe settled deeper into his chair. "I didn't do any better with marriage myself."

"I'm surprised you even gave it a whirl. You always said you wouldn't be any good at it."

"Turned out I was right."

"One thing you should know," Jed said quietly after a while. "Dell Sadler still thinks you pushed his sister over that cliff. You might want to stay out of his way while you're here in town."

"Thanks for the tip."

"Sure. What are friends for?" Jed looked down the length of the broad front porch that encircled the mansion. "What are you going to do with this place?"

"Open an inn and a restaurant."

"Whew!" Jed was clearly impressed. "Talk about big plans! Gonna cost a bundle, though."

"Not a problem," Rafe said.

chapter 4

Hannah stood on the rocky beach below the Harte cottage and watched Winston chase seagulls in Dead Hand Cove. The tide was still out this morning. The five tall, finger-shaped stones that had given the cove its name thrust upward from the wet sand in a pattern that was eerily reminiscent of the outflung hand of a corpse. Or so she and Nick and Lillian had concluded years ago. When the tide came in a few hours from now, all but the very tip of the forefinger would be submerged.

The cove had been a favorite playground for all three Hartes in their youth. In addition to the macabre rock formation, it boasted an intricate network of small caves in the cliffs that framed the tiny beach. Together with Nick and Lillian, Hannah had spent hours exploring the rocky passages. The caves weren't dangerously deep or convoluted, and they had made excellent hiding places for adventurous children.

Out in the cove, Winston dashed off after another seagull. He was certainly enjoying the stay in Eclipse Bay,

Hannah thought. What surprised her was that she was strangely content also, in spite of the looming problem of Rafe Madison.

She and Winston had been here for the better part of a week, but she was no closer to resolving the sticky situation involving Dreamscape than she had been that first afternoon. Rafe refused even to discuss the possibility of selling his share of the mansion. A war of nerves was taking shape. They couldn't go on like this indefinitely, she told herself. Sooner or later one of them would have to make a move toward ending the impasse.

Out on the sand, Winston found a piece of driftwood, seized it in his jaws, and pranced triumphantly back toward Hannah. Halfway across the cove he came to a sudden halt and looked up toward the cliff path.

Simultaneously a whisper of awareness tingled through Hannah. She sensed Rafe's presence just before he spoke.

"Nice to see that Winston doesn't stand on formality all the time," he said.

Hannah braced herself for the little shock of excitement she always got when she first encountered him. She turned and saw that he had reached the bottom of the path. He came toward her with that supple masculine grace that was so much a part of him.

Time had not refined Rafe. The cool, savvy intelligence in his green eyes was more intense and more dangerous—the result of hard experience, no doubt. The bold, sharp planes and angles of his lean face had always had a strict cast, but the years had added an aura of brooding asceticism.

He had left behind the few traces of young manhood that had still clung to him that night on the beach. Nevertheless, for some reason he actually looked better than ever in a pair of jeans. Beneath the tautly stretched fabric of the black, long-sleeved T-shirt he wore, his shoulders seemed broader and stronger. His stomach was still very flat.

What was the matter with her? she wondered. For eight years she had excused herself for her small, youthful, short-lived crush on Rafe Madison. After all, he had been the bad boy of Eclipse Bay, and he had once walked her home after midnight. That was enough to induce a few lusty imaginings in any healthy young woman. But she was far too mature for that sort of romantic nonsense now. Wasn't she?

She had never admitted the crush to anyone, of course—not even Lillian, although she suspected that her sister had guessed the truth. She had a right to her private little fantasies, she told herself. And it wasn't as if she had spent the past few years wondering what she had missed. In fact, she had all but forgotten Rafe Madison until Isabel's lawyer had called to give her the news about the will.

"Good morning, Rafe. Fancy meeting you here. Come to talk about Dreamscape?"

"I make it a policy not to talk business before noon."

"Do you talk about it much after noon?"

"Only if I feel real energetic." He leaned down to greet Winston. "I'm on my way into town to check the mail. Thought I'd see if you and the mutt wanted to go along."

Her first reaction was surprise. This was the first overture of any kind that he had made since the initial confrontation at Dreamscape. Maybe he was going to blink first.

Or maybe she ought to be very, very careful.

On the other hand, sooner or later they had to start communicating.

"I do need to do some grocery shopping," she said warily.

"Might as well go into town together." He gave her

an unreadable smile. "Give the good folk of Eclipse Bay a thrill."

She held her blowing hair out of her eyes and peered at him closely. She could not tell if he was joking.

"All right," she said finally.

He startled her with a fleeting grin. "That's one of the things I always admired about you. You were never afraid of the Big Bad Wolf."

She waved a hand toward Winston. "These days I've got my own wolf."

Rafe eyed Winston with an assessing expression. "Five will get you ten that I can take the dog with one hand tied behind my back."

"Don't count on it, tough guy."

An hour later Hannah emerged from Fulton's Supermarket with a sack in each arm. She looked down the rows of pickups and SUVs parked in the small lot and saw the silver Porsche. Rafe had collected the mail and was waiting for her. He lounged against a gleaming fender, arms folded. A pair of mirrored sunglasses added to the gangster look.

Winston stood on his hind legs in the driver's seat, front paws braced against the edge of the door, nose thrust through the open window. It warmed Hannah's heart to see that he was watching for her return. You could always count on your dog.

She was halfway back to the Porsche when, to her astonishment, Rafe gave her a cool, arrogant smile. Very deliberately he uncrossed his arms and reached out to scratch Winston behind the ears.

It was glaringly evident that Winston did not object. Hannah saw a pink tongue emerge to lick Rafe's hand. Irritation shot through her. Winston never got chummy with strangers, especially male strangers. Winston had standards.

Somehow, during the short time that she had been inside the grocery store, Rafe had co-opted her dog.

"Uh-oh."

She quickened her steps, so intent on the spectacle of Winston and Rafe's buddy-bonding that she never saw the big man who had climbed out of a battered pickup until he was directly in her path.

"Heard you and Madison were back in town," Dell Sadler said. "Come back to screw on the beach for old times' sake?"

Hannah skidded to a halt, barely avoiding a collision. But the abrupt stop sent a shudder through her that dislodged her grip on one of the grocery sacks, and it slipped out of her grasp. She heard an ominously squishy thud. The tomatoes, she thought. Luckily the eggs were in the other bag.

"Hello, Dell," she said quietly.

She knew very little about Dell Sadler other than that he operated a towing service and a body shop on the outskirts of Eclipse Bay. He was a heavily built man in his late thirties with thinning hair and beefy hands. There had always been a grim, morose air about him, as though he had found life to be a serious disappointment and did not expect matters to improve.

"You two got a lot of gall coming back here after what you did."

"If you'll excuse me, Dell—"

He stepped toward her, hands balled into fists. "Think I'd be gone by now? Or that I'd forget what happened to Kaitlin? Or don't you even give a damn?"

"This isn't a good place to talk." With an effort she kept her voice calm and soothing. "Maybe some other time."

"Just because everyone else in this town bought that story about you and Rafe Madison getting it on at the beach the night my sister died, don't think I did. I know damn well he killed her and you lied for him."

"That's not true, and I think that deep down inside you know it." Hannah took a cautious step back, preparing to dart around him. "Please get out of my way."

He thrust his face forward, raised a hand, and stabbed a finger at her chest. "Don't you tell me what to do. Maybe everyone else around here kowtows to you Hartes, but I sure as hell don't. Far as I'm concerned, you and Madison are both scum."

"I'm sorry about what happened to Kaitlin," Hannah said. "Everyone was. But I promise you, Rafe had nothing to do with it."

"He must have screwed you silly to get you to cover for him the way you did."

"Stop it."

"I hear you're back in town on account of that big house. Word is Madison wants the whole place for himself. Probably thinks if he does you long enough and hard enough, you'll turn over your share."

Hannah retreated again, clutching her one remaining sack of groceries. She came up hard against the unyielding fender of a big SUV. Dell closed in on her.

"Get out of my way," she said very steadily, preparing to make a run for Rafe's car.

"When I'm good and ready. I want you to know something. I won't ever—"

Dell broke into a yelp as a hand locked on his shoulder from behind.

Rafe used the grip to spin Sadler neatly out of Hannah's path. With seemingly little effort, he pinned the big man to the door of the pickup.

Simultaneously, Hannah heard a low, fierce growl. She

glanced down and saw Winston. The Schnauzer stood braced in front of Dell Sadler.

"She asked you to get out of the way, Sadler," Rafe said in a very soft voice.

"Screw you, you sonofabitch. You killed Kaitlin, I know you did."

"I didn't kill Kaitlin. I had no reason to kill her. If you ever decide you want to talk about it, come and see me. But don't bother Hannah again. She had nothing to do with what happened to your sister."

Dell scowled. "Take your hands off me, you bastard."

Rafe shrugged, released him, and stepped back. He scooped up the sack of groceries that Hannah had dropped and took her arm.

"Let's go," he said.

She did not argue. They walked quickly back to the Porsche, Winston marching beside them. When Rafe opened the door, the Schnauzer jumped into the small space behind the seats. He kept his nose close to Hannah as Rafe switched on the ignition.

Hannah was acutely aware of several curious onlookers. "That little scene will keep tongues wagging for a day or two."

Rafe drove out of the small lot onto Bayview Drive. "Told you we'd give the folks a thrill."

A short silence fell. Hannah opened her purse and found her sunglasses. She put them on. Winston licked her ear. She stroked him soothingly.

"Two-timer," she muttered. "I saw you licking Rafe's hand earlier."

Winston rested his chin on her shoulder and sighed in content.

"Your dog and I decided not to duel at dawn after all," Rafe said.

"You both chickened out?"

"We prefer to think of it as a negotiated settlement."

"Huh. Translated, I think that means that neither of you was willing to exert yourself to do battle in my honor."

Rafe glanced at her, his gaze unreadable behind the shield of his sunglasses. "When a guy reaches a certain age, he has to pick and choose his battles. I think it's called getting smart."

"Excuses, excuses." She peeked into the sack that had landed on the pavement. As she had suspected, the tomatoes were little more than pulp inside the plastic vegetable bag. The lettuce and mushrooms looked badly bruised too. "So much for dinner."

Rafe said nothing for a moment. He drove with easy skill, but he seemed to be concentrating on the road with an unnecessary degree of attention.

"Got an idea," he said after a while.

"I'm listening."

"Why don't you and Winston eat at my place tonight? I've got plenty of food."

Another overture? Maybe he really was weakening. She tried not to look too eager.

"Seeing as how there isn't much that's very exciting in the other sack of groceries, I believe I can speak for both Winston and myself when I say that we'd be pleased to take you up on that offer."

"Okay. Fine. It's settled."

She watched him out of the corner of her eye. "You appeared to have some hesitation in putting forth your invitation. Was it such a big deal to ask me over to dinner?"

He flexed his hands on the chunky steering wheel. "Had to work up my courage."

"I beg your pardon?"

"I was afraid you'd turn me down."

"Why would I do that?" She gave what she hoped was a very blasé sort of shrug. "We've got to talk about our mutual business problem sooner or later. Might as well be tonight."

"Wasn't planning to talk about the house tonight."

She stilled. "What do you plan to discuss?"

"Old times, maybe?"

She contemplated that for a moment. Then she gently cleared her throat. "You and I have only one incident between us that could conceivably be classified as old times."

"True. But you've got to admit it was a hell of an incident. I could have gone to jail if it hadn't been for you. That would have really messed up my big career plan. I told you that day I called to say good-bye that I owed you."

"Still feel that way?" She smiled sweetly. "Sell me your half of the house and we'll call it even."

"Not feeling quite that grateful," he said.

Rafe walked back into the solarium just as the September sky finally faded all the way to black. Hannah noticed that he did not turn on any lights. Winston, flat on his belly on the floor, looked up hopefully but lost interest when he saw the two snifters Rafe carried.

Rafe lowered himself into the wicker lounger next to Hannah and handed one of the glasses to her.

She watched the darkness settle over the bay and thought about the arugula, beet, blue cheese, and walnut salad and the pasta she had just finished. Rafe had glazed the walnuts with a little sugar and salt and heated them in the oven before adding them to the salad. The pasta had been flavored with an incredibly rich truffle-infused olive oil. A taste of heaven.

"Okay, so you can cook," she said.

"Man's gotta have a hobby."

"I'm with you on that." She took a sip of brandy. "For the record, you can fix dinner for me anytime."

"Thanks. I'll remember that." He cradled his snifter in both hands and gazed out the windows into the deepening night. "Sorry about that scene with Dell Sadler this afternoon."

"It wasn't your fault."

"Depends how you look at the situation, I think. If you hadn't been with me the night Kaitlin died, you wouldn't have had the run-in with Sadler today."

"Well, there is that." She was very conscious of him sitting there, not more than a few inches away. The darkness intensified the sense of intimacy. "About that night—"

He took a sip of brandy and waited.

"We never really talked about it." She drew a breath and took the plunge. "You knew Kaitlin as well as anyone. What do you think happened? Do you think she committed suicide? Or was it an accident?"

He was quiet for a long time. "I'm almost positive that she did not jump."

"What makes you so sure?"

He studied the brandy glass in his hands. "When she kicked me out of her car that night she was pissed as hell. She was angry, not depressed or desperate."

"How angry?"

He tilted his head against the back of the lounger. "Very. Said she'd had it with Eclipse Bay and everyone in it. Said she couldn't wait to blow this burg."

"Making plans for the future."

"Yes."

"So her death must have been an accident."

Rafe said nothing.

Hannah cleared her throat. "I said, her death must have been an accident."

"That's certainly the most convenient explanation for all concerned."

Shock held Hannah absolutely still for a few seconds. She finally found her breath and let it out very deliberately. "You want to elaborate on that?"

"No point." Rafe sipped his brandy. "Not now."

"You're probably right. I guess we'll never know what really happened that night."

"No."

Rafe was quiet for a while. She had the feeling that he had moved onto some other subject in his mind. Whatever it was, he did not seem to be inclined to discuss it, either.

She tried not to be so acutely aware of him reclining there so close beside her, but it was hopeless. Probably time to go home, she thought. Make that *definitely*. She was about to mention that it was getting late when Rafe spoke.

"Somthing I've been meaning to ask you."

"Umm?"

"What went wrong with Mr. Right?"

For some reason that was the last question she had expected. She hesitated, not certain how far she wanted to go down that particular road.

"It didn't work out. What about you?" she added quickly to change the subject. "Heard you got married."

"For a while."

"What went wrong?"

"I told you that the men in my family aren't real good at marriage," he said.

"As I recall, I told you that was an excuse."

Without warning, Rafe sat up on the edge of the

lounger and rested his forearms on his knees. "Mitchell called today."

Hannah blinked. He could switch topics quickly, too. "Your grandfather?"

"He wants me to come to dinner tomorrow night. Octavia Brightwell will be there. Says he wants me to meet her."

Hannah thought quickly. "Brightwell. The owner of that new art gallery near the pier?"

"Yeah." Rafe set his glass down on the table. "Apparently they're involved, so to speak."

"Good grief. I saw her on the street the other day. She's young enough to be his granddaughter."

"So I'm told." He met her eyes in the shadows. "The thing is, I need a date."

She nearly fell out of the lounger. "You want me to go to dinner at Mitchell Madison's house?"

"Got anything better to do?"

"Well, gee, when you put it like that, I guess not. As you once observed so pithily, the entertainment options in Eclipse Bay are somewhat limited." She paused. "Your grandfather won't be exactly thrilled to see you walk into the house with a Harte."

"Don't worry. He'll be on his best behavior because of his new girlfriend."

"Mitchell Madison making nice with a Harte." She smiled slowly. "Now that should be interesting."

"Well?"

"Okay," she said.

It was his turn to be wary. "You'll do it?"

"Sure. On one condition."

"What's that?"

"You have to promise me that afterward we'll have our little chat about how we're going to handle Dreamscape."

He thought about that for a few seconds. One shoulder rose in a negligent motion. "It's a deal."

She felt a distinct chill all the way down her spine. But it was too late now to wonder if she'd just been had by Rafe Madison.

She came awake very suddenly, listening to the silence with all of her senses. Her first thought was that an intruder had entered the darkened house. But in the next heartbeat she reminded herself there was no way anyone could have broken in without alerting Winston.

She sat up slowly. "Winston?"

There was no response. She could not feel his weight at the foot of the bed. It struck her that during the past two years she had grown very accustomed to his companionship at night.

She swung her feet to the cold floor and stood. "Winston? Come here, pal."

She did not hear his claws on the hardwood in the hall. Anxiety raised the hair on her arms. She grabbed her robe and stepped into her slippers, listening all the while for the smallest sounds.

Nothing.

She went to the door.

"Winston." Louder this time.

A soft, answering whine came from the foot of the stairs. Winston was in the living room. He did not seem hurt or scared. Instead she thought she caught the unmistakable anticipation of the hunter in the low sound.

The relief was shattering. Not an intruder, after all. Winston had heard some small creature foraging around outside and had gone downstairs to investigate. Here in Eclipse Bay life was rich for a dog who had been raised in a high-rise apartment.

Taking a couple of deep breaths to get rid of the light-headed sensation, she hurried out into the hall and went down the stairs.

Winston was poised in front of the door. He glanced briefly at her and immediately returned his attention to whatever was prowling around outside. He scratched at the wood hopefully.

"It's okay, pal. You're a city dog. You're not accustomed to the kinds of critters that hang around garbage cans out here in the boonies. Trust me—you don't want to actually catch one of them."

She reached out to pat his head. As soon as she touched him she realized that predatory tension was vibrating from one end of his sleek little body to the other. He ignored her hand. Everything in him was concentrated on whatever it was that had awakened him and drawn him downstairs.

Hannah went to the window. She pulled the curtain aside and discovered that sometime during the night a heavy fog had rolled in off the bay. She had left the porch light on, but its glow did not penetrate far into the thick mist that enveloped the house.

She told herself that she ought to go back to bed and leave Winston to his nocturnal amusements. But for some reason that she could not explain, she lingered at the front door and waited for him to lose interest in whatever skulked in the shadows.

It seemed a very long time before Winston relaxed, licked her hand, and led the way briskly back upstairs.

chapter 5

"Think you can get Bryce to tell you about the trips to Portland?" Gabe asked.

"Not a chance." Rafe propped the phone between his shoulder and his ear, freeing his hands for the job of chopping the onion that sat on the cutting board. "You know Bryce. He takes orders only from Mitchell."

"And Mitchell has told him not to talk about the Portland trips."

"You got it."

Silence hummed briefly on the line. Rafe had a mental image of his older brother at his desk in the president's office at Madison Commercial. It was a good bet that Gabe was dressed in one of his hand-tailored shirts and a pair of expensive trousers. He would likely be wearing a silk tie and Italian leather shoes. He had no doubt arrived at his headquarters at seven-thirty that morning, right after the conclusion of his six a.m. workout at the health club. He would not leave until seven o'clock tonight at the earliest, and when he finally did go back to his austere condominium, he would have a briefcase full of papers with him. Madison Commercial was Gabe's passion. He had devoted himself to it with the sort of single-minded intensity that only another Madison could comprehend.

"It's been more than ten months," Gabe said. "Every Friday. Regular as clockwork."

Rafe finished cutting up the onion and tossed the pieces into the food processor. "I know what you're thinking."

"You're thinking the same thing."

"We might be wrong." Rafe added the pitted olives, three different kinds in all, to the onion. He dumped the rinsed capers and some freshly squeezed lemon juice into the bowl. "But we both know that if he is getting some kind of regular medical treatments, we'll be the last ones to find out."

"Trying to protect us, I guess." Gabe hesitated. "How does he look?"

"Healthy as a bull, except for the arthritis. I'm going to see him tomorrow night at dinner." Rafe paused. "I'll get to meet the new girlfriend."

"Is she really young enough to be his granddaughter?"

"That's what I'm told," Rafe said.

Gabe groaned. "It would be embarrassing if it wasn't so downright amazing."

"Yeah."

"Probably ought to look on the bright side," Gabe said morosely. "If he's able to keep up with her in bed, he can't be at death's door yet."

"There is that," Rafe agreed. He snapped the lid onto the food processor. "Not to change the subject, but how did things go last Saturday night with the lovely Ms. Hartinger?"

"I'd rather not discuss it, if you don't mind."

"Another disaster?"

"I don't like to admit it, but it was excruciatingly clear that she was interested only in my portfolio."

"Thought you said she was perfect."

"I was wrong, okay? Get off my case."

"I still say you're going about this business of finding yourself a wife the wrong way."

"I'm trying to approach it in a non-Madison way. I explained my theory to you."

"I understand what you're trying to do. I'm just saying I don't think it's going to work. It isn't like acquiring a new office tower for Madison Commercial. You can't use the same techniques."

"When did you become an expert?"

"Good point. Forget it." Rafe drummed his fingers on top of the food processor. "I'm taking a date to Mitchell's house tomorrow night."

"Someone local?" Gabe sounded only casually interested.

"You could say that. Hannah Harte."

"*Hannah?* Are you kidding me?"

"No."

"She agreed to go with you?"

"Uh-huh."

"Why ?"

"I'm not sure, if you want the truth. Probably thinks it's a step toward getting her hands on Dreamscape."

"You, uh, led her to think that might be the case?" Gabe asked carefully.

"Sort of."

"But you've got no intention of giving up your claim on that mansion."

"No," Rafe said, "I don't."

"What the hell is going on there?"

"I'll let you know when I find out. I've got to go now. Talk to you later."

Rafe hung up the phone and switched on the food processor. He thought about Hannah while the machine turned the mixture inside the bowl into *tapenade*. An old proverb flickered through his mind, something about bringing a long spoon when you dined with the devil. Madisons had used it to describe the risks of dealing with Hartes for years.

chapter 6

Rafe wrapped his hands around the porch railing and gazed out over his grandfather's magnificent garden. A lot of people in Eclipse Bay gardened, but none of them could match Mitchell's spectacular display of lush ferns, herb borders, and rosebushes. A large greenhouse dominated the far end of the scene. Inside it were more horticultural wonders. A vegetable plot occupied a section near the house. Even in early fall when blooms were fading, Mitchell's garden was a work of art.

In the dark months after the death of their parents, Mitchell had taken his two grandsons into the garden a lot. The three of them had spent countless hours there. Mitchell had shown Rafe and Gabe how to prepare the ground, water the tomatoes, and trim rosebushes. They hadn't talked much, but Rafe knew that they had all found some solace in the work of growing things.

Mitchell had lived a turbulent life by anyone's standards. The years had seen the financial and personal devastation brought on by the destruction of Harte-Madison

and the ensuing feud with his old army buddy, Sullivan
Harte. The turmoil of four divorces and the breakup of
innumerable affairs had taken a toll. The loss of his only
son, Sinclair, had been a cruel blow. Rafe knew that the
unexpected burden of raising two grandsons had come
as a shock to a man who, until then, had not worried
overmuch about his family responsibilities. But through
it all, Mitchell had never lost his interest in gardening.

Gardening was Mitchell's passion. As everyone knew,
when it came to a Madison and his passion, nothing was
allowed to stand in the way.

Rafe went down the steps. "How'd you meet Octavia
Brightwell?" he asked, partly out of curiosity and partly
in a bid to find a neutral topic. Conversations between
himself and Mitchell were fraught with problems.

For as long as he could remember, he had been at
odds with his grandfather. In recent years they had
achieved a prickly détente, but that was only because
both of them had tacitly abandoned the open warfare that
had characterized so much of their earlier communica-
tion. Some would say that they had matured, Rafe
thought. But he and Mitchell knew the truth. They had
both given up butting heads for the most part because it
had become obvious that it was a pointless exercise.
Which was not to say that they did not occasionally engage in the activity from time to time, just to stay in
practice.

They had both been on their best behavior throughout
dinner this evening, he reflected. True, things had been
a little tense for a few minutes after he walked in the
front door with Hannah, but to his credit, Mitchell had
recovered quickly. Rafe's theory was that the older man
was determined to play the genial host in front of his
new girlfriend.

Octavia Brightwell was, indeed, young enough to be

Mitchell's granddaughter. She came as a surprise to Rafe. She had proved to be warm, friendly, and intelligent. He could tell that Hannah had liked her on sight. During the course of the conversation at dinner Octavia had explained that the gallery she had opened in Eclipse Bay was her second. The first was in Portland. This summer she had divided her time between the two locations.

"She stuck her head over my garden fence one morning at the beginning of summer and told me that I was handling my roses all wrong." Mitchell snorted. "Told her I'd been dealing with roses since before she was born. She brought me a book on how to grow roses. Told me to read a few pages. I told her the author of the book was a damn fool. You might say we just hit it off."

"I see." Rafe watched Mitchell pause to remove a dead bloom from a rosebush.

Something twisted deep inside him at the sight of his grandfather's hawklike profile. It hit him that the old warrior with whom he had fought so many battles would not be around forever. It was difficult to imagine the world without Mitchell.

The tough, irascible Mitchell had the usual Madison flaws, Rafe thought, but he had been the one solid anchor in his grandsons' lives since the day their father's motorcycle had collided with a truck.

Rafe thought about the mysterious weekly trips to Portland. If there was something seriously wrong, it did not show. Mitchell used a cane, but he still looked strong and fit. He could have passed for a man fifteen years younger. There was a sharp glint in his slightly faded green eyes. The hard lines of his face had softened little with age. There was a slight stoop to his shoulders these days, and he had lost some muscle with the years, but the physical changes were well concealed by his undiminished will and determination to control his world and everyone in it.

"I take it you and Octavia spend a lot of time together," Rafe said as casually as possible.

"Some." Mitchell nipped off another dead rose.

This was not going to work, Rafe decided. If Mitchell did not want to discuss his relationship with Octavia Brightwell, that was the end of the matter. His grandfather had never talked much about his affairs and liaisons over the years. When it came to women, he lived by an old-fashioned code. A man did not kiss and tell. He had drilled that same cardinal rule into both Rafe and Gabe.

Rafe went down the steps and came to a halt on the path beside Mitchell, who was examining a cluster of ferns.

"I understand you've been going into Portland on a regular basis," Rafe said. "To see Octavia?"

"Nope." Mitchell snapped off another dead flower.

Rafe knew that was the end of that conversation. Gabe would have been better at this, he thought

Mitchell squinted at him. "What the hell are you and Hannah Harte going to do with that damned house?"

"We haven't decided."

"Huh. Just like Isabel to do something crazy like this in her will. She had some romantic notion about you and Hannah patching up the old feud. Told her she was an idiot."

"Telling her that she was an idiot was probably not real helpful."

Mitchell grunted again. "Nobody more contrary than a Harte."

"Except a Madison."

Mitchell didn't deny it. "You look pretty friendly with Hannah."

"I wouldn't say we've reached the friendly stage, but her dog likes me. That's a start."

"Heard she built herself a nice little business in Portland. Organizes weddings or some such nonsense."

"Yeah. She says she gets a lot of repeat clients."

"She's a Harte, and that's not an easy fact to overlook. But I've got to admit that she's got gumption." A thoughtful expression gleamed in Mitchell's eyes. "Never forgot what she did eight years ago. Always felt like we owed her something for the way she backed you up."

"I know."

"There was some nasty talk around town for a while. The folks who believed her when she said she'd been with you on the beach that night assumed you'd seduced her just to score some points against the Hartes."

"I heard that."

Mitchell tapped his cane absently against the base of the sundial. "There are still one or two who think Hannah Harte flat out lied for you that night. They think you really did push Kaitlin Sadler off that cliff."

Rafe felt the tension knot deep inside him. He'd always wondered if Mitchell had been one of those who secretly believed that he had been responsible for Kaitlin's fall.

"Bottom line," Mitchell continued, "is that we're beholden to Hannah Harte."

"Yeah."

"Hate being beholden to a Harte," Mitchell sighed. "Like a bur under a saddle."

Rafe looked at him. "Didn't know it bothered you all this time."

"It did."

"It's not your problem. It's mine."

"You can say that again." Mitchell narrowed his eyes.

"What are you going to do about it? Give up your half of Isabel's house?"

"No."

"Didn't think so." Mitchell started off in the direction of the greenhouse. "Come on. I'll show you my new hybrids."

Rafe glanced back at the screen door. There was no sign of rescue. Reluctantly he trailed after Mitchell.

"I talked to Gabe a few days ago," Mitchell said.

Rafe steeled himself. "Did you?"

"He said he could find a place for you at Madison Commercial." There was not a lot of hope in Mitchell's voice.

"Give me a break. Would you work for Gabe?"

"Hell, no." Mitchell's brows bristled. "He expects everyone to jump when he gives an order."

"That pretty much sums up my problem with him, too."

Mitchell grunted. "Well, it was worth a try."

They walked the length of the garden in silence. Just before they reached the greenhouse, Mitchell launched a salvo in an entirely new direction.

"Don't you think it's about time you got married?" he said.

Rafe felt as if he'd been hit in the head with a ball peen hammer. It took him several seconds to recover. He spent the intervening time with his mouth open.

"Married?" he finally managed. "Are you out of your mind? I tried it once, remember? It didn't work."

"You're going to have to bite that bullet again, sooner or later. You've put it off long enough. If you wait too much longer you'll be so set in your ways you won't be able to adjust to marriage."

"Since when did you become an expert on marriage?"

"I've had some experience."

"You can say that again," Rafe muttered. "For your information, I'm already set in my ways."

"Bullshit. You're still young enough to be flexible."

The door on the back porch opened. Both men spun around so quickly that Rafe was sure they looked guilty of something.

An ethereal-looking woman with a mane of fiery red curls stood in the opening.

"Coffee's ready," Octavia Brightwell called cheerfully.

Rafe did not hesitate. He noticed that Mitchell didn't pause either. He figured his grandfather was just as relieved by the timely interruption as he was.

Side by side, they went swiftly back along the path toward the house.

Hannah slid her key into the front-door lock. "Not that you've got any reason to consider my opinion on the subject, but I liked Octavia."

Beside her Rafe shrugged. "So did I. So what? She's still way too young for him. Gabe's right. It's embarrassing."

Hannah was amused. "That's almost funny, coming from a Madison. No offense, but the men of your family aren't known for feeling shy or awkward about their sex lives."

"It's different when it's your grandfather's sex life," Rafe said glumly.

Hannah listened to the sound of dog claws prancing madly on the hardwood floor on the other side of the door. "Well, if it's any consolation to you, Octavia told me that she and your grandfather are just friends. I believe her."

"Yeah?"

She gave him a quick, searching glance as she opened the door. He had been in a strange mood since return-

ing from the after-dinner walk in the garden. Rafe had
never been an easy man to read, but now there was a
dark, brooding aura emanating from him that had not
been present earlier in the evening. She wondered what
had been said between him and his grandfather.

Winston bounced through the open door, torn as always, between the demands of professional dignity and
blatant emotionalism.

"Such a handsome dog." She bent down to pat him.
"The finest specimen of Schnauzerhood in the known
universe."

Winston glowed.

Rafe watched them with an expression of morbid interest. "He actually believes you when you say that, you
know."

"So what? It's true." She stood back to allow Winston
to trot across the porch and down the steps. The dog
paused briefly to thrust his nose into Rafe's hand, and
then he disappeared discreetly into some bushes.

Hannah reached around the edge of the door and
flipped a light switch. "I'm probably going to kick myself for getting involved, but I feel compelled to ask.
Did things go okay between you and your grandfather
out there in the garden?"

"Sure." Rafe glided, uninvited, through the opening
into the front hall.

"I see." She was not quite certain what to do with him
now that he was inside her house.

She held the door open for Winston. He pranced across
the porch and into the hall. He headed straight for Rafe.

Hannah closed the door and leaned back against it.
Rafe crouched to scratch the dog's ears. Winston
promptly sat down and assumed a blissful expression.

"There was the usual stuff," Rafe said after a moment.

"The usual stuff?"

Rafe kept his attention on Winston, who was clearly ready, willing, and able to absorb an unlimited amount of it. "Mitchell reminded me that it wasn't too late to join Madison Commercial."

"Ah, yes. The usual." She straightened away from the door and walked into the kitchen. When in doubt, make a cup of tea. "And you gave him the usual response, no doubt."

"Well, sure. That's how Mitchell and I communicate. He tells me what I should do, and I tell him I won't do it. We understand each other perfectly."

"Aunt Isabel always said that you and your grandfather had problems from the day you hit puberty because the two of you were so much alike." She filled the kettle and set it on the stove.

"I've heard that theory before." Rafe gave Winston one last pat, got to his feet, and came to stand in the arched doorway. He propped one shoulder against the frame and crossed his arms. "Neither Mitchell nor I believes it."

She was intensely aware of him taking up space in the kitchen. She could feel his disturbing gaze following her every move as she went about the business of preparing a pot of tea.

"It's true, you know," she said gently. "You're both strong-willed, arrogant, independent, and downright bullheaded at times. The two of you probably have the same motto."

"What's that?"

"Never apologize, never explain."

He contrived to look hurt. "Had it occurred to you that I might have something in common with your dog?"

"Such as?"

He smiled humorlessly. "I might actually believe you when you tell me what you really think about me."

She raised her brows at that. "I can't see you giving much credence to anyone else's opinions."

"Shows how much you know. I'm only human."

"Got proof of that?"

"Okay, I'll accept strong-willed, arrogant, and independent." He gave her a derisive look. "But I object to the last part. What makes you say I'm bullheaded?"

She smiled with cool triumph. "Your refusal to talk about how we're going to deal with the problem of Dreamscape."

"Huh. That."

"Yes, that."

He raised one shoulder very casually. "Well, hell, nobody's perfect."

"Except Winston, of course," she added swiftly, in case Winston had overhead the remark and had started to worry.

There was a short silence.

"Mitchell said something else while we were in the garden," Rafe said eventually.

She glanced at him over her shoulder as she dropped a large pinch of tea into the pot. "What was that?"

He watched her with shuttered eyes. "He told me it was about time I got married."

For some reason her stomach tightened. She hoped it wasn't the grilled salmon they'd had at dinner. It had tasted so good going down, but fish could be tricky.

"Well," she said. "Talk about pressure."

"Yeah."

"I'm sure you responded by telling him to stay out of your personal affairs." She concentrated hard on the teakettle, willing it to boil quickly.

Rafe said nothing.

A tiny shriek rose from the kettle. Close enough, she

decided. Grateful for the small distraction, she hastily poured the hot water into the pot.

It was okay, she thought a moment later. She was cool now. But when she turned around with her most polished smile firmly in place, she discovered that Rafe had left the doorway and was now standing less than two feet away.

Much too close.

"I didn't come straight out and say it in so many words." Rafe's eyes never left her face. "But you're right. I made it clear that I'd do what I wanted to do."

"As usual."

"Yeah."

She tried to think of something clever to say in response to that. She wound up clearing her throat instead. "And what do you want to do?"

"Right now I want to kiss you."

chapter 7

She went very still. The really scary part, she realized, was that she wanted the same thing. She had a hunch that he could see it in her eyes.

She licked her lips and asked the only question that mattered. "Why?"

"Does there have to be a reason?"

"Yes." She could feel the counter pressing against her lower back. She put her arms out on either side and gripped the curved tile edge. "Yes, I think so. Especially given the situation here."

"Situation?"

"You. Me. Dreamscape."

"What happens if I can't come up with any reason except the fact that I want to kiss you?"

"The important thing," she explained very carefully, "the really crucial thing, is that the reason, whatever it is, must have nothing to do with Dreamscape."

He raised his hands and slowly folded them around the nape of her neck. His palms were warm and heavy against her skin. She could feel the strength in him but sensed the control. The combination was electrifying.

His thumbs moved gently just behind her ears. He eased her head back slightly and lowered his mouth to hers.

"This has nothing to do with the mansion," he said against her lips. "You have my word on it."

The kiss was a real one this time, not the chaste, meaningless little brush of the lips he had bestowed on her that night when he had walked her home. And it was just exactly what she had always suspected it would be: devastating.

Excitement sparked along every nerve ending. The effect was not unlike touching a match to extremely dry kindling. The flames erupted without warning, fierce and intense. A liquid heat welled somewhere in the region below her stomach. She was aware of the beat of her own heart. The breathless sensation would probably have warranted a trip to the emergency room under other circumstances.

Rafe deepened the kiss with slow deliberation.

The stuff of teenage fantasies, she thought. Except that no teenager could have appreciated just how good the kiss really was. Only an adult woman who had learned the hard way that real life was seldom this great could savor the finer points and the little nuances here.

Rafe crowded her gently up against the counter. She could feel the unmistakable shape of his erection pressed against her thigh.

Okay, so not all of the nuances here were little.

His mouth slanted across hers. He drew his palms down her throat and covered her breasts. A great urgency went through her. With an effort, she managed to let go of the counter edge. She heard him say something that probably would have gotten him arrested if he had said it in public. He made no effort to conceal his hunger. The knowledge that he wanted her played havoc with the last shreds of her common sense.

Just a kiss, she thought. How much damage could one kiss do?

She heard someone moan softly. Probably her, she decided. Not real cool. It was only a kiss, after all. But at the moment she did not care if she was demonstrating a distinct lack of worldly sophistication. The only thing that mattered was getting her arms around Rafe's neck.

The instant she achieved her goal she heard a husky groan. Not her this time. Rafe.

His hands tightened abruptly. She could feel his control slipping away. She wondered if he was aware of it. Then she wondered what she would do if it vanished altogether. Would she care? Should she care?

The world tilted on its axis. She realized vaguely that Rafe had scooped her up into his arms. A shiver went through her.

He paused briefly to switch off the lights. Then he carried her out of the kitchen into the living room. There he put her down on the aging sofa and lowered himself on top of her. His lips went to her throat. She could have sworn she felt his teeth. Another zinging thrill shot through her. She was shivering now. The weight of his body crushed her into the cushions.

At the sound of dog claws scratching on wood, she opened her eyes for a split second. In the shadows she caught a glimpse of Winston hurrying up the stairs to the second floor. Embarrassed by the unseemly behavior taking place on the sofa, no doubt.

She ought to be embarrassed too, she thought. And maybe she would be. Later.

In the meantime, her body was singing a fascinating melody. She had caught a few chords of this particular tune from time to time over the years, but she had never experienced the grand finale.

She felt one of Rafe's hands slide beneath her sweater. The clasp of her bra dissolved at his touch. When his thumb lightly touched her nipple she almost screamed. It was as though every inch of her had been sensitized. She was in some never-never land where the line between acute pleasure and pain was murky.

"I've been thinking all day that it would be like this," Rafe muttered into the curve of her shoulder. "I was going crazy waiting to find out."

His hand moved over the curve of her hip. She felt his fingers on the zipper of her slacks. Things were moving swiftly. Much too swiftly. But she could not seem to summon up a lot of good reasons for calling a halt.

She heard Winston on the stairs again. For some reason the knowledge that her dog had returned to the scene cleared some of the fog from her brain.

"I think this is far enough," she managed to get out.

"Not nearly." Rafe peeled up the edge of her sweater and kissed one of her breasts. "I've been wanting you since you got here."

"That's nice."

He went very still. Then he raised his head and looked down at her with gleaming eyes. "Nice?"

"I'm flattered. Honest."

"Flattered," he repeated carefully. "Great. Flattered. Shit."

She swallowed. "I don't want you to think I'm a prude, or anything, but—"

"But you're still Miss Goody Two-Shoes, is that it?"

"Not exactly." She was starting to grow annoyed. "It's just that in a lot of ways you and I are strangers."

"You're a Harte. I'm a Madison. The way I look at it, we've known each other most of our lives."

She blinked. "That's certainly an interesting viewpoint. Maybe it's even true in certain ways. But something of an oversimplification, don't you think?"

"Do you always talk like this on a date?"

"That wasn't a date we had tonight. I did you a favor."

His smile was infinitely slow, infinitely seductive. "Well, in that case, allow me to repay it." He started to lower his mouth to hers once more.

She braced her hands on his shoulders to stop him. "My point—"

He gave her a look of polite surprise. "You mean you've actually got one?"

"My point," she continued grimly, "is that, although we've known of each other's *existence* most of our lives, it's stretching things to imply that we've been anything more than distant acquaintances. I still say we're strangers as far as this kind of thing is concerned."

"Shush." He covered her mouth with the palm of his hand.

"Mmmph?" Outraged, she grabbed his wrist and tried to yank his hand away from her lips.

She was so intent on telling him in no uncertain terms that she did not find this kind of stuff a turn-on that it took her a few seconds to realize he was not paying any attention to her. She finally noticed that he was lying much too still, his head turned toward the front door.

She heard a very soft whine. Winston was standing at the door again, just as he had done last night. His alert, watchful tension radiated clear across the room.

"He hears something." Rafe took his hand away from Hannah's mouth. He kept his eyes on the dog as he sat up on the edge of the sofa.

"Probably an animal prowling for garbage." Hannah hastily pulled her clothing back into place. "A skunk, maybe. Or cats."

"Probably." Rafe watched Winston intently.

Hannah sat up slowly. "He did this last night, too."

Rafe got to his feet and crossed the room to where Winston vibrated at the door. He halted at the window and pulled aside the curtain. "Fog's so thick now you can't see past the edge of the porch."

Winston whined softly. He glanced at Rafe and then at the door and then back at Rafe. The message was clear. He wanted to go outside to investigate.

A cold chill went through Hannah. It was the same disturbing sensation she'd experienced last night.

"Whatever it is, it's not coming too close to the house," she said quickly. "Winston would be barking like crazy if there was a critter in the bushes at the edge of the porch."

"Sure." Rafe reached for the doorknob. Winston strained forward, preparing to streak through the crack in the door as soon as it appeared.

Real fear galvanized Hannah. Everything in her was suddenly focused on the danger of opening the front door.

"What, are you crazy?" She leaped to her feet and rushed across the room. She bent down to seize Winston's collar. "You can't send him outside. He was raised in a high-rise apartment in the middle of a city, for heaven's sake. He knows nothing about wild animals. Whatever's out there might be a lot bigger and meaner than he is."

Winston tried to pull free of her grasp. He was trembling with eagerness. His nose did not waver from the crack between the door and the frame.

Rafe glanced down at him. "Okay, city dog. Stay inside and be a sissy. I'll handle this on my own."

"Oh, no, you don't." Exasperated, Hannah released

Winston and threw herself in front of the door, arms spread wide. "You're not going out there, either."

Rafe looked amused. "Doubt if whatever is out there is bigger or meaner than me. This is Eclipse Bay, remember? Crime rate around here is almost nonexistent."

Winston whined again and bobbed restlessly at Rafe's heels.

Hannah glared at both of them. She did not budge from her position in front of the door. Frantically she searched for a rational, sensible reason for refusing to allow either male outside.

"Cut the raging testosterone, you two. Let's have a little common sense here, shall we? It is entirely possible that there's a skunk outside. Does either of you have any idea of just how long it would take to get rid of the smell if you got sprayed? You'd both have to sleep on the beach for a week."

"Don't think it's a skunk." Rafe looked thoughtful. "A skunk would head straight for the garbage cans. We'd have heard the clatter by now."

"If it's not a skunk, it might be something worse," she said through her teeth. "Maybe somebody's pit bull or Rottweiler got loose. For all you know, there's a whole pack of vicious dogs out there."

"Speaking of common sense," Rafe said mildly, "I think that theory is a bit weak."

"I don't care. It's my theory and I'm sticking to it. Neither of you is going out there and that's final. Besides, you just got through saying that the fog was so thick you couldn't see beyond the edge of the porch. It makes no sense to go floundering around in the stuff."

Rafe looked at her. She realized that he was laughing silently.

"What?" she said.

"Nothing." He pulled the curtain aside again and

peered thoughtfully out into the darkness. "Just occurred to me that if you don't let me outside, I won't be able to get home tonight, that's all."

She hesitated. "You can leave after Winston relaxes."

"Can't see a damn thing in that muck."

"You can leave your car here and walk home."

He dropped the curtain. His eyes gleamed.

"*Now* what?" she snapped.

"What if someone drives past your house early tomorrow morning and sees my car parked in front?"

She sighed. "Half the town already thinks the worst, anyway."

"Okay, then what about the pack of maddened Rottweilers and pit bulls I'll have to confront if I walk home?"

She moved just far enough from the position in front of the door to lift the curtain. A single glance outside showed that the fog was an impenetrable barrier. The light from the yellow lamp over the door was reflected back from what looked like a solid gray wall.

She looked at Winston. He was now pacing restlessly in front of the door. Whatever it was that he sensed was still out there. She made an executive decision.

"We'll drink the tea I made," she said. "If nothing has changed by the time we finish, you can sleep on the sofa tonight."

"Okay," Rafe said much too easily.

Winston lost interest in whatever lay out in the fog about the same time they finished the tea. But when Rafe checked the view from the window he was pleased to see that the mist had not dissipated. If anything, it was thicker than ever.

Luck was with him tonight.

Hannah came to stand behind him. She peered over his shoulder. "How does it look?"

"Like a great night for mad dogs and skunks."

"Not funny." She hugged herself and rubbed her arms briskly, as though warding off a chill. "I guess you'll have to stay here."

"Don't go overboard with the gracious hospitality routine. I don't mind walking back to Dreamscape. It's not that far."

"No." She turned away abruptly. "You can have the downstairs guest room. I'll get some blankets and a pillow."

He watched her climb the stairs. She had been a little too quick to suggest that he stay here, he decided. The expression in her eyes was wrong, too. He wondered how much of this new, brittle tension derived from the scene on the sofa earlier and how much came from Winston's prowling at the door.

Logic told him that a few kisses wouldn't have rattled her this much. She wasn't a teenager, after all. She was a confident woman who had built a thriving business. It would take more than a sexy tussle on the sofa to throw her. In any event, he was pretty sure that if she really *had* been upset by the small skirmish, she would have been more than delighted to let him walk home in the fog.

Instead, she had insisted that he stay here.

He glanced at Winston. The dog was stretched out on his belly on the rug, nose on his paws, dozing. Hannah had said that it was the second night in a row that he had gone on alert.

Hannah and Winston were both accustomed to life in the city, Rafe reminded himself. They had merely over-reacted to whatever small creature had wandered too close to the house. But if Hannah wanted him to stay here tonight, who was he to argue?

An hour later he was still awake. Arms folded behind his head, he stared up at the deep shadows on the ceiling. He was intensely aware of the fact that Hannah was just out of sight upstairs. He pictured her in a nightgown. Maybe a frilly little see-through number that showed a lot of skin. Fat chance. More likely a sober, long-sleeved flannel thing that fell to her ankles.

Either one sounded interesting, now that he considered the matter. Very interesting, in fact. He was hard as a rock.

Logic told him that a few kisses shouldn't have rattled him this much. He wasn't a teenager, after all. It took more than a sexy tussle on the sofa to throw him.

Right.

chapter 8

He awoke at dawn when a cold nose was thrust against the bottom of his bare foot. The shock brought him to a sitting position in a hurry.

"Sonofa—" He broke off when he saw Winston. "No point in calling you that particular name, is there? You are a son of a bitch. And don't think it hasn't occurred to me that the big dramatic act last night at the door might have been just your deliberate attempt to disrupt the mood of the evening."

Winston gave him a meaningful look.

"Things were going pretty damn good until you showed up and made like Mr. Macho Watchdog."

Winston turned and trotted to the door. There he sat down and stared intently at Rafe.

"Okay, okay. I get the point."

Rafe shoved aside the blankets and got to his feet. He found his trousers and reached for his shirt. After a short search he discovered his low-cut boots fooling around with some dust bunnies under the bed.

"All right, let's go."

He opened the door to a damp, fog-bound morning. Winston stepped smartly outside and headed for the bushes at the edge of the porch. Rafe went down the steps and followed the little path that led to the storage locker used to house the garbage cans. There were no signs of animal tracks in the vicinity and no claw marks on the wooden lid.

Having concluded his personal business, Winston hurried over to see what was going on at the garbage can locker. Rafe watched him closely.

Winston sniffed a bit, but his interest in the locker appeared casual at best. After only a couple of minutes he headed on down the long drive toward the trees that veiled the house and gardens from the narrow road.

Rafe followed, watching to see if the dog paid any unusual attention to any particular point along the way. Winston's progress was slowed by numerous pauses, but none appeared to be any more intriguing to him than another. When he got close to the edge of the property, Rafe decided it was time to call him back.

"Hannah will chew me out but good if she finds out I let you play in traffic." Not that there was much on this quiet road, especially at this hour of the morning.

Winston ignored him, displaying a breathtaking disdain for a clear and reasonable command. Rafe concluded that the attitude was either the result of generations of fine breeding or something that had rubbed off from Hannah. He was inclined to credit the latter.

"Come back here." Rafe walked more quickly toward Winston, intending to grab him before he reached the road.

But Winston stopped of his own accord before he got as far as the pavement. He veered left toward a stand of dripping trees and began to sniff the ground with great authority.

"Just like you knew what you were doing," Rafe said quietly.

Winston flitted briskly from one tree trunk to another, pausing to sniff intently in several places. Eventually he lifted his leg. When he was finished he turned to Rafe as if to say that he was satisfied.

Rafe walked into the stand and took a close look at the tree Winston had marked. He knew that his human senses were abysmally inadequate for the task at hand.

He crouched to get a closer look at the ground at the base of the tree. Unfortunately the pebbles that covered the earth made it impossible to detect any footprints. Always assuming that there were any there to detect, Rafe thought.

He looked at Winston, who was watching him with an inquiring expression. "You know, if one of us had gotten both your nose and my brain, we'd be in great shape."

Winston gave the equivalent of a canine shrug, then turned and went quickly along the drive toward the house.

Rafe straightened. He was about to set off after the dog when he caught a glint of silver foil out of the corner of his eye. A closer look revealed a tightly wadded candy wrapper lying on the ground near the point Winston had marked.

Not exactly a major discovery. A stray breeze could have blown it into the stand of trees. It might have been tossed from a passing car or fallen off the garbage truck.

Or it might have been dropped by someone standing in this very spot about midnight last night.

He picked up the discarded wrapper and went back down the drive to where he had parked the Porsche. He unlocked the door, opened the glove compartment, and rummaged briefly inside. No luck. He looked at Winston, who was waiting, head cocked, on the porch.

"Used to be a time when I carried a spare razor and a few other basic necessities with me for just this sort of occasion," he explained. He shut the door and pocketed the keys. "But I got out of the habit."

His social life had never really picked up again after his divorce, he reflected. Probably because he had not worked very hard to get it up and running. He'd had other interests to occupy him.

He stopped once before he went up the steps and plucked a few sprigs of the mint that were growing beneath the garden's water faucet.

Back inside the house he spent a few minutes in the downstairs bathroom, where he discovered that none of the Harte males had left a razor behind.

"Thoughtless," he told Winston. "But, then, what do you expect from a Harte?"

He listened to the silence upstairs for a moment before he wandered into the kitchen and started opening cupboard doors. He found the usual assortment of aging condiments and spices that tended to get left behind in a vacation cottage. Salt, pepper, sugar, a half-empty bottle of vanilla extract, and an unopened jar of maple syrup. The last item was the real thing, not caramel-colored sugar water, he noted.

He took the vanilla extract and the syrup out of the cupboard and went to check the contents of the refrigerator. The eggs and milk were fresh. The loaf of dense, rustic-style bread baked by the New Age crowd who had taken over the old bakery near the pier was a day old.

Perfect.

The bride's gown was three sizes too big. She tried desperately to pin it into place, but it was hopeless. She knew that no matter what she did the dress would never look right. The client was in tears. The groom kept looking at his watch.

She glanced at the clock and saw that the reception was supposed to start in a few minutes. But the caterers had not yet arrived. None of the tables had been set up. The flowers were limp. She opened a case of the premium-quality champagne that she had ordered and discovered bottles of mouthwash inside. She looked around and realized that the musicians had not yet appeared

On top of everything else, there was something dreadfully wrong with the room. The reception was supposed to be in an elegant hillside mansion overlooking the city. Instead, she was standing in an empty, windowless warehouse.

The tantalizing smell of something delicious being cooked nearby distracted her from the chaos. She realized that she was very hungry, but she could not abandon the client to go get something to eat. She was a professional, after all . . .

Hannah came awake with a start and found herself gazing into the depths of the impenetrable fogbank that hovered outside the window. For a few disorienting seconds she thought she was still in Portland trying to hold together the unraveling threads of a disastrous wedding reception.

Then she smelled the exquisite aromas from downstairs. Reality returned, jolting her out of bed.

Rafe. He had not vanished discreetly at dawn as she had expected. He was down there making himself at home in her kitchen. She had been so sure that he would be gone by the time she awoke.

She looked at the foot of the bed. There was no sign of Winston. What had become of her faithful pal?

Now that was a really dumb question, she thought. Winston was a truly fabulous dog in many respects. But in the end, he was still a dog. If she wanted to find him, she had only to follow the smell of food.

She staggered into the bathroom, the last wisps of the familiar anxiety dream trailing after her. She'd been plagued by the wedding-reception-from-hell nightmare for months before she had made the decision to sell Weddings by Harte.

She gripped the edges of the white pedestal sink and stared at herself in the mirror. Her hair hung in lanky tangles. There was a sullen, surly look in her eyes, and the flush in her cheeks was unbecoming, to say the least. She could not face Rafe in this condition. Her only hope was a shower.

She whipped the long-sleeved nightgown off over her head and stepped beneath the hot spray. Seizing the shampoo in both hands, she went to work with near-violent determination. It had not been a good night.

When she emerged a short time later she felt infinitely better. She pulled on a sweater and a pair of jeans, brushed her freshly washed hair behind her ears, and anchored it with a headband.

She took another look in the mirror just before she left the room. With dismay she realized that she still looked a little too pink. Probably because of the shower, she decided. All that heat and steam. The effect would surely fade quickly.

She squared her shoulders, opened the bedroom door, and stepped out into the hall.

By the time she got downstairs her mouth was watering. She saw Winston sitting just inside the kitchen doorway. He rose to greet her with his customary gallantry, but it was clear that he was distracted by what was going on in the vicinity of the stove.

Rafe looked just as she had known he would look in the morning. Incredibly sexy, right down to and including the shadow of a beard that gave the hard planes of his face an even more dangerous cast than usual.

It really was not fair. A gentleman would have been gone by dawn. But, then, no one had ever called Rafe Madison a gentleman.

"Right on time." Rafe's eyes gleamed as he surveyed her with one swift, all-encompassing look. He picked up an oven mitt. "You can pour the coffee."

She watched as he removed a pan from the oven. The faint scent of vanilla teased her. "What is it?"

"French toast." He put the pan on the stove and tossed the mitt onto the counter. "Baked instead of fried. Sort of a cross between a bread pudding and a soufflé."

She gazed at it longingly. "It's beautiful. Absolutely beautiful."

He grinned. "Thanks."

So the man could cook. She already knew that. It was not a sufficient reason to fall in love. Lust, maybe, but not love.

She dragged her gaze away from the golden-brown French toast and saw that Rafe was watching her with an odd expression.

"I'll get the coffee." She whirled around and seized the pot.

Rafe arranged the French toast on two heated plates and carried the food to the table. Hannah studied the casually elegant fashion in which the puffy, golden-brown triangles had been positioned. There were little sprigs of fresh mint on top of the toast. The syrup in the small pot in front of her was warm.

She picked up her fork. "You know, there's a theory

in some quarters that you turned to a life of crime in order to support yourself after you left Eclipse Bay."

He nodded. "I've heard that theory."

"But after dinner the other night and breakfast this morning, I think the evidence is clear that you went to a blue-ribbon culinary academy instead of jail."

He looked up very quickly.

She paused with a bite of French toast poised in midair. "Good heavens, I was joking. Did you really take cooking classes?"

He hesitated. Then shrugged. "Yes."

She was fascinated. "When?"

"After I got married. In the back of my mind, I think I always had this idea that when you were happily married, you ate at home most of the time. But Meredith wasn't big on cooking, so I took over the job. The better I got at it, the more restless and unhappy Meredith became." Rafe made a dismissive gesture with one hand. "After a while I realized that she wasn't real big on staying at home, either."

She gazed at him in disbelief. "Meredith left you because you're a fantastic cook and because you like to eat at home?"

"Well, those weren't the only reasons," Rafe admitted. "She might have been willing to tolerate my cooking if I had agreed to go to work at Madison Commercial. But I refused, so in the end she gave up on my future prospects and left."

Hannah savored another bite of French toast while she thought about that. "I'm sorry your marriage didn't work out."

"You should be. I figure it's your fault that it bombed."

She nearly dropped her fork. "*My* fault. How in the world can you blame me?"

He met her eyes across the short expanse of the table.

His mouth curved slightly. "That night on the beach you told me I didn't have to follow in my father's and my grandfather's footsteps when it came to marriage, remember? So a couple of years later, I figured I'd give it a try. I mean, after all, it was advice from Miss Overachiever herself. How could it be wrong?"

"Now, hold on one dang minute here." She aimed the fork at him. "You can't blame me just because you chose to follow my perfectly good advice and then messed it up by picking the wrong woman."

"I'm a Madison. I was bound to pick the wrong woman."

"That's a cop-out excuse if I ever heard one and you know it. You will not use it again, do you hear me?"

He halfway lowered his lashes. "Yes, ma'am."

She subsided slightly. "It's not like you're the only person on the face of the earth who made a mistake when it came to selecting the right mate, you know. I didn't do any better."

"Yes, you did. You just got engaged. You never got married."

She made a face and forked up another bite of toast. "I'll let you in on a little secret. The only reason I didn't make the mistake of actually marrying Doug was because he very kindly dumped me before we got to the altar."

"What was he like?"

"He's a lawyer, a partner at a very prestigious firm in Portland. We met when I did his sister's wedding. We had lots of things in common."

"He fit all the criteria on the Mr. Right list you gave me that night on the beach?"

She winced. "You remember that list?"

"Never forgot it. Made a profound impact on me."

"Why?"

He picked up his coffee mug and swallowed meditatively. "Probably because I knew I'd never come anywhere near to meeting even half the requirements and specifications on it."

His words blindsided her. "It really bothered you that you couldn't make my Mr. Right list?"

"Uh-huh."

"Good grief, that's crazy. You were never interested in me. To you I was just some naïve, prissy little overachiever. Miss Goody Two-Shoes, remember?"

"It wasn't the fact that I personally couldn't make your Mr. Right list that bugged me. It was the fact that there *was* such a thing as a Mr. Right list and you knew all about it."

"I beg your pardon?"

"See, I didn't even know the damn list existed," Rafe explained patiently. "That put me at a serious disadvantage. And when I found out that women like you had one and the kind of stuff that was on it, I knew I was in deep trouble."

She shook her head once, dazed. "I don't get it. What do you mean?"

He exhaled slowly. "I'll tell you something, Miss Goody Two-Shoes. That night on the beach you were all those things you just said—naïve and prissy and all that. But I figured you were also an authority on one important thing. You knew what it took to make a good marriage."

"Me? But I'd never been married."

"True, but you'd been raised in a family that looked pretty damn perfect to me. Happily married parents and grandparents. No divorces. No scandals. I assumed that you knew what it took to make it all happen."

Understanding dawned. Rafe had no firsthand knowledge of how a good marriage functioned because, unlike her, he'd never witnessed one close up. Divorce ran as strongly as green eyes in the Madison clan.

"I see. Well, if it makes you feel any better, I have concluded that my original Mr. Right list was flawed," she said.

"Yeah? Why?"

She propped her elbows on the table and rested her chin on the heels of her hands. "I'm going to tell you something that I've never told anyone else. I swear, if this gets out I will throttle you, Rafe Madison."

"Sounds interesting."

"The truth is, Doug had his own list, and I failed to meet all of his specifications and requirements."

Rafe blinked. Then his mouth curved slowly into a grin. "The guy had a Ms. Right list?"

"Yep. He was decent enough to point out the areas in which I was deficient. He made suggestions for improvement. I got ticked."

Rafe's grin metamorphosed into a chuckle. The chuckle erupted into a full-throated roar of laughter.

She watched him, wondering if he was going to fall out of his chair. Winston, ears cocked, looked intrigued. Rafe's howls filled the kitchen.

It took a while for him to pull himself together. Hannah filled the time by pouring herself another cup of coffee and feeding Winston a scrap of leftover French toast from her plate.

Rafe's shoulders eventually stopped shaking. He sprawled in the chair, one hand on his flat belly, and subsided slowly into a grin.

"Sorry." He didn't sound sorry at all.

"I'm glad you find it so amusing."

"I have to know," Rafe said. "Where did you fall short?"

"Why should I tell you?"

"Because I just cooked breakfast for you."

"Hmm." He had a point. "I fit most of the criteria, you understand. I came from a successful family. I was well educated. I had demonstrated initiative and determination by founding my own business. I was well connected in the community. I shared a lot of Doug's interests."

"But?"

She made a face. "But it turned out that Doug was making long-range plans to enter the political arena. He's a good man. I think he really has something to contribute. But he needed a wife who could handle the sort of social and personal demands that go with that kind of job."

"Hence the list."

"Yes. The more I realized that he was serious about a political career, the more we both came to the conclusion that I couldn't handle being a politician's wife."

Rafe reached for the coffeepot. "Welcome to the select club reserved for those who fail to make the Mr. and Mrs. Right lists."

"Gee, thanks. Is there a merit badge?"

"No. So, tell me, what did you do with your own list?"

She hesitated. "I amended it."

He glanced at her with a strange expression. "You mean you've still got one?"

"Yes. But it's a lot shorter now."

"Huh. What's on it?"

"I really don't think—" She broke off at the sound of a car turning into the drive.

Winston was at the door in a flash. He gave the appropriate warning *woof*. Alert but not yet alarmed. On the job.

The low rumble shattered the fragile intimacy that had enveloped the kitchen. Rafe turned his head to check the drive. Hannah followed his gaze. The fog had burned off enough to allow her to see the vehicle that was approaching the house. A green Volvo.

"Anyone you know?" Rafe asked.

"I don't recognize the car."

"Want me to hide in a closet?"

"Don't be ridiculous." She pushed back her chair and got to her feet. "I'm sure it's just a friend of my folks' who found out that I'm in town and stopped to say hello."

He looked at her. "Whoever it is, he or she will have seen my car by now. Probably recognized it."

"The fact that you are having coffee with me is no one's business."

"Wasn't just coffee," Rafe said as she went past him into the living room. "But who's going to argue?"

She was saved from having to respond because she was already halfway to the front door. She patted Winston, who looked like a ballet dancer, poised and ready on his paws.

"It's okay, pal. I don't think a burglar would arrive in a Volvo."

She opened the door. A polished, good-looking man emerged from behind the wheel of the Volvo. He wore a navy blue polo shirt, a pair of gray trousers, and loafers. There was a designer logo stitched on the left side of the shirt. The pants appeared to have been hand-tailored, and the loafers had little tassels. She was almost certain that the hair had been styled in a salon located somewhere other than Eclipse Bay.

When her visitor spotted her waiting in the doorway, he gave her a dazzling smile that lit up the foggy morning like a lighthouse beacon.

"Looks like Perry has started bleaching his teeth," she murmured to Winston.

Winston rumbled deep in his throat and trotted after her as she went out onto the porch.

"Hannah." Perry Decatur jogged toward the steps. "Heard you were in town. Great to see you again. You look fabulous."

At the last minute she realized his intention and braced herself. He swept her into an embrace that would have been more appropriate for lovers who had been separated for years by war and star-crossed fates. She felt the breath go out of her lungs as his arms closed around her.

A low growl reverberated across the porch. For one horrible moment, Hannah was not sure if the sound had come from Winston or Rafe.

"Cute dog."

Perry released Hannah, bent down, and thumped Winston lightly on his broad, intelligent head without going through the civilized formality of allowing Winston to sniff his fingers first.

Winston's silvery brows bristled with indignation, but he was too well behaved to make a scene. He did, however, display a discreet glimpse of fang. Could have been an accident, Hannah thought.

Perry straightened quickly. "Dogs love me."

"No kidding." Hannah looked at Winston. "Thank you, Winston. I can handle this. You may go back inside and finish your breakfast."

With a last glare at Perry, Winston turned and stalked back into the house.

"Fine-looking animal," Perry said approvingly. "Do you show him?"

"Show him what?"

"I meant, is he a show dog?"

She stared at him. "Put Winston in a ring and make him perform stunts for a bunch of judges? Are you mad?

I wouldn't dream of doing such a thing. He would be mortified."

Perry managed a forced chuckle. "I see. Well, how have you been, Hannah?"

"Fine."

"Great. That's just great." He angled his chin in the general direction of Rafe's car. "I see you've got a visitor."

"We're having coffee."

"Coffee sounds terrific."

She chose to ignore the unsubtle hint. "I'm a little busy, Perry."

The bright light of his smile dimmed a bit. "Hannah, I really need to talk to you."

"Call me this afternoon."

"This can't wait." Perry paused a beat and lowered his voice. "It's important. Not just to me but to a lot of people here in Eclipse Bay."

She wavered. "What is it?"

"It's too involved to explain out here."

He moved past her with a breezy arrogance that made her want to stick out a foot and trip him. She avoided the temptation. If Winston was capable of good manners and restraint in the face of extreme provocation, she could do no less.

She went thoughtfully back into the house and closed the door. Perry was already in the kitchen, introducing himself to Rafe.

"I don't think we've met." He thrust out his hand. "I'm Perry Decatur. I'm with the institute. Sorry to interrupt breakfast. Hannah and I are old friends."

"Rafe Madison." Rafe kept his fingers wrapped around his coffee mug and managed to overlook Perry's outstretched hand. "I know all about your old friendship with Hannah. I was the one who walked her home that night eight years ago when she decided to end her date with you a little early. But I'm sure you heard all about that."

Perry blinked a couple of times and dropped his hand. But if he found the moment awkward, he gave no hint. "What a coincidence, the three of us getting together over coffee after all this time."

"Yeah, life's funny that way, isn't it?" The gleam in Rafe's eyes was diamond-hard. "So, what do you do at the think tank?"

"Vice President of Finance and Administration."

Perry removed a small gold case from his pocket and produced a card. When Rafe did not reach for it, he put it down on the table next to the empty syrup jug. He took one of the chairs, twitched it around, and sat down back to front. Very confident. Very much at home in this house. Hannah ground her teeth.

"I'm the guy who deals with the donors and contributors who fund the research projects," Perry said.

"In other words, you hustle cash for the institute," Rafe said.

Hannah raised her eyes toward the ceiling, but there was no help from that quarter.

If Perry was insulted by Rafe's description of his job, he managed to conceal it behind a small chuckle. "It's a bit more complicated than that, but I really don't have time to go into it now."

Hannah dropped down into her chair. "Why don't you tell me exactly why you're here, Perry?"

"Well, I'd like to invite you to attend the reception for Trevor Thornley at the institute tomorrow night," Perry said.

"Thanks," Hannah said, "but I'm not big on political receptions."

"This is an important event," Perry said seriously.

"Thornley's going to formally announce his intention to enter the U.S. Senate race."

"So?"

Perry pursed his lips. "Well, the thing is, when I heard that you were back in town, I more or less assured the director of the institute that I could convince you to come to the reception. It would look very good to have a Harte there, if you know what I mean. Your family has always carried a lot of weight here in Eclipse Bay."

Rafe gave a rude grunt and reached for the coffeepot.

Hannah eyed Perry with renewed caution. "You promised your boss that you would produce me tomorrow night, didn't you? And he's going to be annoyed if I don't put in an appearance."

Perry sighed. "I would take it as a great personal favor, Hannah. Tomorrow night is very, very important to me, careerwise."

"Who else is on the guest list?"

Perry appeared briefly surprised by the question. But he switched gears swiftly. "The usual local honchos, of course. Plus all the folks who backed Thornley's previous campaigns. We've also got some heavy-duty movers and shakers from Portland coming in. The big catch of the evening is Tom Lydd."

"Tom Lydd of Lydd-Zone Software?" Hannah asked.

"One and the same." Perry tried and failed to look modest. "I've been courting him for months, trying to get him to endow a research fund at the institute. I don't mind telling you that the fact that he agreed to attend tomorrow night is a very, very good sign. I'll have his name on an endowment agreement by the end of the week if all goes well."

"Big coup for you, I imagine," Hannah said politely.

"Doesn't get any bigger than Tom Lydd." Anticipation glittered in Perry's eyes. "I think it's safe to say that if

I land an endowment from him, my position at the institute will be rock solid. I'll be in line to take over as director when Manchester retires next year."

"Wow," Hannah said. She paid no attention to Rafe, who was watching her with a bemused expression.

Perry chuckled. "I think we can agree that 'wow' is the operative word. I've got plans for the institute. Big plans. When I take over I'm going to turn it into one of the most influential social policy think tanks in the country. We'll be able to make or break political candidates. Anyone in the Northwest with an eye on political office will come to us for consulting advice."

"All right," Hannah said. "I'll do it."

Perry patted her hand with the same air of condescending approval that he had exuded when he patted Winston's head. Hannah had the same reaction Winston had had. It was all she could do not to bare her teeth.

She could tell from the glint in Rafe's eyes that he had caught her reaction. Perry, however, did not appear to notice. Goal accomplished, he was already halfway out of his chair.

"I'll be very busy tomorrow evening," he said en route to the front door. "I won't be able to swing by here to pick you up. Why don't you meet me at the institute? Say, eight o'clock? Dressy but not formal attire. I'm sure you know the drill."

"Sure, Perry." She followed him back outside onto the porch.

He paused on the second-to-last step and glanced over her shoulder, evidently assuring himself that he could not be overheard by Rafe. Then he lowered his voice to a confidential tone.

"What's with you and Madison?"

"You must have heard by now that Aunt Isabel left

her house to both of us. Rafe and I are discussing how to handle Dreamscape."

A concerned frown furrowed Perry's brow. "Everyone in town heard about that will. Isabel must have been going senile there at the end. Why didn't you let the lawyers work it out?"

"Rafe didn't want to involve lawyers."

"Is that right?" Perry slanted a thoughtful glance at the door. "Probably thinks he can get a better deal on his own. You're lucky that I'm the one who happened to drop by this morning. Anyone else might have taken one look at that domestic little scene in the kitchen and jumped to the wrong conclusions."

"What conclusions?"

"You know what I'm talking about. You, Madison, the breakfast dishes. Hell, it isn't even nine o'clock yet. Looks like the two of you just spent the night together. If that kind of talk got around—"

She folded her arms, leaned one shoulder against the post, and looked at him. "Are you going to spread the rumor that I'm having an affair with Rafe Madison?"

"Of course not. Hell, I'm probably the one person in town who doesn't believe that you let him seduce you on the beach the night Kaitlin Sadler died."

"I appreciate your faith in my virtue. But what makes you so sure I didn't let Rafe seduce me that night?"

Perry chuckled indulgently. "As I recall, you were a bit naïve, not to say, downright inhibited about sex in those days."

"In other words, because I wasn't interested in getting into the backseat with you that night, it's highly unlikely that I fooled around with Rafe Madison later? Is that your logic?"

Perry gave her a knowing look. "As I said, I realize that there's nothing going on between the two of you, but a word to the wise. Eclipse Bay is still one very small town. You'd better be a little more careful about appearances in the future. Someone else might get the wrong idea."

"Thanks for the advice, Perry."

"One other thing you should know." He glanced toward the door behind her again and then leaned forward and dropped his voice still lower. "There's some serious question about Rafe Madison's source of income."

"What exactly are you implying, Perry?"

"I'm not one to make accusations, but there's talk that he may be involved in some less-than-legitimate investments, if you catch my drift."

"You mean he may be a gangster?"

Perry's lips thinned. "I'm just saying he might be skating a little close to the edge of the legal ice. Who knows what he's been up to during the past eight years?"

"Why don't you ask him?"

"None of my business." Perry went hastily down the last step. "Well, got to be on my way. Lots to do before tomorrow night. See you at the reception."

"Don't worry," she said softly. "I wouldn't miss it for the world."

She stayed where she was, lounging against the post, until the Volvo disappeared at the end of the drive. When she finally turned around, she saw Rafe and Winston gazing at her through the screen door.

"You'll be happy to hear that Perry doesn't believe for one moment that anything went on here last night," she said.

"Hell of a relief," Rafe said. "Someone who wasn't quite so high-minded as Decatur might have drawn all the wrong conclusions."

"Yes."

"He's still a jerk," Rafe said.

"Yes."

A speculative look gleamed in his eyes. "Are you serious about going to that political reception?"

"Very serious. Luckily I packed a black dress and a pair of heels. There's just one more thing I need."

"Yeah?" Rafe looked at her. "What's that?"

"A date."

"I got the impression that Decatur thinks he's going to be your date for the evening."

"He couldn't even be bothered to pick me up. I don't count that as a date."

"Got someone else in mind?"

She gave him her brightest smile. "I figure you owe me."

chapter 9

"What caused the feud?" Octavia asked after a while.

Mitchell paused in the process of removing dead blooms from the rosebushes. "A woman. What else?"

Octavia folded her arms on top of the fence and rested her chin on her hands. She watched him nip off another faded flower. "What was her name?"

"Her name was Claudia Banner."

"Was she very beautiful?"

Mitchell opened his mouth to say yes, but then he hesitated, thinking back through the years to his first impression of Claudia. "She was fascinating," he said finally. "I couldn't take my eyes off her. But I never really thought of her as beautiful. I just knew that I wanted her so badly that nothing else mattered. Unfortunately, my partner, Sullivan, wanted her too. For a while."

"What do you mean, for a while?"

Mitchell snorted softly. "Sullivan Harte was always too logical and too coolheaded to let himself be led around by his balls for long. He figured out what Claudia was up to long before I did. I refused to believe him. We fought. End of story."

"How did it happen?"

Mitchell tossed a dead bloom into a sack. "Sullivan and I set up Harte-Madison right after we got out of the army. We had us some mighty big dreams in those days. The plan was simple. We'd pick up a few cheap parking lots in downtown Portland and Seattle and then sit on 'em for as long as it took."

"As long as it took for what?"

"For the boom times to come, naturally. We both knew that sooner or later the Northwest cities were going to be important. What with the Pacific Rim trade taking off, property values were bound to skyrocket. We figured that when the time was right, we'd sell the parking lots to developers and make our fortunes. In the meantime, we'd have income off some very low-maintenance properties in the heart of the cities."

"How did Claudia Banner get involved?"

"Things started happening faster than we expected. We hired Claudia to help us negotiate the first sale. She'd had experience in that kind of thing, you see. Sullivan and I were novices."

"She did the deal for you?"

"Yep." Mitchell moved on to the next rosebush. "And it was a hell of a deal. Sullivan and I were suddenly rolling in dough. Both richer than we'd ever been in our lives. Couldn't wait to sell the next parking lot. Claudia found us a buyer right off the bat. More money fell down out of the sky. We were golden. Couldn't miss."

"What went wrong?"

"Somewhere in the middle of the sale of the third lot, a big one in downtown Seattle, Claudia pointed out that Harte-Madison could structure the deal in such a way that we'd be able to keep a stake in the future profits of the office tower that was slated to be built on the site."

"Uh-oh."

"Yep." Mitchell dropped another dead rose into his sack. "Uh-oh pretty much sums it up. Sullivan and I had financial stars in our eyes. We trusted Claudia. She took us for a ride and then vanished with the company profits on all three parking lots. Harte-Madison got left with a stack of leveraged debt, and the firm was suddenly out of business."

"And you and Sullivan were at each other's throats," Octavia mused.

Mitchell looked at her across the fence, squinting faintly against the weak sun. "I was sure he had somehow seduced Claudia into doing what she did. He figured I was working with her. Sullivan and I cornered each other outside Fulton's Supermarket one day, and the rest, as they say around these parts, is history."

"Did you love her very much, then?"

Mitchell shrugged. "She was my passion. Naturally, I made a fool of myself over her. Making fools out of themselves over females is something Madison men do."

"Is she still your passion?"

Mitchell examined the dead rose he had just pulled off a bush. "I'll let you in on a little secret. When you find yourself within spitting distance of ninety, you start viewing things from a slightly different perspective. If Claudia Banner walked back into my life today, I'd ask for my money back."

"And that's all?"

"Yep." He smiled slightly at the dead rose. "That's all. I've got other passions these days. That's another thing I've learned over the years. If he gives himself a chance, even a Madison can develop a little common sense when it comes to his passions."

Octavia was quiet for a while, watching him work. Eventually she stirred. "You know, if you leave some of the dead blooms on the bush you'll get rose hips. They make a very healthy tonic."

"I can't stand rose hip tea," Mitchell said. He snapped off another dead bloom and stuffed it into his sack. "I've got some good ten-year-old whiskey I use when I need a tonic."

chapter 10

At eight-thirty the following evening, Rafe stood with Jed Steadman at the edge of the crowd and watched Hannah dance with Perry Decatur. Decatur, he was pleased to note, did not appear to be enjoying himself.

The whole scene bordered on amusing. Rafe could almost feel sorry for Thornley and his retinue. The reception was ostensibly in the politician's honor, but most of the guests were too busy sneaking covert glances at Hannah and Rafe to pay much attention to Thornley. That was due to the fact that most of those present were locals, including the mayor and his wife, all of the members of the town council, and the owners of several Eclipse Bay businesses.

Rafe recognized a lot of faces. He knew that the majority of these people had been around long enough to be familiar with the legend of the famous Harte-Madison feud, and virtually all of them had been living in Eclipse Bay eight years ago when Hannah had provided him with his alibi for the night of Kaitlin Sadler's death. In addition, the entire town was no doubt aware of the terms of Isabel Harte's will.

When Rafe and Hannah had walked into the reception together shortly after eight, they had caused any number of heads to swivel and jaws to drop. A ripple of murmurs had spread through the crowd. An amazing number of people had found an excuse to cross the room to greet them and make conversation.

Definitely not a banner night for Thornley, Rafe thought. How could his staff have known that their man's forthcoming announcement of his intention to run for the U.S. Senate seat would take second place to the latest development in the Harte-Madison feud?

Jed munched a cracker slathered in cream cheese and smoked salmon. "Thornley might be the next senator from the great state of Oregon, but he's having a hard time getting anyone's attention tonight."

"Only so far as the locals are concerned. The out-of-town crowd hasn't got a clue about the reason for the buzz."

"True, but almost everyone here is from Eclipse Bay." Jed eyed Perry and Hannah with an assessing gaze. "Decatur certainly doesn't look thrilled. Probably didn't expect you to show up with Hannah."

Rafe watched Perry and Hannah come to a halt on the dance floor. "I'm not real concerned with Decatur's feelings."

"From what I hear, he's got a lot at stake tonight too. Word is he's trying to position himself to take over the institute next year."

"Not my problem." Rafe picked up a feathered toothpick that had an olive, a bit of cheese, and a mushroom impaled on it. He put the tiny skewer in his mouth and removed the edible portions with his teeth.

Jed shot him a curious look. "So what's up with you and Hannah, anyway?"

"We're conducting negotiations."

Jed looked amused. "Yeah, I heard about that. Your Porsche was spotted at the Harte place night before last. Word is you're doing your negotiating in bed."

Very deliberately, Rafe turned to look at him. He said nothing.

Jed grimaced and put up a hand, palm out. "Sorry. Can't help the curiosity. I'm a reporter, remember?"

"Yeah," Rafe said, "I remember."

"I get the message. No more questions of a personal nature about you and Hannah Harte. But speaking as an old friend, I'll just say that you'd better hope that her family doesn't get wind of the talk that's going around town."

"I'm not worried about the rest of the Hartes. This is between Hannah and me."

"Sure. Whatever you say." Jed reached for another canapé and another topic of conversation. "Some big bucks in this crowd tonight. Just saw Tom Lydd and his new bride arrive. I understand the head of the institute is hoping Lydd will endow a research fund."

Rafe followed his gaze to the man with the boyish face and the techie glasses on the far side of the room. Tom Lydd was not yet thirty, but he was already worth millions. "Very smart guy. Took his company public at the right time. His security software is some of the best on the market. Wouldn't be surprised if there's a buyout on the horizon."

Jed glanced at him. "You follow that kind of business news?"

Rafe shrugged. "It's a hobby."

Jed nodded, satisfied. He turned back to his survey of the crowd. "Not a bad turnout for the institute. A rising politician, a sprinkling of big money, and the right people from the political end of the spectrum. Got to admit, this operation has come a long way since it first opened its doors."

Rafe glanced at the tall, photogenic man talking to Tom Lydd. "And so has Trevor Thornley."

"You can say that again. He'll do okay in Washington. He's got all the right instincts, including good timing."

"You always said that timing was everything."

"It sure as hell is in politics. Thornley is also into long-range planning. Another big asset. In addition, he's smart enough not to neglect his home base here in Eclipse Bay. Pols that take their local support for granted always get into trouble fast."

"The fact that he married Marilyn Caldwell didn't hurt him either," Rafe said dryly.

Jed grunted. "You can say that again. Her father's money has come in real handy. Like I said, the guy knows how to plan."

"He sure pays a lot of attention to the institute."

"With good reason. He was its first important political client, and he's still the most faithful. The higher he climbs, the more prestige and power this place acquires."

"And the more it backs him."

"That's how it works." Jed swirled the wine in his glass. "I remember covering his first public relations events here. I knew even then that he had what it takes to make it big in politics."

Rafe thought about the night he had walked Hannah home. The institute had been ablaze with lights that evening. He had seen them from Bayview Drive. Hannah had mentioned that her parents were attending a reception for a politician named Thornley who had just announced that he was running for the state legislature.

Rafe hadn't paid much attention. Politics had been of little interest to him in those days. In any event, he had been too busy obsessing on Hannah's list of criteria for Mr. Right that night.

The memory made him look around for his date. He spotted her coming toward him through the crowd. The sight of her sparked a thrill of intense awareness deep in his gut. She looked great, he thought. The snug-fitting little black number she was wearing underscored a whole lot of her best assets, including the neatly curved breasts, slim waist, and full hips. Her hair swung in a sleek, gleaming curve every time she moved her head. Her legs were incredibly sexy in dark stockings and black high heels.

The most exciting woman in the room, no doubt about it. At least so far as he was concerned.

He watched her weave her way toward him. She had Decatur in tow, but Perry looked more irritated than ever, so that was okay for now, Rafe concluded. Irritated was good. Irritated meant that Decatur had not liked the fact that Hannah had brought her own date tonight. The jerk had probably counted on taking her home after the reception, maybe even planned to take up where he had left off that night in the front seat of his car eight years ago.

Not bloody likely.

Hannah came to a halt in front of Rafe. She looked flushed and glowing, and there was a sparkle in her eye. He was almost positive that Decatur had nothing to do with the look. She was up to something. He had sensed it when he'd picked her up earlier. She had a scheme cooking tonight. He was content to stand back and watch it unfold.

She smiled.

"We're back," she said.

"Yeah, I can see that," Rafe said.

"You'll have to excuse me," Perry muttered. "Got to say hello to some very big people. I'll catch up with you later, Hannah."

"Yes, you will," she said very sweetly. "I'll look forward to it."

Perry hurried off into the throng.

"He doesn't look real happy," Rafe said. "What did you do? Step on his toes?"

"I'm saving that for later."

Jed looked interested. "That sounds promising. Anything you want to tell the press?"

"Not yet, Jed." Hannah smiled. "But stay tuned."

"If we've got some time before the excitement starts," Rafe said, "may I have the next dance?"

"You may."

"Hannah!" A man's voice rose above the din of nearby conversation. "Hannah Harte! Is that you?"

In the next instant, a small knot of people unraveled to allow Tom Lydd to pass between them. He had his wife, a wholesome-looking blonde, in tow. Both were smiling at Hannah with genuine delight.

"What a terrific surprise," the young Mrs. Lydd said. She threw her arms around Hannah and then stepped aside so that Tom could do the same.

"Didn't know that you'd be here," Tom crowed. "This is great. Nice to see a familiar face."

"I'm delighted to see you," Hannah murmured. "Allow me to introduce Rafe Madison and Jed Steadman. Rafe, Jed, meet Tom and Julie Lydd. Fair warning—Jed is the editor of the *Eclipse Bay Journal*."

"Not a problem. I've got no quarrel with the press. Always been good to Lydd-Zone." Tom pumped the hands of both men with his trademark boyish enthusiasm. "Great to meet you both."

"Any friend of Hannah's." Rafe slanted a quick glance at her. She winked at him. That clarified one thing, he thought. The Lydds were part of whatever plan she had concocted.

"Hannah is more than a friend," Julie Lydd confided. "She was our wedding consultant. A true magician, as far as we're concerned. Tom and I had a vision of what we wanted, but we didn't have the vaguest idea of how to pull it off. Hannah made it all happen."

"Everything went off like clockwork." Tom beamed at his wife. "Isn't that right?"

"It was amazing," Julie agreed. "We wanted the whole thing staged on an alien world, you see. The one Tom created for his first big computer game."

"We're talking waterfalls, lagoons, architectural features, the works," Tom continued. "Did the whole thing on our private island up in the Sans Juans. Hannah was brilliant. You can imagine the logistical nightmare involved. Very impressive organizational talents. After we got back from the honeymoon, I called her up and tried to hire her. There's always room for that kind of management skill at Lydd-Zone."

"I told him that if the bottom ever falls out of the wedding business, I'll take him up on his offer," Hannah said.

"Anytime," Tom assured her genially.

Hannah smiled warmly. "I love doing weddings for couples who are matched by my sister's agency."

Jed cocked a brow. "Your sister's a matchmaker?"

Julie Lydd answered, "Tom and I met through Private Arrangements. That's the name of Lillian Harte's agency. She uses a very sophisticated computer program to make her matches. Not everyone likes that approach, of course. A lot of folks think it takes the romance out of the process. But it appealed to both Tom and me."

Rafe looked at Tom. "I hear you're thinking of endowing a research fund here at the institute."

"Looking into it," Tom agreed. "I'm a big fan of the think tank concept." He turned to Hannah. "You're from this neck of the woods. What's your take on the folks running this place?"

Hannah's smile brightened to a blinding glare. "I'm so glad you asked, Tom. I do have some opinions on this operation. Why don't we find a private place to talk?"

"Great." Tom took his wife's arm. "I noticed a small conference room just outside in the main hall. Doubt if anyone would mind if we used it."

Jed watched the three vanish back into the crowd. He turned to Rafe, his eyes gleaming with interest. "What do you think that was all about?"

Rafe picked up a knife, dipped it into a bowl of what looked like cheese spread, and smeared some on a cracker. "How the heck should I know?"

But he had a pretty good idea, he thought. Hannah was making her move. He couldn't wait to find out what happened next.

"What's wrong?" Jed asked.

Rafe grimaced. "The cheese spread is bland. Could have done with some feta and walnuts."

At ten-thirty Hannah emerged from the rest room in time to see Trevor Thornley take the podium to make his big announcement. The lights dimmed over the crowd. Onstage, the politician stood in the center of a dramatic spot. His wife, Marilyn, stood a little behind and just to the right, glowing with wifely pride.

Hannah had a hunch that Marilyn could take a lot of the credit for the fact that her husband was about to launch a campaign for the U.S. Senate. Marilyn had always been ambitious.

Trevor Thornley raised his hands for silence.

"I want to thank everyone here tonight, starting with the faculty of this outstanding think tank. The cutting-edge work done here at the institute in the areas of social and public policy has had a profound impact, not only on how the pundits discuss the issues, but, more importantly, on how politicians and voters think about the challenges that face our nation today.

"The greatness of this country lies in its people. I have always . . ."

"What the hell do you think you're doing, Hannah?" Perry's voice hissed out of the shadows behind her. His hand closed over her arm. His fingers tightened painfully. He spun her around to face him. "I just got through talking to Tom Lydd."

"Such a nice man. And so smart." She smiled into Perry's fuming eyes. "I like his wife, too, don't you?"

"Lydd just told me that he wouldn't even consider endowing a research fund here at the institute unless Professor Brad McCallister of Chamberlain College received a joint appointment to the faculty."

Hannah widened her eyes. "That shouldn't be a problem. I hear that Brad McCallister has already been nominated by the selection committee. He'll make a terrific addition to your staff."

Perry's face was suffused with an angry red color. "Damn it, you had no business interfering in the professional affairs of the institute."

"But I didn't interfere." Hannah smiled. "I merely told Tom that Brad was brilliant and that the selection committee should be applauded for choosing him."

"Lydd told me that he wants McCallister to run the department created by the endowment." Perry started to sputter. "The whole damn department."

"An excellent idea. Brad is the very soul of integrity.

With him in charge, Lydd and the institute will have the satisfaction of knowing that Lydd's money is spent the way he wants it spent."

Perry's face worked furiously. "Pamela McCallister is your friend, isn't she? You knew that Brad was being considered for a joint appointment here."

"I also heard that you were trying to block it because you're jealous of Brad's professional abilities. You're afraid he'll outshine you once he gets on the institute staff, aren't you?"

"That's got nothing to do with it."

"Good. In that case you shouldn't have any problem with the selection committee's choice."

"You planned this. You agreed to come here tonight because you knew the Lydds would be here."

"I believe it was you yourself who mentioned that they had been invited."

"That's beside the point." His voice rose. He grabbed her other arm. Rage flashed in his eyes. "You think you can pull a stunt like this with me just because you're a Harte?"

"Perry, you tried to use me and the Harte name tonight. I let you do it. In exchange, I used the opportunity you dropped into my lap. I'd say we're even."

"You little bitch! You got a kick out of playing the tease eight years ago, and you're still at it, aren't you?"

It occurred to her that Perry had not learned to curb his temper in the past eight years. It flared as quickly and intensely as it had in the old days.

"Let me go," she said coolly. "This scene is starting to remind me of another discussion we had once."

"If you're talking about that night you staged the big drama in my car and then jumped out when I got tired of your cock-teasing—"

Her own temper kicked in. "I'm talking about the night

you decided that since you couldn't seduce me into having sex with you, you would try force instead. What were you thinking, anyway? Were you working on the theory that once I discovered what a great lover you were I'd agree to marry you?"

"Damn it—"

"Or did you convince yourself that if I had sex with you, I'd feel that I had to marry you just for the sake of my reputation?"

His eyes narrowed. "If I ever thought you cared a damn about your reputation, you sure straightened me out when you told Chief Yates and anyone else who would listen that you'd spent the night on the beach with Rafe Madison."

Hannah's turbocharger switch suddenly tripped and her temper went into overdrive. "Let me tell you something, Perry Decatur. You are very, very lucky that I did not tell my folks or my brother how you really behaved in the front seat of the car that night. All I ever said was that we'd argued. I never told them how you tried to force yourself on me."

His eyes bulged. "How dare you accuse me of that sort of behavior? No one has done more for women's issues here at the institute than me."

"Forget the political agenda. We both know what you had in mind that night."

"We were on a date." Perry's voice was choked with outrage. "You freaked out when I tried to kiss you. That was all there was to it."

"That's not quite how I remember it." She stabbed her finger against his elegantly knotted white silk tie. "You thought you could coerce me into marrying you."

"You're crazy. Hell, I knew that you were naïve and inhibited in those days, but I didn't think you were *so* naïve and *so* inhibited that you couldn't recognize a grown man's normal, healthy sex drive when you saw it."

"I saw it, but I gotta tell you, Perry, it didn't look normal or healthy to me."

"It was your fault that there was a small misunderstanding."

She gave him an icy smile. "Yes, it was on the small side, but I wasn't going to mention it."

"There's a word for women like you. You can't blame me for trying to take you up on what you were offering."

"I didn't offer you anything, and you know it."

"I cared for you." His jaw jerked a couple of times as if he were on the verge of being overcome by emotion. "I wanted to marry you."

"Sure. But only because I was a Harte."

"That's not true."

"It was true. I wasn't nearly as naïve in those days as everyone seems to think. Do you really believe that you were the first man who latched on to me because he saw it as a way to marry into Harte Investments?"

"I resent the implications of that statement," Perry said furiously. "I'm an academic. I live for the world of ideas, not the world of business."

"Give me a break, Perry. You're a hustler. You always have been a hustler. Eight years ago you saw marriage to me as a quick, easy way to get access to the deep pockets of my father's company. You also figured you'd have a lot of use for the social and business contacts that my family could provide, didn't you?"

"Your parents liked me."

"Mostly because they thought you were bright, charming, and ambitious. Really ambitious. My family admires ambition in a person. Sometimes we admire it a little too much."

"There's nothing wrong with ambition. It's the American way."

"What you seem to have overlooked is that there's a line between ambition and hustling. I'll admit that it can be mighty thin at times, but it's there if you care to check for it." She paused deliberately. "Something tells me that you haven't looked for it in years, Perry."

"You're just as preachy and prissy as ever, aren't you?" His mouth tightened. "Do you know how incredibly self-righteous and officious you sound when you go into your lecturing mode? No wonder your engagement fell apart. What man in his right mind wants to go to bed every night with a woman who can't stop lecturing?"

She caught her breath. Then she glanced very pointedly at the hands he had clasped around her arms. "Let me go, Perry."

He ignored her. His fingers squeezed tighter. "I've got news for you. The Miss Virtue act doesn't work here in Eclipse Bay anymore. You screwed your image eight years ago when you provided Rafe Madison with his alibi. And what do you think will happen when word gets out that the two of you are *negotiating* the details of your aunt's will over cozy little breakfasts at your folks' place?"

"You know, it won't be as easy to knee you in the crotch tonight as it was the last time, because this skirt is much tighter than the one I had on that night. But I think I can manage it, and I will if you don't let me go right now."

He released her and jumped back as if he'd just touched an electrically charged wire. "Bitch!"

"I think this is about where I came in last time," Rafe said from the shadows behind Perry. "But the big difference is that Hannah won't have to walk home tonight. I've got my car."

"Madison." Perry jerked around to face Rafe and then took another hasty step back. "This is a private conversation."

"I got the impression that Hannah didn't want to continue it any longer." Rafe glided forward with a deceptively lazy movement. His eyes never left Perry's face. "Was I mistaken?"

"This is none of your business." Perry's voice squeaked slightly. "If you touch me, I'll file charges."

Alarmed by the glint of predatory anticipation in Rafe's eyes, Hannah stepped quickly between the two men. "That's enough, Rafe. Everything is under control."

"I know, but it would be sort of fun to bounce him around a little. Please?"

"Rafe, I'm serious." It occurred to her that in her career as a wedding consultant she had honed to a fine art the ability to nip embarrassing public scenes in the bud. Now she was standing in the middle of one that she herself had created. "I do not want anyone hurt here."

"I could take him somewhere else." Rafe looked hopeful. "Pretty quiet down at Eclipse Arch this time of night. No one would hear him squawk."

"You're crazy." Perry backpedaled several more steps. "How dare you threaten me! Do you have any idea of just who is out there in that reception room? There's a future U.S. senator out there. Not to mention a lot of other very important people."

"He's right," Hannah said firmly. "We do not want to cause a disturbance that will only result in embarrassment for all concerned."

"I don't mind a little embarrassment," Rafe assured her. "I'm a Madison."

"Stop threatening me," Perry howled.

"I didn't threaten you." Rafe looked at Hannah. "Did you hear me threaten him, Hannah?"

She seized his arm. "You and I are leaving. Now. The main goal of the evening has been accomplished. Perry has just assured me that he will not stand in the way of Brad's joint appointment at the institute. In fact, he will do everything he can to ensure that it goes through. Isn't that right, Perry?"

"I won't be intimidated," Perry said forcefully. "Furthermore, I am not in charge of the selection committee. You have to remember that."

"Sure, sure, we understand." Rafe winked. "But just among the three of us, Brad McCallister's appointment looks like a sure thing, right?"

Perry cleared his throat and somehow managed to look down his nose even though he was at least three inches shorter than Rafe. "If Lydd goes through with his plans to endow a research fund here at the institute, and if he feels strongly about McCallister's appointment, he will, of course, be able to bring a great deal of influence to bear on the matter."

Rafe glanced at Hannah. "Are you sure you don't want me to bounce him around a bit?"

"Positive. We don't need lawsuits." She tugged on his arm. It was like trying to hoist the anchor of a container ship by hand.

Rafe gave Perry a look of wistful regret. "You know, you're right about one thing, Decatur. When she starts in with the lectures and the good advice, she does sort of take all the fun out of things, doesn't she?"

"That's enough, Madison." Hannah gave up tugging, wrapped her hand around his arm, and leaned forward instead.

"Whatever you say." Without warning, Rafe suddenly reversed course, squeezing her hand against his side.

Hannah, already off balance, with her fingers now

trapped under his elbow, had to run a few steps to avoid being dragged.

"*Rafe.*"

"Sorry." He slowed to a normal pace. "You okay?"

"Of course I'm okay." She shoved her hair out of her eyes and yanked hard on her skirt. "Let's get out of here."

"I'm with you. I don't think I'm going to become a big fan of political receptions. The speeches are boring and the food is bad."

For some inexplicable reason she started to laugh.

chapter 11

With the exception of a few stray chuckles, she had herself under control by the time they got outside. Rafe glanced at her as they walked to the far side of the lot where the Porsche was parked.

"Told you he was still a jerk." He opened the passenger door for her.

"You were right." She slanted him a quick glance. "How long were you lurking there in that hallway outside the rest rooms?"

"Long enough to hear most of the conversation."

She paused, half in and half out of the cockpit. Then she straightened and went up on her toes. Leaning over the top of the car window, she brushed her mouth very quickly against his cheek.

"It really was sweet of you to offer to beat Perry up for me," she said.

He lifted his fingers absently to the place where her lips had touched his skin. In the weak glare of the parking lot lamp his eyes were shadowed, impossibly enigmatic. "That's me, a real sweet guy."

She stepped back quickly and sank into the rich leather upholstery. "But I really didn't need rescuing."

"'Course not. You're a Harte."

"And Perry is just a jerk with a temper who's always looking for an angle."

Rafe folded his arms on the top of the window frame and looked down at her. "Got news for you. It wasn't you I was trying to rescue back there."

She stilled. "I beg your pardon?"

"I just figured I'd better break up that little one-sided skirmish before you cast any more nasty aspersions on Decatur's masculinity."

She was not quite sure how to take that. "Oh." She narrowed her eyes, trying to see his face against the pale light. "You, uh, care about Perry's fragile male ego?"

"Not particularly. But intimidation is a precious tool. Push a guy like Decatur too hard, and it can backfire on you. He might try to take revenge."

"Hah. There's nothing he can do to me."

"Not to you maybe, but he could sure make life hell at the institute for your friend's husband."

She stared at him for a beat or two as the implications sank in. "You're right. If Brad gets the appointment, he'll have to work with Perry, won't he?"

"Maybe not directly, but he won't be able to avoid him altogether. They'll be colleagues, after all. I'm sure Brad can take care of himself, but why make things any harder than necessary for him?"

"Damn." She drummed he fingers on the edge of the seat and gazed morosely through the front windshield. "I got a little carried away back there, didn't I?"

"Perfectly natural reaction," he assured her. "Victory can make a person giddy."

"Apparently." She frowned. "So how come it was okay for you to threaten to bounce him around, but it wasn't okay for me to make rude remarks?"

He exhaled with an air of long-suffering patience. "Because I'm a man and I was making a direct threat."

"Ah, yes, I get it." She nodded wisely. "Macho challenge stuff."

"A challenge that Decatur was never forced to answer or back down from because you intervened, thus saving both his bacon and his pride."

She thought about that. "You did that on purpose, didn't you? You knew I'd put a stop to anything that looked as if it would turn into real violence."

"Pretty sure, yeah."

"How did you know that?"

He grinned. "Instinct."

"Yours or mine?"

"Yours."

She pursed her lips. "You mean you just assumed that because I'm female I would automatically move to stop a couple of males from getting into a brawl?"

"It had nothing to do with the fact that you're female. Believe me, I've met women who love to watch men fight. But I figured that any successful wedding consultant would have developed finely-tuned radar when it comes to scenes. The last thing anyone wants at a wedding is a brawl, right?"

"Well, yes, that's true, of course."

"I figured you'd be good at intervening in a confrontation," he concluded a little too innocently.

"Hmm."

"And you did get in a few zingers," he reminded her. "I heard them. Decatur took some well-placed hits."

She thought about Perry's words. *No wonder your engagement fell apart. What man in his right mind wants to go to bed every night with a woman who can't stop lecturing?* The invisible balloon of her triumph began to deflate.

She exhaled deeply. "Perry got in a few good thumps of his own."

"That's okay. You can handle them. You're tough, aren't you?" He started to close the door. "Hey, you're a Harte."

"Right. I'm a Harte." She continued to gaze out into the darkness on the other side of the windshield. "And what's more, I'm—"

She broke off, startled, when an apparition materialized out of the night directly in front of the car. In the cold glare of the parking lot lamp she saw a figure garbed in black pants, black running shoes, and black gloves. The hood of a black sweatshirt was pulled down over a face smeared with daubs of dark paint.

Rafe glanced over his shoulder, nodded casually. " 'Evening, A.Z. Nice night for recon work."

"Heard you were back in town, Rafe," Arizona Snow said. "Always figured you'd return someday to expose the bastards who tried to frame you for the Sadler girl's murder."

"Well, now that you mention it, that wasn't exactly the reason I came back," Rafe replied. "You see, Hannah and I have this little inheritance problem."

"Dreamscape," Arizona said briskly in a cigar- and whiskey-roughened voice. "I know all about that, too. Isabel was a good friend of mine. If you ask me, it makes a great cover for you." She peered into the Porsche. "Nice to see you, Hannah. Come back to help Rafe flush out the rats?"

Hannah smiled slightly. "Good evening, Arizona."

"My, don't you look fancy tonight." Arizona squinted.

"What the devil are you two doin' hanging around with this crowd at the institute? Part of your investigation?"

"Our being back in town has nothing to do with Kaitlin's death, A.Z.," Rafe said gently. "It was an acci- dent. You know that."

"Bulldooky. Suckers here at the institute offed her for some reason. She probably knew too much about somethin' going on up here."

"How would she have known anything about the institute?" Hannah asked curiously.

"Kaitlin slept around a lot," Arizona said. She shot a piercing look at Rafe. "Reckon you know that."

Rafe cleared his throat but did not say anything. Hannah glanced at him, but he deftly managed to avoid her eyes.

"Always figured poor Kaitlin slept with the wrong guy," Arizona continued. "Someone connected to the institute. Probably talked in his sleep. Or maybe she just saw some papers or something. They figured they had to get rid of her. The killers must have panicked when Chief Yates started investigatin', so they decided they needed a fall guy and tried to pin it on you, Rafe. Probably picked you on accounta everyone knew you'd been seeing a lot of Kaitlin that summer."

"An interesting theory," Rafe said neutrally.

"But thanks to Hannah here, the big plan fell apart." Arizona clenched a fist and pumped it into the air. "Once in a while we throw a wrench into the bastards' plans. Gives me hope that someday we'll expose the whole damned pack of weasels."

Rafe glanced at the black plastic binder in her hand. "What are you doing here tonight?"

"Keeping my logbooks up to date, of course." Arizona tapped the binder with one black-gloved finger. "Until the rest of you wake up and smell the coffee, someone has to keep an eye on what goes on up here at the institute. Someday folks will realize that this so-called think tank is a cover for a secret government operation that operates outside the law. When that day comes, everyone's going to be real glad to have my logs."

Hannah leaned slightly out of the car. "Did you put Rafe and me in your log tonight?"

"Honey, I took down the license plate, make, and model of every car in this lot when it arrived, and that includes friends as well as suspects. Got to keep the record accurate."

"Something to be said for accuracy," Hannah agreed.

"I also noted the number of people in each vehicle and, where possible, the identities." Arizona scowled. "Got to admit, I don't always recognize everyone these days. Every year more strangers show up for meetings and parties here at the institute. In the old days I knew just about everyone who came and went. But not anymore. The web is widening daily."

Rafe eyed the logbook. "Are you going to write down the time that we leave?"

"You bet. It's the details that make the difference, you know. When the truth finally comes out, it will be the accumulation of a lot of tiny facts in these logs that will show how the phantom project operated undetected for so long."

Hannah wrinkled her nose. "You don't really think that Rafe and I are involved in the conspiracy, do you?"

Arizona snorted. "'Course not. You're just a couple of naïve, innocent dupes like most everyone else around here. But I gotta put you in my logs because I gotta have a complete record of all comings and goings. If I start skipping a couple of cars here and there, the government lawyers might try to claim that the logs are incomplete

or inaccurate. Can't give 'em any room to squirm when
the truth comes out."

Rafe inclined his head in sober acknowledgment of
that logic. "Makes sense."

"You better believe it. I've monitored every reception,
every meeting, every special event held here at the institute since the day the place opened." She held her log
aloft again. "All part of the record."

Rafe glanced at his watch. "Well, you can log us out
at precisely ten-forty-three. We're on our way home now."

Arizona's head jerked up and down once in acknowledgment. "Got it." She clicked a black pen and opened
her notebook. "You two drive carefully."

"We will." Rafe started to close the passenger door.

"Say, Rafe." Arizona glanced up sharply. "Why don't
you stop by the café when you get a chance? About time
we updated that menu you worked out when you used
to cook for me. The college crowd seems happy enough,
but after all these years I'm getting a little tired of fix-
ing the same stuff day in and day out."

"All right, I'll drop by soon," Rafe said.

"Appreciate it." Arizona aimed the pen at Hannah.
"You come with him. Always did like the notion of you
two gettin' together. Told Isabel so."

Hannah braced one hand against the door to keep Rafe
from closing it. "My aunt discussed her intention to leave
the house to us with you?"

"Well, sure." Arizona's beefy shoulders rose and fell
beneath the black sweatshirt. "Me and Isabel went back
a long way. She talked to me about her plans for Dreamscape because she knew that everyone else would think
she was crazy for trying to end the feud."

"But not you," Hannah murmured.

"Nope, not me. I told her to go for it. Always knew
the feud had been caused by the sonsabitches who opened

the institute. The bastards probably wanted to break up Harte-Madison because they knew the company would try to block their plans to establish this damned think tank." Arizona sighed. "Unfortunately, their scheme worked all too well."

"Good night, A.Z." Rafe closed the car door very firmly.

Hannah watched Arizona disappear back into the shadows. Rafe circled around the tail of the Porsche and got in behind the wheel.

"You think we're a couple of naïve, innocent dupes?" Hannah asked.

"Sure, but what the hell." Rafe turned the key in the ignition and put the car in gear. "I'd rather be a happy, carefree dupe who gets to go home at ten-forty-three than an ever-vigilant guardian who has to spend nights running around in black sweats recording license plates."

Hannah glanced at the rows of parked cars as Rafe drove out of the lot. "Still, it's hard to believe anyone could get a lot of satisfaction out of writing down license plate numbers. Just think, she's been doing it for years."

"She's dedicated to the cause of ultimately exposing the secret government conspiracy operating here at the institute. As hobbies go, it probably beats watching television."

Hannah contemplated that as she gazed at the scene spread out below the hillside. There was no fog tonight— at least, there wasn't any yet. The bay was a sweep of midnight velvet ringed and studded with the lights of the town and the pier.

She could make out the neon sign that marked the Total Eclipse Bar and Grill. On the opposite side of the street, the town's single gas station was closed for the night. Near the pier was a row of darkened shops that featured rustic antiques, inexpensive beach souvenirs, and seascapes. The neighboring marina was largely unlit. The boats sheltered there were invisible against the dark expanse of the water.

"Arizona Snow is a nice person in a lot of ways, and she's definitely interesting," Hannah said after a while. "But she's not what anyone would call normal."

"The older I get," Rafe said, shifting gears to negotiate the curving road that led down from the institute, "the more I'm convinced that the only good, working definition of 'normal' is the fact that you're still walking around outside and not locked up in a padded cell."

"Okay, I'll buy that definition. It's as good as any other I've ever heard."

"Thanks. You know, for a guy who never made it through his second year of college, I say some smart stuff sometimes."

She smiled wryly. "And so modest, too."

He shot her a quick glance. "What's with the sudden depression here? Losing the glow of victory so soon?"

"You know the old saying, all glory is fleeting."

"Damn." He accelerated at the foot of the hill. "You *have* lost the sparkle."

"I hate when that happens."

"Me, too. Victory over the jerk should buy you more than a moment of exuberance. But don't worry, I've got a surefire cure for what ails you."

She turned her head on the back of the seat and studied his hard profile from beneath lowered lashes. It felt good to be here with him in the intimate confines of the powerful car. She wondered what her family would say if they knew where she was tonight.

For some reason the answer did not matter at that moment.

"What's the cure?" she asked softly.

A wicked expression, barely visible in the eerie light given off from the instrument panel, flickered across his face. "Come home with me, my sweet, naïve little dupe, and I will show you."

She knew the smart answer to that invitation. The only intelligent, sane, reasonable, logical, suitably Harte-like response was to tell him that she had to get home to her dog.

"Okay," she said instead.

She finished the last of the key lime pie and put down her fork with a sigh of mingled satisfaction and regret. The pie had been delicious, tangy and smooth on the tongue, with a flavor that conjured up images of the trop- ics. The slice had been arranged with artistic precision on the plate and trimmed with a paper-thin almond wafer and a slice of lime.

She looked at Rafe, who was sitting on the other side of the old oak table. He had removed his tie, unbuttoned the collar of his pristine white shirt, and rolled the sleeves up to the elbows. Nothing had changed since that night on the beach, she thought. He wasn't the handsomest man she had ever met, but he was far and away the sex- iest.

"The pie was incredible." She tried to focus on some- thing other than sex. It wasn't easy when she was near Rafe, she had discovered. And the problem seemed to be growing worse.

"You don't think I went a little overboard with the lime zest?" he asked.

"You can never have too much zest, I always say."

He nodded. "It's sort of like sparkle, I guess."

"You know, when it comes to cooking, you've got a real talent. Why haven't you ever opened a restaurant?"

"I've been waiting until the time was right."

She put her elbows on the table. "Okay, I can't stand the suspense any longer. If you aren't the owner of a five-star restaurant, how did you finance the Porsche and all this free time you seem to have on your hands?"

He gave her a cryptic smile. "Starting to wonder about all those rumors you've heard concerning my career as a gangster?"

"It never crossed my mind for one second that you might be a gangster."

"Yeah?" He thrust his legs out in front of him, leaned back in the chair, and crossed his feet at the ankles. "Why not?"

"Wrong clothes. Everyone knows gangsters wear shiny suits with big lapels."

"That's East Coast gangsters you're talking about. Out here on the West Coast, your average wise guy prefers a more laid-back look."

"Huh. Well, that blows that theory. So what have you been doing for the past eight years? And don't give me that line about working in a hotel."

"I did work in a hotel. For a while. I've also done a little investing." He paused. "Day trading."

Computer stock trading took nerves of steel and a fine sense of timing, she thought. "I've heard that's an easy way to lose your shirt."

"It is." He shrugged. "But I didn't."

She grinned. "Of course not."

"I'm out of the market now," he said evenly. "I took my profits a few months ago and stuck them into nice, boring bonds and my own portfolio of high techs."

"Stop." She held up a hand. "You're scaring me. It's disconcerting to hear a Madison talk seriously about sound financial planning. Ruins the image of wild, impulsive behavior."

"If you think I'm bad, you ought to talk to Gabe sometime. He's obsessed with making money and doing deals."

She smiled. "A cold-blooded Madison? Hard to imagine."

"Gabe has his share of the Madison hot blood. But he's channeled it into Madison Commercial."

"I'll take your word for it." Hannah hesitated. "Ever cooked for your grandfather?"

He looked genuinely startled. "No. Bryce does all the cooking at Mitchell's house."

"Why don't you invite Mitchell to dinner here at Dreamscape?"

His jaw tightened. "What put that idea into your head?"

"I'm not sure. It just occurred to me that your interest in cooking parallels his in gardening. Creative outlets that you both approach with passion."

"Huh."

"I think you should invite him to dinner."

Rafe contemplated her for a long, brooding moment. "You just can't help yourself, can you?" he said at last. "You can't resist handing out the advice."

She exhaled slowly and sank back into her chair. "You're right. I can't seem to stop. Do you think I should seek professional help?"

"Waste of money. You'd probably end up giving advice to the therapist on your own dime." He got to his feet and stacked the dishes. "Go on into the solarium. I'll bring the coffee out there."

Bemused and feeling oddly flattened, she got up from the table and walked out of the kitchen.

She wandered into the glass-walled room, not bothering to turn on the lights. Drawn by the darkened view, she went to stand at the windows. Rafe was right. She really ought to stop handing out advice to all and sundry. Nobody ever took it anyway.

Morosely she gazed out across the expanse of the curving bay toward the lights of the small harbor and the pier. Music stole softly into the dark shadows of the solarium, curling around her with a lover's touch. It was a slow, sultry number that sounded as if it had been born in a smoky nightclub and had never seen the light of day.

Rafe came through the doorway with a tray in his hands. Without a word he set the coffee and the mugs down on a table. Then he straightened and walked toward her.

A chill of intense awareness swept through her.

So it was dark and there was a torchy tune swirling in the air. So there was a sexy man who could cook like an angel in the immediate vicinity. So what?

Think of Winston.

Rafe came to a stop directly behind her. "Did I tell you how good you look in that dress?"

"Mmm." Noncommittal. That was always a safe way to play it.

He put his hands on her shoulders and turned her slowly around to face him. "You look fantastic in it."

Think of Winston.

Rafe took her into his arms and began to move, very slowly, to the very slow music.

He might as well have been making love to her, she thought. The effect was the same. It felt like things were melting down below. Unable to resist the temptation, she put her head cautiously on his shoulder.

His arms tightened very deliberately around her. His thumb touched the base of her spine.

Think of Winston.

She cleared her throat. "Would you mind if I asked you a purely hypothetical question?"

He put his mouth against her temple. "I live to answer hypothetical questions."

"In your considered opinion, do you think that the average man would be hesitant to become involved in a romantic relationship with a woman who was prone to lecture him in an officious, prissy manner?" She swallowed. "Even though she was right most of the time?"

He said nothing for a moment, dancing in thoughtful silence.

"The average man, maybe," he finally conceded.

Gloom settled on her, darker than fog. "I was afraid you were going to say that."

They danced for another moment or two. Then he brought her to a halt near the window.

"My turn to ask you a hypothetical question," he said. "Do you think I'm average?"

She raised her head very swiftly from his shoulder. "No. No, definitely not. You're a lot of things, Rafe Madison, but you are not average. Not in any way."

She could feel him smiling into her hair.

"Then I don't see that we have a problem here," he said.

He tilted her chin up and kissed her.

She stopped thinking of Winston.

chapter 12

She wanted him. He could feel it in the way she held him. The fine trembling in her body told him of her gathering excitement. He could not recall the last time a woman had shivered in his arms like this.

He realized his own hands were not completely steady.

Somewhere inside him there was a cloudburst. A hot rain poured down, drenching regions that had been parched and dry for what seemed like forever. Suddenly there was a rain forest where there had been only desert. The raw power, the driving need, and the exquisitely painful anticipation that shafted through him was the pulse of life itself.

He had promised himself that when this moment came he would take his time and savor the experience. He wasn't a kid with his girlfriend in the backseat of a car. He was a man who had some experience. He knew the risks of rushing things. But the urgent hunger was an ungovernable force that threatened to overwhelm his will.

"Rafe?" Hannah speared her fingers through his hair

and then tightened them around his neck. "I never intended . . . I mean, I didn't expect to end up like this tonight."

"Are you going to tell me it's too soon?" He kissed her throat. "That we don't know each other well enough?" He counted delicate little vertebrae with his fingertips until he reached the hollow of her back. "Because if you want to stop this, you'd better say something fast."

"No."

He froze, his palm on the curve of her hip, and raised his head to look down at her. "No, you don't want to do this?"

She smiled slowly. "No, I don't want to stop."

He shuddered and pulled her close again. "Don't scare me like that. My heart won't take the shock."

Her laugh was tiny and fraught with nervous energy. It sent sparkles of light through him. In the next moment the small sound transmuted into a sweet, anxious murmur. Her kisses became extravagant, quick, eager. Delicious.

He was tight and hard and edgy now. Every muscle straining. He could no longer think clearly. The fragrance of her body was a disturbing, disorienting incense that clouded his brain. He knew that he was swiftly losing control, but he could not seem to work up any real concern about the problem.

She wanted him.

That was all that mattered.

"Upstairs," he said against her mouth.

"I don't think I can make it that far."

She fumbled with his shirt. Somewhere in the shadows a button bounced and pinged on the tile floor. Her fingers spread across his chest, warm and soft.

"Let's try real hard to make it up the stairs," he said.

Her response was muffled against his bare skin.
"Okay."

He guided her toward the door. Simultaneously he
found the zipper of her dress and lowered it the length
of her back. The top half of the garment fell to her waist.
He saw that the manufacturer of her silky little black bra
had skimped on fabric. The garment did not cover the
top half of her breasts.

Gathering her against his side, he worked feverishly
on the clasp of the bra. At the same time he half carried, half dragged her across the hall. It was an awkward process. What the hell was the matter with him
tonight? He usually didn't have so much trouble doing
two things at once.

The bra finally fell away. He had her as far as the
stairs now. He heard a soft clatter and realized that one
of her high heels had come off.

She lost the second one just as he got them both to
the third step.

"Oh, yes." Her hands gripped his shoulder, small nails
tattooing his skin. She kissed him wildly. *"Yes."*

Slowly, he worked his way up the stairs with Hannah
in his arms. It wasn't easy. She wasn't helping him. He
missed a step when she sank her teeth lightly into his
bicep. She nearly lost her balance when he retaliated by
kissing one taut nipple. Both of them grabbed the banister to keep from falling.

Hannah was quicksilver in his grasp. She slipped and
slithered around him. He groaned aloud when he felt her
hand on the buckle of his belt. Halfway to his goal, he
looked up at the landing. It was lost in distant shadows.

"Not much farther," he said hoarsely. He was lying to
both of them, he thought. The top of the stairs was in
another universe.

"Close enough." She had his belt undone now. Her fingers were on his zipper.

"Better wait until we get upstairs," he whispered.

"Can't wait." One nylon-clad foot glided up his leg.

He felt the heat from the inside of her thigh and sucked in his breath. They were never going to make it at this rate. It was time to take unilateral action.

He picked her up, settled her across his shoulder, and clamped one arm across the back of her legs to hold her there.

"Rafe."

He ignored her breathless, sensual laughter. With total determination he took a firm grip on the banister and hauled them both to the top of the stairs. There he turned right and went down the hall to the bedroom he had chosen the day he arrived. It was a big one, with a sweeping view of the bay.

He went swiftly through the doorway and dumped her onto the quilt that covered the old-fashioned four-poster. She lay there amid the pillows, then reached for him with both arms. He fell on top of her.

He kissed her throat while he rummaged with one hand in the drawer of the nightstand. He knew the box of condoms was in there somewhere. He had put it there this evening before leaving the house. Optimism had been riding high at that point. Probably because he had had several engaging fantasies in the shower and had emerged semi-erect. A man was always at his most optimistic when he had a hard-on.

When he couldn't immediately locate the condoms, alarm set in.

"What the hell . . . ?"

"What's wrong?" Hannah's eyes widened." Are you all right?"

Mercifully his fingers closed around the box. A sense

of victory soared through him. "Yeah, sure. I'm fine. Nothing's wrong."

"Good."

"Very good," he whispered. "Excellent, in fact."

She slid her hands inside the wings of his unbuttoned shirt. Her palms were silken on his skin. Breathing took serious effort now.

By the time he was ready, most of their clothing had magically disappeared. He lowered himself between her legs. She raised her knees and tightened her thighs around him.

He cupped her with his hand. She was wet and hot and swollen. When he used the pad of his thumb on the small bud, she quivered violently. His own body nearly exploded in response.

"Now," she ordered, clutching furiously at him. "Now, please, yes. Do it now."

He needed no further urging. If he didn't do it now, it would not get done at all.

He fitted himself to her and started to enter her carefully. She was snug and tight and damp. He tried to take it slow, but when she lifted herself against him, he abandoned all attempt at sophistication and restraint.

There was nothing sophisticated or restrained about how he felt at this moment.

He thrust deeply into her, losing himself in a world of intense sensation. He heard her soft, exultant cry and felt her body grip him with fierce satisfaction. Her head tipped back. Her lips parted in a soundless scream.

She climaxed immediately. He wanted to indulge himself in the pleasure of her release before he surrendered to his own, but he had only a few seconds to enjoy the experience. The small shivers that went through her were more than he could stand. He tried to swallow his own roar of triumph and exultation, but he did not succeed.

• • •

She did not doze, but she was vaguely aware of a sense of detachment from time and reality. It was a pleasant interlude that she knew would not last forever. Nevertheless, she was reluctant to emerge from it.

Rafe sprawled on his back beside her, big and warm enough to heat the whole bed to a cozy temperature. He had one arm behind his head, the other around her. She opened her eyes partway and studied him in the shadows. He looked as relaxed as a large cat after a successful hunt. She raised her head for a better look. Her glance fell on the green numbers of the radio clock.

"*Winston*." She sat up quickly.

"Huh?" Rafe slitted his eyes. "What's wrong?"

"I've got to get home to Winston." She shoved aside the quilt and scrambled off the bed. "He'll be worried."

Rafe looked amused. "You think your dog worries when you're a little late coming home?"

"Okay, so maybe he won't be worried, exactly." She spotted her panties on the floor and dove for them. " 'Concerned' might be a better word."

"I doubt it."

"Well, he'll certainly need to go outside by now." She stepped into the panties and looked around for her bra. It was nowhere to be found. "He's been cooped up in that house for hours."

"Take it easy." Rafe thrust aside the quilt and got up from the edge of the bed. "I'm sure Winston is fine. He's probably sound asleep."

He was right, she thought. This panicky sensation nibbling at her insides had nothing to do with Winston. She was experiencing some sort of bizarre reaction to what had just happened here in this room. What in the world was wrong with her?

"Have you seen my bra?" she asked. She was glad the lights were still off. She could feel the heat in her cheeks.

He paused in the act of fastening his trousers and reached out to turn on the bedside light. He swept the room with a deliberate look. "Nope. Must have left it back there on the stairs."

She shot him a suspicious glare, almost certain that he was teasing her. She glanced down and saw the toe of her panty hose sticking out from under the bed. Even from here she could see the massive run in the foot of the stocking. With a sigh she shimmied into her dress and groped wildly for the zipper.

"I'll get it for you." Rafe's voice was softer now. He walked across the room to stand behind her. His fingers caught hold of the zipper tab and raised it straight to the base of her neck in a single motion.

"Thank you." Her voice sounded stiff and prim, even to her own ears.

"Sure. Anytime."

She did not dare look at him now. Instead she began to hunt for her shoes.

Rafe shrugged into his shirt. He did not bother to button it. Folding his arms, he lounged against the bedpost and watched her frantic search.

"I don't think your shoes made it upstairs, either," he offered eventually.

"Good grief." She straightened quickly, shoved the hair out of her eyes, and bolted for the door.

He followed her at a more leisurely pace. She ignored him, horrified by the sight of bits and pieces of her clothing strewn on the stairs and in the hall. What had come over her? She didn't do things like this. She must have lost it, big time.

By the time Rafe got downstairs she had retrieved her shoes and her bra and had the door in sight. Clutching her lingerie in one hand, she focused intently on the only thing that mattered at that moment: escape from the scene of her wild, frenzied, totally uncharacteristic passion.

Rafe's voice stopped her cold just as she was about to twist the knob.

"You want to tell me what's wrong, Hannah?"

For a second she could not breathe. She looked down at her trembling fingers. "I think I'm having an anxiety attack."

"Yeah, I can see that. The question is, why?"

His laconic tone chased away some of the panic. Anger rushed in to fill the empty space. This was all his fault. If he hadn't fed her that incredible key lime pie, if he hadn't turned on the music, if he hadn't danced with her in the darkness . . .

If . . .

She whirled around, hands behind her on the knob, and glowered at him.

"Panic attacks happen," she said grimly. "Not my fault."

He studied her for a long, brooding moment. "Second thoughts already?" he finally asked.

She drew a deep, steadying breath. A semblance of reason returned. She could not blame any of this on him. She was the one who had gone crazy here. *Act like a grown-up*.

She cleared her throat. Her fingers tightened on the doorknob. "Sorry. I'm not being real cool, am I?"

"No, but that's not the problem. Nobody ever said you had to be cool." He did not move, just stood there in the hall, watching her. "But for the record, I'd really like to know what went wrong."

"I'm not sure." She released her death grip on the doorknob and shoved her fingers through her hair. She met his eyes. "No, that's not right. Rafe, I need to ask you a question, and you have to tell me the truth."

"What's the question?"

"This." She swept out a hand to indicate the searing passion that had begun in the solarium and ended in his bedroom. "What just happened between us. It didn't have anything to do with Dreamscape, did it?"

His eyes narrowed. "You tell me."

She flinched. "What's that supposed to mean?"

"You've had your wicked way with me, and now you're trying to leave as quickly as you can. Some dumb excuse about a dog, I think. I'll bet you're not even going to call me in the morning, are you?"

"Damn it, Rafe—"

"What the hell am I supposed to think?"

She stared at him, stunned. "Do you really believe that I just . . . I just—" She broke off because her voice was threatening to get lost in a squeaky soprano. She swallowed and tried again. "You think that I just *seduced* you in order to manipulate you into selling your half of this place to me?"

He let her wait a beat. She felt perspiration between her shoulder blades.

Then he smiled slightly. "No."

She sagged back against the doorjamb. "I should hope not. Good Lord, I don't do things like that."

"Neither do I," he said simply.

She looked at him for a long time. Gradually the tension inside her began to seep away. She had gone mad, she thought.

"No. No, of course not." She rubbed her brow. "I don't know why I freaked. I guess I'm just a little stressed."

"You've had a busy night."

"You can say that again." She straightened away from

the door, composed herself. "Speaking of which, I think it's time you took me home."

"All right." He fished keys out of a pocket. "On one condition."

She jerked back around. "What condition?"

He walked past her and opened the door. "You gotta promise to call me in the morning."

He was gone, out into the night, before she could think of an appropriate response. She heard the less than civilized growl of the Porsche engine. The lights came on, blinding her.

A vivid mental image of a hapless deer paralyzed by the beams of an oncoming car galvanized her into action.

She slammed the front door shut behind herself. Hand held high to shield her eyes from the merciless glare of the lights, she rushed toward the passenger side door.

Winston greeted her with a yawn and his customary good cheer. He bestowed an equally enthusiastic welcome on Rafe. Then he trotted across the porch, went down the front steps, and disappeared into the privacy of the bushes. It was obvious that he was in no great rush to use the facilities.

Rafe looked at her, eyes gleaming. "You're in luck. He doesn't look like he's been worrying too much."

She felt the heat rise in her cheeks. "You've made your point."

"You think so?"

"I've already admitted that my little panic attack back there was an overreaction to stress."

"Stress, huh? Sounds like another excuse."

"Good night, Rafe."

He caught her chin on the heel of his hand and kissed

her very deliberately. He stopped just as she felt the breathlessness setting in again.

"Good night," he said. His eyes were shadowed and intense in the yellow porch light. "You've got my number at Dreamscape and my cell phone number. Call me if Winston goes into his alert mode again tonight, okay? I can be here in less than ten minutes."

"His alert mode?" She had forgotten all about Winston's nocturnal prowling. "Oh, right. That's very kind of you, but I really don't think—"

"I know you're having trouble thinking tonight. You've already explained that." He went down the steps. "Just call me if he does the sentry thing."

She held the door open for Winston. Rafe waited until they were both inside the house before he drove away into the darkness.

Twenty minutes later she emerged from the bathroom clad in her primmest nightgown. It was a Victorian number, pure white, with long sleeves, a ribbon-trimmed neckline, and a hem that fell to her ankles. She glanced once at herself in the mirror and was satisfied with the demure gown. It was definitely not the sort of nightwear favored by women who were in the habit of leaving their undergarments strewn on the staircase while they indulged themselves in a mad, passionate fling with the most exciting man in town.

Make that the most exciting man she had ever met.

An aberration. That was what it had been. It had been much too long since she'd had anything resembling a normal sex life. Aberrant behavior was to be expected under such circumstances.

With a sigh, she switched off the lamp. Winston was already in position at the foot of the bed. He raised his head from his paws when she went to the window that overlooked the bay. She could feel him watching her as she opened the drapes.

"Weren't you even a little bit concerned about the fact that I was so late getting home?" she asked.

He did not dignify that with a response.

"I was afraid of that."

She padded through the shadows to the side window and pulled the curtains wide. She was about to turn back to the bed when she glimpsed the sheen of moonlight on metal between two trees.

"What in the world?"

She gripped the window ledge and peered more closely at the glint. A closer look verified her first impression. There was a car parked in a stand of trees near the road. In that position, whoever was in the vehicle had a clear view of the house and the entrance of the long drive.

She glanced at Winston. He had his muzzle on his paws. Not in alert mode.

She closed the drapes again, switched on the light, and picked up the phone. She punched in one of the numbers she had jotted down on the pad beside the bed.

Rafe answered on the first ring.

"What are you doing out there in the bushes?" she asked.

"Nothing for which I could get arrested."

A small thrill of pleasure rippled through her at the sound of his voice; low, sexy, and just rough enough around the edges to bring back some very recent, very heated memories.

She turned off the light again. Carrying the phone, she went back to the window and opened the drapes a second time. She gazed out into the darkness, searching for the metallic gleam of the Porsche's fender.

"Are you sure about that?" she asked.

"Positive."

Talking to him now on the phone was a lot easier than facing him after that interlude in his bedroom, she discovered. There was a strange intimacy to the experience, but at the same time the distance allowed her to finally relax.

"You're keeping watch, aren't you?" she asked. "Waiting to see if whatever alarmed Winston shows up again."

Silence hummed briefly on the other end.

"Just thought I'd stick around for a few minutes," he said.

"That's not necessary. I told you I'd call if Winston starts prowling. Go home, Rafe. We'll be fine, honest."

"I'll only hang around for a little while. Whatever it is showed up between midnight and two the last couple of times, right?"

"Yes."

"It's almost two. I'll leave soon."

"Rafe—"

"Go to sleep," he said softly.

She clutched the phone more tightly. "Rafe, about tonight—"

"What about it?"

"I apologize for acting like a complete idiot. Asking you whether or not what happened between us was all about Dreamscape was inexcusable. I knew better than that."

"Whatever is going on between you and me, it's not about the house."

She hesitated. "A lot of people in town will think it is."

"Everyone in Eclipse Bay thinks that I seduced you on the beach eight years ago, too." The dismissive shrug in his voice was loud and clear. "Do you really care what people think?"

She contemplated the question for a long moment. "No."

"Neither do I."

"Rafe?"

"Yeah?"

"If what happened tonight wasn't about Dreamscape, what was it about?"

"Good question. When you figure out the answer, let me know."

"Rafe?"

"Yeah?"

"Sometimes you remind me an awful lot of Winston when it comes to communicating."

"Probably a guy thing."

"Good night, Rafe."

"Don't forget to call me in the morning."

She hung up the phone and climbed into bed. She did not even attempt to close her eyes until she heard the muted purr of his car's engine recede into the distance sometime later. She glanced at the clock. It was two-fifteen.

At the foot of the bed, Winston was sound asleep.

chapter 13

The next morning she waited until ten o'clock to call.

"Don't want to look too eager," she told Winston as she punched out the number on the kitchen cordless. "Guys sense it if you're too eager."

Winston looked bored. He went to the door and looked back at her with an expectant expression.

"You've already been out twice this morning." She listened to the phone ring on the other end. "I think you're getting addicted to the beach."

It was true, she thought. Winston's approval of their new lifestyle was evident. He loved running around in Dead Hand Cove with its myriad smells and odd inhabitants. He clearly delighted in his off-leash freedom.

Rafe finally answered the phone.

"This is Madison." He sounded impatient, as if his attention was on something vastly more interesting than a phone call.

She frowned briefly at the instrument in her hand and then held it to her ear again.

"Sorry if I'm interrupting anything important," she said dryly. "I thought you were expecting my call."

"'Morning, honey." Rafe's voice warmed measurably. "I'm a little busy at the moment. Can I get back to—hang on a second." He broke off abruptly and spoke to someone else. "Take a good look at the wiring in that panel, will you, Torrance?"

"Honey?" Hannah pondered the simple endearment. Rafe had never called her honey, not even last night in the middle of making love to her. Of course, he had not made a lot of conversation in bed.

"Hell, there should be insulation in that wall," Rafe continued in a muffled voice. "Yeah, I can see the pipes. That's why I want insulation in it. Who wants to listen to every flush and shower?"

"Pipes?" Hannah stopped trying to tease out the little nuances of "honey" and focused on the more disturbing word. "Rafe, what's going on there? Is something wrong?"

"I'm getting an assessment of the condition of the plumbing and wiring," he said casually. "The good news is that Isabel had it all brought up to code a few years ago." His paused to speak to someone else again. "Is that copper?"

"Rafe, who are you talking to?"

"The Willis brothers are here," he said into the phone. "I'm having them go over the place from top to bottom."

"You've got Walter and Torrance Willis there?" She shot up from the kitchen chair. "Why?"

"Just getting together some preliminary estimates to see how much it will cost to put in the inn and restaurant," he said with breathtaking innocence.

"You can't do that." She grabbed her keys and broke into a run, heading to the door. "Not without my permission, damn it."

"We both agreed we wanted to open an inn here at Dreamscape."

"We haven't even decided how we're going to deal with the legalities of ownership. Don't you dare touch a thing until I get there."

Winston saw her heading for the door. He started to bounce a little.

"I told you, I'm just getting some preliminary figures together," Rafe said.

"I am coming over there right now. You listen to me, Rafe Madison. I own half of that house. Don't you dare touch a single thing until I get there. And don't let the Willis brothers touch anything, either."

"It's a little late to call them off," Rafe said reflectively. "They're already pretty deep into the plumbing."

"I don't believe this."

She tossed the cordless phone down on the hall table and rushed outside to the car. Winston followed. He leaped into the passenger seat and sat back with an air of anticipation.

"I knew last night was all about Dreamscape," she told him.

She sailed through the front door of the big house a short time later, ready for battle. Winston trotted in right behind her, greeted Rafe briefly, and began a tour of the kitchen.

Rafe glanced at his watch as Hannah came to a seething halt in front of him. "Six minutes and twenty-two seconds. You made good time."

She planted her hands on her hips. "What is going on here?"

Rafe was saved the necessity of responding to the question by the small, neatly made man who chose that moment to wander out into the hall.

Compact and completely bald, Walter Willis had always

reminded Hannah of an android. There was a mechanical precision about his movements that lacked the casual human element. His speech was clipped and crisp. The starched creases in his work clothes never softened. It was as if he had been designed and constructed under controlled, sterile conditions in a high-tech manufacturing plant.

"Hannah." Walter wiped his hands on a spotless rag that dangled from his belt. "Good to see you again. Heard you were back in town."

Hannah was amazed by her self-mastery. She managed to veil the fuming expression she knew had been blazing in her eyes. She even summoned up what she hoped looked like a genuinely pleasant smile of greeting.

"Hello, Walter," she said. "It's been a while."

"Certainly has." Walter turned his head and called to his brother over his shoulder. "Torrance, come on out here and say hello to Hannah."

Torrance stepped out of the laundry room. His expression brightened instantly. He hoisted a pipe wrench in greeting. "Hey, there, Hannah. Welcome back."

The Willises were identical twins, but it was easy to tell them apart because, sartorially speaking, they were polar opposites. If Walter had been engineered to precise specifications on a futuristic computerized assembly line, Torrance had been someone's home garage project.

Rather than shaving off what little hair he still possessed as Walter did, Torrance wore his thin, scraggly locks in a ponytail that stuck out through the opening at the back of his cap. The trailing end of a snake tattoo slithered out below one sleeve. His coveralls were stained with what looked like several eons' worth of grease, grime, and pizza sauce. The only things that were clean and shiny about him were the tools in the wide belt that he wore low on his hips.

"Isabel always said the two of you would come back for good someday." Torrance turned to Walter. "Didn't she say exactly that?"

"She sure did," Walter agreed. "If she said it once, she must have said it a hundred times. I believe the last time was the day she had us out here to install the washing machine in the laundry room."

Torrance nodded. "Believe it was." He winked at Hannah and Rafe. "Told us she wanted to leave everything in good working order for you two."

Willis shook his head indulgently. "That Isabel. Always did have a real romantic streak."

Hannah narrowed her eyes. "Don't you two have some plumbing you should be looking at?"

"Plumbing. Whoa. Almost forgot. You heard the lady," Torrance continued. "Reckon we better get back to work."

"Right." Walter's head jerked once in a mechanical nod. "Plumbing. Listen, you two, don't pay any heed to the talk that's going around town these days. Bound to be some for a while, given what happened the night the Sadler girl died and all and now this business with Isabel leaving you the house. But it'll fade quick enough."

"Let's hope so," Hannah said.

Torrance clapped Rafe on the shoulder. "Just want you both to know that me and my brother here never once thought you'd had anything to do with Kaitlin Sadler's death."

"I appreciate that," Rafe replied.

Walter pursed his lips. "Torrance and I always suspected that she got killed by some sex maniac from Seattle. Isn't that right, Torrance?"

Torrance bobbed his head several times. "Yup. That was how we figured it, all right. Not that Chief Yates paid any attention to us."

"Yates just wanted to close the case as fast as possible," Walter said somberly. "He was getting ready to retire. Last thing he wanted to do was leave behind a nasty unsolved murder. Would have spoiled his record."

"Murder." Hannah met Rafe's eyes for a few seconds. He gave her an enigmatic look. She turned back to Walter. "Are you serious? Do you really think Kaitlin was murdered by a sex maniac?"

Walter traded glances with Torrance. "Can't blame us for wondering, given what we found the day we fixed her washer. Right, Torrance?"

Torrance's head went into nodding mode again. "Right. Gotta wonder."

Rafe looked at Walter "What exactly did you find the day you fixed her washer?"

To Hannah's astonishment, Walter blushed a bright shade of red.

"Kinky stuff," he muttered.

"What kind of kinky stuff?" Rafe asked.

Something in his voice made Hannah glance sharply at him. But she could read nothing in his expression.

Torrance rolled his eyes. "You know. Frilly undies."

Hannah thought about the little demi-bra she had lost on the stairs last night. When her gaze collided with Rafe's, she knew he was thinking about it too.

"What's so kinky about a woman wearing frilly underwear?" she demanded

"Well, the stuff we found wasn't exactly little," Torrance said. "Big enough to fit a man."

"Definitely a heck of a lot bigger than Kaitlin," Walter confided. "She was real petite, if you recall."

"There was also a sexy nightgown that was much too big for her," Torrance continued. "And some really large sparkly high heels."

"Don't forget those videotapes," Walter added.

Hannah stared at him. "You found all that stuff inside her washer?"

"Not exactly inside the washer." Torrance hesitated. "Well, see, once we got goin' on the washer, we realized that her dryer exhaust hose probably hadn't been cleaned in a long time."

"Dangerous things, exhaust hoses," Walter put in seriously. "If they get clogged with lint, they can cause fires. Anyhow, we figured we'd do Kaitlin a favor, so after we finished with the washer, we pulled out the dryer to check the exhaust hose. That was when we found the large-sized undies and the videos and all."

"*Behind* the machine?" Rafe asked carefully.

Torrance nodded violently. "Someone had cut out a big chunk of drywall and stuffed the videos and the ladies' things into the space between a couple of studs."

"Knew right off the female stuff didn't belong to you, Rafe," Walter assured him hastily.

"What was your big clue?" Rafe asked. "Wrong size?"

Torrance guffawed with laughter. "Heck, everyone knew you'd been seein' a lot of Kaitlin that summer. But me and Walter never figured you for one of them transistors."

"Transvestites," Rafe corrected mildly.

Torrance nodded. "Never figured you for one of them."

"You were right about my taste in underwear. I'm a pretty traditional kind of guy."

Torrance's laughter faded. "Anyhow, after Kaitlin died, Walter and I remembered that stuff we found in the wall. That's what made us think she'd been done in by some out-of-town sex maniac."

"From Seattle," Walter concluded.

"Why Seattle?" Hannah asked.

Torrance snorted. "Not the sort of thing they do in Portland."

Hannah looked at Rafe.

He shrugged. "The man has a point. You know what they say about those folks up in Seattle."

She turned back to Walter and Torrance. "You said you told Chief Yates about the videos and the lingerie?"

"Yup, figured it was our civic duty," Torrance said. "But he told us to keep our mouths shut. Said there was enough gossip goin' around as it was. Town didn't need any more."

"Besides, the stuff was gone when we took the chief to Kaitlin's house to show it to him," Walter added. "I don't think he believed us."

Rafe frowned. "The lingerie and videos weren't there when you went back?"

"Nope." Torrance sighed. "That's the main reason Walter and me didn't talk too much about what we'd found. Didn't have any proof, and Chief Yates said we could get in a lotta trouble if we started spreadin' false rumors. Right, Walter?"

"Right," Walter said crisply. "We're not blabbermouths. But we always thought Kaitlin was murdered by that sex maniac she must have been seein'." He looked at Rafe. "No offense, but everyone knew she was fooling around with other men."

"Yes." Rafe did not look at Hannah. "Even I figured it out. Why do you think the guy who was into the lingerie murdered her?"

"Who knows?" Torrance said.

"Maybe he didn't like the fact that she had those videos," Walter said. "Could be they were films of him dressed in the lingerie."

Rafe's gaze went to Hannah. She saw the glint of curiosity in his eyes. She didn't blame him. She was reluctantly fascinated, herself.

"You think this guy from Seattle went back to Kaitlin's house after he murdered her and stole the lingerie and videos?" Rafe asked.

"Makes sense, doesn't it?" Walter asked. "He wouldn't want to leave any evidence around that might point back to him."

"It's certainly an interesting theory," Hannah allowed cautiously.

"That's all it'll ever be now," Walter said. "Kaitlin's been dead and buried for a long time. No one's going to reopen that old case. Probably for the best." He turned with military precision. "Well, you'll have to excuse us, we've got work to do. Don't we, Torrance?"

"Yup." Torrance's head bobbed up and down half a dozen times with great enthusiasm. "Turnin' this place into an inn with a restaurant attached is gonna be a big project. But you know, it makes a lotta sense. What with the institute and the college and the plans to renovate the old pier and put in more shops, Eclipse Bay is attractin' a lotta visitors these days. Don't have many nice places for 'em to stay. Just the motel out on the highway. Way it is now, folks have to drive on up the coast to find a classy place."

He swung around and lumbered off after his brother.

Hannah waited until both Willises were out of sight. Then she looked at Rafe.

"A sex maniac from Seattle?" she said softly.

"I have a hunch that everyone in town has a personal theory of what happened that night."

"Frilly lingerie in sizes big enough to fit a man?"

"Don't look at me." He held up both hands, palms out. "I never saw any of that stuff."

"What about the videos?"

He shook his head. "Nope. No videos. Hannah, I only went out with Kaitlin a few times before it became real obvious that she was just amusing herself with me while she hunted for her real meal ticket. I never got to know her well enough to learn about her little quirks and eccentricities."

"Hmm. You do realize what this means, don't you?"

He leveled a finger at her. "Nothing. It means absolutely nothing. We only have the Willis brothers' word on what they found in the wall behind her dryer. And no offense to either Torrance or Walter, but they're not the most sophisticated guys to come down the pike. I doubt if they've been any farther than Portland in their entire lives. What looked like kinky clothing and dirty videos to them might be nothing more than a little late-night entertainment to other folks."

"Kaitlin wasn't exactly shy about her own sexual activities. I can't see her going out of her way to protect the reputations of the men she dated, either. If she went to the trouble of hiding that lingerie and those videos to protect a boyfriend, she must have had big plans for the poor guy."

Rafe hesitated. "Kaitlin's supreme goal in life was to marry someone with enough money to help her escape Eclipse Bay."

"So, maybe this particular boyfriend had money. Maybe she saw him as a hot prospect for marriage."

"Why hide the undies and the tapes?"

"Who knows? Maybe he was already married. Maybe she wanted to protect him because she was hoping he'd get a divorce and marry her. Maybe—"

"Whoa," Rafe said. "Lots of maybes here."

She made a face and planted her hands on her hips. "You're right. Got a little carried away there for a minute, didn't I?"

"Imagination is a wonderful thing. But in this case it's wasted. It's been eight years. We'll never know for sure what happened to Kaitlin that night. Like Walter said, that's probably just as well."

Reluctantly she pulled her thoughts back to the matter

at hand. The instant she refocused on her chief problem, her irritation returned.

"Let's get something clear here," she said. "You're not going to do anything to Dreamscape until you and I have come to some agreement about how to handle the legal aspects of Isabel's inheritance."

Rafe pondered the view of the hall. "I could open the restaurant in my half of the house."

"That's crazy. There's no way you can turn half of this place into a restaurant. How would we divide the kitchen? What about all the people who would use *my* half of this hall to get to *your* restaurant? And who gets the solarium?"

"I thought it would make a nice dining room. In the summer I'll set up tables outside on the veranda, too."

"Not without my permission, you won't. Rafe, you just can't run roughshod over the legal technicalities of this inheritance. We're talking several hundred thousand dollars worth of mansion here. We have to settle things first. You know that as well as I do."

"Well," Rafe said a little too casually, "speaking of settling the minor details, I've got a suggestion."

Sensing danger, she went very still. "What is it?"

"How about a partnership?"

She stared at him, momentarily speechless.

"You?" she managed at last. "Me? Partners in Dreamscape?"

"You don't think it would work?"

"What about last night? Are you just going to pretend it never happened?"

"What's last night got to do with it?"

Suddenly she could no longer breathe. "*Everything*. How can you talk about a business partnership after—" She waved a hand, unable to finish the sentence.

"Ah." Understanding lit his eyes. "You're worried about us mixing business with pleasure?"

There was a distant ringing in her ears now. Was that all it had been to him? A pleasant interlude? She struggled to regain her composure.

"Aren't you?" she asked in as cold a voice as she could manage.

"Well, sure," he said far too readily. "Naturally I'll have a problem with it because I'm a Madison. Madisons always have problems when they get their financial affairs mixed up with their sexual affairs. But it shouldn't be a stretch for you. You're a Harte. You can compartmentalize."

He was goading her, she thought. She had to get out of here before she lost it. Hartes did not do that kind of thing. Not in public, at any rate.

"You're right," she said. "I could probably handle it. But as you just pointed out, you're a Madison. You'd screw it up for sure."

She spun on her heel and walked swiftly outside. Winston, ever faithful, trotted out of the kitchen to follow her. Together they went down the front steps without a backward glance.

She yanked open the car door. Winston bounded inside and took up his post on the passenger seat. She got in behind the wheel and slammed the door shut.

The last thing she saw in her rearview mirror was Rafe lounging against the porch railing watching her roar out of the driveway. He had enjoyed seeing her come so close to the edge, she realized. He had deliberately pushed her, just to see what would happen.

A wave of uncertainty swept through her. All of her grandfather's warnings about Madisons flashed through her mind. What kind of game was Rafe playing?

chapter 14

Rafe brought the Porsche to a halt in the drive, switched off the engine, and sat for a while, staring at the front door of Mitchell's house.

Asking his grandfather to come to dinner was a crazy idea. If he had any sense he would fire up the engine and drive straight back to Dreamscape. But then he would have to explain to Hannah why he had chickened out.

The thought of going through another scene with her after the one that had taken place this morning when she had arrived to find the Willis brothers hard at work was not appealing. He had taken a chance, pushed his luck, and, predictably enough, things had exploded in his face. He would be more cautious next time. Who said a Madison couldn't learn from his mistakes?

He climbed out from behind the wheel and walked toward the porch steps.

The front door opened just as he raised his hand to knock. A cadaverously thin figure with a buzz cut and a face that looked as if it had been hewn out of the side of a mountain stared at him.

Bryce had worked for Mitchell for nearly ten years. No one knew where he had come from. He had started out as a part-time handyman and had gradually carved out a position as full-time majordomo. If Bryce had a last name, it had been lost in the mists of time. As far as Rafe knew, he had no close relatives. Bryce had brought order to the chaos of Mitchell's household. He was unswervingly loyal to his employer. Beyond that, he was a mystery.

"Hello, Bryce."

"Good afternoon."

"I'm looking for Mitchell."

"Your grandfather is out in the garden."

"Thanks."

Rafe nodded in a friendly manner and walked off down the porch. No point exchanging further pleasantries. Bryce was not one for extended conversations.

Rafe opened the gate and entered the lush wonderland. When he didn't see Mitchell, he took the narrow gravel path that led toward the greenhouse at the far end of the garden.

He found his grandfather inside the opaque structure, tending to a tray of plants. Mitchell had a long-spouted watering can in one hand and a small spade in the other.

Rafe took a breath and stepped into the humid atmosphere of the greenhouse. He recalled Hannah's comment. *Your interest in cooking parallels his in gardening. Creative outlets that you both approach with passion.*

The idea of having something in common with Mitchell was a hard concept to digest.

"Lookin' good in here," he said. He told himself Hannah would have been proud of him for trying to start things off on a civil note. Then again, maybe not. She was pretty pissed at him right now. "You ever think about opening a commercial nursery?"

"Hell, no. Last thing I want to do is turn a good hobby into a business. Ruin all the fun." Mitchell set down the watering can with a thunk and scowled ferociously. "Speaking of business, what's this I hear about you opening an inn and a little restaurant out there at Dreamscape?"

"Word gets around fast."

"If you wanted to keep it a secret, you shouldn't have called the Willis brothers out to give you an opinion on the condition of the plumbing and wiring in that old place."

"You're right." Rafe examined a row of tiny pots containing small green plants with glossy leaves. "On the other hand, not much point trying to keep the plan a big dark secret here in Eclipse Bay."

Mitchell gave him a sharp glance from beneath bushy brows. "You're serious about opening an inn?"

"Yeah." Rafe moved on to a tray of feathery ferns. "Been thinking about it for a year now."

Mitchell whistled softly. "Well, shoot and damn. Why the hell didn't you ever say anything?"

"Got to work things out with Hannah first."

"Huh. That's a fact."

Rafe looked up from the ferns. "Aren't you going to tell me that turning Dreamscape into an inn and restaurant is just about the dumbest idea any Madison has ever had?"

"Dumb is beside the point. Madisons don't concern themselves with dumb. They concentrate on what they want." Mitchell's eyes crinkled at the corners as he squinted at Rafe. "You really want this?"

"Yes."

Mitchell studied him for a long moment. Then he nodded once and stripped off a garden glove. "Go for it."

"I beg your pardon?"

"You heard me. If you want it that bad, there's no point in me trying to talk you out of it. You're a Madison. Nothing's going to get in your way. Hell, you've got a better chance of pulling off an inn out there at Dreamscape than most folks."

Rafe was thunderstruck. He stared at Mitchell until he finally got his jaw back in place.

"Are you telling me you think opening an inn and a restaurant is a *good* idea?" he finally managed.

"Didn't say that." Mitchell tossed the glove down on the workbench. "Don't know if it's a good idea or not, to tell you the truth. Just said I could see that nothing was going to stop you. You've got a good head for business when you choose to use it. You could make this inn-restaurant thing work."

Rafe lounged back against a waist-high potting bench, slightly shaken. This was the first time that Mitchell had ever given even halfhearted approval for any idea that did not involve going to work for Madison Commercial.

"Where does Hannah Harte fit into this big plan of yours?" Mitchell asked.

Rafe did not move. He did not even blink. "What do you mean?"

"Last I heard, she still owned half of that old house. Has she agreed to let you buy her out?"

"No."

"Then what the hell are you going to do with her?"

Rafe examined the hibiscus next to him. "I've suggested to her that we form a partnership to operate the inn and restaurant."

"A *partnership*?" Mitchell's face worked in astonishment. "With Hannah Harte? Have you lost every damned marble you've got?"

So much for getting Mitchell's unqualified support.

"You don't have to shout," Rafe said. "I can hear you just fine."

"Now you listen to me. You're a Madison. You can't have a business partnership with a Harte. It'll never work. Never in a million years."

"Okay, so it might be a little more complicated than the usual business partnership," Rafe said.

"Well, shoot and damn." Mitchell grabbed a pair of pruning shears. "The rumors are true, aren't they? You are foolin' around with her, aren't you?"

"We have started what some people might call a relationship. Sort of."

"A relationship?" Mitchell went to work on the hibiscus with the shears. "That mean you're shacking up together?"

Rafe realized that he was standing closer to the hibiscus than was comfortable. He moved a couple of steps aside to give Mitchell and his shears plenty of space.

"I don't think I'd use that term."

Mitchell snipped off a straggling branch and glared. "Well, just what term would you use?"

"Like I said, the situation is a little complicated at the moment."

Mitchell aimed the shears at Rafe. "Pay attention for once in your life. What I got to say is important. That woman put her reputation on the line for you eight years ago. Saved you a lot of grief."

"I know that."

"You can't fool around with her. It's not right."

"I'm not fooling around with her." Rafe searched for the right words, but they eluded him. "Whatever is going on, it's serious."

Mitchell frowned at him for a long, considering moment. "It sure as hell better be serious." Abruptly, he turned back to his pruning. "Why'd you come here today?"

"Came over to see if you want to have dinner with Hannah and me tomorrow night." Rafe hesitated. "Feel free to bring your friend Octavia with you, if you want."

"Octavia's gone back to Portland."

"Invitation still stands."

"Huh." Mitchell clipped off another small branch. "Hannah Harte can cook?"

"I don't know. She's never done any cooking around me. I'll be doing the cooking."

"Should be interesting," Mitchell said.

"Does that mean we can expect you for dinner?"

"I'll be there. Be a change of pace from Bryce's grub." Rafe exhaled slowly. "Okay. Fine." He straightened and headed for the door. He felt as if he had just weathered a storm. "See you around six."

"Should be *damned* interesting," Mitchell muttered again.

Waste of time, Rafe thought. But what the hell. Maybe Hannah would cut him some slack. He should get some points out of this. After all, it had been her suggestion to invite Mitchell to dinner.

He wondered if it was a bad sign that he was trying to please her.

Rafe paused in the office doorway and studied the scene. There was a computer on the desk. The telephone had several lines. The hardware was nearly buried amid piles of notebooks, photos, and newspapers. The bookcase was crammed with volumes. Several framed front-page editions of the *Eclipse Bay Journal* hung on the walls. One of them featured a photograph of Trevor Thornley standing with the former owner and editor of the newspaper, Ed Bolton, and his smiling wife, Bev.

"I always wondered what a newspaper editor's office looked like," Rafe said.

Jed grinned and leaned back in his chair. "This is what this particular newspaper editor's office looks like. Have a seat."

"Thanks." Rafe cleared a heap of out-of-town newspapers off a chair and sat down.

"Want some coffee?" Jed gripped the arms of his chair as if about to push himself up and out of it. "One thing we've got a lot of around here is caffeine. Part of the mystique."

"No, thanks." Rafe glanced at the computer. The screen showed a page of text. He glimpsed the words. *"Thornley stated that he will run for the Senate on a platform that calls for social and personal responsibility."*

"You got a one-on-one interview with Trevor Thornley?" Rafe asked.

"Did it this morning before he left for Portland. I'm writing an editorial for tomorrow's edition."

Rafe settled back into the chair. "What's it like talking to a future U.S. senator?"

"Not a whole lot different than it was talking to a future member of the state legislature eight years ago. Only he's much more polished these days. But it's still tough to get a straight answer out of him."

"Probably why he's come so far, so fast."

"Probably. Well, like they say, he may be a sonofabitch, but he's our sonofabitch. I think Eclipse Bay can count on him to remember his roots even when he winds up in Washington, D.C." Jed propped his elbows on the chair arms and linked his fingers across his small paunch. "What brings you here today?"

"Idle curiosity."

"The best kind, I always say. That's what makes good reporters." Jed chuckled. "What are you curious about?"

Rafe steepled his fingers. The decision to pay a visit to the offices of the *Eclipse Bay Journal* had seemed a spur-of-the-moment thing. He'd been on his way back to Dreamscape when it struck. But now that he thought about it, he realized that it had been nibbling at the back of his mind all morning, ever since Walter and Torrance Willis had voiced their theories about Kaitlin Sadler having been murdered by a sex maniac from Seattle.

"I've got a favor to ask," he said. "I want to take a look at some old editions of your paper."

Jed's eyes darkened with sudden interest. "How old?"

"Eight years."

Jed whistled tunelessly. "Well, I'll be damned. You want to see the coverage of Kaitlin Sadler's death, don't you?"

"Is that a problem?"

"Hell, no." Jed's chair squeaked as he sat forward abruptly. He fixed Rafe with an intent look. "What's up?"

"Nothing. I told you, I'm just curious, that's all. I didn't pay any attention to the stories that appeared in the paper at the time. I was too busy trying to keep from getting arrested. As soon as I was cleared, all I wanted to do was get out of town."

"An understandable reaction." Jed picked up a pen and absently tapped the edge of the computer keyboard. "Sure you're not looking for something in particular?"

"I'm sure."

"Hey, this is your old buddy, Jed Steadman, boy reporter and pool pal, remember? If you've got a line on what really happened that night, the least you can do is fill me in."

"Think it would still be news after all this time?"

Jed raised his eyebrows. "If you've got anything to

indicate that what happened to Kaitlin was something other than an accident, yes, it sure as hell would be news. No one here has forgotten that incident." He paused. "We've only had one real murder in Eclipse Bay in the past decade, and that was when a couple of tourists got into a quarrel out at the RV park and one of them shot the other."

"I don't have a line on Kaitlin's death," Rafe said swiftly. "Just a couple of questions."

"Such as?" Jed paused ever so briefly. "I hate to remind you, but this is my newspaper now."

"I could try the public library."

Jed's grin came and went. "Yes, you could. All right. I've stuck with the agreement." He got to his feet. "Come on, I'll dig them out for you. Can't blame me for trying to find out if you've got an angle on that old story, can you?"

"Guess not." Rafe shoved himself up out of the chair and turned to follow Jed through the doorway. "I'll tell you what I'm looking for, if you'll promise to keep it quiet."

Jed raised one hand as he went down the hall. "Word of honor."

"I want to see if whoever covered the story mentioned the fact that Kaitlin Sadler was seeing someone other than me that summer."

Jed came to a halt in another doorway and gave Rafe a quizzical frown. "Everyone knew she was seeing other men. Hell, *you* knew it. It was no big secret that she was running around."

"I just want to see if the names of any of the other men she dated came up in the course of the investigation."

"Aha." Jed's hand tightened on the edge of the doorjamb. He gave Rafe a knowing look. "You want to see if there were any other serious suspects besides your-self, don't you? What is this? You think maybe one of her other boyfriends really did push her off the cliff that night?"

"I haven't got a single thing to go on here, Jed. I'm curious, that's all. Are you going to let me see those old papers or not?"

"Sorry. Force of habit. Come on, I'll get you set up on the machine."

A short time later Rafe found himself seated in front of a microfilm reader, scanning eight-year-old editions of the *Eclipse Bay Journal*. He paused when he came to the front-page headline that had been printed the morn-ing after Kaitlin's death: LOCAL WOMAN FOUND DEAD AT HIDDEN COVE.

"That's it." Jed hung over his shoulder, one hand grip-ping the back of Rafe's chair. "I didn't cover the story. I was busy writing up the piece on Thornley's reception at the institute."

Rafe glanced at the byline. "Did you know Ben Or-chardson well?"

"No one knew him well, but I learned a few things from him. He was a halfway decent reporter in his day. Worked for a couple of the big-city dailies for several years. But he had a problem with the bottle. Wound up here at the *Journal* for a while, but Ed had to let him go after a few months."

"Is Orchardson still around?"

"Are you kidding? He was sixty-three when he cov-ered the Sadler story. He retired and moved away just before I married Connie. Haven't heard from him since he left Eclipse Bay. I remember him saying something about heading for Mexico or maybe Costa Rica where he could live like a king on his Social Security check while he wrote the great American novel. Doubt if he ever sobered up long enough to buy a computer and go to work, though."

Rafe read through the first story that had appeared, searching for names other than his own. The first one that leaped out was Hannah's. He paused to study the short paragraph that had covered his alibi.

> *Hannah Harte, daughter of longtime Eclipse Bay summer visitors Hamilton and Elaine Harte, stated that she had been with Raphael Madison at the time of Sadler's death. "We met on the beach near Eclipse Arch a few minutes after midnight," she said. "We talked for a while. Then he walked me home. It was a long walk. We arrived shortly before two."*

The words were simple enough, but they had cost Hannah a lot at the time, Rafe reflected. He could imagine what her parents had had to say about the events of that night. But that was Hannah for you. Not a woman to stay silent when she had something to say.

Jed leaned closer. "Something I've always wondered about . . . ?"

The story jumped to an inside page. Rafe advanced the film. "Yeah?"

"Is talking really the only thing you and Hannah Harte did that night on the beach?"

Rafe leaned back and met Jed's eyes. "Yes."

Jed straightened quickly and took a step back. He cleared his throat. "Hey, just a reporter's natural curiosity, you understand."

Rafe turned back to the article and continued reading.

> *Yates said that he is still investigating
> Sadler's movements on the night of her death.
> "No one seems to know where she went or
> what she did after Madison got out of her
> car near the Arch. No one has any idea why
> she was on Hidden Cove Trail at that hour
> of the night. The trail is closed at sunset.
> There are no lights . . ."*

"Whatever happened to Chief Yates?" Rafe asked as he went on to the next story. "Is he still around?"

"Didn't you know? He died of a heart attack a couple of years ago."

"Wonder if there's any way of getting a look at his old file on the case?"

"The new chief of police is named Sean Valentine. He's a solid guy. He'll probably let you look at the old files, but I doubt that you'll find anything. Orchardson went through them thoroughly at the time. I remember him saying that with you in the clear, there was no other viable suspect. He said he was fairly sure Kaitlin's death had been an accident or suicide."

"I don't buy suicide," Rafe said.

Jed shrugged. "Neither do I. But I can see her having a few drinks and losing her balance on that trail."

"But what was she doing there on the trail in the first place?"

Jed considered for a moment. "Think maybe she went there to treat herself to a couple of beers after she ditched you?"

"I don't know. She didn't have any booze in the car when she dropped me off at the Arch, I can tell you that."

"She could have picked someone up after she left you."

"Yeah." Rafe studied the article on the screen. "Maybe. But Kaitlin was not a big drinker."

Jed crouched down behind the chair and rested an elbow on the back. He eyed the screen over Rafe's shoulder. "You're serious about this, aren't you?"

"Curious, not serious."

"There's a difference?"

"I'm not sure," Rafe admitted. He went back to the front page of the story he had been reading. He paused when he saw a night shot of the brightly lit facade of the Eclipse Bay Policy Studies Institute. "I see Thornley's big event at the think tank that night got squeezed below the fold."

Jed made a face. "Don't remind me. My first big story, and I lost the lead because of the Sadler piece."

Rafe followed the reception story to an inside page and found a photo of the crowd that had attended the Thornley reception. "Looks like most of Eclipse Bay was there."

"Everyone in town was invited, but it was understood that if you went you were expected to donate to Thornley's campaign. That limited the guests to the upwardly mobile among us, the local movers and shakers, and the hustlers who felt they had a stake in getting Thornley elected."

Rafe smiled slightly. "Not a lot of guys like me there, I take it?"

"Not that I recall." Jed grinned. "I was the youngest person there, and the only reason I attended was because I was covering it for the paper."

Rafe leaned back in the chair, thinking. "What time did the reception end?"

"I don't remember precisely. It ran late because Thornley was a little long-winded in those days. And because there was plenty of free booze."

The lights had still been on at the institute when he walked Hannah home along Bayview Drive, Rafe thought. "So, it would probably be safe to say that everyone who attended the Thornley reception that night has a reasonably solid alibi."

Jed slanted him a speculative glance. "Yes. I could probably dig up the old guest list if you want to look at it. As the only representative of the local media at the event, I'm sure I got a copy. It might be in my files. But Kaitlin didn't move in those circles, Rafe. Why would anyone from that crowd want to kill her?"

"Good question." Rafe thought about the oversized lingerie, the high heels, and the videos that the Willis brothers claimed to have discovered behind Kaitlin's dryer. No point in mentioning them, he thought. He had nothing hard to go on yet. "You're right. There's nothing here, Jed. Sorry I wasted your time."

"No problem," Jed replied. "Keep me in mind if you get any other wild hairs, okay? This is a slow news town. I wouldn't mind a big exposé on the Sadler death, especially if it involves an eight-year cover-up. Pulitzers have been won on less."

"Don't worry," Rafe said. "If I get any more brainstorms, you'll be the first to know."

chapter 15

"It was one of the more embarrassing moments of my life." Hannah propped her heels on the ottoman, sank deeper into the brown leather sofa, and sipped glumly on the hot green tea Pamela had given her. "I couldn't believe that I was standing there in the front hall of Dreamscape, yelling at him. I know the Willis brothers were listening to every single word. The story will be all over town by now."

Pamela, ensconced in the big recliner on the other side of the coffee table, curled one leg under herself. She wrapped her hands around her own mug and smiled wryly. "Very un-Harte-like."

"Very."

"One could almost call it outrageous. For a Harte, at any rate."

A searing vision of her black bra lying on the staircase at Dreamscape flashed before Hannah's eyes. If Pamela only knew, she thought, just how outrageous she had been in the past twenty-four hours.

"I'm glad you find it so amusing," Hannah muttered into her tea. "I'd like to remind you that half of Dreamscape belongs to me. I had a right to scream some when I realized what he was doing."

"Of course you did."

"You're not taking this seriously, are you?"

Pamela raised one brow in a very knowing fashion. "I'm waiting for the other shoe to drop, as it were."

Both shoes had dropped last night before she even got upstairs, Hannah recalled. "What's that supposed to mean?"

"You're involved in a sticky situation with a Madison," Pamela said. "So far, all you've done is yell at him in front of witnesses. That may be a big scene for a Harte, but I doubt if it even ruffled Rafe Madison's hair. The question here is, What happens next?"

Hannah swallowed more tea and submerged herself deeper into the pool of gloom. "He's proposed a partnership in an inn and restaurant."

"A partnership?" Pamela's eyes widened behind the lenses of her glasses. "You and Rafe Madison? Oh, my."

"It's impossible, of course."

"Of course."

"It would never work."

"Never in a million years. I can't even begin to imagine what your family would say about the notion of you and Rafe opening an inn together."

"I prefer not to think about it."

Pamela looked as though she was attempting to suppress a smile.

"What?" Hannah demanded.

"I'll say one thing about you and Rafe Madison," Pamela murmured. "You two don't get together often, but when you do, it's never dull."

The sound of a vehicle in the drive saved Hannah from

having to come up with a response to that observation. Two small whirlwinds, both dressed in jeans, T-shirts, and miniature running shoes, blew into the front room. They flew toward the door. A massive beast that went by the wholly inappropriate name of Kitty followed in their wake.

Kitty was the reason Winston had remained at the cottage that afternoon. Kitty did not care for Winston. Hannah was fairly certain that the feeling was reciprocated. On the one occasion when Winston and Kitty had been introduced, she had caught Winston eyeing Kitty with a peculiar gleam in his eye. It was the same gleam that he got when he chased seagulls on the beach. For her part, Kitty had hissed and growled and generally made it clear that she was not a dog lover.

"Daddy's home, Daddy's home," the whirlwind named Rose chanted happily as she stretched both hands overhead and tried to seize the doorknob.

Mark, Rose's older brother, grabbed the knob before she could get a grip on it. "I get to show him my new maze before you make him look at your stupid drawing."

"My drawing isn't stupid." Rose looked at Pamela for confirmation of her artistic ability. "It isn't stupid, is it, Mom?"

"It's beautiful," Pamela assured her. "We're going to hang it on the refrigerator with the others just as soon as you finish it."

Rose whirled back to her brother. "Told you so, you big dummy. You don't know what you're talking about."

Pamela gave Hannah an amused glance. "I think she takes after me. Not at all reticent about standing up for herself."

Hannah grinned. "It's so thrilling to see the genes pass down to another generation."

"Ever think about producing your own little bundle of Hannah genes?"

Hannah watched the two children battle over who got to open the door for Brad. A pang of deep longing twisted through her. She gazed at Mark and imagined a little boy with Rafe's eyes. For the first time she wondered if her growing restlessness this past year had something to do with her ticking biological clock.

"Funny you should ask," she said softly. "Of course, there's one small problem. I need more than just Hannah genes to create the final product."

The front door opened, and Brad walked into the hall. He was a fair-haired man with earnestly intelligent eyes framed by wire-rimmed glasses. There was a deceptively quiet, deeply thoughtful way about him that belied a quick, razor-sharp brain. He was fashionably rumpled in what passed for academic chic. His button-down shirt and khaki trousers were both wrinkled. The loud, awkwardly knotted tie, scuffed leather shoes, and bulging book bag accented the young, professorial look.

He barely had time to wave a hand toward Hannah before the two whirlwinds and Kitty descended on him.

"Daddy, wait until you see the maze I built."

"Daddy, Daddy, I want to show you my picture."

Brad crouched to greet his children and the family cat. There was genuine pleasure on his face.

Hannah watched the intimate little family ritual of greeting daddy and was horrified when she detected a hint of dampness on her own lashes. She blinked hurriedly and looked away. What was wrong with her today? At this rate she would soon be an emotional basket case. She had to get a grip on herself. Pamela was watching her with gathering concern.

"Are you okay?" Pamela pitched her voice below the hubbub taking place in the front hall. "Something wrong?"

"No, of course not. I'm fine." Hannah took a long, reviving swallow of tea. "I've been a little tense since the scene with Rafe this morning, that's all. I've got to do something about the problem of Dreamscape, Pam. The situation is a mess. It has to be resolved."

It was Brad who responded. He wandered into the living room, Rose and Mark bobbing around his legs. "From what I heard this afternoon, Rafe Madison has his own plans for Dreamscape. What's going on? Are you going to sell him your half of the house?"

"He isn't offering to buy it," Hannah said dryly. "He's proposing a partnership."

Brad considered that. "Maybe he can't afford to buy out your half."

"From what I can tell, money is not a problem for Rafe," Hannah said.

Brad met her eyes. "Then what's the issue? Pamela has told me something about the history of the Hartes and the Madisons. I got the impression that there was no love lost between the two clans."

"I'll admit that we haven't socialized much in the past three generations."

"Why would Rafe Madison want to get involved in a business partnership with you?" Brad asked.

"Beats me." Hannah decided it was time to change the subject. "How's tricks with you, Brad?"

"As a matter of fact, I have some good news. I got a call from the director of the institute this morning. He offered me the joint appointment. I start the first of the month."

"Yahoo!" Pamela leaped off the recliner and threw her arms around Brad. "Congratulations! I knew you'd get it."

Brad grinned at Hannah over Pamela's head. "I think I may have had a little help from my friends. Rumor has it that Perry Decatur mysteriously withdrew his objection to the appointment."

"That little S.O.B." Pamela made a face. "I knew he

was the one who was holding up the process. He's jealous as all get-out. He's afraid you're going to show him up for the lightweight he is once you're on the faculty there. Which you will, of course. Wonder what made him back off?"

"Why don't you ask Hannah?"

Pamela swung around, a hundred questions in her eyes. "What's going on?"

"Not much," Hannah said mildly. "Perry asked me to attend the Thornley reception last night. He wanted to impress everyone at the institute with his contacts. You get the picture."

"Got it," Brad said. "The Hartes are one of the most important families in town. Having a representative from the family there last night would have been a coup for Decatur."

"As it happened," Hannah continued, "I discovered that a former Weddings by Harte client was also scheduled to attend the reception. Perry was angling to get him to endow a research fund at the institute."

"Tom Lydd," Brad said.

Hannah nodded. "You are good. Something tells me you'll go far at the institute."

"And you had a word with Lydd, I take it?"

"All I did was mention that I knew the institute's selection committee had your name under consideration for a joint appointment and that you would make a wonderful addition to the faculty. Tom Lydd took it from there."

Brad exhaled deeply. "Decatur must have blown a gasket."

Pamela slapped a palm across her own mouth and then exploded with laughter. "A classic Harte tactical maneuver. Your folks would be so proud of you."

"I owe you," Brad said to Hannah. He looked serious.

"No, you don't." She grinned, feeling somewhat cheered

for the first time since the scene at Dreamscape that morning. "Perry Decatur owed me for something that happened eight years ago. It was payback time."

Brad shook his head. "You Hartes sure do have long memories."

Hannah wasn't sure that he meant it as a compliment.

She drove back to the cottage later that evening after sharing dinner with the McCallister family. The meal, with all its noise and chaos, had done wonders to improve her mood, she realized.

Maybe she could finally do some clearheaded thinking tonight. She needed to put things in perspective. Not that it was easy to gain any sort of real perspective on Rafe Madison. But the good news was that she was no longer feeling as unsettled as she had for the better part of the day. She was a Harte. As Pamela had reminded her, she was supposed to be good at strategic planning and tactics. Hartes did not allow themselves to get tangled up in messy emotions when it came to business. That was a Madison characteristic.

She had to start concentrating on the business aspects of Dreamscape. She could not allow Rafe to muddy the waters again.

Something told her that would be easier said than done. Madisons were very good at muddying things, she reflected as she pulled into the driveway in front of the darkened house.

She switched off the engine, climbed out from behind the wheel, and started toward the front door with a vaguely wistful sensation. She didn't have a loving husband and a couple of lively kids waiting to greet her, but at least she had Winston.

Faithful, loyal, lovable Winston.

She put her key in the lock and waited for the muted

sounds of doggy welcome. But there was no muffled scratch of toenails on hardwood, no happy whine.

The first tingle of unease shot through her. Winston was an alert dog. His hearing was almost preternatural. Surely he had caught the sound of the car in the drive.

Quickly she unlocked the door, opened it, and stepped into the hall.

"Winston?"

There was no response.

"Winston? Where are you? Here, Winston. Look, I'm sorry about Kitty. I admit that I patted her on the head a couple of times, but that was all, I swear it."

Winston did not come trotting around the corner.

She switched on a light and walked into the kitchen. Most of the water she had left in one of the twin stainless-steel bowls on the floor was untouched. The expensive chewing bone had been abandoned under the table.

Unease turned to concern that was only a little shy of panic. Something was wrong.

"Winston?"

She hurried back into the living room and started up the stairs. Perhaps he had gotten himself trapped in a bedroom or a bathroom when a door had accidentally closed. Frantically she tried to think of reasons why an inside door would suddenly swing shut. A draft? But if Winston was locked in an upstairs room, why wasn't he barking furiously to let her know where he was?

By the time she reached the top of the stairs, she was running. A single glance down the hall showed her that all of the doors stood wide open.

She darted from room to room, checking under beds and inside closets. There was no sign of Winston.

It occurred to her that he must have somehow gotten out of the house on his own and wandered off. It was a very un-Winston-like thing to do, but for all his canine cleverness he was still a dog and dogs were born explorers.

She went slowly back downstairs and came to a halt once more in the hall, pondering the mystery of how he might have escaped the house. The front door had been locked when she returned. That left the kitchen door and the mudroom door.

A quick check in the kitchen revealed that that door, too, was still securely locked. With mounting trepidation she walked back out into the hall and turned right. Automatically she switched on lights as she went toward the rear of the house.

The small mudroom was swathed in darkness. She hit the light switch and glanced quickly around the neat clutter. Rain gear, umbrellas, beach shoes, and a stack of old towels filled most of the space. Two brooms and an aged mop stood in the corner.

She studied the door. It was closed, but it was unlocked. She could not have forgotten to lock up before she left for Pamela's earlier in the day, she thought. It simply wasn't possible. She had lived alone in the city too long to neglect such simple precautions.

Even if she had left it unlocked, how had Winston gotten it open? He was a brilliant dog, but he had paws, not hands. It was pushing credibility much too far to believe that he had somehow managed to twist the doorknob and open the door. A specially trained dog might have accomplished the feat, but Winston had never been taught to do fancy tricks.

It was hard to believe that she had left this door not only unlocked but ajar. But she must have done just that. It was the only conceivable way that Winston could have gotten out of the house.

Despair engulfed her. Winston was somewhere outside

in the darkness, possibly lost and terrified. If he reached the road, he might get hit by a car.

She whirled around, yanked open a cupboard, and grabbed a flashlight. She would need it. Although there was a moon, the fog was thickening rapidly.

She seized a faded windbreaker from a wall hook, pulled it on, and opened the mudroom door. She stepped out onto the rear porch and switched on the flashlight.

"Winston."

A faint bark sounded in the distance. It was barely audible above the muted rumble of the light surf at the base of the cliffs, but her heart leaped in relief. Winston was in Dead Hand Cove.

She plunged down the steps and entered the ghostly tendrils of gathering fog. The beam of the flashlight infused the surrounding mist with an unearthly light. With the ease of long familiarity, she made her way toward the path that led down the rocky cliff to the beach.

"Winston. Talk to me. Where are you?"

This time she got a series of hard, sharp, excited barks. They definitely emanated from the cove, but they did not sound as if Winston was moving toward her. She wondered if he had somehow managed to trap himself inside one of the small caves at the base of the cliff.

At the top of the path she paused to shine the flashlight down on the rocky beach. The beam pierced the mist in places, revealing a wide swath of damp sand. The tide was coming in, but it had a ways to go before the water filled the cove. She could still make out the tips of the five fingers. But sprays of foam were already dampening the rocky monoliths. In another hour or so the water would cover all but the tallest of the stones.

Winston barked again, louder this time. She was definitely getting closer to him, she realized. But he was not making any headway toward her.

She started cautiously down the pebble-strewn path that led to the tiny beach. Only the fact that she had used the trail for years and knew it better than she knew the streets of Portland made it possible to navigate it at night with some confidence. The foggy darkness and the slippery rocks made for slow going. Twice she lost her footing and had to grab at a stony outcropping to save herself from a nasty fall.

She was breathing hard by the time she reached the rough beach. Immediately she shone the light along the dark voids that marked the caves.

"Winston!"

Another series of barks sounded in the mist. Behind her now. But how could that be? Fresh alarm swept through her.

She turned quickly to face the fingers. Aiming the flashlight toward the thumb, she started cautiously across the damp sand.

Spray dampened the front of her windbreaker. A wave broke at the entrance to the cove. Cold seawater swirled around her feet. Should have taken time to put on a pair of boots, she thought.

More loud, demanding barks punctuated the mist. Winston was getting impatient. Perhaps he had bounded up onto a finger before the tide returned and was now reluctant to jump down because he would get wet. But that didn't make any sense. Winston wasn't afraid of a few inches of water. She gasped when another swirl of cold foam lapped at her ankles.

She started toward the nearest finger and aimed the beam of the flashlight at the top. There was no dog there. Methodically she shone the light on the next monolith. The spray had thoroughly dampened her hair and face now. She would take a hot shower when she got back to the house. She definitely did not need a case of hypothermia.

It was getting harder to see through the ever-thickening fog, but she managed to make out the shape of the second finger. There was something wrong about it.

Another string of tense barks echoed in the fog. Definitely coming from the vicinity of the second finger.

She hurried forward, ignoring the cold water now swirling around her calves. The beam of the flashlight fell on a large square animal cage perched atop the monolith. Winston was inside.

"Oh, my God, Winston! What happened?" She sloshed toward him through the slowly deepening water. "Who did this to you?"

She found the door of the cage and yanked it open. Winston exploded into her arms. He was damp and trembling. She staggered backward under the impact, slipped, and barely managed to keep her footing. Winston lapped happily at her face. The flashlight beam arced wildly in the darkness as she clutched at him.

"After this little incident, I'm going to have more gray hair than you do," she whispered into his wet fur. "What on earth happened here?"

But Winston had no answers for her.

She carried him quickly toward the beach. "I'm going to call the police. This is a small town. The chief will know which one of the local punks would pull a vicious trick like this. I'm going to press charges. I swear it."

Winston licked her ear.

She set him down at the water's edge. "Come on, let's get you home and dried off. I wonder how long you were out there on that rock? I can't wait to get my hands on whoever did this. I'll—"

Winston interrupted her with a low, startlingly savage growl. She flashed the light down at him and saw that his whole attention was focused on the darkness that cloaked the cliff path. The tension in him was the only warning she got.

"Winston, no!" She grabbed his collar just as he leaped forward. "No. Winston, stay."

He obeyed instantly, but she could feel him quivering with predatory urgency. There was someone in the vicinity of the cliff path. Someone Winston did not like.

Fear crashed through her. She had to assume that whoever was on the trail was the same person who had caught Winston and set him out on the monolith to drown.

At the same instant it occurred to her that although she could not see the person watching from the shadows, he could certainly see her. The flashlight in her hand made a very effective beacon.

She turned off the beam and crouched down beside Winston. "Hush." She closed her fingers lightly around his muzzle. She did not think his low growls could be heard above the sound of the incoming tide, but if he started barking again, he would give away their location.

Winston shuddered under her hands. His attention never wavered from the cliff path.

One thing was certain, Hannah thought as she waited for her eyes to adjust to the new level of darkness. They could not go up the path. They would run straight into whoever waited there. Nor could they just stay here in the cove like sitting ducks.

Keeping her fingers around Winston's muzzle, she tugged on his collar to guide him.

"This way," she whispered. "Heel, or whatever it is dogs are supposed to do at times like this."

If Winston was offended by the command, he was gracious enough not to complain. He paced obediently along beside her. She bent low, not daring to take her fingers off his muzzle as they made their way toward the dense darkness of the cliff caves. She relied on the sighs and splashes of the returning seawater to cloak whatever noise she made as she scrambled over the rocks with Winston.

The biggest danger would come from tide pools that littered the cove. At night, without a flashlight, each one was a potential trap. Things slipped and slithered under her feet, but Winston detoured safely around the edges of the pools.

The deeper darkness of a cave entrance loomed in her path. The scent of rotting seaweed enveloped her. But for once Winston showed no interest in the fascinating odors that assailed his nostrils. He was alert and focused. She did not dare release her grip on his muzzle.

"Hush," she said again. "Please, hush."

He gave a low, almost inaudible whimper and quivered tensely.

She put out one hand and felt for the wall of the cave. When her palm made contact with the damp rock she started cautiously forward. Winston must have sensed her intention or perhaps he was merely responding to some ancient den-seeking impulse. Whatever the reason, he willingly took the lead as they made their way deeper into the convoluted cavern.

As soon as they rounded the corner, they lost what little fog-reflected moonlight there was coming through the mouth of the cave. The quality of the darkness took on a deeper, thicker feel. Hannah could see nothing now. She stumbled awkwardly along, blindly following Winston. But after she bumped her head on a rocky outcropping and scraped a knee, she decided to risk the flashlight again.

She kept the beam pointed straight down toward the rising floor of rock. Winston trotted forward through the sandy rubble that littered the bottom of the cavern. He no longer seemed inclined to bark. Cautiously, she released his muzzle.

The path led through a series of small, damp chambers. She stumbled over the remains of an old pink-plastic sandal. Probably one that she or her sister had lost when they had come here to play years ago, she thought.

The cavern branched off in several directions. Some of the tunnels were too narrow for any human to pass through, although Winston could have made it. She selected a passage she had often used in the past. Her brother, Nick, had marked it with an **X** painted in red. Here in the endless gloom the paint had faded little over the years.

Winston strained forward more eagerly now, perhaps sensing the fresh air that wafted in from the far end of the twisted passage. They rounded a bend. There was a difference in the density of the light at the far end of the cavern. She realized she was looking at night and fog now, not at rock wall.

Hastily she doused the flashlight beam again and allowed Winston to draw her quickly toward the exit. His mood had altered. He was still eager, but he seemed excited and cheerful, no longer the hunter confronting danger.

"Hannah."

The shock of hearing her name called loudly just as she and Winston emerged from the cavern sent a jolt through her. The realization that it was Rafe's voice that echoed in the mist brought a nearly paralyzing sense of relief.

"Over here, Rafe."

Winston whimpered and bounded up the slope that led to the top of the cliff. She rushed after him. They were both running now.

Hannah did not slow down when she saw Rafe silhouetted against the glare of the flashlight. She kept going at full speed, straight into his arms.

chapter 16

An hour later Rafe heard her stalk back into the kitchen behind him. He removed the pan of steaming cocoa from the stove and glanced over his shoulder.

She had washed and dried her hair and tucked it back behind her ears. A thick white toweling robe was belted around her narrow waist. Her face was pink and flushed. He knew that the high color in her cheeks was not from the hot shower she had just taken. She was still fuming.

He hadn't entirely recovered from the roller coaster of emotions he'd been through in the past hour either, he realized. Hannah and Winston had been through a bad experience, but the whole event had not been a picnic for him. He'd endured his own private ordeal.

First there had been the nightmare images he had envisioned when he knocked on the front door of the house and received no answer. Given the fact that Hannah's car was in the drive, he'd started out with the worst-case scenario—that she was upstairs in her prissy little bedroom with another man. When he'd finally climbed out of the dark pit into which that vision had cast him, he'd summoned up some common sense and logic. Even if Hannah had been engaged in passionate sex upstairs, he reasoned, Winston would have come to the door.

Winston had not come to the door. Ergo, Winston and Hannah had gone for a walk. Given the fog and the late hour, however, that conclusion had induced other, equally disturbing scenarios. The tide was coming in. It was a damfool time to go walking on the beach.

When he'd finally spotted them coming toward him from the vicinity of the caves, the relief that had flashed through him had been stunning. Then Hannah had launched herself into his arms, and he'd realized that she was scared and shivering. Her clothes and hair were wet.

She'd told him the full story on the way back to the house, and he'd been chilled to the bone by the tale. A hundred variations on disaster had assailed him. She could have been swept up in the churning waters of the cove while attempting to rescue Winston. What if whoever she thought had watched her from the path had pursued her and the dog into the caves?

After the visions had come the questions, the primary one being, What the hell was going on? He'd made the cocoa partly as therapy for himself. Cooking always centered him and allowed him to think more clearly.

He'd done a lot of thinking while he stirred the hot chocolate and waited for Hannah to come back downstairs. He'd even managed to reach a few conclusions. He was calm and cool again, he told himself. He was back in control.

"Sit down," he instructed. "I'll pour you a cup of this stuff. Winston has already had his treat."

She looked at Winston, who was flopped under the table. Rafe had dried him off and fluffed his fur with some of the old towels in the mudroom. He looked none the worse for his ordeal. In typical dog fashion, he appeared to have forgotten the entire experience.

The same could not be said of Hannah, Rafe thought.

"I still can't believe that that twit at the police station actually said they could not spare an officer to investigate what happened to Winston tonight." She dropped into a chair at the kitchen table. "The woman acted as if I had phoned in a complaint about some stupid childish prank."

"Try not to take it personally." Rafe poured the cocoa into a mug and put it on the table. "This is a small town, remember? There aren't many officers on the force. The dispatcher explained that they were all busy out at Chamberlain tonight because of the big rally."

"I *am* taking it personally. Winston would have drowned if I hadn't found him in time."

"Maybe, but once you told the dispatcher that you and the dog were okay and that there was no sign of forced entry here at the house, you lost your status as an emergency."

"I know, I know." She heaved a sigh and then, frowning slightly, she sniffed. She looked down at the mug of cocoa he had put in front of her. "That smells good."

"Drink it."

Obediently she took a sip. "Just what the doctor ordered. Thanks."

"You're welcome." He sat down across from her. "I went back to the edge of the cliffs and looked for that cage or animal trap or whatever it was. But it's gone."

"Knocked off the finger by the incoming waves, no doubt." She took another sip. "Maybe it will get washed ashore or left on the sand when the tide goes out tomorrow. I'll watch for it. It's the only evidence I've got."

"Even if you find it, I doubt if it will prove useful.

There won't be any fingerprints left on it by the time the sea gets finished with it."

She looked dismayed. "You're probably right."

Rafe glanced down at Winston. "Someone must have opened the back door and enticed him into the trap."

"Probably wouldn't have been too hard." Her mouth tightened. "A nice chunk of raw steak would have gotten his attention."

"The real question is, How did the mudroom door get unlocked?"

She pursed her lips. "I've been thinking about that. It's no secret that Mom and Dad leave a spare key with a realtor here in town who looks after the place when no one in the family is using it. It's not too much of a stretch to imagine someone stealing the key or copying it."

He thought about it. "Maybe. But it seems like more trouble than the average kid would go to just to play a nasty prank."

She looked at him with troubled eyes. "You think this was something more than a vicious stunt?"

He shoved his hands into the front pockets of his trousers. "If you put this incident together with the possibility that someone may have been watching your house at night on and off this past week, you've got the makings of a stalker scenario."

She shuddered. "That occurred to me while I was in the shower. But it would have to be someone who had followed me from Portland, and I honestly can't think of anyone there who is obsessive about me."

"The ex-fiancé?"

She looked genuinely taken aback by the suggestion. Then she shook her head with grave certainty. "No, definitely not Doug. He's not the type."

"I'm not sure the type is always obvious."

"Our engagement ended a year ago. Why would he start stalking me now? And why follow me here to Eclipse Bay to do it? He doesn't know his way around this town. Whoever trapped Winston and stuck him out on that finger knows a lot about this place."

"Good point. Got to be someone from Eclipse Bay. Someone who knew about the fingers and the tides in Dead Hand Cove. Someone who knew how to get a key to this house."

"What are you thinking, Rafé?"

"I'm thinking Perry Decatur."

"Perry?" She sat back, startled. "Oh, no, that's ridiculous. Why would he do something like that?"

"To get even for the way you finessed his move to keep Brad McCallister off the faculty at the institute?"

She chewed on her lower lip for a few seconds and then shook her head again. "I suppose it's possible. But I don't think so. Not his style. Perry's a conniving little twerp, but I don't see him pulling a stunt like this."

"Why not?"

"Well, for one thing, whoever carried that cage out to the finger had to get wet and dirty doing it. Perry isn't the type to get wet and dirty if he can help it. Plus there was a real risk of getting caught in the act if I came home early. Perry doesn't take risks if he can avoid them. He prefers to maneuver behind the scenes."

Rafe was unconvinced. "I don't know. He was plenty pissed last night."

She exhaled heavily. "It just doesn't feel like the kind of trick he would pull. More likely it was a local kid. A budding little sociopath who has graduated from setting fires to torturing animals."

Rafe said nothing.

"You've got a problem with my logic?"

"I'm just thinking," he said.

"I can see that. And it makes me nervous."

"Me, thinking, makes you nervous? Why?"

"Because the last time you did some serious thinking you decided to make us partners in Dreamscape."

"That's different."

"Bull."

"It's going to work. You'll see, partner."

She pointedly ignored that. "What, exactly, are you thinking about what happened tonight?"

He hesitated and then decided there was nothing to be gained by keeping silent. "I'm thinking that whatever is going on here might not be about you."

"Not about me? That was my dog out there on the finger."

"What I meant was it might not be about you alone." He paused. "It might be about us."

"Us? You mean someone doesn't like the idea that we're—" She broke off and made another run at it. "Someone doesn't like the rumors that are going around about us? But why on earth would anyone care if we're, uh—"

"Sleeping together?" he offered helpfully.

"One time," she said swiftly. "There was only one time. That does not exactly constitute a flaming affair."

For some reason he found that observation both extremely irritating and strangely depressing. "Can't argue that."

She sipped her cocoa for a moment, then put the mug down. "I just had a thought. Maybe whoever did this is one of your old flames. A jealous lover from your misspent past?"

"Doubt it."

She was undeterred. "Good grief. If I'm right, we've got more suspects than we can count."

His incipient depression vanished in the heat of a sudden, fierce anger. He sat forward quickly, flattening his palms on the table. "My reputation in this town was always a hell of a lot more exciting than the reality."

She blinked. "Now, Rafe—"

"Trust me on this. I was there."

She cleared her throat. "Well, yes, of course you were, but everyone knows about your reputation in those days."

"This may come as a stunning surprise to you, but contrary to popular opinion, I don't have a legion of old flames hiding in the bushes here in Eclipse Bay."

"I don't believe I used the word 'legion.'"

"Close enough. For the record, virtually all of my dates—and there were not as many of them as everyone seems to think—were weekend or summer visitors who came here for the beach, the boardwalk, and a good time. They knew what they were doing and so did I. There was nothing serious with any of them, and I've never seen any of them again."

Her jaw clenched visibly. "There was Kaitlin Sadler."

"Yes. There was Kaitlin Sadler. She was a year older than me, experienced, and she could take care of herself."

"I never implied that you took advantage of her. No one ever said that."

"I didn't have a lot of rules for myself in those days, but I had a few and I stuck to them. I never got involved with anyone who was married or too young or too naïve to know the score. Hell, you ought to know that better than anyone else."

"Me?" She gripped the edge of the table. "Why should I know anything about the history of your love life?"

"Because I never laid a hand on you eight years ago, that's why."

For the space of two or three heartbeats she simply stared at him in utter astonishment. Then she pulled herself together with an obvious effort. "Of course you never touched me. I wasn't your type. You wouldn't have looked twice at me if we hadn't been stuck out there at the Arch together that night."

A cold, mirthless amusement shafted through him. "You weren't my type, and you were squarely in the 'don't touch' category as far as I was concerned, but that doesn't mean that I didn't look twice."

Her eyes widened. "Because I was a Harte? Was I some sort of challenge?"

"The fact that you were a Harte had nothing to do with it."

"Then why did you look twice?"

"Damned if I know. Pure masochism, probably, because I sure as hell knew that you'd never look twice at me."

"That's not true." She shot to her feet. "I had a crush on you. Every girl in Eclipse Bay did."

"That's supposed to thrill me?" He was suddenly on his feet, too, although he had no recollection of getting out of his chair. "To know that for you I was just the interesting bad boy with the bike and the leather jacket and the dangerous rep? The kind of guy your parents always warned you about? The kind of guy it might be amusing to fool around with but definitely not the kind you would ever marry?"

A fresh tide of hot color rose in her face. He could have sworn he had embarrassed her. Good. Served her right. But her gaze did not slide away from his.

"How did you know what kind of man I'd marry?" she asked evenly.

"You told me that night, remember? You were only nineteen and you already had your damned list of requirements for a husband made out."

"I was twenty, not nineteen, and I swear, if you mention that list one more time—"

He reached for her. He closed his hands around her shoulders and hauled her up against his chest. "As far as I'm concerned, I don't care if I never hear about that damned list of yours again for as long as I live. Furthermore, I'm not real keen on hearing about your new, updated version of it, either."

"Uh, Rafe, you're acting a little weird here. Maybe the stress—?"

"Yeah. Maybe."

He covered her mouth with his own, letting the fierce tension that was eating him up inside pour into her. She made a soft, muffled sound, and then her arms closed tightly around him and she was kissing him back with all the passion that had infused her anger a few seconds earlier.

"My God," he muttered against her throat. "Do you have any idea of the scare you gave me tonight?"

"Scare?" Her own voice was muffled because she was frantically kissing his jaw. "Why were you scared?"

"First, because I thought maybe the reason you weren't answering the door was that you were with some other man."

"No. Really?" She went very still. Then she pulled back slightly and looked at him with wide, fascinated eyes. "You were actually afraid that I might be in bed with another man? Did you think that I might have a few old flames of my own here in Eclipse Bay?"

"Let's not go there." He refused to be sidetracked again by that possibility. "My other big fear was that you'd gone for a walk with Winston and fallen on the rocks."

"Like Kaitlin Sadler?"

"I wasn't thinking of Kaitlin," he said bluntly. "All I could think about was you." He wrapped his fingers around the back of her head. "Lord help me, I haven't been able to concentrate on anything else except you since I got that letter from the lawyer."

"Don't give me that." Fresh outrage erupted. "If you've been concentrating on me, it's because I'm connected to Dreamscape. You have to deal with me before you can get your hands on my property. *That's* why you suddenly started focusing on me. Admit it."

He cast about briefly for the words he needed, but he could not find them.

"We both want the same thing for Dreamscape," he said finally. "We ought to be able to work together."

"And sleep together?"

"We both want that, too. I really don't see the problem here, Hannah."

"Probably because you're thinking like a Madison."

"You know something?" he said through his teeth. "I've had it with you implying that just because I'm a Madison, I can't handle a sexual relationship and a business relationship simultaneously."

"I've had it with you classifying our relationship as *sexual*."

"Well, what would you call it?"

She stilled. "I don't know."

"Fine. Great. That's a lot of help."

She raised her chin. "I just know that for me there has to be more than sex."

That stopped him cold. "More?"

"And don't you dare tell me that a business partnership will fill in the empty places," she added icily.

He was annoyed. "I wasn't going to say that. That sounds like something a Harte would say, not a Madison."

"If I'm not allowed to insult your family, you can't insult mine."

"Sure, right. Take all the fun out of the argument. Damn it, Hannah, I've had enough of this. You know that what we've got is more than just a sexual thing. I want you. I think you want me. Can't we just go with that for now?"

She put her hands on his shoulders as if to steady herself. "I don't understand what's happening here. But I do know that adding sex to the mix complicates things."

"In the most interesting way," he muttered against her throat.

"Rafe—"

"Give whatever we've got going for us a chance, okay?" He drew his finger down the curve of her neck. "That's all I'm asking."

"I really don't think that's a good idea, Rafe."

He cradled her chin in his palms. "Tell me something."

She searched his face. "What?"

"Do you ever stop talking?"

"Not as long as I have something to say."

"Just wondered." He kissed her again.

For a few seconds she hesitated and then, with a tiny sigh, she softened.

Maybe she no longer had anything to say, he thought. A man could always hope.

Afraid to risk any more conversation, he kept his mouth on hers as he maneuvered her through the kitchen door. When they went past the light switch, he reached out and flipped it to the off position. Heavy shadows descended. The only light now was a dim, welcoming glow at the top of the stairs. He started toward it with Hannah tucked safely against his side.

His breathing was heavy and ragged by the time he got both of them to the bedroom at the end of the hall. He did not turn on the lamp, but the light from the corridor was sufficient to allow him to see that the room, with its white wicker furniture, white bedspread, and bleached wooden floors, was just as he had imagined it all those years ago: a pristine retreat for an untouchable princess. He felt like the intruder he was.

Not that that was going to stop him, he thought.

Exultation raced through him. Nothing could stop him as long as he knew that Hannah wanted him as badly as he wanted her. The passion between them was mutual. He could work with passion. He was a Madison.

He stopped beside the bed and untied the belt that bound the robe around her waist. She wore a long-sleeved, high-necked, prim white gown underneath it. Womanly armor, he thought. Did she know the challenge it presented?

She mumbled something against his mouth as he slipped the robe off her shoulders. He did not catch the precise words, but he had no trouble at all understanding the meaning. She was as swept up in the moment as he was.

Her arms tightened fiercely around his neck when he started to unfasten the tiny little buttons of the flannel nightgown. She smelled so good. He knew that when he threaded his fingers through the triangle of hair at the apex of her thighs she would be moist. He could hardly wait.

She unbuttoned his shirt and spread her palms across his chest. "I love the feel of you," she whispered.

He was already hard, but her touch and the sultry desire in her words made him absolutely rigid. Electricity flashed through his senses.

He released her long enough to sit down on the edge of the white bed and remove his running shoes. When he looked up he saw that she was watching him with hungry attention, as if every move he made fascinated her.

He rose and lowered the flannel gown to her waist. It

slipped low on her hips but it did not fall all the way to the floor. He caressed the tips of her small breasts. Her nipples were stiff and full. He closed his eyes briefly against the torrent of need that threatened to drown him.

She undid his belt, and then she lowered his zipper. When her fingers closed lightly around him he stopped breathing for a few seconds. The sensations tearing through him were so intense that he was sure he could live without oxygen for a while.

She slid her hands beneath the waistband of his trousers and pushed slowly downward. The pants hit the floor at his feet.

"*Rafe.*"

He stepped out of the trousers and quickly sheathed himself in the condom he took from his back pocket. Then he grabbed her around the waist and fell back across the white bedspread with her. She sprawled atop his chest and thighs, the bottom of her gown tangling in his bare legs.

She rained kisses on his flesh. Her fingers circled his upper arms. He shuddered under the gentle assault. Then he rolled onto her back, leaned over her, and tore the gown off altogether. It vanished into the darkness below the bed.

He curved his hand around her hip and kissed the gentle swell of her belly. She trembled beneath him and reached for him.

"No," he said. "Not yet."

He found the tight, hot place between her legs. And she was wet, just as he had anticipated. He inhaled the secret scent until he could no longer think clearly. Then he separated her thighs and kissed the exquisitely soft skin he found there.

She shivered again. Her nails dug into his shoulder as she tried to pull him up along the length of her. But he was not yet ready to be lured into the climax.

He drew a fingertip along the tight nub hidden in the silky thatch of hair and felt her quiver in response. She was clawing at him now.

He bent his head and touched the tip of his tongue to her full, taut clitoris. She tensed.

"Rafe." It was a plea and a protest. "Wait. Don't do that."

"Come for me."

"I can't. Not like this. It's too—*Rafe*."

"Come for me." He kissed her again, intimately, and simultaneously eased two fingers into her, stretching her gently.

Her hands twisted in the sheets. "No, wait. I want—"

"Come for me."

"I . . . Oh, no. Oh, yes. *Yes!*"

He felt her climax take her. The sensation was so intoxicating he nearly went with her.

He held himself together until the tremors had begun to subside. Only then did he shift his position to lie on top of her.

"Open your eyes," he whispered. "Look at me."

Languidly she raised her lashes and smiled at him, a dreamy smile that was somehow smug and all-knowing and filled with invitation.

He plunged into her body, driving himself to the hilt. She closed around him and took him deeper still, straight down into uncharted depths and unknowable waters.

"Come for me," she said into his mouth.

He gave himself up to the tides of a mysterious sea.

A long time later he roused reluctantly from the cocoon of warmth that enveloped them, levered himself up on his elbow, and looked down at her.

"I just want to know one thing," he said.

She raised her lashes halfway and yawned. "What?"

"Are you sleeping with me because you've got some kind of kinky thing about finding out what it's like to do it with the kind of guy your parents would hate?"

"That would be extremely immature."

"Yeah."

"Hartes do not act out just for the hell of it, nor do we take risks merely for the sake of novelty. We are not immature. We're the logical, reasonable, rational ones, remember?"

"Yeah." He kissed her breast. "So why are you sleeping with me?"

She studied him with an enigmatic expression. "You had all the answers earlier."

"Earlier I was trying to talk you into bed."

She punched him lightly on the arm. "We are not amused, Madison."

"I'm serious. I know why I'm sleeping with you. I want to know why you're sleeping with me."

She searched his face. "Is it that important to you?"

Anger stirred deep inside him, dissolving much of the warm afterglow that had enveloped him. "Hell, yes, it's important. You think I'd be trying to get through a stupid conversation like this if the answer wasn't important?"

"Well, I'll tell you one thing," she said. "I'm certainly not doing this because I still have a teenage-type crush on you or because you're the guy my parents always warned me about."

He rolled onto his back, put one hand behind his head, and gazed moodily up at the dark ceiling. "So what's the reason?"

She rose partway off the bed and leaned over him in the shadows. When she spoke, her voice was low and steady.

"I am sleeping with you because, among other things,

I am a mature, unattached adult who happens to be physically attracted to you and also because—"

An eagerness that bordered on desperation swept through him. Get a grip, he thought. "And also because—?"

He sensed that she was on the verge of saying something crucial. But in the next heartbeat the intense, important thing disappeared beneath a breezy smile.

"And because my dog likes you, and I trust Winston's judgment implicitly," she said demurely.

So what the hell had he expected her to say? He wondered. "Sonofabitch."

"Yes, but we do not refer to him in those terms in his presence."

"Huh."

"In my experience, Winston is never wrong in these matters."

He thought about that for a while. "Winston didn't like the ex-fiancé, I take it?"

"Winston was civil, but he never warmed up to Doug." Hannah paused. "There was an unfortunate incident one evening toward the end of the relationship that more or less summed up his opinion."

"What sort of incident?"

She cleared her throat. "Winston mistook Doug's leg for a fire hydrant."

"Winston and I are pals," Rafe said. "I don't think he'd make the same mistake with me."

"He seems to like you very much."

"Guess that'll have to do. For now."

She tilted her head slightly. "I guess so. For now."

He lay there unmoving, intensely conscious of the warmth of her hip where it rested against his thigh and the elegantly sensual curve of her shoulder. He could not shake the feeling of destiny that rippled through him. It was the same sensation that had come over him the day he opened the letter from Isabel's lawyer.

"What are you thinking?" she asked.

Don't let the feeling run away with you, he warned himself. Stay on top of it. Stay in control. Don't think about the future. Stay with the present.

But the future was so important now.

He inhaled slowly, centering himself. "I was thinking about the subject that we were discussing before we were so delightfully interrupted."

"I believe you were holding forth on a theory that whoever tried to murder Winston might have been attempting to express his displeasure over our relationship."

"You don't have to say it in that tone of voice. It's a good theory. But I never got a chance to explain the finer points."

"I'm listening."

"I didn't mean to imply that whoever tried to off Winston did so because he was pissed about the fact that you and I are sleeping together. What I was going to suggest was that he or she might be worried about something else altogether."

"Such as?"

"Think about it," he said patiently. "Ever since we arrived here in Eclipse Bay, there has been talk. It hasn't all been focused on the speculation that one of us is trying to screw the other out of Dreamscape."

She winced. "What a delicate way to put it."

He ignored her. "There's also been gossip about what happened eight years ago."

"Oh, for pity's sake. You actually think that some people still care whether or not we had sex on the beach that night?"

"No. The conversations have circled around the subject of Kaitlin Sadler's death. You heard the Willis brothers. Others are talking, too. I overheard a couple of folks in the vegetable aisle at Fulton's chatting about how no one was really sure what happened that night. One of them suggested that Yates might have closed the case a little too quickly, for lack of suspects."

Hannah's lips parted as understanding struck. "Kaitlin died a long time ago. Who would care if there was fresh talk going around about an old tragedy?"

"Someone who thinks that I really did murder Kaitlin might care. A lot."

She froze. "Dell Sadler. But why would he try to harm my dog?"

"As far as Dell is concerned, you covered for me that night. You're involved."

"You think he would have tried to harm Winston as a way of taking some revenge?"

"I think," Rafe said deliberately, "that we'd better talk to him."

chapter 17

The faded sign over the gate read SADLER'S AUTO RE-BUILD. Beneath it, in slightly smaller letters, were the words 24-HOUR TOWING. And below that was the phrase SPECIALIZING IN INSURANCE WORK. But the chain-link fence that enclosed the metal carcasses of ruined automobiles and the big dog with the massive head sprawled in front of the trailer sent a slightly different message. This was a junkyard.

Hannah took one look at the huge dog and decided to leave Winston in the car. "Whatever you do, don't let him out," she said as Rafe opened the door on his side.

Rafe eyed the animal lying in the shade of the tattered awning that shielded the trailer door. "Have a little faith. We're talking brains versus brawn here. My money's on Winston."

"We are not going to put that to the test." Hannah looked at Winston through the two-inch crack she had left between the window and the top of the car door frame. "Don't do anything to provoke that beast, understand?"

Winston whined softly. His rear legs were planted on the seat she had just vacated, his front paws braced against the door. Ears alert, nose quivering, he stared through the window, his whole attention concentrated on the other dog.

Hannah shuddered at the thought of what might happen if Winston got out of the car. She checked the passenger door to make certain that it was firmly shut and then sent Rafe a warning glance over the low roof of the Porsche.

"Be sure you close that door firmly."

"You worry too much," Rafe said. He gave the Porsche door a rather casual push. "Winston's smart. He can handle that guy."

She watched the big dog heave his bulk to his feet. "I'm sure I'm a lot smarter than that monster, too. But I wouldn't want to get into a fight with him."

"Okay, okay. Winston stays in the car." Rafe walked to the gate and leaned on a grimy button.

A few seconds later the door of the trailer opened. Dell Sadler appeared, silhouetted in the gloom. He gazed at Rafe and Hannah, his face shadowed by the brim of a greasy billed cap. After a while he apparently came to a decision. He started toward the gate. The dog paced stiffly after him, moving with the painfully awkward stride of an animal who was either very old or had been badly injured.

Dell crossed the yard, weaving his way between piles of tires, crumpled fenders, and assorted mutilated auto parts. When he reached the gate he made no move to open it. He stared balefully at Rafe through the chain links. The dog came to a halt beside him and stared too. Dell did not look down, but he put his hand on the creature's head in a gesture that was at once calming and absently affectionate. The bond between man and beast was evident.

"It's okay, Happy," Dell said.

Quite suddenly Hannah found it difficult to believe that this man had tried to murder Winston last night.

"What d'ya want?" Dell asked gruffly.

"We need to talk to you, Dell."

"What about?"

"Kaitlin."

Dell's shoulders stiffened visibly. He hesitated for a long time. Then he reached for the latch. "You better come inside."

The gate swung open. Dell led the way through the piles of dead automobiles.

The tidy interior of the trailer was a surprise. Hannah glanced surreptitiously around as she sat down on the worn vinyl-covered couch. There was a good reading lamp on the built-in end table. A pile of magazines bearing recent dates was stacked beside it. A new mystery novel by a familiar author lay on the miniature coffee table.

Dell hovered in the little kitchen. He appeared nervous, uneasy, as if he was not sure how to handle guests. "You want something to drink? I got some soda and beer."

"Soda's fine," Rafe said. "Whatever's handy."

"Soda sounds great," Hannah said gently.

"Sure." Dell opened the refrigerator and hauled out two cans. He carried them into the living room portion of the trailer and set them on the table in front of Rafe and Hannah.

Hannah glanced through the screen door of the trailer, studying the dog sprawled outside. "What happened to your dog?"

"Happy got run over by some drunk bastard on the highway while we was out on a tow job one night. Messed up his rear legs pretty bad. Vet told me I oughta put him down, but I just couldn't do that. Cost me a fortune, but what was I gonna do? Me and Happy are partners, y'know?"

"I know," Hannah said. Definitely not a dog killer, she thought. But if Dell Sadler wasn't the one who had put Winston out on the rocks in Dead Hand Cove, who had? "Someone tried to kill my dog last night."

"Why would anyone wanna kill a dog?"

"We think it may have been meant as a warning of some kind," she said quietly.

"Shit. That's why you're here, isn't it? You think maybe I tried to hurt your dog on accounta what happened to Kaitlin?"

"It crossed our minds," Rafe admitted. "You're the only one I can think of who might have wanted to avenge Kaitlin's death."

"Shit," Dell said again. He sank down onto a threadbare chair and stared at the logo on the can in his hand. "I wouldn't hurt no dog. That little pooch of yours didn't have anything to do with what happened to my sister."

"You're right." Rafe leaned forward, legs spread. He held the can of soda loosely in his fingers between his knees. Serious but nonthreatening. Man to man. "I'll come to the point, Dell. I know you think I killed Kaitlin. I didn't. That's the God's honest truth. You'll believe what you want to believe, but in the meantime, I really need to know why you're so sure I'm guilty."

Dell turned the can between his hands. Eventually he looked up. "I always figured it was you because you were the last one with her that night. Everyone said you were pissed that she was playing around."

Hannah stirred. "But why were you always so sure that it was murder in the first place? Why couldn't it have been an accident?"

"Because they found her in Hidden Cove. Said she must have been up on the path in the middle of the night. Doesn't make sense. Why would she go out there?"

"To meet a man?" Hannah suggested gently.

Dell gave her a derisive look. "She had her own house. And a car, too. She didn't have to go to someplace like Hidden Cove to fool around."

"Unless she didn't want to be seen with whoever she met there," Rafe said bluntly. "Which lets me out. She sure didn't mind having people see her with me."

Hannah pursed her lips, thinking. "Maybe she didn't go out there to meet anyone. Maybe she just went there to meditate."

"Meditate?" Dell looked at her as if she had lost her mind. "Kaitlin wasn't into that kinda weird stuff."

"Everyone needs to get away to a quiet place to think about their future once in a while," Hannah persisted. But she noticed that Rafe was now looking at her strangely too. Obviously neither of these two considered Kaitlin to be the thoughtful, introspective type.

"Not Kaitlin." Dell took a swallow from his can of soda and wiped his mouth with the back of a stained sleeve. "She had her future down cold. Didn't need to do any meditating on it. Kaitlin always had big plans, y'know?"

A tingle of expectation shot through Hannah. She and Rafe exchanged nods. She turned back to Dell.

"Why do you say that Kaitlin didn't have to do any meditating on her future?" she asked carefully.

"She already knew what she was going to do. Called me that night." Dell studied his soda can intently. "Said she'd had enough of this town. She was gonna leave first thing in the morning and never come back."

"Are you telling us that you spoke with Kaitlin just before she died?" Rafe asked.

"Yeah. Like I said, she called me. Woke me up. She was still really mad at you, y'know? Said she'd had it with everyone here. All losers, she said."

"How did she plan to finance this final exit?" Rafe asked.

Dell sucked in a deep breath and took another swallow of soda. He lowered the can slowly and peered into the middle distance. Looking into the past. "She told me that she was going to use her nuclear option."

Rafe did not move. "What the hell was that?"

Dell hesitated. "I'm not sure, to tell you the truth. She never was real clear about it. I got the feeling that she had some cash stashed away. Figured one of her boyfriends had given it to her. Or maybe someone gave her a piece of fancy jewelry she thought she could sell."

Hannah's mouth went dry. She said nothing.

"Let me get this straight." Rafe sounded as if he was choosing his words with exquisite care. "You're saying that she left me on the beach that night, went home, and called you to tell you that she was going to go nuclear and then leave town?"

"The next thing I know," Dell said dully, "Yates is pounding on my door. Come to tell me Kaitlin's dead."

"And you told him you were pretty sure I'd killed her—is that it?"

"Well, yeah," Dell muttered.

"Follow your own logic for a while here," Rafe said. "How did I know she was headed for Hidden Cove?"

"I figure you went to her place. You killed her there and then dumped her body in Hidden Cove."

Rafe groaned. "Well, it's a theory. I'll give you that much."

"Kaitlin wasn't like me," Dell pleaded to Hannah. "She wanted to get out of this town. Be someone. She had dreams, y'see? Lots of 'em. Big ones."

"I understand," Hannah said.

"But none of 'em ever worked out for her." Dell gave a sad sigh. "Seemed like everything always went wrong. I was her brother, y'know, but there was never anything I could do to fix things for her."

Rafe frowned. "It wasn't your fault you couldn't straighten out her problems, Dell."

"Maybe. But it just seemed like I shoulda been able to do something, y'know?"

"Yeah," Rafe said. "I know. Sometimes you've just got to live with the fact that there wasn't anything you could do."

Dell nodded bleakly. "Thought I'd put it all behind me. Told myself it was finished. Then you two showed up in town together. Made it clear you planned to hang around awhile. People started talking about what happened that night again."

Rafe looked at him. "When Yates came around asking questions, did he say whether or not he had searched Kaitlin's house?"

"He went through the place real thoroughly. Her car, too. I was with him when he did it," Dell said morosely. "Said he was looking for a suicide note, but he tore that place apart, y'know? Why would he do that if he was just lookin' for a note? I mean, if she'd left one, she would have put it in plain sight, don't you think? Why leave a note if you don't want it to be found?"

"You're right," Rafe said. "She'd have left it in plain sight."

Hannah gripped the edge of her chair very tightly. "Do

you recall whether or not Yates pulled out her washer and dryer to check behind them?"

Dell nodded. "And the refrigerator, too. Like I said, he really went through her stuff. But I know she didn't jump off that cliff. There was no note. I told him she wasn't the type to commit suicide. Asked him what he was really looking for."

Hannah watched him. "What did he say?"

"Said he'd know it if he found it. But he didn't find anything."

They all sat in silence for a time. After a while Dell sighed heavily and drained the last of his soda. "I didn't try to kill your dog, Hannah."

"I believe you," Hannah said. "You wouldn't hurt an innocent animal."

Dell nodded and said nothing.

"There's something else," Hannah said. "Rafe didn't kill Kaitlin. I really was with him that night on the beach near the Arch. There was no way he could have followed your sister home, let alone kill her and take her body to Hidden Cove. You have my word on it."

Dell did not move for a long time. Then he looked at Rafe. "If it wasn't you, who was it?"

"Good question," Rafe said.

Back in the car, Winston draped the front half of his body over the back of the seat and nuzzled Hannah's shoulder. She scratched his ears and glanced at Rafe.

"Are you thinking what I'm thinking?" she asked.

"About that lingerie and the videos the Willis brothers found hidden behind Kaitlin's dryer?" Rafe steered the Porsche in a tight circle and drove down the dusty, rutted road that led away from Sadler's Auto Rebuild. "Yeah, that's what I'm thinking. Maybe those videos were her nuclear option."

"Blackmail material?"

"Maybe," Rafe said again. "And maybe Chief Yates suspected something. Maybe that's why he tore her place apart that night."

"But he didn't find anything."

Rafe turned right onto the main road. "Which means that whoever killed Kaitlin managed to recover the videos and the lingerie."

Hannah shivered. "Do you realize what we're saying here?"

"We're saying that Dell Sadler was right all along. Kaitlin didn't die in an accidental fall. And she sure as hell didn't jump off the Hidden Cove path. She was murdered by someone she was attempting to blackmail."

Hannah took a breath. "We're making some huge assumptions here."

He shrugged. "After what almost happened to you and Winston last night, I'm willing to take some very big leaps."

"If we're right, someone murdered Kaitlin because she had possession of compromising videos."

"The question is, who in this burg would have committed murder just to keep her quiet about an affair involving some frilly lingerie? Cross-dressing isn't that big a deal."

"Come on, Rafe. You want possibilities? How about some desperate assistant professor at Chamberlain who might have been afraid that his chance at tenure was about to go up in smoke because of those videos? Or try a minister at a local church who would lose his congregation if his taste for ladies' underwear became public knowledge. And then there's the crowd up at the institute. Arizona Snow has always been convinced that there are some very unsavory characters up there. Maybe she's right."

Rafe sank deeper into the leather seat. "You're right. A long list of possibilities."

"Then there's the Willis brothers' theory that the killer was someone from out of town. Which gives us an even longer list."

Rafe's dark brows met above his shades in a thoughtful frown. "Don't think so. Her decision to use her nuclear option, as Dell put it, was apparently an impulse. Her victim had to be someone she could reach on the spur of the moment that night. Not someone who had to be summoned from Portland or Seattle or Salem."

"Makes sense." Hannah pondered for a minute. "Okay, let's try this from another angle. Surely not everyone in Eclipse Bay is into ladies' lingerie. And not everyone here who is into women's underwear would commit murder to keep a blackmailer quiet."

"Your point?"

"All we need to do is find out who fits the profile, as the cops say. Someone who is into female undies and who would also be willing to kill to get his hands on the compromising videos."

"To do that we need to talk to someone who knows this town better than you and I do."

"Got a name in mind?"

Rafe's mouth curved in a humorless smile. "As a matter of fact, I do. Our dinner guest tonight."

chapter 18

Rafe rinsed the red radicchio leaves under running water and dropped them gently into the colander on top of the arugula and cilantro. Mentally he ran through his plans for the meal. Three carefully chosen ripe avocados sat in a bowl at the far end of the counter. He would cut them in half just before serving, spoon balsamic vinegar into the hollows and sprinkle them with some coarsely grated sea salt. The pasta would be a straightforward dish using olives and tomatoes and goat cheese.

When he finished rinsing the lettuce for the salad, he went to work on the hummus. He tossed a sizable quantity of cooked garbanzo beans into the food processor and added tahini, lemon juice, and a bit of garlic.

He snapped on the lid, flipped the switch, and thought about what Dell Sadler had said while he listened to the pleasant sound of garbanzos being pulverized. *Kaitlin had intended to use her nuclear option.*

A killer who had thought himself in the clear for the past eight years might have reason to worry now that the old gossip was being dredged up and rehashed all over town. What if someone remembered something important after all this time? What if someone put two and two together in a way that hadn't been done eight years ago? What if someone had seen something that night and belatedly realized that it was a clue?

A murderer who had struck once to keep his secret might be willing to strike again.

A cold feeling closed in on Rafe. The dread that he had been holding at bay all day broke through the dam, and he was suddenly dealing with a nightmarish river. The question he had not raised with Hannah, the one that had been plaguing him for hours, could no longer be avoided.

That question was horrifyingly simple: What if Winston had not been the main target last night? Maybe the attack on the dog had never been intended as a warning. Maybe the Schnauzer had been set out on the finger as bait to lure Hannah into danger. If she had arrived home as little as half an hour later, rescuing Winston would have put her in great jeopardy. The force of the incoming tide could have swept her feet out from under her, perhaps dashed her against the rocks.

He thought about how she had taken Winston into the caves because she had sensed someone watching her from the cliff path. What if the killer had been hanging around, watching to see if his plans were going to work out as he'd intended? What if he had waited on the cliff path with the intention of making certain that Hannah and Winston never made it back from the cove alive?

What if?

Rafe switched off the food processor and removed the lid. He could not afford to take any more chances, he thought as he scooped out the fragrant hummus. Tonight he would have to take drastic steps. He would never be able to sleep if he didn't.

At six-thirty that evening, he picked up the tray of hors d'oeuvres. Winston, who had been supervising the final kitchen preparations with an expression of mingled wistfulness and lust, got to his feet.

"Here you go, mutt." Rafe tossed him a slice of pita bread slathered in hummus. "Chef's privilege."

Winston gnawed happily on the tidbit as he hurried after Rafe. Together they crossed the hall toward the sunroom, where Hannah and Mitchell were sharing a glass of wine and the view of evening fog moving in over the bay.

Rafe glanced at the bowl of hummus and pita toast points arranged on the tray, double-checking the visual appeal of the hors d'oeuvres. The trickle of uneasiness he felt was disconcerting. He was usually confident of his cooking. He knew he had a keen sense of how to blend flavors into intriguing combinations and a flair for presentation. He had planned this meal with great care. He knew everything was perfect. It was the first time he had ever cooked for Mitchell, and he did not want any screwups.

Mitchell's low growl stopped him just as he was about to enter the room.

". . . Don't you worry. Rafe will do right by you," Mitchell said. "I'll see to it."

Rafe froze in the doorway. Winston stopped, too, cocking his head with an inquiring look.

"What the heck does that mean?" Hannah sounded baffled and more than a little wary. "Are you going to force him to give up his claim on this house?"

"Never could force that bullheaded boy to do anything he didn't want to do, and I'm pretty sure he won't give up Dreamscape. Seems to have his heart set on turning it into an inn and a restaurant."

"He certainly does." Hannah's voice was clipped.

"When a Madison's got his heart set on something," Mitchell warned with gruff gentleness, "it isn't easy persuading him to change course."

"That's what I've heard."

"He's got the cash to make it happen. Made himself a bundle in the market, you know." Mitchell sighed. "Always did have a head for business."

"Apparently." Hannah's tone was becoming grim.

"Barring a tsunami or an earthquake or a volcanic eruption that wipes out this section of the coast, I reckon Rafe will see his plans through." Mitchell paused. "Thing is, he's a lot like me when it comes to going after what he wants."

Hannah was quiet for a time. Rafe realized that his hands were clenched around the handles of the hors d'oeuvres tray. He could not seem to move through the doorway. He was waiting for something, but he was not sure what that something was.

"So what did you mean when you said you'd see to it that he would do right by me?" Hannah asked eventually.

"Lord above, woman, don't play dumb with me. There isn't any such thing as a dumb Harte, and we both know it. I'm talking about marriage, naturally."

"Marriage!" Hannah's voice rose to a shrill squeak. "Rafe and me?"

"Well, sure. What did you think I was talking about?"

"Are you out of your mind?"

"Hear me out, now, Hannah. I've been doing a lot of thinking about this, and I'm pretty sure I can swing it."

"Pretty sure? *Pretty sure?*"

"Okay, damn sure. Pardon my language. Not quite the

same thing as making him give up Dreamscape, of course. That would be a real case of hitting my head against a brick wall. But this fear of marriage that he's got, that's just a case of bad nerves."

"Nerves," Hannah repeated in a dazed voice.

"Right. He's convinced that Madison men have a bad time with marriage."

"Well, you do have a history of disastrous marriages in your clan," Hannah muttered. "And Rafe has already screwed up once."

"Okay, so he made one little mistake."

"Little?"

"These things happen."

"You ought to know," Hannah said much too sweetly. "How many times have you been married, Mr. Madison?"

"Don't go tagging Rafe with my lousy track record. I admit that for a long time after Claudia Banner took off with the assets of Harte-Madison, I didn't think real clearly when it came to women. Had a few problems."

"That's putting it mildly, from what I understand."

Mitchell made a rude sound. "Can't blame you for your opinion. You've been brought up to think the worst of me. I know that Sullivan has fed you a lot of wild stories over the years. What I'm trying to tell you is that Rafe and I are alike in a lot of ways but not in every way."

"If you say so."

"If that isn't just like a Harte," Mitchell said heatedly. "Throw a man's mistakes back in his face and don't bother to give him a chance to put things right. You got a lot in common with your granddad, young woman."

"I think we're straying from the point here."

"Look, that divorce wasn't Rafe's fault. Don't hold it against him. He learned from it."

"Uh-huh. From what I can gather, he learned that he doesn't want to get married again," Hannah said dryly.

"Exactly what I'm trying to tell you," Mitchell said quickly. "Like I said, I've been doing a lot of thinking, and I've figured out Rafe's problem. He's got some sort of phobia about marriage, see."

"You've concluded that he's afraid of marriage?" Hannah's voice was oddly weak.

"Right." Mitchell sounded pleased that she had grasped the point so readily. "The way some folks are scared of spiders or snakes."

"A charming analogy."

"I can sort of see how it happened," Mitchell continued earnestly. "I got to admit I didn't set a good example for Sinclair, and things trickled on down to Rafe. But I figure I can get him past it. Figure I owe him that much, since it was me who was responsible for this phobia thing in the first place."

"How do you intend to do that?" Hannah's voice was stronger now, infused with morbid curiosity. "Get out your shotgun and march him to the altar?"

Rafe felt as though he'd been turned into a block of solid marble.

"Is that what you want?" Mitchell asked ingenuously.

"Good grief, *no*. Of course not."

Rafe winced. Did she have to sound so positively negative about the idea?

"It might take a little push from me," Mitchell allowed reflectively. "When it comes to phobias, sometimes you've got to force folks to face up to 'em."

"You just told me that force didn't work well with Rafe."

"I'm thinking more in terms of applying a little pressure in the right spots."

"As it happens," Hannah said, sweet, sharp steel in

every syllable, "I'm in the business of getting people married, and I can tell you that making a marriage work is hard enough when both parties go into it enthusiastically. Any marriage forged by outside pressure would be doomed before the vows even got said."

"You're too young to be so pessimistic," Mitchell complained.

"Mitchell, I'm sure you mean well, but the very last thing I want to do is marry a man who doesn't want to get married. Are we clear on that?"

"Now don't let Rafe's bad nerves put you off the notion," Mitchell replied. "It's true the Madison men have a lousy track record when it comes to marriage, but the right woman could change all that."

"Why do you want to change it?" Hannah demanded, thoroughly exasperated now. "What is this all about, anyway? Why do you want Rafe and me to get married?"

Still stuck in the doorway, Rafe waited for the other shoe to drop.

"Because it's the right thing to do," Mitchell snapped, evidently out of patience himself. "It's the only way to stop people from talking."

"Since when did you start worrying about local gossip?" Hannah asked.

"There's gossip and there's gossip," Mitchell declared. "Everyone in town is saying he's carrying on with you because he wants to get his hands on the other half of this place. That's a damned lie. Reminds me of the talk that went around town the night Kaitlin Sadler died. All those rumors about how he'd seduced you just to get himself an alibi. Pure garbage."

"They certainly were," Hannah said quietly.

"Hell, I know that." Mitchell's voice rang with conviction. "Rafe had nothing to do with that poor girl's death. Madison men got problems when it comes to dealing with the opposite sex, but no Madison man has ever laid a hand on a woman in anger. No man in this family would ever assault a female, by God. And no Madison would seduce an innocent girl like you to cover his own tracks, and that's a fact."

A loud silence gripped the sunroom.

"I know that," Hannah said quietly.

Rafe remembered to take a breath.

"I'm not saying Rafe might not have argued with Kaitlin Sadler," Mitchell continued. "He's a Madison. He's got a temper. But if he had been with Kaitlin that night and if there had been some terrible accident, he'd have gone for help and then he'd have told the flat-out truth about what happened."

"I know that, too," Hannah said again. Her voice was very even. "I'm a Harte, remember? Lord knows that we're well aware that Madisons have their faults, but no one in my family has ever accused anyone in your clan of lying."

"Damn right," Mitchell agreed.

Rafe glanced down at the tray of hummus and pita bread points he held. Mitchell had believed him all those years ago. The old man disapproved of just about everything he'd ever done in his life, but he had never doubted Rafe's word about what had happened the night Kaitlin Sadler died.

Rafe discovered that he could move again. He walked into the sunroom and set the tray down on a table. He noticed that Hannah's cheeks were flushed. She avoided his eyes. He knew she was wondering how much of the conversation he had overheard.

"The hummus looks wonderful," she said a little too brightly.

"Thanks." Rafe picked up the small glass pitcher of very good, very expensive olive oil that sat on the tray.

He poured a liberal stream of the rich, fruity oil over the hummus.

"What's that?" Mitchell studied the hummus with curiosity. "Some kinda bean dip?"

"Yeah," Rafe said. "Some kind of bean dip." He set down the pitcher of olive oil. He pulled the bottle of Chardonnay out of the ice bucket and poured himself a glass. "Glad you left some for me. I need it."

Hannah and Mitchell gazed at him as though he were charming a snake. Both were uneasy. Neither wanted to make any sudden moves. He took his time, savoring the perfect balance of oak and fruit and the elegant finish of the wine.

When he was done, he set the glass down on the table very deliberately and looked at Hannah and Mitchell.

"I hear that wine is good for the nerves," he said.

Two hours later, Mitchell put down his fork with a sigh of satisfaction. Just a few slivers of buttery pastry was all that remained of the kiwi tart.

"Where the hell did you learn to cook?" he asked Rafe. "Sure didn't get it from me. The best I can do is throw a salmon steak on the grill."

"Took some classes," Rafe said. "But mostly I just spend a lot of time fooling around in the kitchen."

"Well, if this inn of yours doesn't work out, it won't be because the food is bad."

Rafe caught Hannah's attention. He knew that they were both aware of what had just happened. Mitchell had bestowed his approval, not only on the food but on the entire inn project. She was probably thinking that she had just lost a lot of ground in her battle to claim his half of the inn. She was right.

"I need to talk to you about something important, Mitchell." Rafe settled back in his chair and contemplated his grandfather across the remains of the meal. "Last night someone tried to drown Hannah's dog."

Mitchell blinked in astonishment. Then he looked at Winston, who was dozing peacefully on the rug beneath the table. "Who the hell would do a thing like that?"

"I don't know," Rafe admitted. "But I intend to find out."

"What's going on here?" Mitchell demanded.

Nobody ever accused Mitchell of being slow, Rafe thought. "I don't know that, either, but we've concluded that it might be connected to what happened to Kaitlin Sadler."

Mitchell gazed at him for a very long time. "You're serious, aren't you?"

"Very. There's some stuff I need to tell you before this conversation goes any further." Rafe gave Mitchell a brief summary of events, including the talk with Dell Sadler.

When he had finished, Mitchell whistled softly. "You realize what you're saying?"

"That it's possible Kaitlin Sadler really was killed, just as Dell Sadler has always believed. And that the reason she was murdered was because she tried to blackmail someone here in Eclipse Bay."

"Well, shoot and damn." Mitchell sounded thoughtful now. "Yates was so damn sure it was an accident."

"Maybe not quite so certain as he let everyone think," Rafe said. "In addition to asking a lot of questions, he did a thorough search of Kaitlin's house and car that night. He must have had a few suspicions."

Mitchell shrugged. "Yates was a good cop in his time."

Hannah sipped coffee from a small cup. She regarded Mitchell very steadily. "We need a little help."

"From me? Now, see here, just what are you two thinking of doing?"

"We're going to try to find out who Kaitlin was blackmailing," Rafe said.

Mitchell frowned. "You want my advice? Don't go poking a stick in a hole. There might be a real nasty varmint inside."

"The problem," Rafe said deliberately, "is that the varmint has already crawled out of the hole. I don't think Winston was the real target last night. I have a hunch that whoever put him out there on that finger may have intended for Hannah to get caught by the incoming tide."

Hannah snapped her head around in surprise. "Rafe, what are you saying? You never told me you thought that someone had tried to—" She broke off.

"I'm not sure that someone did try to hurt you last night. Winston may have been just a warning. But I'm not taking any chances."

"What do you mean?"

"Never mind. We'll deal with that later."

"Deal with what later?" She slammed her coffee cup down onto the saucer. "Now just one damn minute. I want an explanation."

Rafe met Mitchell's gaze and talked over the top of Hannah's simmering words. "If I said to you ladies' underwear in sizes big enough to fit a man, big high heels, Kaitlin Sadler, and some compromising videotapes that were bad enough to serve as blackmail material, what would you say?"

Mitchell's face worked. For a moment Rafe thought that he was going to explode with outrage. But abruptly the ire metamorphosed into something else. Curiosity, or reluctant interest, Rafe decided.

"We're talking eight years ago, aren't we?" Mitchell said thoughtfully.

Rafe watched him. "One way or another, you've been

connected to this town for more than fifty years. Any names come to mind?"

"No," Mitchell said immediately. "But that's no big surprise. I never paid much attention to other people's sex lives. The only one that ever interested me was my own." He paused. "But there was someone who did keep track of that kind of thing, along with every other damn secret in this town."

Hannah groaned. "I hope you're not going to tell us that person was Arizona Snow. It's hopeless trying to get anything out of her. She might know some secrets, but she filters them all through her conspiracy theories."

"Wasn't thinking of Arizona," Mitchell said. "I was talking about Ed Bolton. Owned the *Eclipse Bay Journal* for more than forty years until he sold out to Jed Steadman. Ed knew everything about everyone in this town."

Disappointment coursed through Rafe. "I heard that Ed Bolton died four or five years ago."

"He did," Mitchell said in an oddly neutral voice. "Heart attack. But his widow, Bev, is still around. Lives in Portland now."

"Do you think that Bev Bolton would know the secrets that Ed knew?" Hannah asked.

Mitchell nodded slowly. "Bev and Ed were together for a long time. Fine woman. Good marriage, from all accounts. Yeah, I reckon she'd know what Ed knew."

Somewhere in the back of Rafe's brain something went *click*.

"How do you know so much about Bev Bolton's marriage?" he asked Mitchell.

"Bev and I get together once in a while," Mitchell said very casually. "Talk over old times. You know how it is."

Rafe flopped back in his chair. "Damn. How long have you and Bev Bolton been having an affair?"

Mitchell's brows bunched and quivered in annoyance. "See here, my private life is none of your business."

"Right. Sure. Your business."

"Bev and I go back a long ways." Mitchell paused. "A couple of years after Ed died, I asked her to marry me."

Rafe was astounded. "No kidding? What happened?"

"Turned me down flat," Mitchell admitted.

"I see." Rafe said.

"As I was saying," Mitchell went on, "Bev and I get together whenever I go to Portland."

"I understand." Rafe recalled the conversation with Gabe concerning Mitchell's frequent trips to Portland. "And you've found a reason to go nearly every week for the past ten months."

"What the hell business is it of yours? A man's got a right to his personal life."

Rafe started to smile. The smile turned into a grin before he could control it, and then, without warning, he was laughing so hard he feared he might fall off his chair.

Winston roused himself to thrust his nose inquiringly into Rafe's hand. Rafe scratched him behind the ears and laughed even harder.

Hannah and Mitchell frowned.

"What's so funny?" Hannah asked with a bewildered expression.

Mitchell glowered. "If there's a joke here, you'd better share it."

"The joke is on Gabe and me," Rafe said, subduing the laughter to a wide grin. "We thought all those trips to Portland you've been taking for the past year were to get medical treatment. We were afraid you had some terrible, lingering disease you were hiding from us."

"Huh." Mitchell blinked, and then his eyes gleamed with secret amusement. "One of those trips last year was to see a doctor. But it wasn't because I had come down with anything serious."

"Just a checkup?" Rafe asked.

"You might say that," Mitchell said with a benign smile. "Happy to tell you that everything is in pretty fair working order, considering the mileage I've put on this body."

"Glad to hear it." Rafe realized he felt a lot lighter.

"Unless you do me in with your cooking," Mitchell said, "Dr. Reed tells me I'm likely to be around to pester the rest of you for quite a while yet. Now, then, as I was saying before I was so rudely interrupted, I was planning to go to Portland at the end of the week. No reason I can't drive in with Bryce in the morning instead."

Bryce arrived to collect Mitchell shortly after ten that night. Hannah stood on the front porch with Rafe and Winston, her arms folded, and watched the big SUV lumber off down the drive. It turned left onto the road, and the headlights disappeared into the night.

She braced herself. She had managed to relax midway through the meal, and later when the conversation had turned to the subject of Kaitlin Sadler's death, she had almost forgotten the awkward moments she'd experienced earlier in the evening. But now that she was alone again with Rafe, she could feel the uneasiness stealing back over her.

The unsettling question returned in a rush. Just how much had Rafe overheard of Mitchell's vow to make his grandson do right by her?

"Well, I'd call the evening a resounding success," she

said briskly. She turned away and walked back toward the open front door. "Mitchell liked your cooking, and he seems genuinely interested in helping us figure out what's going on around here. Can't ask for more than that."

"As a matter of fact," Rafe said, "there is one more thing."

"You want help with the dishes?" She paused in the doorway. "No problem."

He leaned against the railing and studied her in the yellow glow of the porch lights. "Thanks. I'll take you up on that. But I wasn't referring to the dishes. I've been doing some thinking."

She realized that her heart was beating much too quickly. Maybe she shouldn't have had that cup of strong coffee after dinner. "What exactly have you been thinking about?"

"I said earlier that I think there's a possibility that whoever stuck Winston out on the rock last night was after you, not your dog."

She felt the world drop away from beneath her feet. "Are you saying that you think someone actually tried to kill me last night?"

"I don't know. Maybe he just hoped there would be a convenient accident. All I know for sure is that I don't think we should take any chances."

She chilled. "You're leaping to a very wild conclusion, Rafe."

He straightened away from the railing and crossed the porch to stand in front of her. He gripped her shoulders with both hands. "Listen, I didn't want to scare you like this, but I couldn't come up with any other way to convince you."

"Convince me of what?"

"That you can't stay alone in your folks' house any longer."

"I'll think about it," she said.

"I'm trying to be real rational and logical here. The way I see it, we've got two options. You and Winston can move in with me here or else I can pack a bag and settle in at your place. Take your pick. Either one is fine by me, but I think you'd be more comfortable here. There's more space. Hell, you can have the entire third floor to yourself if that's what you want."

For a split second she was on the verge of a very primitive sense of panic. It was one thing to spend the occasional night together while they charted their way through uncertain waters in a relationship that might easily founder. It was something else again to actually pack up and move in here with him. She wasn't sure just what the nature of that difference was, but she knew that it was important. She tried to stall while she sorted out the implications.

"People will talk," she said. It was weak. She knew it was weak even before she saw his brows lift.

"People are already talking," he said dryly. "I doubt if the gossip will get any more exciting if you move in here. You can always say that you're just trying to stake your claim to your half of Dreamscape."

It was a perfectly reasonable, eminently pragmatic suggestion she told herself. And there were more bathrooms and more space here. What if someone really had intended for her to drown last night? And she did own half of this place.

"Okay," she said, trying to sound very cool. "I'll go back to the house and pack my things. But I think we need some ground rules here."

"I was afraid you'd say something like that. Let me

guess what you mean by ground rules. Separate bedrooms, right?"

"I think it would be best," she said very primly. "This thing is getting very complicated."

"And sharing a bedroom with me on a routine basis makes it even more complicated?"

She narrowed her eyes. "An occasional night of . . . of—"

"Wild passion?" he offered helpfully.

She stiffened. "As I was saying, an occasional night together is one thing. But sharing a bedroom feels more like . . . like—"

"Like a commitment?" he supplied with an air of amusement.

"Yes," she shot back, goaded. "Like a commitment. Which, I might add, neither of us has made."

"The subject has not arisen."

"That's not the point." She could hear the waspish edge in her own voice. "If I'm going to stay here, it will be on my terms, and that means separate bedrooms."

He moved his hand in a suspiciously careless manner. "Whatever you say. I'll drive you back to your place and give you a hand with the packing."

"That's not necessary."

"It's the least I can do if you're going to help me with the dishes."

Suspicion flickered briefly. He was being entirely too cooperative, she thought. But when she searched his gaze she saw nothing but mocking amusement.

Much later that night she awoke quite suddenly, aware that something was wrong. She stared at the ceiling for a while before she realized that she could not feel Winston's familiar warmth at her feet.

There was a soft whine in the darkness. Alarm zapped

through her. She sat straight up in bed and switched on the light.

Winston was sitting in front of the bedroom door. He looked impatient to get out.

"Oh, damn." She shoved aside the covers, grabbed her robe, and hurried toward the door. "What is it? Is there someone out there watching us here at Dreamscape? I thought we left that problem behind when we moved out of the cottage."

Winston scratched politely at the base of the door. She flung it open for him. He trotted out into the unlit hall. She followed quickly.

On the second floor landing she paused. "We should wake Rafe. He'll want to be involved in this, whatever it is."

Winston ignored her. He trotted down the next flight of stairs to the first floor and disappeared. Hannah peered over the railing to look for him and saw a glow coming from the kitchen. Rafe was already awake.

She hurried downstairs, crossed the hall, and walked into the kitchen. She stopped when she saw Rafe standing in front of the counter with a knife in his hand. He had taken the time to pull on a pair of jeans, but that was all. His sleek shoulders gleamed in the kitchen light. His bare feet looked strong and supple and very sexy.

There was a chunk of leftover feta cheese on the plate that sat on the drainboard. Winston was positioned at Rafe's feet, looking expectant.

Hannah came to a halt in the doorway. "What's going on here?"

"Couldn't sleep," Rafe said. He dropped a bit of the cheese into Winston's waiting jaws. "Came down here to get a bite to eat." He held up the knife. "Want some?"

"No, thanks." She was torn between the urge to let him drop a bite of cheese into her mouth and the knowledge that if she had any sense she would hurry back upstairs. As was so often the case when she was caught between two equally opposing forces, she did nothing. "I was afraid that Winston had heard a prowler outside."

"Nope." Rafe ate some more cheese. "He must have heard me come downstairs a few minutes ago. How about you? Sleeping okay up there on the third floor?"

"I was sleeping just fine until Winston decided to follow you down here."

Rafe studied her with an unreadable expression as he munched cheese. "Hey, that's just great. Lot of people don't sleep well in a strange environment, you know? Sometimes they just lay there staring at the ceiling and think about things."

"Things?"

"Yeah." He sliced off another bit of cheese. "Things."

"Right. Things." The dangerously enigmatic shimmer in his eyes was starting to worry her. It was definitely time to retreat, she decided. She gripped the lapels of her robe and took a step back. "Well, as long as everything is okay down here, I'll go back to bed."

"You ever do that, Hannah? Just lie in bed and think about things?"

She hesitated. "Sometimes."

"I've been doing it a lot lately."

"Is that so?"

He put some cheese on a cracker and then popped the whole morsel into his mouth. "Aren't you going to ask me what kind of things I think about?"

She took another wary step back, not trusting his odd mood. "None of my business," she said crisply.

"Don't be so sure of that. Tonight, for instance, one of the things I was thinking about was who, besides Bev Bolton, might be able to give us a few insights into the

bedroom lives of our friends and neighbors here in
Eclipse Bay. I had an idea."

She folded her arms and propped one shoulder against
the doorjamb. "Don't tell me one of your buddies is the
local Peeping Tom?"

"He would be highly offended at the suggestion. I always had the impression that he sees himself as a lone
crusader for freedom, privacy, and the First Amendment."

"I assume we are not talking about the head of the
public library."

"Nope." Rafe ate more cheese. "I'm going to talk to
my potential informant tomorrow while Mitchell is in
Portland."

"I'm probably going to regret this, but I want to be
there when you talk to this person." She paused deli-
cately. "Who is it we're going to see?"

"Virgil Nash."

She winced. "I don't suppose there's any way we can
talk to him without someone finding out."

"Doubt it. Still want to come with me?"

She decided to be philosophical about the situation.
"Ah, well. It's not as if I have anything but a few tattered threads left of my reputation here in Eclipse Bay,
anyway. What do I care if the whole town finds out that
I was seen entering the local porn dealer's shop with
you?"

"That's the spirit," Rafe said with enthusiasm. "Virgil's Adult Books and Video Arcade is just the kind of
place folks would expect me to take a nice girl like you."

"Nobody ever said you didn't know how to show a
lady a good time." She turned away to seek the safety
of the third floor.

"I was thinking about something else besides Virgil
Nash," Rafe continued in a conversational tone. "I also
thought a lot about phobias."

Her mouth went dry. So he had overheard her awkward conversation with Mitchell. An ominous sensation rolled through her. She turned very slowly in the doorway to face him.

"I was afraid of that," she said.

"You know, my grandfather may be right. Perhaps the best way to get over a phobia is to confront it head-on. Just do it, you know?"

She cleared her throat. "I'm no expert on phobias, but it seems to me that that approach would be likely to trigger severe panic attacks."

"Hadn't thought of that."

"I suggest you do think about it. Now, if you'll excuse me, I'm going back to bed."

"Hannah?"

She looked back unwillingly. "Now what?"

"If I'm the one with the phobia, how come you're the one who looks panicked?"

"Good night, Rafe." She fled toward the stairs.

Winston did not return to the third-floor bedroom right away. When he finally did come back upstairs, his fur was cool and damp. Hannah realized that Rafe had taken him outside for a late-night walk.

"What did you two talk about out there?" she whispered.

Winston did not reply. He settled into position at the foot of the bed and promptly went to sleep.

"Guys always stick together."

She tried to go back to sleep. It was hard work. For a long time, she just stared at the ceiling and thought about things.

chapter 19

Virgil's Adult Books and Video Arcade was located less than a hundred feet beyond the official boundary of the town of Eclipse Bay. When he had established his business fifteen years earlier, Virgil had been careful to select a location that was just outside the reach of local reformers, civic activists, and members of the town council who saw running the local porn store out of town as a sure ticket to reelection.

"It's the old law of real estate," Virgil had once explained to Rafe. "Location, location, location."

While convenience had been of paramount importance, Virgil had also realized that most of his clientele would also appreciate a measure of privacy while they made their purchases. With the aim of providing customers with that treasured commodity, he had placed the small parking lot behind the shop rather than in front, where familiar vehicles might be noted by neighbors, business acquaintances, and parents who happened to drive past.

"I can't believe I'm taking my dog into a place like

this." Hannah scowled at the sign over the shop's rear entrance as she snapped the leash onto Winston's collar. "I can only hope that he doesn't realize what sort of business this is."

Rafe took the keys out of the ignition and unbuckled his seat belt. "It was your idea to bring Winston along."

"I refuse to leave him home alone until we find out who tried to murder him." Hannah glanced swiftly around the nearly empty parking lot. "Thank goodness there aren't too many customers here at the moment."

"There aren't *any* other customers here," Rafe said. "That van in the corner belongs to Virgil."

"Oh. Hard to see how he stays in business. It's two o'clock in the afternoon and there's no one here."

Rafe cracked open his door. "Virgil doesn't get busy until after dark."

"How do you know that?"

"Everyone knows that." He got out of the car and closed the door very quickly before she could think of any more questions.

Hannah opened her own door and climbed out warily. "All right, Winston, let's go. But whatever you do, don't touch anything. Understand?"

Winston sprang lightly out of the car. And immediately paused to sniff curiously at a small plastic wrapper that lay on the pavement.

Hannah glanced down to see what had caught his interest. She gave a half-strangled shriek of dismay. "Good grief, that looks like a used condom. Didn't you listen to me, Winston? I said, *don't touch anything.*"

Rafe watched her drag Winston away from his investigations. "Are you two going to fool around out here all afternoon?" He opened the rear door of the shop. "We've got business to do."

Hannah gave him a ferocious glare. She stalked toward him with Winston in tow. "You certainly seem to know your way around the premises."

"Spent some extremely educational afternoons here when I was a young man."

"I'll bet."

"Virgil always was a pioneer in the field of sex ed."

"Sex ed, my left pinkie. Virgil sells dirty books and movies. I refuse to dignify his profession by referring to him as an instructor in the field of sex education."

"Suit yourself." Rafe led the way into the shop. "But I think you'll like Virgil once you get to know him."

"I doubt if I'll be coming back here much in the future," she said austerely. She followed him into the shop and let the door slam shut with a reverberating bang.

"Okay, be that way," Rafe said.

She did not dignify that with a response. Her attention was on Winston, who was busily sniffing around a display of what looked like small bottles of whipped cream. Rafe glanced at the sign above the display. PASSION CREAM. FOUR EROTIC FLAVORS.

Winston appeared to be particularly fascinated with the Cherry Pie flavor.

"Winston, leave that alone."

Rafe had a feeling that Hannah was going to be saying that a lot while they were in the shop.

"Rafe." The elegantly modulated voice emanated from the far side of the shop. "Heard you were back in town. Good to see you again."

Rafe turned around and greeted the thin, slightly built man seated in the large wing chair near the window. "Hello, Virgil. Been a while."

"It has indeed." Virgil put down the book he had been reading and stood up. "And judging from the latest gossip, I assume that the charming lady at your side is Hannah Harte?"

"Hannah, meet Virgil."

Hannah managed a smooth, brittle smile. She did not give Virgil her hand to shake. Instead she managed to make it appear as though she had all she could do to hang on to Winston's leash and her purse at the same time.

"You haven't changed a bit, Virgil," Rafe said. "I think I recognize that vest."

Virgil's gray eyes twinkled a little behind the lenses of his reading glasses. He glanced down the front of the frayed green sweater vest that he wore over a plaid shirt. "You may be right. Can't even recall when I got this. Probably a birthday gift from some dead relative whose name I have apparently forgotten. Where does the time go, eh?"

There was an oddly ageless quality about Virgil. His background was as cloaked in mystery as Arizona Snow's. No one knew where he had come from or what he had done before he set up the porn shop just outside the town limits. With his gaunt frame, neat silver goatee, slightly stooped shoulders, and thick glasses, he had the look of an absentminded professor who had spent too much time indoors with his books.

The scholarly impression was not far off the mark, Rafe thought. Somewhere along the line Nash had acquired a fine classical education. Virgil's personal library, a sophisticated collection of history, literature, and philosophy, was extensive. Rafe knew that because he had spent a lot of time in it.

Virgil was not anyone's idea of a porn dealer, but he considered himself a professional in a sadly underappreciated line of work. He had once told Rafe that he had dedicated himself to the business of selling what he liked to call erotica years ago and had never wavered from his career choice.

Virgil glanced from Rafe to Hannah and back again. His silver brows rose inquiringly. "I am delighted that the two of you found time to pay me a visit. I've heard all about your plans for an inn and a restaurant out there at Dreamscape. I think it's a wonderful idea."

"Those plans have not been finalized," Hannah said brusquely.

"I'm sure everything will work out." Virgil smiled at Rafe. "Heard you did all right for yourself."

"Didn't go to jail," Rafe said.

"Had a hunch you would turn out okay."

"I understand Rafe spent a lot of time here in the old days," Hannah offered.

"Yes, indeed," Virgil said with paternalistic pride. "I sold him his first condom. Taught him how to use it properly, too, before he left the store."

"I see."

Rafe winced. "Now, Hannah, it wasn't like I came in here every week. Besides, none of the guys wanted to risk buying condoms at the local drugstore. The word would have been all over town by nightfall. Here at Virgil's there was a lot more privacy."

Hannah raised her eyes to the ceiling. "I'd rather not hear too many details about your past, thank you very much."

Virgil chuckled. "Looks like your aunt Isabel was right all along. The two of you were obviously meant for each other."

Hannah stared at him. "You knew Aunt Isabel?"

"Yes, indeed. We had some mutual interests."

"I find that difficult to believe."

Virgil arched a brow. "Did you know that she collected eighteenth-century erotica?"

"Uh, no." Hannah cleared her throat. "She never mentioned it."

"Yes, indeed. I helped her build her collection. I have some excellent contacts in the rare book business, you see. I'm sure you'll run into Isabel's old books and prints when you two start going through her things at Dreamscape. Whatever you do, don't toss or sell any of those books and things until you check with me. Some of those volumes are worth several thousand dollars."

"Good grief," Hannah said weakly. "I'm suddenly getting a whole new picture of my aunt."

Rafe tried not to laugh. It wasn't easy. The bewildered, bemused expression on Hannah's face was priceless.

Virgil crouched and held his hand out to Winston. "Lovely dog."

Hannah frowned as Winston trotted forward to sniff politely. When the dog appeared satisfied, she hesitated and then said, "Thank you."

She still sounded stiff, but Rafe could tell she was softening. Virgil put his hand in the small of his back and straightened with great care.

"Arthritis," he explained. "Or the old war wound. I can never tell the difference."

"Which war?" Hannah asked warily.

"Does it matter? They're all the same, aren't they? At least, they all look the same when you're standing in the middle of one." He looked at Rafe. "What can I do for you? Something tells me that the two of you are not here to purchase the latest issue of *Fetish* magazine or to rent *Alice Does Wonderland.*"

Rafe leaned back against a counter stocked with rainbow-colored plastic dildos arranged in order of size. He shoved his hands into his front pockets and plunged straight into the tale.

"This is about what happened the night Kaitlin Sadler died," he said. "Hannah and I have some reason to think that her death might not have been an accident."

Virgil nodded somberly. "Yes, of course."

Hannah shot him a quick, frowning glance. "You don't look surprised, Mr. Nash."

"Why should I be surprised? I've heard the rumors."

"Exactly what rumors have you heard?" Rafe asked.

Virgil raised his thin shoulders in a small shrug. "Everyone knows that the two of you went to see Dell Sadler yesterday. Given his history with you, Rafe, there could be only one reason why the pair of you would sit down and talk after all this time."

"Okay," Rafe said, "I'll cut to the chase. A few things have happened lately that make us think that someone doesn't want the old investigation reopened."

Virgil said nothing. He just waited.

"We've picked up some indications," Hannah added, "that Kaitlin Sadler may have been blackmailing someone in town. If it's true, it might mean that same someone killed her to silence her."

Glittering curiosity flared without warning in Virgil's gaze. "You don't say."

"We don't have anything solid to go on yet," Rafe said. "But it looks like the blackmail material might have had something to do with someone's sex life."

"It often does." Virgil paused. "But in this day and age, it would have to be a particularly interesting sex life to be worth blackmail payments or murder."

"That's why we came to you," Rafe said. "Know any men in town who like to wear ladies' underwear?"

"At least half a dozen names come to mind," Virgil said without missing a beat. "If that's all you've got, you'll be at this investigation for a very long time."

"You're kidding," Hannah said. "You know half a dozen men in Eclipse Bay who have a penchant for female underwear?"

"The fetish for women's undergarments is not all that

rare or unusual." Virgil adopted a professional tone as he warmed to his lecture. "It is generally considered a harmless quirk, as these things go. Indeed, the history of prominent men dressing in lingerie goes back for centuries. There have been kings, generals, presidents, statesmen—"

"But of the six men here in Eclipse Bay who like to wear lingerie which one would be seriously horrified if the news got around?" Rafe asked before Virgil could get sidetracked by his professional interest.

"I imagine that they would all be embarrassed, to varying degrees."

Hannah looked at him. "Think any of them would be so humiliated that he would pay blackmail or kill to keep the secret?"

Virgil stroked his goatee while he pondered that. In the end, he shook his head decisively. "Frankly, I don't see any of them in the role of murderer. But one never knows, does one?"

"Six men," Rafe repeated.

"Those are just the ones who come to mind immediately because I have had some contact with them over the years," Virgil said. "There are no doubt several others who don't shop at my store."

Hannah sighed. "It's hopeless. Sounds like we can't even get a complete list, let alone verify the whereabouts of all the men on it for the night Kaitlin died."

"You don't need to find all of them," Virgil pointed out. "Just the ones who knew Kaitlin intimately."

"From what I've heard, that would still be a mighty long list." Hannah shot Rafe a dark glare.

"Don't look at me," Rafe said calmly. "I prefer lingerie on ladies."

"And he is the only suspect who had an ironclad alibi that night," Virgil reminded her. "Thanks to you."

"I know." Hannah scowled. "Still, there must be some way to narrow the list."

"For starters, I imagine that you can eliminate any man who wasn't reasonably affluent at the time," Virgil said. "After all, no point blackmailing someone who can't afford to pay."

Rafe was intrigued. "You're right. That might cut the list down a little."

Hannah frowned. "If he was rich enough to pay blackmail, chances are he would have been wealthy enough to be invited to the political reception up at the institute that night. But if he was there, he's also got a solid alibi."

"I'm not so sure about that," Rafe said slowly. "The institute was crowded that evening. Everyone who was anyone in Eclipse Bay was there. Someone could have slipped away long enough to murder Kaitlin and then returned to the reception with no one the wiser."

"I don't see how you could possibly ascertain that information," Virgil said quietly.

Rafe glanced at Hannah. He knew they were both thinking the same thing.

"There just may be a way to do that," he told Virgil.

"Indeed?" Virgil looked intrigued. "Fascinating. You do understand that under normal circumstances I would not even consider providing you with this list. But given what you say may have been an attempt on your life, Ms. Harte, I will try to help. There is just one thing I would like for you both to keep in mind."

"What's that?" Rafe asked.

"When it comes to blackmail," Virgil said very seriously, "there are sometimes others besides the victim who have a motive to kill the blackmailer."

Hannah's brows snapped together. "Such as?"

"Such as anyone who has a great deal invested in the victim," Virgil said.

Rafe looked at him. "Hell, do you think maybe we should be looking at all the *wives* of these guys you know who like to run around in lacy unmentionables?"

"Never forget the old saying about the female of the species being just as deadly as the male. The wife of a prominent, wealthy, or powerful man who could be brought low by blackmail would certainly have reason to get rid of a potential threat to her future income and position."

They all pondered that for a moment. Then Virgil turned away and walked to the counter. He picked up a pen and started to write names down on a sheet of yellow paper.

Hannah moved closer to Rafe and lowered her voice. "Are you thinking what I'm thinking about how to figure out who might have left the reception and returned between midnight and two?"

"A.Z.'s logbooks."

"Yes." Hannah watched Virgil. "You know her better than I do. Think she would let us look at them?"

"I might be able to talk her into it."

"But, Rafe, even if we come up with a good suspect, what can we do with the information? Officially there was no murder, and we don't have anything that resembles proof."

"We'll work on that part after we get the good suspect."

They stood in silence for a while, waiting for Virgil to finish his list. After a time Rafe got restless. He wandered over to a pile of padded leather handcuffs. He picked up one and examined the Velcro fastener.

Hannah gave him the same sort of look she had given Winston when he tried to investigate the condom wrapper out in the parking lot.

"Don't even think about it," she said.

• • •

Mitchell settled into the overstuffed easy chair with a familiar sense of contentment. The chair had been new and a little stiff a year ago when he had first started visiting Bev on a regular basis. But he had spent a lot of time in it during the past months, and the leather upholstery had shaped itself to his body. It was comfortable and welcoming. Sort of like Bev herself, he thought.

But there was a lot more to Bev than warmth and comfort. There was stimulation, both mental and physical. He loved to argue with her. Loved to play cards with her. Loved to go for long walks along the river with her. She made him feel good in ways that no other woman ever had, not even in the wild years following the breakup of Harte-Madison when he'd chased the illusion of passion the way other men had chased wealth or fame, or adrenaline.

Bev walked into the living room with the coffee tray. He turned away from the view of the river to look at her. A deep pleasure reverberated somewhere inside. There was wisdom and warmth and laughter in her eyes. Her own personal standards were high, always had been. But unlike some folks he knew who had made it this far in life, himself included, she was not inclined to judge others harshly. She accepted people as they were.

A fine figure of a woman, he thought, watching her pour the coffee. Bev was a great believer in vitamins and exercise, and the results were obvious. There was a healthy, energetic aura about her. She had not magically escaped the common chronic problems that came with the years. Six months ago he'd noticed the bottle of blood pressure pills in the kitchen cupboard above her sink. There was another bottle of tablets for the relief of arthritis in her bathroom, the same brand his own doctor had prescribed for him. But Bev's natural optimism and zest for living subtracted years from the calendar.

She had always had an instinct for style. Today her silver hair was swept back from her forehead in a short, sophisticated bob. She wore a good-looking black-and-white pantsuit that accented her healthy figure. Little silver rings dangled from her ears.

She smiled and handed him a cup of coffee. "How are things going over there in Eclipse Bay? Are you and Rafe getting along okay?"

"As well as we ever did." Mitchell sipped the coffee. Just enough sugar and a splash of milk. Bev knew how he liked it. "Better, maybe. But he's still one stubborn, muleheaded son of a gun."

Bev took her seat and crossed her legs in a graceful, unconsciously feminine movement that sent a whisper of anticipation through him. A few months back, his doctor had written another prescription for him, one that worked hydraulic marvels. He and Bev had gotten a lot of use out of it lately.

"Sounds like a chip off the old block," Bev said.

"Why the hell does everyone keep saying that?"

"Probably because it's true."

He bristled a little. "Well, I'm working on seeing to it that Rafe doesn't make all the same mistakes I did."

Bev chuckled. "A worthy project. Good luck."

"Thanks. I'm gonna need it." He frowned. "He's carrying on with Hannah Harte."

Bev's brows rose in surprise. "Carrying on, as in having an affair with her?"

"That too. It's Isabel's fault. If she hadn't left that damn house to both of 'em none of this would have happened."

"What exactly has happened?"

"I just told you—they're sleeping together."

"Are you sure?"

"Hell, everyone in town knows it."

"Hmm." Bev tilted her head slightly to the side as she contemplated that information. "I wouldn't worry about it too much if I were you. Isabel was a very, very smart woman. She probably knew what she was doing when she drew up that will."

Mitchell grunted. "Maybe yes, maybe no. Either way, it all comes down to the same thing. Rafe's carrying on with Hannah, and her family hasn't got a clue. When Sullivan Harte finds out, he's gonna shit . . . uh, he's gonna blow his top."

"Rafe and Hannah aren't kids anymore. They're full-grown adults. They'll make their own decisions."

"Huh. Far as I'm concerned, Rafe's already made his, and he's by God gonna follow through if I have anything to say about it. Hannah's a nice young woman, even if she is a Harte. If he thinks he can fool around with her and then walk away, he's got another thing coming."

Bev peered at him with a mixture of amusement and curiosity. "Are you saying you feel Rafe ought to marry Hannah?"

Mitchell balanced the cup and saucer on the broad leather arm of the big chair. "Yep. That's exactly what I think."

"Since when did you become such a zealous believer in old-fashioned morality?"

"Since I started watching the two of 'em together. You ought to see the way he looks at her, Bev. Damn near painful."

"What about Hannah?"

"She looks at him the same way. Thing is, they're scared to death of each other."

"You think you can play Cupid?"

"Figure it's my responsibility to straighten things out." Mitchell looked at the river. "I put my son, Sinclair, through hell when he was a boy. Set a real bad example. Sure enough, he turned right around and did the same thing to Rafe and Gabe. I figure it's up to me to stop this cycle before it goes on to another generation."

"And you're going to do it by marrying Rafe off to Hannah?"

"If I can." Mitchell paused to take another swallow of coffee. "But before I can see about getting Rafe to the altar, I've got to help him and Hannah fix another little problem that's come up."

"What's that?"

Mitchell looked at her. "Rafe has convinced himself that someone may have tried to kill Hannah and her dog a couple of nights ago."

Bev's shock left her mouth hanging open for a few seconds.

"Are you serious?" she finally managed.

"On the surface, it looks like some bastard tried to drown her dog, but Rafe thinks it may have been an attempt to get Hannah, too. He's sure it's got some tie back to what happened to Kaitlin Sadler."

"But that's ridiculous," Bev sputtered. "Kaitlin's death was an accident. Everyone knows that. And if it had been something worse, heaven forbid, why would the killer make a move against Hannah now?"

"Ever since Rafe and Hannah returned to Eclipse Bay to sort out the business with Dreamscape, there's been talk. Some of it is about the fact that they're carrying on together, naturally. But some of it is about the past. Rafe and Hannah have started asking questions themselves, and now, what with the incident involving the mutt, they're beginning to dig a little deeper." Mitchell met her gaze. "To tell you the truth, I'm afraid they just might uncover some old bones that would probably be better off left buried."

"But Rafe, being Rafe, won't listen to your advice to leave well enough alone, is that it?"

Mitchell shrugged. "He never did listen."

"So you've decided to help him look into the matter?"

"That's about the size of it."

Bev studied him for a long moment. Then she gave him a knowing smile. "You're enjoying yourself, aren't you? I think you like the idea of playing Dr. Watson to Rafe's Sherlock Holmes."

"Be the first thing Rafe and I have done together since he was a kid." Mitchell was aware of an oddly wistful feeling. "We got along pretty good for a few years after he and Gabe came to live with me. But from the day Rafe hit his mid-teens, he and I locked horns. It's been a little better in the past few years, but it's like we're walking on eggshells. Doesn't take much for either one of us to set the other off. My fault, I reckon."

"Don't be too hard on yourself, Mitch. You did all right by your grandsons. Sinclair wasn't much of a father to his boys."

Mitchell gripped the mug hard. "That's because he had me for an example."

"The point is that after your son's death, you stepped in and did what you had to do. You stopped your running around—"

"Well—"

Bev chuckled. "All right, let's just say you cut way down on your running around. You paid attention to the job of raising Rafe and Gabe, and neither one of them has screwed up his life. I'd say you did okay."

Bev always had a way of making him feel better about things, Mitchell thought. She had a way of giving him a slightly different perspective.

"Let's get back to the reason you're here." Bev put her coffee aside and sat forward. "You say you want to help Rafe find out what really happened to the Sadler woman. But what if there isn't any conspiracy to uncover? What if Chief Yates was right about her death being an accident?"

Mitchell shook his head. "I started into this thinking that Rafe and Hannah were going off the deep end. But now I'm not so sure. Bev, you knew everything that Ed knew about the goings-on in Eclipse Bay, and Ed knew a hell of a lot. If I said that there's a possibility that Kaitlin Sadler might have been having an affair with someone who wanted to keep it a big, dark secret, do any names come to mind?"

"Kaitlin got involved with more than one married man." Bev made a face. "She was not very popular with the ladies of Eclipse Bay, I can tell you that."

"How about if I throw in some dirty movies and some female underwear in a man's size? Does that narrow the list a bit?"

Bev angled her chin. "Hmm," she said thoughtfully.

Mitchell waited.

"Unfortunately," Bev said slowly, "there is one name that does come to mind. Ed once told me about some rumors he'd heard shortly before Kaitlin's death. Naturally he ignored them. Ed was an old-fashioned kind of journalist. Unlike this modern bunch, he didn't believe in printing the details of people's sex lives on the front page of a family newspaper."

Mitchell could feel himself getting revved up. This investigating business was fun. He was starting to understand why Rafe was so eager to poke a stick into this particular varmint hole. "Can I have the name of this guy Ed didn't want to put on the front page?"

Bev hesitated. "I'll give it to you, but it won't do you any good. He has an ironclad alibi for that night."

"How do you know that?"

"Because I can vouch for his whereabouts that evening, as well as the whereabouts of most of the rest of the good, upstanding citizens of Eclipse Bay."

"Well, shoot and damn." Disgust replaced the anticipation Mitchell had been savoring. "Don't tell me you saw him at that reception up at the institute that night?"

"I'm afraid so," Bev replied. "Still want the name?"

"Sure." A thought struck Mitchell. "You never can tell. Maybe he ducked out long enough to murder the Sadler woman. In a crowd of that size, he might not have been missed for a while."

"Trust me, he would have been missed if he had vanished for any period of time longer than what it would take to go to the men's room," Bev said. "The name is Trevor Thornley. Soon to become Senator Thornley, if all goes according to plan."

Mitchell groaned. "Well, shoot and damn."

chapter 20

"Trevor Thornley? In lingerie and high heels?" Hannah sank back into the depths of the wicker chair. "There's an image I could have done without."

Rafe paced back across the solarium. "But it makes sense. Dell told us that Kaitlin had claimed that she was going to score big. None of the names on Virgil's list would qualify as big scores. She might have pried a few bucks out of some of them, but not enough to finance a fresh start outside of Eclipse Bay."

"But a politician with a bright future in front of him might have looked very tempting to her," Hannah said quietly.

"Sure would be embarrassing as all get out if Kaitlin actually had movies of him running around in ladies' undies," Mitchell said. "Thing like that would have cost him the election eight years ago. Seeing as how he was the conservative on the ticket and all."

Rafe continued his pacing. "Might have been worth murder to Thornley."

"Never did trust him," Mitchell said.

Rafe was almost amused. "Big deal. You've never trusted any politician in your life."

"It's a grand theory, gentlemen." Hannah picked up her wineglass. "But let's not get too carried away here. As Bev pointed out to Mitchell, Thornley is the one person who could not have disappeared from the reception without being missed that night."

Rafe came to a halt and rested a hand on the windowsill as he contemplated the steel-colored waters of the bay. "Remember what Virgil told us. In a blackmail case there are others besides the victim who have a motive to kill. Anyone with an investment in the person being blackmailed might be moved to do something drastic to stop the extortionist."

Hannah swirled the sauvignon blanc in her glass. "Are you suggesting Thornley's wife might have murdered Kaitlin?"

Rafe thought about it. "Marilyn Thornley is as dedicated to her husband's career as he is. A decade ago she had a reputation for getting what she wanted. Doubt that's changed much in the last few years."

"I won't ask how you know that," Hannah grumbled.

Rafe shrugged. "Don't give me that look. Marilyn never wanted me. She knew I wasn't headed for big things."

Hannah frowned. "So how do you know that she had a way of getting what she went after?"

It was Mitchell who answered. "He knows because for a while Marilyn wanted Gabe."

"Aha." Hannah pondered that fact. "Did she, uh, get him for a while?"

"You know, I never came right out and asked him," Mitchell said laconically. "But to tell you the truth, if they did have a fling, it wouldn't have meant much to him. The only thing he cared about in those days was reviving Madison Commercial. Still is, come to that. I swear, if that grandson of mine doesn't figure out that there's more to life than doing deals and making money, he's gonna wind up missing all the stuff that really matters."

Rafe shot him a narrow-eyed look. "Gabe resurrected Madison Commercial for you, Mitchell."

"You don't have to tell me that. I admit I steered him in that direction. But I never meant for him to make the damn company his entire life."

Rafe shrugged. "The company's his passion. What did you expect?"

"We all know what happens with a Madison once he's fixated on his great passion in life," Hannah murmured into her wine.

"You make it sound like Gabe doesn't have time for a wife, but that's not true," Mitchell continued. "The only reason he hasn't married is because he's got a problem with women."

Hannah was interested. "What kind of problem?"

"He expects them to work the same way his company works." Mitchell's voice dripped with disgust and frustration. "Don't know where he got the notion that women operate like an accounts receivable department or that you could treat one of 'em like a branch of the head office. Certainly not from me."

"We're getting a little off track here," Rafe said. "Why don't we get back to the problem at hand?"

Hannah straightened in her chair. "Right. Okay, let's see what we've got so far. We think that Trevor Thornley might have been Kaitlin's blackmail target. But we also know that he couldn't have killed her that night because he was the star of the institute reception. That leaves us with the extremely weak possibility that someone who didn't want Thornley compromised might have gone out to meet Kaitlin and silence her."

"Makes sense to me," Mitchell said. "What do we do next?"

Rafe turned the glass in his hands. "We talk to Arizona Snow. See if she'll let us look at her logbooks for that night."

"Let's just hope she wasn't home sick with the flu that evening," Hannah said.

"Thank you, Miss Optimism," Rafe growled.

"Well, to be honest, I keep wondering what we can do even if we do come up with a really terrific scenario for the murder of Kaitlin Sadler. It's not like we can hope to find any proof after all this time. Say that we're successful. What are our options?"

Rafe hesitated. It was Mitchell who sat forward, determined and eager.

"I'll tell you what you do," he said. "You blow the whole damn story wide open so there are no more secrets to be kept. You go to Jed Steadman down at the *Journal* and give him the facts. He always wanted to be a real investigative reporter. This is his big chance, and I'm betting he'll take it. If he runs with it, you can pretty much guarantee that every paper in the state will start digging into the Sadler woman's death."

"He's right," Rafe said. "Jed might not find hard proof, but the entire Thornley camp will be on the defensive. Hell, the lingerie rumors alone will be enough to keep them fully occupied. Whoever's behind this will be too busy proving Thornley's innocence on both counts to bother with any more attacks on you or Winston."

Hannah looked at each man in turn. The same ice-cold intent glittered in both pairs of sea-green Madison eyes. She shook her head. "And you two wonder why everyone says you're so much alike."

• • •

After dinner Rafe walked out onto the porch with Mitchell. Winston padded along at their heels. Together the three of them gazed at the big SUV lurking in the shadows of the drive, looking for all the world like some modern-day *Tyrannosaurus rex* waiting for prey. Probably hoping some slow-witted, herbivorous little compact would wander within range, Rafe thought. The silhouette of Bryce's figure behind the wheel was just barely visible in the gathering shadows. The dinosaur's brain.

"Well, thanks for dinner," Mitchell said.

"Sure. Anytime."

"Still can't get over the fact that you can turn out first-rate grub like that."

"Maybe you've just been eating too much of Bryce's cooking. "

"Could be. But I'm used to it."

Rafe leaned against a post. "I haven't thanked you for the information you brought back from Portland."

"No problem." Mitchell tapped the end of his cane on the edge of the step. "Sort of interesting, if you want the truth. Haven't ever done anything along those lines."

"Neither have I. Lucky for us, you and Bev Bolton are such good friends."

"Uh-huh."

There was another short silence. Winston yawned.

"Sure hope to hell we know what we're doing here," Mitchell said after a while. "If we're right, we're talking about blowing apart the campaign of a hot-shit candidate for the United States Senate. Lawsuits could be the least of our worries when this is over."

"Since when did a Madison ever let the small stuff get in the way?"

Mitchell nodded. "You've got a point there."

"The important thing is that we put a stop to whatever

is going on around here." Rafe folded his arms. "Hannah's safety comes first."

"Can't argue that one," Mitchell said. "What's a political campaign compared to protecting a lady? Speaking of Hannah—"

Rafe braced himself. "Were we?"

"We sure as hell were. I didn't want to say anything in front of her, but we both know the two of you can't stay shacked up here like this indefinitely."

"Shacked up?" Rafe managed a politely blank expression. "I don't believe I'm familiar with the term."

"Bullshit! You know damn well what I'm talkin' about. When are you going to do the right thing by that girl?"

"When are you going to do the right thing by Bev Bolton?"

Mitchell's face tightened. Rafe was startled to see a flash of pain in his grandfather's eyes. The expression vanished swiftly behind glittering outrage.

"I'd marry Bev Bolton tomorrow if I thought she'd have me," Mitchell said ferociously. "But I've got a reputation to live down. She doesn't think I know how to make what she likes to call a commitment."

Rafe looked at him, saying nothing.

Mitchell blinked once or twice. The outrage faded to dawning chagrin. "Well, shoot and damn. You're in the same leaky boat, aren't you, son?"

"I don't think Hannah bought that story you gave her about my bad nerves," Rafe said. "She's got the same problem with me that Bev Bolton has with you."

"Your checkered past?"

"Yeah. But in my case it's not only my own that I've got to live down. I've got yours and Dad's in the way, too."

"Well, shoot and damn." Mitchell gazed unhappily at the tip of his cane, then at Rafe. "Don't suppose you've got any good ideas on what to do about this problem Madisons seem to have with females?"

"No."

"Well, shoot and damn."

"Yeah," Rafe said. "Shoot and damn."

"No sense asking Gabe. He's no better with women than we are."

"Apparently not."

Mitchell glanced at Winston. The Schnauzer cocked his head in polite inquiry.

"No point asking him for advice, either," Rafe said. "Hannah had him neutered."

The night coalesced swiftly around them, deepening the somber atmosphere.

"I think there's some irony here somewhere," Rafe said eventually. "But I can't be sure, because I never finished college."

"Told you you'd regret dropping out."

"I know. Look at me now. Doomed to go through life without knowing about stuff like irony and postmodernism. It's almost enough to make a man regret a misspent youth." Rafe paused. "But I'll probably get over it."

Mitchell nodded. "Fix yourself a whiskey and soda and take a long walk on the beach. Always worked for me." He roused himself and went down the steps. "Tell you one thing," he said over his shoulder as he strode toward the waiting SUV.

"What's that?"

"You may not have finished college, but you're a Madison."

"So?"

"So, no Madison ever let anything stand in his way once he made up his mind to go after what he wanted. Remember what I said. You can't shack up with Hannah forever. It's not right. You've got to come up with a fix for this mess. Hear me?"

"I hear you."

Mitchell opened the passenger-side door of the SUV and climbed in. Rafe and Winston watched the monster vehicle lumber off down the drive.

When the taillights disappeared, Rafe looked down at the dog. "You know, Winston, one of the reasons you and I get along so well is that you never hand out unsolicited advice."

Winston yawned again, rose, and ambled back inside the house.

Mitchell peered at the road through the windshield. "I think those two need a little kick in the right place to get them moving in the right direction."

"My advice is to stay out of the matter, sir," Bryce said. "The conduct of close interpersonal relationships is not your strong point."

"I don't pay you for advice."

"You have made that clear many times over the years."

"Never seems to stop you from interfering."

"That's why you keep paying me, sir."

"Hmmph."

"I hate to ask," Bryce said, "but do you have a plan to apply this kick you seem to feel your grandson and Miss Harte require?"

Mitchell drummed his fingers on the dash, thinking furiously. "I'm working on one."

Bryce nodded. "I was afraid of that."

Rafe was brooding. Hannah could feel the vibes. He had been in a strange mood since he came back into the house after seeing Mitchell off. She had helped him with the dishes. There had been very little conversation. The few words that had been exchanged had been centered on speculation about what they might or might not learn from Arizona Snow.

"She's so weird," Hannah said. "Lord only knows what those logs of hers will look like, assuming she'll even let us see them."

"I think she'll let me have a look at them." Rafe finished drying a pan and shoved it into a cupboard. "She and I always got along pretty good in the old days."

"I know." Hannah glanced at him. "Why did the two of you hit it off so well, anyway?"

"I don't know why she liked me, but I can tell you why I took to her."

"Why?"

"She was the only one who never tried to tell me what I should do with my life."

Hannah winced. "Okay, I can see the appeal there. Did she ever tell you anything about her past?"

"Nope."

"Ever wonder about it?"

"Sure." Rafe shut the cupboard door. "Everyone in town wonders about her past. Most people figure she's just one hundred percent bonkers."

"When I was younger," Hannah said slowly, "I imagined that she was an ex–secret agent who was forced to retire after her mind cracked under the strain of undercover work."

"That's as logical as any of the other theories I've heard over the years."

When they finished the dishes they wandered out into the darkened solarium. Rafe put two glasses on the table between a pair of wicker loungers and filled each with gently steaming water. He picked up a bottle of orange liqueur and splashed some into two balloon glasses. Then he cradled the bowls of the balloon glasses over the hot water to warm the liqueur.

When he was finished, he lowered himself into one of the loungers and handed one of the balloon glasses to Hannah.

She accepted the pleasantly warm glass and took a sip of the sultry liqueur. Winston stuck his head over the edge of the lounger. She stroked his ears. An air of doggy bliss emanated from him.

The darkness grew heavier. So did Rafe's mood. Hannah resisted the urge to break the silence. She was determined that he would be the one to do that. If he wanted to brood, that was his business. It wasn't like she was his wife or even a close friend, she reminded herself. It wasn't her job to cheer him up when he was down or jolly him out of a bad temper. Sure, they had made love a few times, but that didn't mean they were lovers.

Instead of rallying her, that thought lowered her own spirits.

Wonderful. Now she was brooding too.

For a while she thought Rafe might not speak at all. She was telling herself that she was getting accustomed to the silence when he finally started talking. The first words out of his mouth startled her so much that she was the one who was momentarily speechless.

"Ever since the night Kaitlin died," he said, his voice seeming to come from a distant place, "I've always wondered whether or not Mitchell believed that I might have killed her."

Hannah opened her mouth and then closed it again. She was so taken back she could not think of an appropriate response. Maybe there wasn't one.

"He never said a word." Rafe turned the heated glass between his palms. "But that didn't mean anything. His first loyalty is to Gabe and me. I've always known that.

Even when we were going toe-to-toe about everything from my lousy job prospects and the motorcycle to my choice in girlfriends, I knew that he would stand by me no matter what. He might disapprove. He might be disappointed. He might be furious. But he would be on my side in a fight. Just like Gabe."

Hannah stared at him. "You actually thought that all these years Mitchell has been wondering what really happened that night? You weren't sure he believed your story?"

"I was never certain." Rafe's jaw tightened. "And I was too damn proud to confront him and ask him straight out."

She pondered that for a moment. "Maybe you were afraid of the answer."

He looked out at the lights on the far side of the bay. "Maybe. Or maybe I just didn't want him to be put in the position of having to pretend that he never doubted me. Mitchell and I have had our problems, but we've always been straight with each other. Didn't want that to change."

She thought back to what Mitchell had said about Rafe the first night they had invited him to dinner. *He's a Madison. He's got a temper. But if he had been with Kaitlin that night and if there had been some terrible accident, he'd have gone for help and then he'd have told the flatout truth about what happened.*

"Your grandfather knows that you had nothing to do with Kaitlin's death," she said. "He never doubted you."

"I know that now."

Hannah exhaled slowly. "Well, if nothing else good comes from this situation, it sounds like you and he are working out some sort of long overdue reconciliation. That's worth something."

Rafe gave her a laconic, sidelong look. "Why do you

care whether or not Mitchell and I patch up our differences?"

"I live to bring joy and happiness to those around me."

"Try again."

She made a face. "Don't pin me down."

"Right." He took another swallow of the liqueur.

She gave him a few seconds. When he did not volunteer anything further in the way of conversation, she tried another tack.

"I promised myself I wasn't going to ask what happened between you and Mitchell outside on the porch a while ago, but my curiosity has gotten the better of me."

"No surprise there."

She ignored that. "Look, you just told me that you're no longer worried that Mitchell might be harboring some deep, dark suspicions about what happened on the night of Kaitlin's death. And the two of you have decided that you'll work together on our little investigation. Heck, you're even having your grandfather over for dinner these days. Obviously your relationship is improving rapidly. So what went wrong out there on the porch?"

"Nothing went wrong."

"Don't give me that baffled, befuddled male stare. I'm not buying it."

He sank deeper into his lounger and wrapped his long-fingered hands around the balloon glass. "I thought I was pretty good at doing baffled and befuddled."

"Not funny, Madison. When you went outside you were in a reasonably good mood. You came back in a lousy mood. You can't blame me for wondering what transpired on the front porch."

For a moment she thought he would not answer. Then he tilted his head against the back of the lounger and closed his eyes. "Mitchell made it clear that he didn't like the fact that you and I are, and here I quote, *shacking up* together."

"Shacking up?" Hannah sucked in an outraged breath. "He actually used that term?"

"He did, yes."

"Ridiculous. No one uses that phrase anymore."

"I mentioned that."

"It's old-fashioned. Downright archaic. It implies an outdated value system that demeans and insults two rational, intelligent adults who choose to make their own decisions in an extremely private area of life."

"Damn right."

"It's a stupid phrase implying low morals and a complete disregard for societal norms."

"You can say that again—I think."

"It takes absolutely no allowance for alternative lifestyles, freedom of association, and the right to life, liberty, and the pursuit of happiness."

"Well, Mitchell never was what anyone would call politically correct, even on his good days."

"Besides," Hannah concluded, "it's not even true."

"Sort of hard to explain the facts to Mitchell."

"We are *not* shacking up." She batted at the air with one hand while she fumbled for words. "We're not even sharing the same floor here at Dreamscape, let alone the same bedroom."

"Believe me, I am well aware of that."

"We haven't even *done* anything," she raced on wildly. "Not since I moved into Dreamscape, at any rate."

"That fact has not escaped my notice, either." He sounded disappointed.

"I own half this house." She gripped the arm of the lounger. "If I want to use part of it, that's my business."

"You're entitled, all right."

"Furthermore, it was *your* idea for me to move in here."

"I take full responsibility," Rafe said piously.

"Oh, stop being so bloody reasonable about it." She flopped back in the lounger in disgust. "You're a Madison. You're not supposed to be reasonable."

chapter 21

"You want the logbook from the night Kaitlin Sadler died?" Arizona Snow squinted her eyes against the smoke that rose from her cigar. She regarded Hannah and Rafe across the expanse of the wide table that dominated the space she fondly called her war room. "Well, now, isn't that an amazing coincidence?"

Hannah tensed. She felt Rafe, sitting beside her, do the same. Winston, apparently sensing the suddenly charged atmosphere, paused in the act of sniffing around the base of a metal file cabinet. They all looked at Arizona.

"Okay, you've got our attention, A.Z.," Rafe said. "What's with the crack about a coincidence? Are you saying that someone else has been here asking for that particular log?"

"In a manner of speaking." Arizona shoved her hands into one of the half dozen pockets of her khaki cargo pants. She chewed thoughtfully on the fat stogie she had stuck between her thin lips. "But he didn't exactly ask politely. The institute sent an agent to break into my place a week or so after Kaitlin's death. Took only one thing. Give you two guesses what that one thing was."

Hannah leaned forward, stunned. "The log that covered that particular night?"

"You got it," Arizona said. She removed one hand from a pocket and slammed the table with the flat of her palm. "I knew right then and there something big had gone on that evening. But the next morning the only thing everyone in town could talk about was Kaitlin Sadler's so-called accident and the possibility that Rafe, here, might have offed her. Now, don't that tell you somethin'?"

Rafe studied her warily. "You still think Kaitlin was killed by someone up at the institute?"

Arizona gave him a grimly triumphant look. "The way I figure it, there's only two possibilities. Either that poor gal was murdered by an agent in order to create a distraction for whatever the hell they were doin' up there at the institute—"

"Or?" Hannah prompted cautiously.

Arizona lowered her voice to a whisper laden with portent and dark implication. "Or like I said the other night, the Sadler girl saw somethin' she wasn't supposed to see. Either way, it's obvious that the institute got rid of her before she could spill the beans, and then they set Rafe up as the fall guy. If it hadn't been for you, Hannah, he might have gone to prison."

Hannah's heart sank. She did not dare to meet Rafe's eyes. They had both known that it would be difficult to talk to Arizona Snow. But neither of them had allowed for the fact that her logbook for the fateful night might have gone missing.

"You got any ideas of who might have taken your log?" Rafe asked.

"I just told you who took it. One of the institute agents."

"Huh." Rafe flicked a glance at Hannah.

She smiled encouragingly at Arizona. "I don't suppose you remember any cars that left the institute parking lot that night sometime around midnight and returned before the reception ended?"

Arizona shook her head regretfully. "Been eight years now. All I recall is that there was an awful lot of activity up there that night. The parking lot was full most of the evening. Lots of coming and going. There was the media, some out-of-town institute agents, and all the innocent dupes of Eclipse Bay who paid good money to cheer for Thornley."

Rafe sat back. "Damn. Told you years ago that you should start entering your data on a computer, A.Z."

Arizona gave a snort of disgust. "Can't trust computers. Any kid can break into them and help himself to anything he wants."

"Filing your information in hard copy sure didn't do us much good," Rafe muttered.

Arizona raised one massive shoulder in a shrug. She regarded her guests with a crafty gleam in her eyes.

Hannah turned to Rafe. "Got any more bright ideas?"

"Let me think." He rubbed the back of his neck. "Jed Steadman mentioned that he might be able to dig up an institute guest list for that night."

"Checking the whereabouts of everyone on the list for that two-hour window would take days and days of work," Hannah said. "Even assuming it could be done at all. And we couldn't ever be sure of the accuracy. Like Arizona said, it's been eight years. No one's going to recall many details."

Rafe studied the large topographic map of Eclipse Bay and the surrounding vicinity that was laminated to the surface of the war room table. "Jed might be able to help us out there, too. He covered the reception. He might still have his notes."

Hannah thought about that approach and shook her head. "He might have some old notes regarding the most newsworthy people in attendance. But he certainly wouldn't have kept tabs on everyone in the crowd."

"If we're right, we're looking for someone who may have been newsworthy, or at the very least, attached to the Thornley campaign." Rafe rose from his chair. "It's just barely possible Jed will be able to help us. Worth a try."

"Well, it's not like we have anything else to go on." Hannah started to rise. "Without Arizona's log for that night—"

"Didn't say there wasn't a log for that night," Arizona drawled.

Halfway to her feet, Hannah paused. "What?"

Rafe planted both hands on the laminated map and leaned across the table. "A.Z.? You told us that log was missing from your file."

A deep, hoarse chuckle rumbled through Arizona. "The original was stolen, like I told you."

"Original?" Rafe waited.

"I didn't just fall off the turnip truck," Arizona said with cool satisfaction. "I've been in this business a long time. First thing I do when I get back from a recon job is make a copy of my log."

Rafe started to grin. "I should have guessed."

Hannah felt a small flicker of hope. "Where's the copy of your missing log, Arizona?"

"Hidden in the bunker along with all the other copies." Arizona glanced at the massive multifunctional steel watch on her wrist. "Take a couple of hours to drive to the site, dig out the log, and get back to town. What d'ya say we meet up out at Dreamscape at 1100 hours?"

"We'll be waiting." Rafe straightened. "Thanks, A.Z. I really appreciate this."

"Sure. Any time." Arizona gripped the arms of her desk chair and shoved herself to her feet. "Just glad to see some folks from around here finally start paying attention to what's going on up there at the institute."

"Innocent dupes of the world, arise," Hannah murmured. "You have nothing to lose but your innocence."

Rafe took her arm and headed toward the door. "We'll keep you informed of everything we discover, A.Z."

"You do that." Arizona hesitated, concern furrowing her forehead. "And you two take care, hear? You're tangling with the institute crowd now. That means you're dealing with some ruthless types. Someone up there ordered the Sadler's girl's death to cover up something. Whoever did it might be willing to kill again."

A chill went through Hannah. She cleared her throat. "Well, on that cheerful note—"

"By the way," Arizona interrupted rather casually, "how long are you two gonna shack up together out there at Dreamscape?"

Anger surged, temporarily submerging the little thrill of dread Hannah had felt a few seconds ago. She jerked to a halt, spun around, and glared at Arizona.

"We are *not* shacking up."

Rafe tightened his grip on her arm. "Hannah, this isn't the time to go into it."

"The heck it isn't." Hannah grabbed the edge of the door as Rafe tried to haul her forcibly out into the hall. "I want to set the record straight before we leave. Listen, Arizona, Rafe and I are *sharing* Dreamscape until we negotiate a way out of the mess Isabel left us in. We are not shacking up there."

"Sorta hard to tell the difference," Arizona answered through a cloud of smoke.

"Not from where I stand," Hannah retorted. "We're sleeping on separate floors."

"Sounds uncomfortable," Arizona said.

Hannah was a bundle of simmering outrage. Rafe could feel her vibrating on the seat beside him. Winston had draped himself over the back of the seat and licked her ear repeatedly in an effort to console her, but she refused to be restored to a more reasonable mood.

Rafe tried distraction first.

"A.Z.'s got a strange view of the world, but she doesn't make things up out of thin air," he said. "She thinks that logbook was stolen. I'm inclined to believe her."

"It's been eight years. She probably misplaced it."

"Not A.Z. She's one well-organized conspiracy theorist. Trust me." He downshifted as he drove past the pier. "Makes you wonder, doesn't it?"

"I'll say it does. It was bad enough when people suspected that we were having an affair. But now the whole town apparently thinks that we're living together openly out there at Dreamscape."

"We are. Sort of."

"Doesn't it bother you?"

"Well, no, not really. Hannah, I'm trying to hold a rational conversation here. We were discussing the missing logbook, if you will recall."

"It bothers me. I realize that you Madisons are accustomed to being gossiped about here in Eclipse Bay. But we Hartes try to avoid being the subject of idle rumors and speculation."

She was tight and wired, Rafe realized. Her arms were crossed beneath her breasts. Her face was pinched with irritation.

"People have been talking about us since the day we arrived," he said evenly. "It didn't seem to bother you so much at first. Why are you going ballistic now?"

"I'm getting tired of it." She looked out at the bay. "I thought everything would be settled by now. It all seemed so simple back at the beginning. I would buy out your share of Dreamscape and start work on my inn. But things just keep getting more complicated."

"By 'things,'" he said carefully, "I assume you are talking about our relationship, not the possibility that we may have awakened a sleeping murderer?"

"Yes, I am talking about our relationship."

He gripped the wheel and braced himself. "Okay. You want to discuss that instead of the missing logbook?"

"No."

He drew a deep breath. He should be feeling relieved, he thought. But for some reason, he was vaguely disappointed.

"Well, that simplifies matters," he said. "Let's get back to the logbook."

"Why bother? There's nothing we can do until Arizona finds her copy."

He flexed his hands on the wheel. "Whatever you say. I need gas."

"So? Get some."

"Yes, ma'am."

He drove past the library and the small park next to it, then turned the corner into the town's main shopping area. Chamberlain College and the institute had had an impact here. For years the post office, together with the hardware, drugstore, and grocery store had formed the core of Eclipse Bay's tiny business district. But lately a smattering of new shops, including a bookstore and a restaurant, had appeared to cater to students and faculty.

He pulled into the Eclipse Bay Gas and Go, stopped

at the first pump, and switched off the engine. He realized that his own temper was starting to fray.

"I wish you'd stop that," he said.

"Stop what?"

"Stop fuming. You're starting to make Winston and me tense."

"I'm angry. I've got a right to be angry. I intend to stay angry for as long as it suits me."

That did it. He turned halfway around and flung his arm over the back of the seat. "What the hell is going on here, anyway? I don't know why you're letting a simple crack about us shacking up together upset you like this."

"I hate that term."

"Shacking up?" He shrugged. "You've got to make allowances for the older generation."

"Now you're starting to say it, too. For the last time, we are not 'shacking up.'"

"Okay, okay, take it easy." Rafe watched a vaguely familiar figure garbed in grease-stained coveralls emerge from the garage and amble toward the car. "Son of a gun. Is that Sandy Hickson?"

The question got Hannah's attention for a moment. She peered through the windshield. "Yes, I think so."

Rafe popped the door. "He sure hasn't changed much, has he?"

"No." Hannah's mouth thinned. "He still looks like the kind of guy who checks out rest room walls for the names of potential dates."

"A man has to use whatever resources are available." Rafe climbed out from behind the wheel and closed the door. He braced one hand against the roof of the Porsche and leaned down to look at Hannah through the open window. "Better stop glaring at me like that. Sandy might come to the conclusion that we've having a lovers' spat.

If you think the gossip is unpleasant now, just imagine what it will be like if word gets out that we're fighting."

Hannah chose to ignore him.

"Hey, Rafe."

Rafe straightened and nodded at Sandy. "Sandy."

"Heard you were back in town. How's it hangin'?" Sandy leaned down to speak through the open window. "Hi there, Hannah."

"Hello, Sandy."

Sandy gave Rafe a keenly interested glance. "What can I do for you?"

"I just need gas." Rafe pushed himself away from the car. "What have you been up to, Sandy?"

"Doin' okay." Sandy beamed proudly. He hoisted a rubber-bladed scraper out of a bucket of dirty water and went to work on the front window of the Porsche. "Bought the station from old man Carpenter a couple years ago."

"No kidding?" Rafe noticed the sign that pointed customers toward the rest rooms. He thought about what Hannah had said a moment earlier. "That's gotta be convenient."

"What's that?"

"I said, Congratulations. I'll bet you do pretty good during the summer months."

"You can say that again." Sandy winked. "Looks like you're doin' all right for yourself, too."

"Getting by." A dark cloud of premonition settled on Rafe. Maybe stopping for gas had not been such a swell idea.

But it was too late to change course. Sandy's grin was only a decimal point away from a leer. He dropped the wiper back into the bucket and moved closer to Rafe. He lowered his voice to a conspiratorial whisper.

"Heard you and Hannah were having yourselves some good times together out there at Dreamscape."

"I heard that, Sandy Hickson," Hannah shouted through the open window. "It's not true. Furthermore, if you repeat that one more time I will wrap one of those gas hoses around your throat. Do you hear me?"

Sandy blinked and took a quick, startled step away from the fender. "Hey, Hannah, I didn't mean nothin', honest. Just passin' the time of day."

"Bull," she said. "Just because you own your very own rest rooms now and have access to an unlimited source of phone numbers, don't think that everyone else gets involved in the same kind of limited, one-dimensional relationships you apparently prefer."

"Sure, sure." Sandy threw Rafe a desperate look.

"I'm finished here," Rafe said quickly. "What do I owe you, Sandy?"

"Uh, eleven-fifty," Sandy said.

A classic finned Cadillac pulled into the neighboring aisle. A petite woman with a helmet of steel-gray curls got out. "Is that you, Rafe Madison?"

"Yes, ma'am, Mrs. Seaton." Rafe grabbed his wallet. Speed was of the essence.

Edith Seaton examined him from head to toe with an expression of frank feminine admiration. "My, my, you did fill out nicely, didn't you?"

Rafe could feel the sudden heat in his face. He had a nasty feeling that he was turning a dull red. There wasn't much that could make him blush, but Mrs. Seaton had managed the trick.

"Nice to see you again, Mrs. Seaton." Damn. He didn't have fifty cents in change. He concentrated on plucking a ten and two ones from his wallet. "I see you've still got the antique shop on the corner."

"Oh, yes. Wouldn't know what to do with myself if

I didn't have the shop." Mrs. Seaton glanced into the car. "Is that you, Hannah?"

"Yes, Mrs. Seaton." Hannah's voice sounded strained and slightly muffled.

"Thought so. Heard all about you and Rafe inheriting Dreamscape. I talked to Isabel shortly before she made her transition, you know. She was very excited about the whole notion of leaving that place to the two of you." Mrs. Seaton winked. "She was always such a romantic at heart."

"Uh-huh," Hannah said. Her voice dripped icicles.

The crowd was growing rapidly. Across the street the door of the Total Eclipse Bar and Grill opened, and two of the patrons emerged. They stood for a few seconds beneath the neon letters that spelled out the bar's slogan, *Where the sun don't shine*. Then, curiosity obviously aroused, they jaywalked toward the gas station to see what was happening.

A familiar green Volvo rolled up to a pump. The window on the driver's side was down. Perry Decatur, dressed in a slouchy jacket and dark glasses, sat behind the wheel. His head swiveled toward the car.

The audience continued to swell. It was definitely time to leave. He tossed the gas money at Sandy. "Here you go. Keep the change. See you later." He reached for the door handle.

But escape eluded him. A battered white pickup pulled up to the pump just ahead of the Porsche, and a burly man dressed in denim jeans held up by a belt fastened below his belly got out. He adjusted the billed cap that covered his thinning hair.

"Rafe Madison." The big man's eyes crinkled with genuine pleasure. "Long time no see."

"Hello, Pete."

Pete Levare hitched up his jeans and screwed his features into a good-natured expression of avid curiosity. "Heard you and the Harte girl each got a chunk of Dreamscape. What the hey's going on out there, anyway? Is it true the two of you are—"

He never got to finish the sentence. The passenger door of Rafe's car flew open.

"That does it." Hannah erupted, Mount St. Helens fashion, from the Porsche's cockpit. Sensing an exciting new game, Winston leaped to follow her.

Together dog and woman whipped around the front of the car and started toward the hapless Pete. A sense of impending disaster settled on Rafe. It was like watching a film in which events are spinning out of control. All he could do was stand there and wonder how bad it would get.

"Whoa." Pete held up both hands, palms out, and backpedaled furiously toward the safety of his pickup. "Calm down, Hannah. What did I say? What did I say?"

"It's not what you said, it's what you were about to say," Hannah yelled as she charged toward him. "You think Rafe and I are shacking up together, don't you?"

"Shacking up? No, no, I never said that. Did I say that, Rafe?" Pete cast a helpless, beseeching glance at Rafe.

Rafe ignored him. He was too busy admiring the sight of Hannah in a full-blown temper. Invisible waves of energy shimmered in the air around her. The stylish acid-green scarf she wore around her throat snapped in the breeze. Who would have thought a Harte would demonstrate so much passion in public?

Winston pranced at her heels, his little legs moving so rapidly that all that could be seen in the vicinity of his paws was a silvery blur.

It was a thrilling sight, but one that he knew would have some repercussions.

Rafe cleared his throat. "Uh, Hannah—"

She paid him no heed. He groaned, folded his arms, and lounged against the car door. He'd tried. Later, when she was pissed at him for having caused this scene, he would remind her of that singular fact. Whatever was about to happen here was definitely not his fault.

"Pay attention, Pete." Hannah came to a halt in front of the big man and planted her hands on her hips. "Rafe and I are not—repeat, *not*—shacking up together at Dreamscape. Is that clear?"

"Sure, you bet," Pete said quickly. "Right. Not shacking up."

Mrs. Seaton looked fascinated. "I heard the two of you are planning to get married."

"*What?*" Hannah whirled around to stare at her. "Where did you hear that?"

"At the post office this morning," Mrs. Seaton said brightly. "Ran into Mitchell collecting his mail. He said he thought you and Rafe made a wonderful couple. Said you'd probably have something to announce any day. Is that true?"

"*No!*" Hannah's voice rose. "There will be no announcements."

Rafe kept his mouth shut.

Everyone looked expectant.

"Are you sure?" Mrs. Seaton asked.

"I am absolutely positive," Hannah ground out between set teeth. "Rafe and I have never discussed marriage."

From out of nowhere a lightning bolt of anger sizzled through Rafe. He stirred against the side of the car. "Strictly speaking, that's not true."

Hannah swiveled to pin him with a dangerous look. "What are you talking about?"

"I'm just saying that subject has come up between us."

"The hell it has," she shouted.

"I'll agree that we haven't come to any definitive conclusions yet, but you can't say that we haven't talked about it."

"Don't you dare get cute on me here, Rafe Madison." She took a step toward him. "You have never once asked me to marry you."

"You know what Mitchell said about my phobia."

"Don't give me that stupid excuse about having a phobia. You're the one who said the best way to deal with a phobia was to confront it head-on. I haven't noticed you trying that approach."

"Okay." He felt his stomach clench. "I'm asking."

For a second or two he didn't think he would get an answer. He heard Mrs. Seaton catch her breath. The others gazed with rapt attention. Even Perry Decatur was staring, transfixed by the scene.

Hannah pulled herself together with a visible effort. She glanced hurriedly around, as though finally coming to her senses. Rafe saw the gathering dismay and anger in her eyes.

"That was not a real proposal." There was a strange edge to her voice now. "That was a joke. At my expense. I don't appreciate it, Rafe."

"No joke," he said softly. "The proposal was real to me." He held her complete attention. "Do I get an answer?"

She stared at him, her face frozen. And then, to his horror, he saw the glint of moisture in her eyes. Her lips parted, trembled ever so slightly.

"Oh, shit." He knew instinctively that if she burst into tears in front of all these people she would never forgive him.

He pushed away from the car door and wrapped one arm around her waist. "Sorry, folks. We've got an appointment."

He got her around the hood of the car and into the passenger seat before anyone had quite realized what was happening.

"Winston," he said firmly.

Winston scrambled nimbly into the car. Rafe closed the door behind him, circled back around the front of the Porsche, and got behind the wheel. He twisted the key in the ignition, wrapped one hand around the gearshift, and pulled out of the station onto Bay Street before the crowd could react.

When he checked the rearview mirror, he saw a row of excited faces. He knew only too well that the news about his gas station proposal would be all over town by five o'clock that evening.

He glanced uneasily at Hannah. She was blinking rapidly and dabbing at her eyes with a hankie, but she appeared to have the potential flood of tears under control. Winston rested his muzzle on her shoulder.

"Sorry about that," Rafe said eventually.

"Oh, shut up."

He tried to look on the positive side. At least she hadn't said no.

chapter 22

The letdown was far worse than the anger or the tears. It bordered on outright depression, Hannah thought. She retreated to the upstairs veranda as soon as she was inside the house. Rafe did not try to stop her.

Half an hour later, stretched out in a wicker lounger, with Winston hovering loyally beside her, she tried to sort out her mangled emotions and jumbled thoughts. She gazed at the restless surface of the bay and told herself that she had overreacted. She had, in fact, come unglued in a way that was most unusual for her.

Obviously she had been under more stress lately than she had realized.

She had every right to be furious with Rafe for that scene at the Eclipse Bay Gas and Go, she decided. But why had she let events get to her like that? She had been screaming at Pete Levare. She had nearly burst into tears in front of all those people.

What was the matter with her?

The answer was out there, but she knew she did not

want to deal with it. She almost welcomed the sound of Rafe's footsteps behind her. Anything was better than looking at the hard facts of her situation. ʹ

"You okay?" he asked.

She took some satisfaction from the fact that he sounded worried.

"I'm pissed," she said.

"Yeah. I know." He handed her a glass of iced tea. After a second's hesitation she took it from him. He seemed relieved. He lowered himself onto a wicker chair and rested his elbows on his knees. "It was my fault."

"We've already established that." She examined the glass in her hand. The tea was not ordinary black tea over ice. It was a luscious green-gold in color. There was a sprig of mint draped artistically over the rim and tiny little mint leaves frozen inside each ice cube. A crisp straw poked over the edge of the glass. An impossibly thin slice of lemon floated in the crystal-clear depths. "There's no little paper umbrella," she said.

He examined the glass critically and then shook his head once, decisively. "An umbrella would have been over the top."

"Just like that scene at the gas station." She sipped the tea through the straw. It was perfect. Cold, strong, and invigorating. "Why did you do it?"

"Do what?"

"Ask me to marry you in that dumb, tacky way."

"You sure you want to reopen that conversation?"

"I want an answer."

He looked out at the silver surface of the bay. "All right. I wanted to marry you the day you got out of the car here at Dreamscape, but I knew you wouldn't take a chance on me. At least, not right away."

Tea sloshed over the side of her glass. She sputtered wildly, "You *what* . . . ?"

He did not respond to her interruption. Instead he plowed ahead with a sort of dogged determination. She got the feeling that having launched himself on this venture, he was bound to see it through to the conclusion, even if that conclusion was ill-fated.

"During the past few days I thought maybe we were getting closer. Making progress."

"Having sex, you mean."

He nodded agreeably. "That, too. But I didn't want to push it."

"The sex?"

"The relationship."

"Oh, that." She scowled. "Why not?"

"Mostly because I figured you'd get nervous and back off."

"Me? You're the one who claims to have a deep-seated fear of having inherited a genetic tendency to screw up relationships."

"I had every right to play my cards close to the chest. I wasn't sure what I was dealing with. After all, you told me you'd drawn up a new list of qualifications for a husband. Hell, you wouldn't even tell me what was on the revised version."

She dropped her head against the back of the lounger. "That stupid list."

"Yeah. That stupid list. Worrying about it has been a real source of stress for me, Hannah."

Her hand stilled on Winston's head. "It has?"

"That damned list has driven me nuts. At any rate, this afternoon at the gas station when you started to tell everyone that the subject of marriage had never even come up between us, I guess I got a little irritated. Hell, I lost my temper." He paused. "And whatever common sense I've got."

She slowly lowered the glass. "Are you serious?"

He turned his head back to look at her. "Dead serious."

"You've been thinking about marriage since I first got here?"

"Before that, if you want the truth." He looked down at his loosely clasped hands for a moment. When he raised his head again his eyes were bleak. "Maybe since I got the news about Dreamscape from Isabel's lawyer and realized that you were still single."

"I don't understand," she whispered. "What put the notion of marriage into your head? Did you have some crazy idea that it would be the simplest way to deal with our inheritance?"

"Hell, no. Marriage is not a simple way of handling anything. I know that better than anyone."

"Then why?" Her voice was rising again. She'd have to watch that. She was a Harte, after all.

Rafe's jaw tightened. "It's hard to explain. It just seemed right somehow. When I got the letter from the lawyer things started to fall into place. For the first time in my life I knew exactly what I wanted. It was as if I'd been groping my way through a fog bank for years and suddenly the fog evaporated."

"What, precisely, do you want?"

He spread his hands. "Nothing too bizarre. You. The inn and the restaurant. A future."

She waited for him to add undying love and mutual devotion to the list. But he didn't. "I see. Some people would say that a marriage between a Harte and a Madison would definitely qualify as bizarre."

He watched her intently. "Look, I don't know what's on this new list of yours, but I've done some changing during the past eight years. I still don't meet all the requirements you gave me when you were nineteen—"

"I was twenty that night, not nineteen."

"Whatever. The thing is, I do meet at least some of those specifications, and I'm willing to work on the rest."

"Why?" she asked bluntly.

He leaned forward, intense and earnest. "You're a Harte. You ought to see the logic in us getting married. Hey, we'd be going into this deal with our eyes wide open. We know a hell of a lot more about each other than most people know about their potential spouses. We've got some history together. Three generations of it. We'd have Dreamscape to work on together. Sharing a business enterprise is a very bonding experience."

"You think so?"

"Sure." He was warming to his theme now. "For my part, I can guarantee that this wouldn't be another typical Madison marriage."

She sipped her tea, reluctantly fascinated. "In what way?"

"I just told you." He spread his hands in a gesture of exasperation. "It won't be based on some wild, romantic fantasy of endless lust."

"No lust at all?" she asked around the straw.

His jaw locked. "I'm not saying I don't find you attractive. You know I do. We're sexually compatible. That's important in a marriage."

"Sexual compatibility is nice," she agreed.

"Right. Real important."

"But what you're proposing here is a marriage of convenience."

"What I'm proposing," he said, his voice tightening, "is a marriage based on the sort of things that are supposed to appeal to a Harte, the kind of crap that was on that original list of yours: Mutual goals. Shared interests, et cetera, et cetera."

The edge in his voice made her look at him quickly, but his face was an unreadable mask.

"Right." She jiggled the straw among the ice cubes. "Crap."

He drew a breath. "Okay, 'crap' was not a great word. Look, what I'm trying to say here is that I think we've got a shot at making a marriage work. Hannah, you told me once that I didn't have to repeat the same mistakes my father and my grandfather made. I haven't been one hundred percent successful, but I have managed to avoid some of the larger disasters. And I did meet the goal I set for myself eight years ago."

"You didn't end up in jail."

"Doesn't that count for something?"

"Huh."

"It's taken me a while to find out what I want in life, but I've got it straight now. I need to know if you can stretch your new list of requirements in a husband to accommodate me."

"Depends." She steeled herself. "You see, the new edition of my list is extremely short, at least compared to the old one. Only one requirement is on it."

He watched her the way Winston watched seagulls. Hope and determination burned in his eyes, but so did the knowledge of potential defeat.

The roar of a sturdy truck engine rumbled in the drive on the opposite side of the house. Winston removed his head from under Hannah's hand and hurried off around the corner to investigate. Rafe frowned, clearly annoyed by the interruption. Then he realized who it was and surged to his feet.

"That will be A.Z.," he said. He started after Winston.

Hannah glared at his back. "So much for declaring undying love and devotion." But she said it very softly so that he would not hear her because it was entirely possible that he did not have either to declare.

Who would have guessed that a Madison would have

ever settled for a marriage based on mutual interests and shared goals?

Who would have guessed that a Harte would have hungered for a little wild passion and romantic love?

The noise of the truck engine ceased abruptly. Hannah got up from the lounger and followed Rafe and Winston around the corner.

"This here's the log for that night." Arizona opened the black leather-bound volume on the kitchen table and swiveled it around so that Rafe and Hannah could look at the entries. "That first Thornley reception was a big event. Lots of folks there, including some from Portland."

"We're looking for a record of a car that left the parking lot and returned between midnight and two." Rafe slid the log closer to get a better look at the tiny, meticulously made notations. "I assume you stayed until the reception ended, A.Z.?"

"Until the last car pulled out of the lot," she assured him. "No point keeping a half-assed record, I say."

Hannah flipped pages. "There are a lot of entries here. It's going to take a while to go through them."

"Take your time." Arizona shoved herself to her feet. "Reckon I'll go out into the sunroom and relax while you two conduct your little investigation. Mind if I pour myself some more of your coffee, Rafe?"

"Help yourself." He reached for a pen and the lined tablet he had set out on the table.

"Thanks." Arizona reached for the pot. "Been a while since I sat in Isabel's sunroom. Miss those visits. Isabel always had something interesting to say."

The sad, faintly wistful note in Arizona's voice caught Hannah off guard. She looked up quickly.

Arizona headed for the kitchen door, chunky mug in

hand. "I could talk to her, you know? She understood when I told her about the goings-on up at the institute. Didn't laugh the way some folks do."

Arizona ambled out into the hall and disappeared in the direction of the solarium. Hannah gazed after her for a moment, aware of a glimmer of curiosity.

"I wonder just how close Arizona and Aunt Isabel actually were," she said quietly. "As far as I know, neither of them ever married. They were friends for a long time. You don't suppose—?"

"None of our business." Rafe wrote down a license plate number. "This will go faster if you take the notes while I read the entries."

"All right." She took the pen from him and positioned the yellow tablet. "Go."

It was a discouraging process. Arizona's log was more than a simple list of license plates, names, and times. It was complicated by extensive notations. Rafe read some of them aloud.

. . . Member of the Inner Circle?
. . . Claims to be from Portland but spotted a copy of the New York Times *on the backseat . . .*
. . . Showed up for last Tuesday's secret meeting at the institute. Probably on the inside. . .

"She's crafted a fantasy world for herself," Hannah whispered. "It's amazing."

"I'm not so sure it's any more amazing than the fact that we're sitting here going through her fantasy world logbooks because we think we can use them to solve an eight-year-old murder."

"Okay, you've got a point." Hannah tapped the pen against the table. "I can see where some people might

conclude that we're as far out in left field as Arizona
herself."

It took nearly half an hour to get through the log for
the night of Kaitlin Sadler's death. Hannah was privately
on the verge of conceding defeat when Rafe paused at
a license plate number.

"Huh," he said.

She looked up quickly. "What?"

"We've been concentrating on plates and vehicles connected with the Thornley campaign."

"So?"

Rafe sat back slowly and shoved his hands into his
back pockets. He studied the open logbook. "None of
them left and returned during that two-hour window.
Maybe we've been coming at this from the wrong angle."

Hannah did not like the dark excitement in his voice.
"You think maybe whoever left to meet Kaitlin borrowed
someone else's car?"

"Maybe." Rafe hesitated. "But there's another possibility. From what we can figure out, Kaitlin was acting
on impulse that night. She had made up her mind to
leave town in the morning. She needed cash in a hurry.
We've been going on the assumption that she tried to
sell the blackmail tapes to someone from Thornley's
camp. But there was another potential market for those
tapes."

"What market is that?"

"The media."

"Well, sure." Hannah tossed aside the pen. "But why
would anyone in the media murder her after agreeing to
buy the incriminating tapes? The last thing a journalist
would want to do is get rid of his source. He'd want
backup for his story."

"Not if," Rafe said slowly, "he planned to use the tapes
to blackmail Thornley himself."

Hannah drew a breath and let it out carefully. "The news of Thornley's interest in lingerie never appeared in the media. You think that's because some journalist who attended the reception that night kept the tapes and has been using them to blackmail Thornley all these years?"

Without a word, Rafe took one hand out of his back pocket and rotated the logbook so that she could see the entry he had marked.

"Not *some* journalist," he said quietly. "One Kaitlin knew well enough to call in a hurry that night. One she had reason to believe might be interested in handling a sleazy story about Thornley. An old acquaintance she thought she could trust."

Hannah looked down at the name written next to a license number. Stunned, she glanced quickly at the notes she had been making. The vehicle had left the reception shortly after midnight. It had returned at one-forty-seven A.M.

"A journalist," Rafe went on very quietly, "who might have known that Arizona Snow had a habit of hiding in the shadows to make notes about events at the institute. One who might have decided that even though no one in town ever paid any attention to A.Z.'s conspiracy theories, it would probably be a good idea to steal the log for that evening."

A chill of disbelief numbed Hannah. "You think Kaitlin tried to sell the tapes to Jed Steadman?"

An hour later Hannah paused halfway across the sunroom to glare at Mitchell, Rafe, and Arizona. All three of them glowered back at her.

"What the heck are we supposed to do now?" she demanded. "The big idea was to take the evidence to Jed Steadman and let him run with the story. Now it looks like he's the chief suspect."

Arizona shook her head and made a *tut-tut* sound. "Should have guessed the local media were involved in covering up institute actions. Explains a hell of a lot, if you ask me. No wonder they've been able to maintain a cloak of secrecy over their activities up there."

"If we're right, this has nothing to do with the institute," Hannah said with a patience she did not feel. "It's a simple case of blackmail and murder. It looks like Kaitlin called Jed that night. He went to meet her on the path above Hidden Cove. Maybe she offered to cut him in on the blackmail deal. Or maybe she simply wanted to sell the tapes to him outright. Either way, he saw a golden opportunity to cash in on the compromising videos."

"But he figured he'd better get rid of Kaitlin," Mitchell said. "Probably didn't trust her to keep her mouth shut. Or maybe he didn't want to split the potential profits two ways."

Rafe massaged the back of his neck. "The bottom line here is that we don't have any hard evidence for any of this."

"You got my logs," Arizona reminded him.

"No offense, A.Z., but we need more than that to take this to the police."

"We've still got the option of turning the story over to the media," Hannah reminded him. "Not the *Eclipse Bay Journal*, obviously. But maybe one of the Portland papers will be interested."

"Maybe. Maybe not." Rafe tapped his finger on the arm of the wicker chair. "I was counting on Jed going with the story and doing the basic legwork because it was a hometown scandal. He had the best reason to get excited about it."

"He'll get fired up about it, all right," Mitchell said morosely. "Probably sue us."

Hannah looked out over the bay. "I wish we had a little more to go on here. Rafe is right. We don't have any hard evidence."

There was a short, stark silence behind her.

"You know who you're looking at now," Mitchell said eventually. "If nothing else, you ought to be able to use what you've got to scare the hell out of Jed Steadman. Make sure he knows that if he makes one false move, a lot of folks will be watching. That should keep him in line."

Arizona grunted. "Why not call up the Thornley crowd and tell them we know who's been blackmailing their candidate all these years? That would stir things up a mite."

"I'm not so sure Jed has been blackmailing Thornley," Rafe said thoughtfully.

Everyone looked at him.

He sat forward and folded his arms on his knees. "When you get right down to it, there's no evidence that Steadman has been living above his income. If he's getting cash out of Thornley, where has the money been going?"

Another silence greeted that observation.

"Well, shoot and damn," Mitchell muttered. "Why would he commit murder for the tapes and then sit on them for eight years?"

A cunning light appeared in Arizona's eyes. "Why waste time prying a few bucks out of a small-time state pol when you can hold your ammunition and use it on a genuine U.S. senator?"

Hannah heard a collective intake of breath.

"You know something, A.Z.?" Rafe's smile held no humor. "For a professional conspiracy theorist, you sometimes make a lot of sense."

"She's got a point, all right." Mitchell whistled softly in admiration. "Everyone knew from the start that Thornley would probably go all the way to Washington." He glanced at Rafe. "You know Steadman better than anyone. Think he's into that kind of long-range planning?"

"Maybe," Rafe said thoughtfully. "He always likes to talk about the importance of timing and planning."

Hannah clasped her hands behind her back. "If Jed has been sitting on those tapes all this time, he must be getting a little antsy now that the big payoff is almost within reach. No wonder he freaked when Rafe and I returned to Eclipse Bay and people started to talk about the past."

"The question is, What do we do with all this guesswork?" Mitchell asked of the room at large.

Rafe looked out over the bay. "We get a little more information, if we can."

Hannah swung around in alarm. "What are you going to do?"

"There's a town council meeting tonight. They're going to be discussing the pier renovations. Jed will cover the session. It will probably run late."

Understanding hit her. She took an urgent step toward him. "You're going to search his house, aren't you? Rafe, you can't take that risk. What if a patrol car goes past his place while you're inside and you're spotted? If you get caught you'll be arrested for breaking and entering. You could end up in jail."

"Now that would be ironic," Rafe said. "Be the fulfillment of a long-standing prophecy."

"That is not amusing." She whirled around to face Mitchell. "I'm sure you don't want him to take this kind of risk. He's your grandson. Help me out here."

Mitchell stroked his chin. His expression of wolfish anticipation was uncomfortably familiar. "Well, I sure wouldn't want him to take such a dumb risk on his own. Reckon I'd better go with him to keep him out of trouble."

Hannah looked from his face to Rafe's and back again. She groaned. "Well, shoot and damn. This is a fine time for the two of you to decide to bond."

Mitchell studied the big house from beneath the branches of a dripping tree. Jed Steadman's home stood dark and silent in the fog-drenched gloom. "You thought about what we're going to do if we set off an alarm?"

"Doubt if there is one," Rafe said. "Not many people here in Eclipse Bay are worried about crime."

"If we're right about Steadman, he isn't exactly a typical resident of our fair town. You and Hannah have made him nervous lately. He might have put in an alarm. All I want to know is if you've got a backup plan in case we run into one."

"You think I'd do something dicey like this without figuring all the angles first?"

"Just tell me what we're supposed to do if we trigger an alarm."

"We run like hell."

Mitchell nodded. "I was afraid of that."

"You want out before we go inside?"

"Hell, no. Haven't had this much fun in years."

Rafe smiled slightly to himself. "I was afraid of that."

Getting inside was easy. Maybe a little too easy, Rafe thought as he slid the unlocked bedroom window open. He eased one leg over the sill and paused for a few seconds, listening to the silence.

"What's the matter?" Mitchell demanded.

"Nothing." Rafe got the other leg over the sill and stood inside the bedroom.

He was conscious of an eerie stillness in the house. A lonely quality permeated the darkness around him. He was only too well acquainted with this bleak, melancholy sensation. He had been aware of the emptiness collecting in his house in San Diego for a long time before he had made the decision to move to Eclipse Bay. Maybe this was how any man's home felt when there was no woman in it to soften the edges and warm the shadows.

"Now what?" Mitchell whispered after he climbed through he window.

"You take this room. Look for a wall safe. I'll go see if I can find a study or a home office. Got your gloves?"

"Sure, but we're not exactly experts at this kind of thing. What if he realizes later that someone went through his belongings?"

"Give him something more to worry about," Rafe said. "If we don't turn up those tapes, giving him a good scare may be the only tactic we've got to use against him."

He left Mitchell in the bedroom and went swiftly down the hall. He stopped in the doorway of another bedroom and clicked on his penlight. The room was beyond spartan in its bareness. It looked as if no one had ever slept in it. He opened a closet door. A mound of old camping equipment was piled inside.

He closed the door and went on down the hall to the next room. A quick glance revealed that Jed used it as an entertainment center. A massive television set took up a large section of one wall. Several thousand dollars' worth of speakers and other electronic equipment were positioned around a large recliner cushioned in black leather.

A wastebasket sat next to the recliner. Rafe glanced inside and saw a small heap of trash. A little square of yellow paper and a bit of foil clung to the side of the basket.

Rafe aimed the penlight closer to the candy wrapper. It looked identical to the one he had discovered beneath the tree at the end of the Harte cottage drive. It wasn't conclusive proof that it had been Jed who had kept watch on the house that night, but the evidence was mounting.

"Rafe." Mitchell's voice echoed softly from the other bedroom. It was husky with urgency. "You better take a look at this."

Rafe swung around and hurried back down the hall. "What is it?" He rounded the corner and aimed the penlight at Mitchell, who was standing in front of a chest of drawers. "Find something?"

"It's what I didn't find." Mitchell waved a hand at three open drawers. "There's nothing in here. Cleaned out."

"Are you sure?"

"Have a look for yourself."

Rafe went to the closet and yanked it open. Three shirts hung limply in the far corner. A pair of worn slippers sat on the floor. The rest of the space was empty. The door of a small safe built into the closet wall hung open. There was nothing inside,

"Looks like he packed up and left." Mitchell hooked his thumbs on his belt. "Maybe he figured out we're on to him."

"How could he have known?"

Mitchell shrugged. "Small town. He might have seen Arizona's truck parked at Dreamscape this afternoon. Wouldn't take much for him to put two and two together. He's got to know you're one of the few people who takes her seriously. Maybe he figured out that she was helping you look into the Sadler girl's death. Wouldn't be a real big leap for him."

"No." Rafe thought about it. "Not if he was already paranoid about that possibility. Maybe he planned for the possibility that someone would come around asking questions someday."

"One thing's for certain." Mitchell turned toward the open wall safe. "If Steadman has cleared out for good, you can bet he didn't leave those tapes behind for us to find."

chapter 23

Rafe was brooding again. Hannah tolerated it as long as she could stand it, but by ten o'clock that evening she was starting to climb the walls. She tracked her quarry down in the solarium, where he was sitting in the shadows. He had one hand on Winston's neck, rubbing the dog absently behind the ears.

"I vote we all take Winston for his evening walk on the beach," Hannah said from the doorway.

At the sound of his name included in the same sentence as the word "walk," Winston moved smartly out from under Rafe's hand and bounced toward the door.

Rafe's hand paused in midair over the place where Winston's ears had been a second earlier. "It's dark, in case you haven't noticed."

Hannah lounged in the doorway, arms folded. "There's no fog. The moon is out. All we need is a flashlight."

"It's late."

She looked at the back of his head. "Just a little past

ten. The first time you and I walked on the beach it was after midnight."

There was a short, stark silence. Without another word, Rafe levered himself up out of the lounger.

They went out of the big house through the French doors that opened onto the lower veranda. Rafe clicked on the flashlight, but Winston ignored the beam. He bounded ahead, zipping down the steps and heading toward the shadowy beach path with the ease of a creature who relies on a variety of senses to get around.

Rafe and Hannah followed in the dog's wake.

The evening was cool but not cold. The bay was a dark mirror beneath the icy white moon. A swath of silver streaked the surface of the deceptively still water. In the distance the lights of the pier and the streets of the small downtown section of Eclipse Bay glittered. Hannah could see the glow of Chamberlain College and the institute on the hillside.

Everything about the night brought back memories of her first walk on the beach with Rafe. She wondered if he was remembering that same evening and if so, what he thought about it.

When they reached the sand they followed Winston toward the rocky pools uncovered by the low tide.

"This is about Jed Steadman, isn't it?" Hannah asked after a while. "I know it must have been hard for you to discover that he may have been the one who murdered Kaitlin. He was your friend, after all."

"Jed was just a guy I knew a long time ago," Rafe said distantly. "Someone I could shoot a game of pool with on a dull night."

She peered at him. "I thought you two were quite close in the old days."

"I hardly thought about him in the past eight years, let alone picked up the phone to call him. And he sure as hell never bothered to get in touch with me. We weren't buddies. Just a couple of guys who did some stuff together on long summer weekends because we had one big thing in common."

"What was the big thing? Kaitlin Sadler?"

"No. The big thing was that neither of us had a father anywhere in the picture."

Hannah shoved her hands into the pockets of her sweater jacket. "I can see where that would have been a bond of sorts."

"I envied him a little, if you want to know the truth. I always figured he was the lucky one. He seemed like he knew what he was doing. Had a plan for his future. Knew where he was going. The kind of guy who wouldn't screw up."

Halfway down the beach, Winston paused to investigate a hunk of driftwood. Rafe aimed the flashlight at him and then let the light slide away toward the foam at the water's edge.

"I was wrong about Jed, you know," Rafe said after a while.

"What do you mean?"

"He wasn't the lucky one. I was. I had Mitchell after my parents were killed. Gabe and I both had him. I went off track for a while, but at least I knew there was a track, thanks to him."

Hannah nodded. "I understand."

"I don't think there was ever anyone there for Jed. His father drank a lot, and one day he just disappeared. His mother remarried two or three times."

"Hmm," Hannah said.

"What's that supposed to mean?"

"Let's not go too far into let's-feel-sorry-for-poor-Jed-who-came-from-a-dysfunctional-family territory. I'm sure it's all true, but I can't believe that he didn't know a few of the rules. The night he murdered Kaitlin Sadler in order to get his hands on those blackmail tapes he broke those rules. I'm sure he was well aware of what he was doing."

"You know, Hannah, that's one of the things I like about you." For the first time that evening there was a trace of wry amusement in Rafe's words. "I can always count on you to cut right to the heart of the matter."

Hannah sighed. "All right, if you're not brooding because of Jed, do you mind telling me why you've been in such a foul mood all evening?"

"I've been thinking."

"No offense, but I'm not sure it's good for you."

"I appreciate the positive feedback."

"Okay, okay. I don't want to argue."

"But you're so good at it."

She tightened her hands inside the pockets of her sweater jacket. "Let's start over. Tell me what you've been thinking about this evening."

He was silent for a couple of heartbeats. She had the impression that he was gathering himself for a big jump.

"I've decided to sign over my half of Dreamscape to you," he said.

For a few seconds she thought she had misunderstood. She reran his simple statement twice through her brain before she finally decided she had gotten it right the first time.

She came to a sudden halt on the beach and swung around to face him. "You're going to do *what*?"

"You heard me." He stopped and looked at her. "Dreamscape is Harte property. It's always been Harte property. I know your aunt had some romantic notions, but the truth is, I don't have any real claim on the place. It's yours. I'm not going to fight you for it."

Panic seized her. She jerked her hands out of her pockets and grabbed fistfuls of his black pullover. "I thought we had a deal."

"You didn't seem interested."

"I never got a chance to respond." She stood on tip-toe and leaned closer. "Arizona Snow arrived with her logbook in the middle of our business discussion, if you will recall. Then came our big deductions concerning Kaitlin Sadler's death."

"Hannah—"

"That was followed by you and your grandfather deciding to engage in a bit of breaking and entering. The next thing we know, Jed Steadman has left town and you're brooding. All in all, it's been a somewhat hectic day. I haven't had a chance to get back to you on your business offer."

"I've known for a long time now that my claim on Dreamscape was the only thing I could use to hold you. I don't want to use it."

"Excuse me if I got this wrong, but I was under the impression that you saw me and Dreamscape as a sort of package deal."

"I can build my restaurant somewhere else."

"Your dream of a restaurant is your passion. Dreamscape is the best possible location for it, and you know it. You can't give it up."

"Got news for you, Hannah. The restaurant is important, but it's not my greatest passion."

"Rafe—"

"I don't want you and the restaurant in a business deal."

"You're the one who made the offer."

"I was getting desperate."

Hope soared within her. Grimly she tamped it down, forcing herself to keep things in perspective. "But now you've changed your mind? You don't want me any-more?"

He closed his free hand around one of her fists. "I want you, Hannah, but it's no good unless you want me. Tonight I realized that taking Dreamscape out of the equation is the only way to find out how you really feel about me."

She couldn't keep the lid on the tide of hope any longer. It surged through her. "You want to know how I feel? I'll tell you how I feel. I love you, Rafe Madison. I want to stay here in Eclipse Bay with you. I want to open a five-star inn and restaurant at Dreamscape with you. I want to have babies and a future with you."

For an instant he did not move. Then he abruptly wrapped one arm around her and pulled her hard against his chest. "Are you sure?"

She snuggled against him. The heat and strength of his body enfolded her. He was her future.

"I'm sure."

"I love you," he said into her hair. "You're my pas-sion, not the restaurant. You know that, don't you?"

"I do now." Relief and joy washed through her. Once a Madison was committed to his passion, nothing else was allowed to get in the way.

"What about your new list?" he asked quietly. "Do I qualify?"

She smiled against his throat. "There was only one item on it. I wanted to marry someone I could love with all my heart. Someone who loved me the same way in return."

"No problem. I meet all the qualifications." He tight-ened his hold on her. "We'll make it work. You and me. Dreamscape. The future. We'll make it all work. I swear it."

"With your dreams and my brains, how can we miss?"

He raised her chin on the edge of his hand. "That night on the beach I told myself I could never have you, but I knew even then that I would never be able to forget you."

"I told myself the same thing about you."

He smiled against her lips. "You and your damned list were always there, somewhere in the back of my mind. You want to know the truth? Part of me wanted you to be happy. But another part hoped like hell that you would never find a man who met all those specifications for a husband."

"You and your big career objective to stay out of jail were always in the back of my mind. The thought of so much potential going to waste was extremely annoying."

"Sounds like we've been a constant source of irritation for each other all these years."

"I can't think of a better basis for a marriage."

He grinned. "Neither can I."

The beam of the flashlight splashed across the sand when his mouth came down on hers. Hannah reveled in the kiss. A singing happiness exploded inside her.

Winston's sharp, harsh bark broke the spell.

Rafe reluctantly raised his head. "I don't think your dog approves of us making out on the beach."

"He'll just have to get used to it."

Winston left the piece of driftwood he had been worrying and dashed toward them. He barked again, louder and more urgently this time. Not a request for attention or an invitation to romp.

A surge of alarm shot through Hannah. "I think something's wrong."

Winston did not stop when he reached the place where Hannah and Rafe stood. He sped on down the beach toward the path that led back to Dreamscape. He was barking furiously now.

"What the hell?" Rafe swung around to follow the dog with the flashlight beam. "Oh, shit."

He broke into a run.

Hannah looked toward the mansion. Shock seized her. The background rumble of the restless bay behind her blotted out any sound that might have drifted down the cliffs from Dreamscape. But she did not need to hear the crackle and hiss of the fire. She could see the flames leaping into the night quite clearly.

Should have taken the cell phone with me, Rafe thought as he raced toward the house. But the possibility that the fire could still be handled with the garden hose was too tempting to allow for a detour into the house to call 911.

He leaped the steps and ran the length of the veranda. Winston was a short distance ahead of him. The dog was in full charge mode. He was no longer sounding the alarm with short, warning barks. The porch lights glinted on bared teeth and flattened ears.

He had been right about Winston the first time he saw him, Rafe thought. Definitely not a froufrou pooch.

"I'll call the fire department," Hannah shouted.

"Right." He did not look back as he rounded the corner of the veranda.

Winston's growl was the only warning he got before he glimpsed the figure silhouetted by the flames. The man was attempting to flee, but the dog had closed his jaws around a pant leg.

Rafe saw Winston's victim raise the gasoline can in his hands and prepare to smash it down hard on the Schnauzer's skull.

"Goddamn dog," Jed yelled.

Rafe slammed into him. The can sailed out onto the grass, away from the flames. Jed went down hard on the wooden boards. He opened dazed, angry eyes. Hatred and rage flared hotter than the crackling fire.

Winston tried to get a better grip on Jed's leg.

"Let go, Winston."

The dog released the trouser cuff and looked at Rafe.

"You sonofabitch," Jed roared. "I had it all planned. Waited all this time. But you had to come back and ruin everything."

He heaved himself upward, hands stretched out for Rafe's throat.

Rafe saw the madness in his eyes and moved back out of reach. "It's over, Jed."

"Why did you have to come back here and screw up everything? Why, goddamn you?"

"It's over," Rafe said again.

In the distance sirens wailed. Winston pranced in agitation and started to bark again. Hannah rounded the corner, the fire extinguisher from the kitchen cupboard in her hands.

"Oh, my God." She halted at the scene in front of her.

"I had it made until you came back." Jed's face crumpled in fury. "Everything was in place. After all these years, everything was in place. And then you came back."

He launched himself wildly across the short space that separated him from Rafe.

Rafe sidestepped the charge and stuck out one foot. Jed tripped over it and fetched up against the wall of the mansion. He clung there a few seconds and then slid slowly to a sitting position.

When he opened his eyes this time, the rage was gone. In its wake was a bleak awareness of abject failure.

"I had it all planned," he whispered.

chapter 24

"Winston was the hero of the hour." Hannah looked proudly at her dog, who was gnawing on a chewing bone. "Thanks to him, the fire damage was minimal. The Willis brothers assured us they could have things in great shape in a couple of weeks."

"I'd allow more like a couple of months, if I were you," Mitchell said. "Construction work never gets done on time, especially when the Willis brothers are handling things."

"Maybe it's just as well," Hannah said. "We wanted to make some major modifications to that wing, anyway. We can incorporate them into the repairs."

"Makes sense." Mitchell leaned back in his chair and cast an assessing glance the length of the veranda. "Got your work cut out for you here. But I think, in the end, you'll have yourselves a nice little inn and restaurant."

"Five stars," Rafe said. His voice was soft with certainty.

"Don't doubt it for a minute." Mitchell chuckled. "Always knew you could do anything you set out to do. Just a matter of applying yourself."

Hannah grinned. "Gee, what a coincidence. I once told him the same thing."

Rafe stacked his heels on the railing and took a swallow from the beer bottle in his hand. "How could I miss with both of you telling me what to do with my life?"

"Took you long enough to live up to expectations, but you finally made it." Mitchell cradled his beer in one fist and squinted into the dying light. "Any more news on Jed Steadman?"

"Just that everything went down pretty much as we figured." Rafe looked out over the bay. "Except, of course, that Jed is claiming through his lawyer that Kaitlin's death was an accident."

"The result of a quarrel over the tapes," Hannah explained.

"Yeah, yeah," Mitchell muttered. "Reckon it's a given he'll end up facing only a manslaughter charge. But what happened to the tapes?"

"Jed claims they went over the cliff with Kaitlin and were swept out to sea. Says he never even viewed them."

"Ha." Mitchell grimaced. "And if you believe that, I've got some waterfront property in Arizona I can sell you."

"I don't think anyone actually believes his story," Hannah said slowly. "But if those tapes don't surface, no one will be able to prove otherwise. The Thornley camp is taking the line that the incident had nothing to do with their man. But there's a rumor going around that Trevor Thornley met Kaitlin when she worked for his first campaign."

"Wonder how many copies there are of those tapes," Mitchell mused.

"Not our problem," Rafe said. "Thornley's the one

who has to worry about opening a tabloid someday and finding a picture of himself modeling lingerie inside. We've got other things to occupy us."

Mitchell cocked a brow. "Such as?"

"Such as planning a wedding," Hannah said smoothly.

For a split second Mitchell looked stunned. In the next instant delight exploded across his weathered features. He gave a whoop that made Winston drop his chewing bone, get up from the floor, and pad over to his chair to see what all the excitement was about.

"Well, shoot and damn," Mitchell said when he finally got his exuberance under control. "I knew you two would get around to doing the right thing. You just needed a little kick in the you-know-where."

"Don't know how we could have managed without your help," Rafe said dryly. "Telling everyone at the post office that Hannah and I were planning to get married was certainly an inspiration for us. Wasn't it, Hannah?"

"Definitely inspirational," Hannah said.

Mitchell was clearly having trouble containing his delight. "Least I could do. Wait'll Sullivan and the rest of those uptight, upright Hartes hear about this. Your family is going to have a combined hissy fit, Hannah."

Hannah winced. "I expect there will be some fireworks when Rafe and I tell them the good news."

"Gonna light up the sky," Mitchell agreed cheerfully. "Sure would like to be there when you spring it on 'em."

"Forget it," Rafe muttered. "You're not going to be anywhere in the vicinity."

"Ah—"

"Speaking of family reaction," Hannah said firmly, "I'll be planning this wedding. I've had a certain amount of experience in the field, but I must admit this particular event presents some unique challenges."

Mitchell chortled. "Worried about a brawl in the church?"

Hannah gave him a repressive look. "I expect some cooperation, restraint, and civilized behavior from everyone. Is that clear?"

"Don't look at me like that." Mitchell contrived to appear deeply offended. "We Madisons aren't going to cause a ruckus."

"Damn right," Rafe agreed. "If there's trouble it won't start on the Madison side."

Hannah gave both men a steely look. "It better not finish there, either."

The wedding was held two months later, in the Eclipse Bay Community Church. Everyone in town was invited, and virtually everyone came. In spite of several ghoulish predictions of carnage, the ceremony went off without a hitch.

Halfway through the reception, which was held at Dreamscape, Mitchell could no longer restrain himself. He sought out Sullivan in order to gloat.

He found his old partner and rival on the veranda. Sullivan stood alone near the railing, a glass of champagne in one hand, a cane in the other.

Well, shoot and damn, Mitchell thought. He's lost as much hair as I have. Seemed like he was taller back in the old days, too. Guess we've both shrunk.

Looking at Sullivan was a little like looking into an old mirror. What had he expected? That they would stay young and dynamic forever? *At least I'm not the only one here with a cane.*

"Hey, Sullivan." He came to a halt a few paces away. "What do you think of your new grandson-in-law?"

Sullivan turned slowly around to face him. Mitchell relaxed a little. His ex-partner might be showing some wear and tear, but a savvy gleam still burned brightly in his eyes. This was the same man who had fought at his side in a long ago military action that no one except those who had been involved in it even remembered. This was the same man who had saved his life in that miserable jungle and whose life he had saved in return.

This was the same man he had teamed up with to risk everything in a financial gamble that had made them both rich for a while. The same man whose teeth he had tried to knock out in front of Fulton's Supermarket.

He met Sullivan's eyes and knew that they were both aware of the truth. The bonds that joined them would never dissolve.

Sullivan glanced down the length of the veranda to where Rafe stood with Hannah. "He'll do. Always said he had potential."

"I sure as hell never heard you say that."

"We haven't talked much for a long time, Mitch."

"Nope. Sure haven't."

"You did okay by Rafe and Gabe."

Startled, Mitchell glanced quickly at him and then turned just as swiftly away. "Can't take all the credit."

"No, but you can take some of it."

They stood together for a while, watching the crowd. Mitchell noticed that Sullivan made no effort to walk away.

"Looks like we're going to be seeing a lot of each other again," Mitchell offered finally. "I hear you Hartes are big on family gatherings."

"Yes." Sullivan looked at him. "We're very big on that kind of thing. How do you feel about your new granddaughter-in-law?"

Mitchell smiled. "She'll do."

"This better work out, Mitch. I swear to God, if Rafe doesn't treat her right—"

"Don't sweat it." Mitchell watched Rafe slide a protective arm around Hannah's waist. "She's his passion. You know how it is with Madisons and their passions."

"Yes." Sullivan sounded satisfied. "I know how it is with Madisons and their passions. Nothing gets in the way."

chapter 25

One month later . . .

The phone rang, shattering the moment. Rafe paused in the act of leaning over to kiss Hannah. She looked up at him from the pillow.

"The phone," she said.

"I knew I should have switched off the ringer before we went to bed tonight."

The instrument warbled insistently.

"You'd better answer it. Might be your grandfather."

"All the more reason to ignore it." Reluctantly he picked up the phone. "This better be important," he said to whoever was on the other end of the line.

"Am I interrupting anything?" Gabe asked politely.

"Yes. Our one-month wedding anniversary."

"It's only nine o'clock."

"Us old married folks go to bed early."

"I've heard that," Gabe said. "Actually that brings me to what I wanted to talk about."

Rafe groaned and flopped back on his pillow. "I really do not want to talk about your thwarted love life tonight."

"I haven't got a love life to thwart."

"Another date go south?"

"Big time."

Rafe glanced at Hannah, who raised one brow. "Told you this idea of using a businesslike approach to finding a wife wasn't going to work very well."

"No, I know I'm on the right track. I just need to fine-tune the strategy. I realized tonight that what I have to do is approach this the same way I would approach a merger or an acquisition. I need to hire a professional consultant."

A premonition of disaster shot through Rafe. "I hope you aren't going to tell me what I think you're going to tell me."

"I'm going to call Hannah's sister first thing in the morning and sign up with her matchmaking agency. I understand she's fully computerized."

Rafe shut his eyes. "This is a bad dream. I know it is."

"I spoke with Lillian briefly at the wedding. She said she's got a very high success rate."

"Gabe, I don't think this is a good idea."

"Why not?"

"Well—" Rafe hesitated. "I don't know. It just feels sort of dicey for some reason."

"What have I got to lose?"

"Uh, well—" Rafe felt a tug on his wrist. "I'm going to hang up now, Gabe. I want to go back to celebrating my one-month anniversary."

"Give Hannah my best. If things work out with the Private Arrangements agency, I'll be celebrating some anniversaries myself one of these days."

"Something tells me it won't be that simple," Rafe warned. "You're a Madison, remember? We don't do simple when it comes to marriage. We always do things the hard way."

"Only when we make the mistake of letting emotion take over. I don't plan to make that mistake."

"Good luck." Rafe disconnected, tossed the phone onto the table, and rolled back toward Hannah.

That was when he realized that his left wrist was bound to the red wrought-iron bed frame. He studied the familiar-looking padded handcuff Hannah had used to chain him with great interest.

"Where'd you get the cuffs?" he asked.

"I bought them from Virgil." She held up the second cuff. "An anniversary present."

"Oh, my." Rafe smiled slowly. "Don't know if I can handle so much excitement."

"Something tells me you're up to the challenge."

"I'll do my best." He reached out for her with his free hand and pulled her down across his chest. "I love you, Hannah."

"I love you, too."

He speared his fingers through her hair. "Should have married you eight years ago."

"Maybe. Maybe not. I think we both needed time to decide what we wanted out of life."

"You could be right." He thought about that for a few seconds. "I told you that night that it would be a long walk home."

"Yes, you did." She brushed her lips across his. "But we both got here safely. That's all that matters."

Turn the page for an excerpt from

SOFT FOCUS

by Jayne Ann Krentz

Now available from Jove Books

Six months earlier . . .

HE SAW HER COMING TOWARD HIM, AN AVENGING warrior princess in a crisp black business suit and high heels. Her dark hair was swept up into a stern knot at the back of her head. The little scarf at her throat matched the diamond-bright fire in her blue-green eyes. One look at her and the white-jacketed waiters leaped out of her path. She strode through the maze of linen-and-crystal-set tables, her gaze never wavering from her target.

The movers and shakers of Seattle's business community sensed disaster, or, at the very least, excellent gossip, in the making. A hush fell across the club's formal dining room.

Seated in the leather-cushioned booth, Jack watched her approach.

"Oh, shit." He spoke very, very softly. It was obviously too late to pray.

One look at the fury that etched Elizabeth

Cabot's intelligent face told him that he had lost his gamble. She knew everything this morning. What had happened between them last night clearly made no difference to her now.

A heavy cloud of stoicism settled on him. He waited for her with the patience of a man who knows he is facing an inescapable fate.

She was almost upon him now, and he knew that he was doomed. It was not his whole life that flashed before his eyes in those final moments, however. It was the memory of last night. He recalled the sweet, hot anticipation and the hungry rush of desire that had flashed between them. Unfortunately, that was all they had shared. The concentrated excitement had taken him by surprise, probably because he had worked so hard to contain it for the past month. In the end it had swept away his self-control and the lessons of experience that any man his age was expected to know. He was well aware of his mistakes. Elizabeth did not believe in faking her orgasms.

She had been very nice about it last night. Polite as hell. As if her failure to climax was her fault and hers alone. Actually, she had seemed quite unsurprised, as far as he could tell. It was as if she had not expected anything more from the encounter and had, therefore, not been disappointed. He had apologized and vowed to make amends just as soon as physically possible. But she had explained that she had to go home. Something about an early-morning meeting for which she had to prepare.

Reluctantly, he had driven her back to the gothic monstrosity she called home on Queen Anne Hill. When he had kissed her goodnight at the door of the mansion he had assured himself that he would get a second chance. Next time he would get it right.

But now he knew there wasn't going to be a next time.

Elizabeth arrived at the booth, vibrating with a degree of passion that had been noticeably missing in the final scenes last night.

"You conniving, two-faced, egg-sucking son of a bitch," she said between her teeth. "What made you think you'd get away with it, Jack Fairfax?"

"Don't be shy, Elizabeth. Tell me what you really think of rne."

"Did you actually believe that I wouldn't find out who you are? Did you think that you could treat me like a mushroom? Keep me in the dark and feed me manure?"

There was no hope of defending himself. He could see that. But he had to try. "I never lied to you."

"The hell you didn't. You never told me the truth. Not once during the past month did you give me any hint that you were the bastard who engineered the Galloway takeover."

"That was a two-year-old business deal. It had nothing to do with us."

"It had *everything* to do with us, and you knew it. That's why you lied to me."

In spite of the hopelessness of the situation, or

perhaps because of it, he started to get mad. "It's not my fault the Galloway deal never came up between us. You never asked me about it."

"Why would I do that?" Her voice rose. "How was I supposed to guess that you were involved in it?"

"You didn't work at Galloway. How was I supposed to guess that you had a connection to the company?" he countered.

"It doesn't matter. Don't you understand? That takeover was as ruthless, as cold-blooded, as anything I've ever seen in business. The fact that you were the hired gun who tore that company apart tells me exactly what kind of scum you really are."

"Elizabeth—"

"People got hurt in that takeover." Her hand clenched very tightly around the strap of her elegant shoulder bag. "Badly hurt. I don't do business with men like you."

Jack saw Hugo, the maître d', hovering uneasily at a nearby table, obviously at a loss to decide how to quell the escalating scene. The waiter who had been on the way to the booth with ice water and bread halted, unmoving, a short distance away. Everyone in the dining room, was listening now, but Elizabeth was oblivious to her audience.

Jack was morbidly fascinated himself, even though he was at ground zero. He would never have guessed that Elizabeth was capable of such drama. For the past month she had seemed so calm, so composed, so controlled.

"I think you'd better cool down," he said quietly.

"Give me one good reason."

"I'll give you two. Number one, we've got an audience. Number two, when you finally do cool off you are going to regret this scene a lot more than I will."

She smiled at him with such freezing disdain that he was amazed there were no icicles in her hair. She waved one hand in a wide arc that encompassed the entire dining room. He took that as a very bad sign.

"I don't give a damn about our audience," she said in ringing accents that no doubt carried all the way into the kitchen. "The way I look at it, I'm doing everyone here a public service by telling them that you are a lying SOB. I won't regret a single thing about this scene."

"You will when you finally remember that we've got a signed, sealed contract for the Excalibur deal. Like it or not, we're stuck with each other."

She blinked once. He saw the jolt of shock in her eyes. In the heat of her outrage, she had apparently forgotten the contract they had both signed yesterday morning.

She rallied swiftly "I'll call the Fund's lawyers as soon as I get back to the office. Consider our contract null and void as of today."

"Don't bother trying to bluff. You can't get out of our deal just because you've decided I'm an SOB. You signed that damned contract, and I'm going to hold you to it."

"We'll see about that."

He shrugged. "If you want to tie both of us up in court for the next ten or twelve months, be my guest. But I'll fight you all the way, and I'll win in the end. We both know it."

She was trapped, and he was pretty sure that she was too smart not to recognize that simple fact.

There was a tense moment while he watched her come to terms with the realization that he had won.

Frustrated rage flared once more in her face.

"You will pay for this, Jack Fairfax." She reached out and swept the pitcher of ice water off the tray held by the motionless waiter. "Sooner or later, I swear you will pay for what you did."

She dashed the contents of the water pitcher straight at him. He did not even try to duck. The only escape route was under the table, and somehow that option seemed more ignominious than staying in his seat.

The icy water splashing in his face ignited the temper that he had been struggling to control. He looked at Elizabeth. She was staring at him, the first signs of shock and horror lighting her eyes. He knew that it was just beginning to dawn on her that she had made an almighty fool of herself.

"This isn't about the Galloway deal, is it?" he said softly. "This is about last night."

Clutching her purse, she took a step back as if he had struck her. "Don't you dare bring up last night. This is not about last night, damn you."

"Sure it is." He swiped a chunk of ice off the shoulder of his jacket. "I take full responsibility, of course. It's the gentlemanly thing to do, isn't it?"

She sucked in her breath in a stunned gasp. "Don't try to reduce this to sex. What happened last night is the least important aspect of this entire affair. In fact, what happened last night was so unimportant and so unmemorable that it doesn't even register on the scale."

Last night had meant nothing to her. He lost what little remained of the control he had been exerting over his anger. His hands closed around the edge of the table. He rose deliberately to his feet, heedless of the fact that he was still dripping ice water. He smiled slowly at Elizabeth.

"On my own behalf," he said with grave politeness, "I would like to say that I didn't know going in that I was dealing with the original Ice Princess. You should have warned me that you've got a little problem in that department. Who knows? With some extra time and effort, I might have been able to thaw you out."

As soon as the words were uttered, he regretted them. But they hung there in the air above the table, frozen, glittering shards of ice. He knew they would never melt.

Elizabeth fell back another step. Her face was flushed. Her eyes narrowed. "You really are a bastard, aren't you?" Her voice was low and much too even now. "You don't care a damn about what happened in the aftermath of the Galloway deal, do you?"

He ran a hand through his hair to get rid of some

of the cold water. "No, I don't. Business is business, as far as I'm concerned, I don't believe in getting emotionally involved."

"I understand," she said. "That's precisely how I feel about last night."

She turned on one needle-sharp heel and walked out of the restaurant without a backward glance.

Jack watched her leave. He did not take his eyes off her until she disappeared through the door.

The twinges of impending fate that he had experienced when she had entered the dining room grew stronger. He knew that she must be feeling them too.

They both knew the truth.

She could walk away from what had happened between them last night, but she could not walk away from the business contract they had signed. For better or worse, for richer for poorer, it bound them together more securely than any wedding license could have done.

And don't miss

LOST & FOUND

The exciting novel by Jayne Ann Krentz

Now available from Jove Books

THE RANKS OF MEDIEVAL WARRIORS, FOREVER FROZEN IN their steel carapaces, loomed behind him in the shadows. Mack Easton's face was as unreadable as that of any of the helmed figures standing guard on the other side of the office window. There was something about Easton that made him appear locked in time, too, Cady thought. A quality of stillness, perhaps. You had to look twice to see him there in the shadows. If it hadn't been for the glow of the computer screen reflecting off the strong, fierce planes of his face and glinting on the lenses of his glasses, he would have been invisible.

Not a youthful face, she thought. Definitely mature. But not *too* mature. Thirty-nine or possibly forty, a good age. An interesting age. At least it looked interesting on Mack Easton.

The weird thing was that, even though she had never been able to imagine an exact image of him with only the telephone connection to go on, now that she was actually face-to-face with him she could see that he fit the voice perfectly. Take the serious, dark-rimmed glasses, for example. Never in a million years would she have thought to add that touch if she had been asked to draw a picture of him based on their long-distance conversations. But when he had removed them from his pocket a few minutes ago and put them on she had decided they looked absolutely right on him.

"We have a photograph," he said. "It was found in the museum's archives."

Museum was not the word she would have used to dignify Military World, she thought. What was she doing here? She must have been temporarily out of her mind last night when she took Easton's call. She was at home in hushed galleries, art research libraries, and the cluttered back rooms of prestigious auction salons. She mingled with connoisseurs and educated collectors.

Military World, with its low-budget reproductions of arm and armor from various wars was very much as she had envisioned it; tacky. Then again, maybe that was just her personal bias showing. She had never been overly fond of armor. To her it symbolized all that was brutish and primitive in human nature. The fact that the artisans of the past had devoted enormous talent and craftsmanship to its design and decoration struck her as bizarre.

The office in which they sat belonged to the two owners of Military World, a pair that went by the names of Notch and Dewey. They hovered anxiously in the shadows, having surrendered the single desk to Easton and his laptop computer.

Mack occupied the space behind the desk as if he owned it. She got the impression that was the way it was with any place he happened to inhabit at any particular moment. Something that just sort of happened to him; something he took for granted.

She wished that she could get a better look at his eyes but the reflection on his glasses concealed them as effectively as the steel helms hid the features of the armored figures beyond the windows.

He pushed the photograph toward her across the battered desk and reached out to switch on the small desk lamp. She watched, unwillingly fascinated, as the beam fell on one large, powerful-looking hand. No wedding ring, she noticed. Not that you could be sure a man was unmarried just because he didn't happen to wear a ring.

With an effort she tore her gaze away from his hand and focused on the photo. It featured a horse and rider garbed in flamboyantly styled armor that looked as if it had been designed for a video game or dreamed up by an artist for the cover of a science fiction fantasy novel. She recognized it as a fairly accurate reproduction of the elaborately embellished armor crafted during the Renaissance. Such impractical styles had never been intended for the battlefield. They had been created for the sole purpose of making the wearer look good in ceremonies, festivals and parades.

"Fifteenth century, judging from the helm and breast plate," she said. "Italian in style." *In style* was a polite way of saying *reproduction.*

"I'm aware of that, Miss Briggs," Easton said with icy patience. "But if you look closely, you can see a portion of another display behind the horse's, uh, rear."

She took a closer look. Sure enough, if she looked past the tail of the fake horse she could just make out the dimly lit image of a standing figure garbed in heavily decorated steel.

"Half-armor," she murmured. It was always good policy to impress the client, even if you weren't particularly interested in the job. Word-of-mouth was important. "In the style of the Northern Italian armorers of the sixteenth century. Looks like part of a garniture meant for jousting at the barriers. Suits of armor from this era often consisted of dozens of supplementary and interchangeable pieces that allowed the set to be modified for specific uses. Sort of like a modern all-in-one tool kit."

"It's the helm that we're interested in here," Mack said.

She peered at it. The bad lighting made it difficult to see much detail. "What about it?"

"It's the only piece that was stolen."

She looked up. "Is there a better photo around?"

One of the two men who hovered near the far end of the desk, the individual who went by the name Dewey, edged closer with a crablike movement.

"Lucky to have that one," he said, sounding apologetic.

She could only guess at Dewey's age. His face was a worn and weathered map that could have belonged to a man of fifty or seventy. He was dressed in military surplus complete with camouflage fatigues, battered boots and a wide leather belt. His graying hair was caught in a scruffy ponytail secured with a rubber band. She would not have been surprised to learn that he commuted to and from work on a very large motorcycle.

It was hard to imagine that he was representative of Lost and Found's typical clientele. How in the world had he and his partner managed to find the very-hard-to-find Mack Easton? More to the point, why had Mack agreed to help them? Surely he was too expensive for this pair. If he wasn't, she certainly was.

"I was going for a shot of the fifteenth-century display," Dewey explained. "We had just finished setting it up, you see. This was maybe two years back, right Notch?"

The other man nodded vigorously. "Right."

Dewey returned his attention to Cady. "I wanted to get a picture for our album. Lucked out and accidentally got a bit of the other exhibit in the shot."

"Never would have guessed that the helmet on the sixteenth-century suit was the real thing." Notch spread his hands. "Like, who knew, man?"

Cady cleared her throat. "How did it come into the, uh, museum's collection?"

"I found it right after we bought Military World from

old man Belford. He had it stashed away in the back room. I polished it up and added it to the rest of the outfit. Seemed to match, y'know?"

"I see." She tapped one finger against the photo while she considered her options. As much as she wanted to take on another assignment for Lost and Found, she had a reputation to maintain. One had to draw the line somewhere. She did not trace reproductions.

Surreptitiously she glanced at her watch. She might be able to catch the one o'clock flight if she left Military World within the next forty-five minutes. She could be home in time for dinner.

She turned back to Easton. Something in the way he was watching her told her that he had noticed her checking the time. She summoned up what she hoped was an expression of professional interest. "What did the insurance people say when you notified them about the theft?"

Notch and Dewey exchanged uneasy looks.

Mack did not move. "There's a slight problem with the insurance situation."

She sighed. "In other words, the helm was uninsured?"

Notch made an awkward sound deep in his throat. "Things have been a little rough lately, financially speaking. Dewey and me had to economize and make some cutbacks, y'know? Sort of let some of the insurance go."

"Not that the insurance company would have covered the helm for anything like its true value, anyway," Dewey said quickly. "If we'd had coverage, it would have been for a reproduction, not the real thing on account of we didn't know it was genuine, if you see what I mean."

"I don't want to be rude," Cady said gently, "but what makes you think the helm is a genuine sixteenth-century piece?"

Dewey and Notch stared at her, open-mouthed.

"You're supposed to be an expert," Dewey said. "Can't you tell from looking at it?"

She made a bid for patience. "This is only a photograph. There is no way I or anyone else can use it to determine whether or not the helm is genuine."

Notch looked stricken. "But Mack here said that you knew your stuff."

"Old armor is very popular right now," she explained. "A lot of the well-heeled early retirees in the software industry are collecting it like mad. Guess it reminds them of all those sword-and-sorcery video and computer games they love to play. Prices are going through the roof. Unfortunately, antique armor is fairly easy to fake. Bury a piece of steel in the ground with some acidic substance for a while and, presto, you get aged armor."

Notch bristled. "Are you sayin' our helmet is a forgery?"

"I'm saying that is an extremely likely possibility." Cady spread her hands. "Even the experts get burned a lot when it comes to armor. And the business of creating counterfeits isn't exactly new. A lot of the best reproductions of antique armor were made in the nineteenth century. By now, the steel has taken on the patina of genuine age and can easily pass for the real thing."

"I still say our helmet is the real thing," Notch declared.

Cady slanted a quick, searching glance at Mack. He moved his head in the smallest of negatives. He was staying out of the argument; letting her handle the clients.

Summoning up her best professional expression, she turned back to Notch and Dewey. "Why are you convinced that the helm is genuine when every other piece in your collection is a reproduction?"

"Simple." Dewey rocked triumphantly on his heels and looked shrewd. "Someone stole it."